THE WRONG PLAYER WORLD SO FAR

The Wrong Player Series

The Wrong Quarterback

The Wrong Play

Merry Me

The Pucking Wrong Series

The Pucking Wrong Number

The Pucking Wrong Guy

A Pucking Wrong Christmas

The Pucking Wrong Date

The Pucking Wrong Man

The Pucking Wrong Rookie

The Wrong Made Men Series

Don't Say Mafia

THE WRONG PLAY

C.R. JANE

Podium

Copyright © 2025 by C.R. Jane
Cover design by Emily Wittig
Photography by Michelle Lancaster
Editing by Stephanie H./Hannotek, Ink

ISBN: 979-8-3470-0429-4

Published in 2025 by Podium Publishing
www.podiumentertainment.com

Podium

For the ones who were told to stay quiet,
who were kept in the shadows,
who were made to feel like secrets instead of something sacred.
This is for you.
You deserve a Jace Thatcher.

Dear Red Flag Renegades,

The Wrong Play explores the shadows of self-doubt, a place I believe we've all wandered—where feelings of worthlessness make us question if we'll ever be enough. We've all felt like a dim flicker in a world of blazing lights, convinced our past defines us, whispering we're not worthy of the love we crave.

But here's the truth I wanted to weave into Riley and Jace's story: sometimes it takes the right person to see who we've been all along. Jace, with his fierce, unyielding love, doesn't just see Riley—he *sees* her, the real her, the one she's been too afraid to let shine. He doesn't care about the labels the world slaps on her, the shadows of her past, or the doubts that haunt her. He sees her light, her strength, her everything, and he fights to make her see it too. That's what real love can do...it holds a mirror to the parts of ourselves we've hidden, showing us we were always enough, even when we couldn't believe it.

I hope Riley's journey resonates with you, reminding you that your worth isn't defined by the voices that try to dim your glow. You are enough, just as you are, and maybe there's someone out there, or already in your life, waiting to show you that truth. Thank you for joining me on this ride, for loving these characters as fiercely as I do, and for being the renegades who embrace the red flags and find beauty in the crazy things these men do for love.

No Drama Llamas Forever.

XOXO,

CR Jane

TEAM ROSTER

OFFENSE

QUARTERBACK:

Parker Davis | #12
Trent Maxwell | #07
Malik Harper | #16
Owen Matthis | #14

RUNNING BACK:

Garrett Harper | #22
Griffin Tillman | #30
Trevon Brooks | #29
Elijah Rivera | #33
Jordan Wright | #20
Marcus "Speedy" Hayes | #28

WIDE RECEIVER:

Jace Thatcher | #77
Hunter Manning | #63
Chris Jordan | #19
Caleb "Ace" Thompson | #11
Ethan Vance | #36
Isaiah Turner | #18
Brandon Holt | #17
Trey Anderson | #84
Quentin Scott | #89

TIGHT END:

Matthew "Matty" Adler | #23
Eric Simmons | #86
Logan Mendez | #80
Cam Richards | #82

OFFENSIVE LINE:

Hunter "Tank" Thompson | #67
Sam Carrington | #65
Connor Wright | #55
Chapman "Chappie" Cordell | #68
Derrick Morgan | #73
Connor Steele | #71
Blake McAllister | #75
Jared Foster | #54
Grayson Lee | #72
Noah Chambers | #74

DEFENSE

DEFENSIVE LINE:

Darwin Harrison | #90
Matt Santiago | #92
Elijah Reed | #99
Anthony Williams | #94
Jacob Tanner | #96
Jalen Fields | #69
Wyatt Cook | #98
Damien Ward | #91
Sean Little | #97

LINEBACKERS:

Brandon Scott | Outside Linebacker | #44
Marcus Steadman | Middle Linebacker | #52
Andre Carter | Outside Linebacker | #41
Malcolm Spencer | #51
Aiden Cruz | #57
Cole Anderson | #53

SAFETIES:

Xavier Hawthorne | Free Safety | #21
Malik Greene | Strong Safety | #93

CORNERBACKS:

Tyrell Brooks | #24
Dante Jefferson | #66

SPECIAL TEAMS

KICKER:

Ethan Collins | #3
Will Torres | #6

PUNTER:

Ryan Matthews | #2

RETURN SPECIALIST:

Chris Reddick | #46

LONG SNAPPER:

Colton Ramsey | #9

COACHING STAFF

HEAD COACH	Clint Everett
OFFENSIVE COORDINATOR	Dale Malone
DEFENSIVE COORDINATOR	Bryce Thompson
SPECIAL TEAMS COACH	Reggie Caldwell
STRENGTH AND CONDITIONING COACH	Travis Richards
QUARTERBACKS COACH	Evan Houston
WIDE RECEIVERS COACH	Trey Winston
RUNNING BACKS COACH	Nathan Grant
OFFENSIVE LINE COACH	Doug "Grizzly" Callahan
DEFENSIVE LINE COACH	Marcus Hayes
LINEBACKERS COACH	Jerome Brooks
DEFENSIVE BACKS COACH	DeAndre Moore

THE WRONG PLAY

PLAYLIST

HUNGER	ROSS COPPERMAN
MAKEDAMNSURE	TAKING BACK SUNDAY
PINK PONY CLUB	CHAPPELL ROAN
SLOW DANCING IN A BURNING ROOM	RILEY GREEN
DEATH WISH LOVE	BENSON BOONE
SUN TO ME	ZACH BRYAN
BUT DADDY I LOVE HIM	TAYLOR SWIFT
ORDINARY	ALEX WARREN
YOU BELONG WITH ME (TAYLOR'S VERSION)	TAYLOR SWIFT
BETTING ON US	MYLES SMITH
THE MANUSCRIPT	TAYLOR SWIFT
CURIOSITY	BRYCE SAVAGE
THE ONLY EXCEPTION	PARAMORE
REMEMBERING SUNDAY	ALL TIME LOW
LOSE YOU TO LOVE ME	SELENA GOMEZ
LOVE THE HELL OUT OF YOU	LEWIS CAPALDI
THE ALCHEMY	TAYLOR SWIFT

LISTEN TO THE FULL PLAYLIST HERE

TRIGGER WARNING

Dear readers,

Please be aware this is a dark romance and as such can and will contain possible triggering content. Elements of this story are purely fantasy and should not be taken as acceptable behavior in real life.

Our love interest is possessive, obsessive, and the perfect shade of red for all you red flag renegades out there. There is absolutely no shade of pink involved when it comes to what Jace Thatcher will do to get his girl.

Themes include football, stalking, thoughts about self-harm, manipulation, dark obsessions, chronic health conditions involving the main character, nonconsent/dubious consent (not involving Jace Thatcher), physical abuse (referenced but not explicitly described, and not by Jace Thatcher), emotional abuse (not by Jace Thatcher), age gaps, drugging, light captor/captivity, and sexual scenes.

There are no harems, cheating, or sharing of partners involved. Jace Thatcher only has eyes for her.

Prepare to enter the world of the Tennessee Tigers ... You've been warned.

THE
WRONG
PLAY

"I LOVE ME SOME ME."

—**Terrell Owens**

PROLOGUE

RILEY

Nineteen Years Old

The moment he left me, I felt it.

The hollow ache.

The sickening weight pressing down on my chest like something inside me had caved in. I barely remembered the drive home; I barely noticed when my feet carried me through the front door of my parents' empty house. The silence was deafening, stretching through the space like a reminder of just how alone I was.

I dropped my bag by the stairs, numb, my head spinning with the words Brandon had said before walking away.

It's not you, Riley. I just need to figure some things out.

I don't want to hurt you.

I think we should see other people.

We need time apart to figure out who we both really are.

And the last one.

You need someone who understands you.

Lies. Each and every one of them. The type of pretty words a guy says when he doesn't have the guts to tell you the truth—he wants someone else.

I sniffed, my throat thick, my vision blurring. I didn't want to cry over him.

But it wasn't *just* him. It was everything. The way my parents were always gone, too distracted by their own lives to notice me. Always off on business trips or at charity galas, smiling for cameras, pretending they had a perfect family waiting at home. But they didn't. I was home. And they weren't.

Because who could even want me?

Brandon had been right to leave. He'd figured it out before I did—that I was too much and not enough all at the same time. Too needy, too desperate, too pathetic. I clung too hard to things that didn't belong to me, to people who were already halfway out the door.

Maybe there was something broken inside me, something unlovable. Something that was constantly chasing after what didn't want to be caught.

Maybe it was the way my body was always working against me. The exhaustion, the pain that never really went away, the days when even getting out of bed felt like a battle. My chronic exhaustion had been a shadow over my life for as long as I could remember—one that I'd stopped talking about, because what was the point? No one wanted to hear about it. No one wanted to deal with the baggage that came with me. Certainly no one wanted to empathize with the fact that I was having to take a gap year between high school and starting my life . . . because my body wouldn't cooperate.

I was always alone.

Always.

I wasn't in love with Brandon. After he'd graduated high school, we'd hung out until I graduated a year later. He was nice. He included me. He filled the spots of loneliness.

Or at least he had.

Even if I wasn't in love with him, this broken connection hurt. It made the loneliness I'd always felt come back . . . full force.

I walked into the kitchen, heading straight for the fridge, ready to drown myself in whatever I could find on the shelves. But I froze.

Because tonight . . . it turned out I actually wasn't alone.

He sat at the kitchen table like he belonged there, fingers lazily flipping through one of my father's leather-bound books. A half-full glass of scotch sat beside him, and I knew if I got closer, its scent would mix with his. The faintest trace of his cologne—warm cedarwood and something deeper, something that always lingered long after he'd left.

"Riley, I didn't hear you come in," he said, lifting his eyes from the book. His voice was smooth and unhurried—like honey laced with something sharp, something dangerous. It was the kind of voice that wrapped around you like silk. Or at least it had always felt that way for me.

Professor Callum Westwood.

My father's best friend.

His gaze ran over me, slow and knowing, like he could see *everything*. The pain. The vulnerability. The pathetic, broken girl standing in front of him with her heart in pieces.

I swallowed, gripping the counter behind me. "What are you doing here?"

He smirked, setting the book down. "Your father asked me to check on the house while they were away."

Of course he had. My father trusted him implicitly. So did my mother. And I did, too.

I pretended not to notice his wording—the insinuation that my parents had asked him to check on the house . . . but not on me. But I felt it. Another reminder that there was no one who cared.

For years, Callum had been a fixture in my life—family dinners, weekend barbecues, holidays. He was brilliant, charming . . . respected.

And dangerous.

At least in my head.

He was handsome in a way that made women stop in their tracks. His dark brown hair had just the right amount of silver at the temples, adding to his air of sophistication. His chiseled, angular jaw always carried a five-o'clock shadow, and his piercing blue eyes held an intensity that made it impossible to look away. He looked every bit the polished professor, the kind of man who exuded effortless charm.

The community adored him—respected him. His tailored suits, composed demeanor, and knowing smiles only added to his allure, painting the perfect picture of a man who carried himself with quiet dignity.

I had always been aware of him in a way I shouldn't have been. There had been times—quick glances, fleeting moments—where I'd felt something. Something dark and consuming. Something that sent a thrill down my spine and left me ashamed of myself.

And now . . . he was here, and I was a mess, and he was looking at me like he knew exactly what I was feeling right now.

"Something wrong?" he asked, tilting his head.

I forced a weak laugh, blinking fast. "Just tired."

He hummed, pushing back from the table, standing with the easy grace of a man who never rushed for anything.

"You've been crying."

I stiffened. "I—"

"Boy troubles?"

I swallowed, humiliated.

"You've been dating some boy from school the last few months, right?"

I blinked at him, surprised that he would know that when I was sure that my own parents didn't.

"Yes," I whispered. "But . . . he broke it off." The words came out filled with pain. Deep pain. Something I shouldn't be showing anyone.

He took a slow step toward me, his voice lower, softer. "Did he hurt you?"

Yes.

No.

I didn't know how to answer that.

Because there were a million ways to hurt someone.

There was the ripping away of something you thought was real.

There was the silence that followed, the emptiness where something warm used to be.

There was the quiet, brutal way someone could make you feel like you were never enough.

My silence must have been all the answer he needed because Callum exhaled through his nose, a slow, controlled breath. His eyes darkened, his fingers flexing at his sides.

"He's a fool," he said.

The words made my stomach twist.

Because . . . it almost sounded like he meant them.

But that was probably me imagining it. Wishful thinking of the highest order.

He took another step toward me, closing the space between us until I could feel the warmth of his body.

The feel of his closeness was steady . . . something to anchor myself to.

And I had been drifting for so, so long.

"He didn't deserve you," he continued, his voice smooth and coaxing.

His fingers skimmed my hand, a whisper of touch—barely there, yet somehow devastating.

A shiver rolled through me.

It wasn't supposed to feel good. Alarms were blaring loudly in my head, in fact.

But it did.

Callum's hand moved higher, his fingers tracing over my pulse, slow and deliberate, like he was memorizing the shape of my veins. "You need someone who can take care of you," he murmured, his voice dangerous in the way a blade glinted just before it struck.

My breath snagged as his grip tightened, just barely. Not enough to hurt. Just enough to make me hyperaware of how easily he could.

"Someone who knows what you need." His tone was rich, laced with something dark, something final, as if he were the only one who truly understood. The only one who ever could.

I swallowed hard, my head spinning.

This wasn't wrong.

It wasn't.

He was just comforting me.

He was just here.

And Callum had always known how to say the right thing, how to make people believe in him.

His fingers slid up my forearm, his touch deceptively gentle. "I can take care of you, Riley," he whispered, his voice slipping through my ribs like smoke, curling into something cold and inescapable.

My breath hitched again.

Because no one else ever had.

His fingers skated up my jaw, tilting my chin up. His touch was light. Too light. Like he was giving me a choice. Like he was waiting for me to close the space between us.

"You don't have to keep pretending," he whispered.

My throat tightened.

Because I was.

I was pretending to be fine.

I was pretending I wasn't hurt.

I was pretending I didn't need someone to put their hands on me just to feel something other than this hollow ache.

And Callum? He knew.

The warmth of his hand spread through me, pulling me in like a slow, steady tide. I couldn't think. I could only feel.

His thumb pressed against the base of my throat. A slow, lingering pause. Like he was waiting. Like he was seeing if I'd stop him.

And I didn't.

Because maybe I wanted to be wanted. Maybe I wanted to feel something, anything other than this ache.

Brandon had wanted me for a while, but anyone would get tired of their girlfriend always needing to cancel plans because of their chronic exhaustion . . . or not being fun enough. And then he'd stopped wanting me.

And now Callum was here.

And maybe . . . maybe he wanted me.

His face dipped lower, his lips just a breath away. "I could make you forget him."

The words coated my skin, sinking deep. The air thickened. I was breathless. Lost.

My pulse thrummed against my skin, erratic, frantic, like it didn't know whether to flee or surrender.

"You're beautiful," Callum murmured, his eyes never leaving mine. Dark and unreadable, but steady—like he was completely confident in what he was doing.

"You always have been."

Heat flushed down my spine, a foreign, disorienting sensation taking root in my chest.

No one had ever looked at me like this.

Like I was something to be devoured. Like I was something worth wanting.

My breath caught as he lifted a hand, his knuckles grazing the side of my face, slow and deliberate. The touch was still light—so light that I felt it everywhere.

He wasn't rushing. He was waiting. Waiting for me to let him in.

"Riley," he murmured, his voice a low, hypnotic hum.

I couldn't move. Couldn't breathe.

I couldn't do anything but stand there, trapped between the past I wanted to outrun and the man standing in front of me, offering something else.

But . . . this was wrong, right?

And he was old enough to be my dad.

I'd thought he was handsome, sure. But Callum had always been a fixture in our house, always there, a shadow in the background of my life. Reliable. Present. Not . . . this.

Not a man who looked at me like he saw something worth wanting.

I swallowed hard as I stared back at him.

I could still walk away.

But his eyes, dark and knowing, held me in place.

And I . . . I wasn't sure if I wanted to.

Callum leaned in, brushing his lips against my temple, lingering. His breath was warm against my skin, each exhale coiling through me, filling all the empty spaces.

"Come upstairs."

A whisper. A promise.

I tensed.

I shouldn't.

I shouldn't.

"I don't—"

Callum's fingers moved down my arm, a slow, steady glide before he took my wrist gently in his grasp.

His thumb pressed against my pulse point again, like he already knew what my body wanted, even if my mind didn't.

"I won't do anything you don't want, Riley."

His voice was smooth. Reassuring. A lullaby of certainty.

"Just let me take care of you."

Take care of me. Like I was something fragile. Like I was something worth handling carefully.

Like I was someone who deserved it.

It was all I had ever wanted.

My chest ached with the need to be seen. To be chosen. To be wanted.

I let out a slow, unsteady breath, and I nodded.

Callum's lips curled in satisfaction, and he didn't say anything else.

He didn't push. He just turned, still holding my wrist, and started walking.

And I let him lead me upstairs.

Inside my room, the air was heavy and charged. I stood in front of him, my breathing uneven, shallow, his presence swallowing up the space around me.

Callum's hands brushed the hem of my shirt, slow, unhurried, his fingertips skimming the fabric in a way that felt deliberate.

Waiting for me to stop him.

But I didn't.

I couldn't.

His hands slid beneath the fabric, his fingers featherlight as they traced along the bare skin of my stomach, moving higher, along my ribs. I shuddered, heat licking up my spine, my skin flaring to life beneath his touch.

His hands were warm, steady. Assured. Like he had all the time in the world to do this, to unwrap me piece by piece.

A shaky breath left me. This was happening.

I wasn't sure what I had expected. Maybe for him to be rougher. Hungrier.

Instead, he was methodical and patient, like I was something to be unwrapped slowly. Like he was memorizing every little reaction, every gasp of breath, every moment of hesitation.

"I've never done this before," I whispered, my hands curling into fists. The words felt fragile, like something I should have kept to myself.

Something dark flashed behind his eyes, and he tilted his head like he was studying a rare find.

"That's okay."

The way he said it . . . it sounded like he already knew. Like it was something he had suspected. Planned for.

A strange sort of sickness rolled through me. Something . . . off.

Callum tilted my chin up with a finger, his gaze locking onto mine with that effortless confidence of his.

And suddenly, the moment felt too big. Too charged. Too irreversible.

"I'll take care of you, Riley," he murmured, his fingers ghosting over my jaw.

I swallowed hard. He sounded so sure, and I wanted that certainty. Desperately.

Because for the first time in weeks . . . in years, someone was looking at me like I mattered. Like I was worth the effort. Like I was worth something.

So, when his lips brushed against mine—soft, coaxing, deliberate—I didn't pull away. I let him kiss me.

And I kissed him back.

———

Pain.

It was the first thing I registered. A deep, throbbing ache between my thighs. A slow, dull pulse that radiated through my limbs like an echo of the night before.

I sucked in a sharp breath, blinking up at the ceiling, momentarily disoriented. My sheets were tangled around my legs, the weight of the heavy comforter pressing down on my overheated skin. The air was thick, stifling, carrying the lingering scent of his cologne.

Callum.

The name sent a shock through my system, a cold rush of nausea tightening my throat.

The memories came back in pieces—his hands on me, his voice low and coaxing, the way he had looked at me as if I belonged to him. As if I were something to consume.

I turned my head, my gaze darting to the other side of the bed. Empty.

A cold, hollow feeling settled in my chest.

I pushed myself up, wincing as another pang of pain lanced between my legs. A slow, sinking dread crept over me as I felt the dampness beneath me, as I saw the dark stain on the crisp white sheets.

Blood.

A sob clawed its way up my throat, violent and raw, and I pressed a hand over my mouth, tears spilling hot and fast down my cheeks.

It was real.

I had let this happen.

A wave of self-loathing slammed into me, suffocating, crushing.

What had I done?

I could still hear him—his voice in my ear, his lips at my throat, the quiet certainty in the way he had touched me, like he had always known this was inevitable.

Like I had always been his to take.

And I had let him.

I had gone upstairs with him. *I* had let him undress me. *I* had kissed him back. A man old enough to be my father.

The weight in my chest only got heavier as I forced myself to move. I threw on clothes, making sure not to look in the mirror before I scrambled back toward the bed.

The sheets—stained, wrinkled, evidence—mocked me as I frantically ripped them off, balling them up in my arms.

The smell of him was still on them. Still in the air. Still in my hair.

I squeezed my eyes shut, my breath catching, my stomach twisting.

Had I wanted this?

Shame curled around my ribs, digging its claws in deep . . . making it hard to breathe.

I had wanted to feel something other than loneliness . . . than rejection.

And now?

Now, I felt *ruined*.

I swallowed the bile rising in my throat and moved.

Down the hall, my steps were uneven, my legs weak, still trembling with the aftermath. I knew the housekeepers would take care of it, they wouldn't even tell my parents what they had seen, but I couldn't let them. I needed to scrub it away myself, to erase the proof . . . to pretend it had never happened.

I shoved the sheets into the washer, fumbling to pour in bleach with shaky hands before slamming the door shut and pressing start. The hum of the machine filled the empty laundry room, drowning out the thoughts screaming inside my head.

I turned to leave, only to freeze.

Voices.

Low, steady, familiar.

I swallowed hard, pulse pounding as I stepped out of the laundry room and followed the sound, my bare feet silent on the hardwood.

The moment I reached the kitchen doorway, my stomach dropped.

There he was.

Sitting at the breakfast table with my parents, sipping coffee, like nothing had happened.

He laughed at something my father had said, casual and at ease, his posture relaxed as if he hadn't taken *everything* from me just hours before.

And my parents—they were completely clueless.

None of them even looked up when I walked in.

It was at least a few minutes of hovering before my mother finally glanced away from Callum and noticed I was standing in the doorway. Her lips pressed together like she'd just caught sight of something distasteful. "Riley, for fuck's sake, fix yourself before coming to breakfast. We have company."

I flinched. The smell of fresh coffee and bacon in the room made me want to be sick.

Callum's eyes flicked to mine, a spark of amusement in their depths, as if he enjoyed this. As if he enjoyed watching me unravel while he sat there, perfectly composed, perfectly untouchable.

"Morning, Riley," my father said, his voice light, unconcerned. "I didn't know you were home."

As if I had anywhere else to be.

I grinned weakly, the smile feeling all wrong on my face considering how I was feeling. Of course he hadn't known I was home. I was surprised that he had noticed me walking into the room at all.

"You look tired," my mother said after a minute, even though she was looking at her phone. "Didn't sleep well?"

I hesitated, my hands curling into fists at my sides. Callum still had that smirk on his face, the one that told me he was finding this all very amusing.

No, actually, I didn't sleep well at all because your husband's best friend took my virginity last night, and now I feel like I might crawl out of my skin.

I swallowed down the words and slid into my seat instead, since I knew that was what they'd expect with company over. "I'm fine," I muttered.

Callum was directly across from me, still the picture of composed elegance as he stirred sugar into his coffee. Completely normal. Like I wasn't barely holding myself together. Like my entire world hadn't shifted overnight.

My hands clenched tighter in my lap as Eleanor, one of our housekeepers, set down a plate filled to the brim with eggs, pancakes, and sausages. I stared at the plate, trying to stop myself from throwing up all over it.

"Not hungry?" Callum's voice was smooth, warm, dripping with the same familial concern that he usually had when he'd spoken to me in the past.

My mother barely spared me a glance before shaking her head in exasperation, like it had been years of her having to put up with me instead of mere minutes. "Eat your breakfast, Riley. The last thing we need is one of your episodes."

My fingers tightened obediently around my fork, my skin hot and clammy. I picked at my food, pushing eggs around my plate without taking a bite. Callum eyed me for a second with his sharp gaze as he lifted his cup of coffee to his lips.

I swallowed down a mouthful of bile.

Breakfast passed in an uncomfortable blur, with my parents exchanging idle conversation about their next trip while I sat in silence. Callum chimed in occasionally, always perfectly at ease.

I couldn't help but watch him. How could he be so normal? How could he act like this was just another morning lost in conversation with his best friends?

Like he hadn't touched me.

Destroyed me.

When I'd cut up my eggs into small enough pieces that it looked like I'd at least eaten a few bites, I pushed back from the table and made a beeline to the hallway—knowing my parents wouldn't even notice I was gone. I needed to get out of the house, get some air, figure out how I was going to recover from this.

My phone buzzed in my pocket, and I pulled it out listlessly, staring at the message.

> **Brandon: How are you?**

Of course he would ask that. Brandon never wanted to feel like the bad guy. He wouldn't want me to be upset with him. I would have leapt in desperation at this text if he'd sent it last night. I would have tortured myself with how to respond and wondered if I could possibly get him to want me again.

But right now, all I felt was . . . numb.

Exhausted.

Like something important inside me had been sucked out.

I'd always thought it would be Brandon who I'd give my virginity to. I'd been so close, and then I'd . . .

A hand suddenly closed around my wrist from the hallway, and I was yanked back into the shadows.

I barely had time to gasp before my back hit the wall.

"Easy, darling." His voice was low, edged with something dark, something possessive. His body pressed against mine, and I could feel his hard length against my stomach.

I should have shoved him away. I should have screamed.

But I didn't. I was frozen.

Trapped in his orbit.

Callum's lips brushed against my jaw, his breath hot against my skin. "You look so pretty when you blush." His fingers moved down my side, stopping just above my hip, pressing in slightly. "I'm sorry I couldn't stay this morning, but I know you understand."

A tremor ran through me. "Callum—"

He hummed, nipping at the edge of my jaw. "I can't wait to be inside you again."

My stomach clenched, that sick feeling once again roiling inside me. I squeezed my eyes shut, my hands coming up to push him away, but he caught them, trapping them against the wall.

His hips rolled into mine, slow, purposeful. My breath hitched, humiliation scorching through me.

"Was it torture to sit across from me like that?" he murmured. "I could barely function having you so close and not being able to touch you."

I shook my head, my throat thick. "Callum—"

He cut me off with a kiss.

Deep. Overwhelming. Taking.

My heart slammed against my ribs, panic and shame warring inside me. My fingers twitched against his shirt.

Footsteps.

They were distant, but growing louder, coming from the other end of the hallway. Stark relief rattled through my bones.

In an instant, Callum pushed away from me, taking a quiet step back, smoothing his shirt like nothing had happened, his expression unreadable as my father stepped into the hallway.

"There you are." My father didn't even glance at me, addressing Callum instead. "Ready to head to the club?"

"Of course." Callum's voice was light, easy. His posture was relaxed, his hands tucked into his pockets.

He was so much better at *pretending* than I was. The fact that he could just head to the country club for a round of golf after all that had happened was inconceivable to me.

"I was just discussing Riley's college applications. She's considering a few out-of-state options, but I think I can convince her that Chapel Hill's her best bet."

I sucked in a breath, my pulse hammering. Chapel Hill. Where he was a professor.

My father nodded approvingly, even though I knew he really didn't care. "That's good," he said absently as he pulled up an email on his phone. "I know Claire would love to have her nearby."

Callum turned his head just slightly, his eyes catching mine. And in them, I saw it.

The warning.

The power.

The control.

I swallowed hard, forcing myself to breathe as my father patted Callum on the shoulder, completely oblivious.

Completely blind.

I was born with something broken inside of me. That was the only explanation I had for what came after.

All I knew was that I never said no.

Once I had given in, there didn't seem to be a way to take it back.

At first, it was under the pretense of helping me with my college applications. My father had been thrilled when Callum volunteered, saying it was an incredible opportunity to have help from someone so respected in academia.

It also meant that my father didn't have to spend any of his precious time helping me. Win-win for him.

I couldn't come up with a fast enough excuse to say no. And even if I had, I knew it wouldn't have mattered.

So, I sat at his desk, pretending to focus on school applications while his presence loomed behind me, always too close, always just barely brushing against me. A hand on my shoulder. A soft breath against my neck when he leaned down to point something out on my laptop. The way his voice dipped low when he praised me, whispering how sexy I was . . . how special I was.

Right before he fucked me on his desk.

He cut me off from everything. From my friends, from school, from anything outside of him.

"You think they care about you?" he'd ask, his voice laced with mock sympathy when I mentioned an invite from friends.

And when I would shake my head, desperate for his approval, he would smile and tuck my hair behind my ear, whispering, "That's my darling."

He made me think I wanted it.

Needed it.

He reminded me constantly that no one else would deal with me.

"No man is going to put up with this, Riley," he murmured one night, his fingers brushing over my wrist where the scar from my IV line still lingered. "No man is going to want a girl who spends half her time sick in bed, too tired to function. That's why you're so lucky to have me. Because I can see past all that."

He was everywhere.

In the mornings, he would want an hour-by-hour outline of my day. If I didn't answer, he'd call, his voice smooth as he asked if I was ignoring him.

When I was with my parents, he would brush his fingers against mine beneath the table, just barely, just enough to make my stomach clench with something confusing, something sick.

When I started pulling away, feeling the weight of what we were doing, he made me feel unlovable.

A burden that only he could endure.

I had never felt more alone.

I hated myself.

But I couldn't stop.

Because he had convinced me that I was his. That no one else would ever want me the way he did.

And the worst part?

I believed him.

―――――――

I had known the moment I woke up that my body wasn't going to cooperate today.

My limbs felt heavy, my mind ached with the familiar pressure of exhaustion, and my stomach churned like I had swallowed glass. I was used to this; it's not like it was the first time. My body had betrayed me for years, pulling me into waves of fatigue and pain I couldn't control.

But today was worse. Today, I felt like a shell of a person, barely able to breathe, let alone move.

I had tried to tell him. Tried to explain that I didn't have it in me, that I was too sick, that I needed to rest. But Callum never listened when he didn't want to.

"Shh," he had whispered against my skin, his weight pressing down on me, suffocating. "Just let me have this."

I had wanted to fight. I really had. But my body was already shutting down, the way it always did when I pushed too hard. And he didn't care. He took what he wanted, his hands rough, his voice coaxing, telling me how good I felt, how lucky I was that he still wanted me even like this.

Even when I was weak. Even when I was broken. Even when I was sick.

After, when he was gone, I lay curled in bed, the sheets pulled up to my chin, staring blankly at the ceiling. My limbs ached, my skin raw and bruised. A single tear slipped from the corner of my eye, trailing down my temple and disappearing into the pillowcase.

I couldn't do this anymore.

I turned my head toward the nightstand, my heart pounding as my gaze landed on the small pair of silver scissors sitting beside my forgotten notebook. My fingers twitched.

It would be so easy.

Just a few seconds—the pain would be something I could control. Something I could see.

Not this endless, gnawing ache in my chest. Not the exhaustion that lived in my bones. Not the way my skin felt too tight, too bruised, too tainted.

I reached for them, my fingers brushing the cool metal, and something in me settled. A terrible, quiet relief.

This was a choice. This was something that was mine.

I curled my fingers around the handle of the scissors, bringing them closer, my pulse slowing as I pressed the tip against the delicate skin of my wrist. Just a test. Just to see what it would feel like.

A single harsh breath left my lungs.

Then—movement.

Out of the corner of my eye, I caught something in the mirror across the room.

I looked up, and everything inside me stilled.

The girl staring back at me was a stranger.

Pale. Gaunt. Dark circles hollowed out her once-bright eyes, her cheeks sunken, her lips cracked. Her collarbones jutted out sharply, her skin washed out beneath the dim glow of her bedside lamp.

She looked sick. She looked lost. She looked . . . already gone.

My breath hitched, and my fingers spasmed, the scissors slipping from my grasp and clattering against the floor.

A choked sob ripped out of me, raw and unexpected.

How had I let it get this bad? How had I let him convince me that this was all I was?

I covered my mouth with both hands, my shoulders trembling.

I thought about the girl I used to be. Broken for sure, but one who dreamed about going to college, about escaping this house and this town and this life that had never really been hers. The girl who used to believe she had a future.

And then I thought about him.

How he had taken that from me.

Piece by piece.

How he had carved out every last shred of self-worth I had, replacing it with his voice, his control, his will.

You need me.

No one else will want you.

No one else will put up with you.

You're too much work, darling. You should be grateful I'm still here.

I squeezed my eyes shut.

I wasn't grateful. Not anymore.

I *hated* him.

And more than that—I hated that I had let him be right for the past year. I didn't have to stay here, in this room, in this house . . . in his grasp.

My heart thundered in my chest as I turned, dragging my aching body toward my desk, my fingers trembling as I opened my laptop.

The screen glowed in the dark, the unfinished college application I had filled out months ago still waiting. The one he didn't know about.

I had never submitted it.

Because I was afraid. Because I thought I needed him.

But maybe I didn't.

Maybe, I never had.

The submit button hovered beneath my cursor, taunting me.

I clenched my jaw, wiped my tear-streaked face with the back of my hand, and with one final, shaky breath—

I clicked it.

A confirmation message popped up, stark and certain, and my body sagged, my breath coming in gasps. For the first time in a year, I felt something that wasn't fear.

It wasn't even relief.

It was *freedom*.

And I wasn't looking back.

———————

I avoided him after that.

I tried to confess everything to my mother . . . to tell her what had been going on, but when I tried, she'd just sighed, pressing a hand to her temple as if I were the problem, as if my words were some unbearable inconvenience she didn't want to believe.

After that, I swallowed the words instead of screaming them.

Because that was the moment I realized—no one was going to save me.

No matter how many times he texted, no matter how often my parents told me I was being ungrateful by not letting Callum "help" me, I locked myself in my room. I let his messages go unread. I ignored his calls, his subtle threats, the way he tried to make me feel guilty for pulling away.

You don't really want this, darling. I know you better than you know yourself.

You think anyone else will want you? You think anyone else will put up with your broken body, your moods, your issues?

I love you. I'm the only one who ever will.

I used to believe that. Maybe some part of me still did, the part he had spent months carefully shaping, molding, breaking down until I was nothing but an extension of his will. Nothing but his dirty secret.

But there was a sliver of something else now, something louder than his voice in my head.

Anger.

It had started small. A flicker of heat under my skin every time I saw his name flash across my phone. A tightening in my chest when my mother sighed dramatically over breakfast, lamenting about how *poor Callum* was so confused by my behavior. That he was only trying to help me, that I was *overreacting*, that I should be grateful for everything he had done for me.

I kept my mouth shut and pushed my meal around my plate, my stomach churning with barely restrained rage.

Grateful.

They wanted me to be grateful?

Grateful that he had stripped me down, taken every part of me and twisted it into something he could control. Grateful that he had stolen pieces of me I could never get back. That I was nothing more than a possession he thought he owned.

I pressed my fork down against the plate until my knuckles turned white. I was done.

I spent the next few days locked in my room, ignoring the knocks at my door, ignoring my mother's passive-aggressive sighs, ignoring the creeping sense of dread every time my phone buzzed.

And the moment the acceptance letter arrived, I didn't even hesitate.

I stared at the email, my breath shallow, my hands shaking so hard I nearly dropped my phone.

Congratulations, Ms. St. James. We are pleased to inform you that you have been accepted—

I didn't read the rest. I didn't need to.

I had an out.

A real, tangible way to escape.

I scrambled out of bed, barely feeling my body move as I yanked my suitcase from the closet, throwing in clothes at random. My movements were rushed, frantic, like I thought the email would disappear if I didn't act fast enough. Like Callum would somehow sense what I was doing and appear in my doorway, that same practiced smile on his face, ready to convince me that I was his and nothing I did would ever change that.

I shuddered.

No.

No more.

I zipped up the suitcase, grabbed my car keys, and slipped out of my room, heart pounding as I moved through the darkened hall. The house was still, silent—the kind of silence that used to make me feel *safe*.

Now, it only made my skin crawl.

I stepped outside, inhaling the crisp night air, the weight on my chest loosening ever so slightly.

I tossed my bag into the passenger seat, gripping the steering wheel so tightly my fingers ached. I stared at the house, at the looming windows, the perfectly trimmed hedges, the home where I had lived my entire life.

I should have felt something. Sadness. Nostalgia. Regret.

But all I felt was the overwhelming need to run.

So I did.

I turned the key, felt the rumble of the engine beneath me, and drove.

I didn't look back.

CHAPTER 1

RILEY

had imagined college a thousand different ways.

Some versions were lonely, but freeing. Some were overwhelming, filled with new people and new experiences. Some were even terrifying, but exciting, like stepping onto a stage without knowing my lines.

None of them looked like this.

I stared at my textbook, my vision blurring as I tried for the third time to reread the same paragraph. My body ached, my chest tight, and my limbs felt heavy, like I was wading through molasses. I was exhausted in a way that went beyond a bad night's sleep. The kind of exhaustion that settled into my bones and refused to leave.

My first month at Tennessee had been a disaster.

I had gotten sick within the first two weeks and hadn't really recovered.

I had barely started the semester before my body betrayed me. A flare-up had knocked me out for almost a month, leaving me stuck in my dorm, barely able to move, let alone attend class. By the time I had dragged myself out of my room, I was already drowning in overdue assignments, missed lectures, and the overwhelming sense that I was falling behind. The professors were understanding—for a while. But sympathy only stretched so far in college.

Now, I was barely holding on to passing marks. Academic probation loomed like a threat I couldn't afford to acknowledge.

The campus was huge, filled with students who all seemed to already know what they were doing, where they were going . . . who they were supposed to be. I, on the other hand, spent most of my time lost—both literally and figuratively. I was always five minutes late to everything, trying to figure out how to navigate the endless mazes of lecture halls and offices. My body was struggling to keep up, and it showed in everything I tried to do.

And then there was my roommate.

Emma was . . . odd.

Not in an endearing, quirky way, but in a deep, unsettling way that made me wonder how she functioned in society.

And that was coming from me—possibly the second most awkward person in the world.

Because Emma had clearly taken the first spot.

She spoke in whispers, even when we were alone in the room, and she had a habit of staring at me while I was sleeping. I knew this because I'd woken up twice to find her sitting at her desk, completely still . . . watching me.

The first time, I'd thought I had imagined it. After the second time, I started locking the bathroom door while I showered and sleeping with one eye open.

She seemed to leave the room only to attend her classes.

Which meant that I never had a moment alone. I didn't have any friends yet, and I wasn't close enough to anyone to go hang out in their dorm. That meant when I wasn't working my two campus jobs, I spent most of my time holed up in the library or pretending to study at the campus café just to get away from the constant feeling of being watched.

I had considered requesting a room change, but what was the point? I could end up with someone worse.

Possibly.

Well, probably not.

I was pretty sure Emma had said, "Sometimes, I wonder what you'd look like if all the light went out of your eyes," the other night . . . but she'd said it so softly . . . and so cheerfully that I couldn't be certain.

But really, what excuse would I give? *Hey, my roommate is a little too ghostlike for my taste. Can I please have someone who blinks?*

I sighed, rubbing my hands over my face.

Despite everything, though, despite the loneliness, the exhaustion, and the looming threat of failing out, there was one thing that made it all worth it—I was free. Free from him. Free from the whispers in my ear, the suffocating grip he had on my life, the constant reminder that I was never enough. The weight of Callum had been lifted, and even though I was struggling, even though every day it felt like another battle, at least it was *my* battle. At least I was finally fighting for myself.

The library was half full, the hum of hushed voices and the soft scratch of pens against paper filling the space. I had taken my usual seat at the far end, where the overhead light wasn't too harsh, and I could spread out my notes without anyone getting in my space.

I had been staring at the same sentence in my textbook for five minutes when someone sat down across from me.

"Do you always look this miserable, or am I just catching you at a bad time?"

I glanced up, blinking at the girl now sitting across from me. She seemed vaguely familiar, her dark curls piled on top of her head, gold hoop earrings glinting under the soft glow of the lamp.

I searched my brain for her name. "Yeah . . ."

She grinned. "Tasha. We have English together," she supplied helpfully. Right. That's where I'd seen her.

She popped her gum and nodded. "And you're Riley. The mysterious girl who never talks in class."

I sighed, rubbing my temple. "Not mysterious. Just . . . shy."

"Same thing." She propped her chin on her hand and smirked. "Anyway, I was gonna leave you alone, let you keep suffering in solitude, but then I fig-ured—what kind of person would I be if I let you waste away in the library when I have the perfect solution to all your problems?"

I raised an eyebrow. "You have some kind of wild study technique that's going to magically save my GPA?"

She snorted. "No. Something much, much better than that. Sorority recruitment."

I stared at her. "I appreciate it, but—"

"Nope." She held up a manicured hand. "Don't say no yet. Just listen. We're hosting an event at the Lucky Strike tonight. It's chill. No pressure. Just a chance to hang out, meet cool girls, maybe have some fun. Which . . . based on that look on your face, I'm guessing you haven't had in years."

I scoffed . . . but couldn't come up with anything to say. Because she was kind of right.

"It's true, isn't it?" She gave me a pointed once-over. "When's the last time you went anywhere that wasn't a classroom or your dorm or the library?"

Her smirk widened when I didn't say anything.

"Exactly. And before you throw out some excuse about how far behind you are, it's basically a scientific fact that in order to study hard, you have to play hard, too. I'm surprised you haven't figured that out yet."

A grin slipped across my lips, one of my first since coming to campus.

"And you know what professors looooove, Riley?" she asked, leaning forward.

"What?" It was ridiculous how much I hated that word—*professor*—but it couldn't be helped. I might never hear that word again without wanting to throw up.

"*Making connections*. Professors like students they recognize. And what better way to get involved than by joining the *best* sorority on campus?"

I hesitated. The last thing I wanted was to spend a night in a loud bar, pretending to be social when all I really wanted was to hide under my covers.

But then I thought about what hiding under the covers actually meant . . .

Being watched.

By Emma.

While I slept.

And I did have that fake ID that Callum had gotten for me so I could drink when I was with him . . .

Tasha leaned forward, watching my expression, a victorious gleam in her eyes. "Come on, Riley. You're not supposed to just survive college. You're supposed to enjoy the whole experience. Live a little."

I sighed, biting the inside of my cheek. She had a point. I had spent my time at Tennessee so far avoiding risk, avoiding people . . . I was missing out on everything.

Maybe it was time to change that.

I let out a slow breath. "Fine. I'll go."

Tasha grinned, clapping her hands together. "Not exactly the enthusiasm I'm looking for, but I can work with it." She stood and stretched. "And hey, if nothing else, there's free drinks."

I laughed, and the sound seemed like a good sign. "You should have led with that," I told her, even though I'd never had more than a few sips of a drink my entire life.

She winked. "See you tonight. You won't regret it."

And with that, she sauntered off, leaving me staring at my textbook, feeling something I hadn't felt in a long time.

Excitement.

CHAPTER 2

JACE

H ey, Matty," I yelled to him as I lined up for the next play. "What did Cinderella do when she got to the ball?"

I could practically hear his sigh over the roar of the crowd. He liked to pretend I wasn't funny . . . but he was obviously wrong.

"She gagged," I yelled just as Parker received the snap, and I took off down the field.

There was something magical about the sound of a football spiraling through the air. Maybe it was the way the crowd held its breath. The way the ball cut through the stadium lights, a perfect arc against the night sky. The way I knew—*knew*—it was meant for me before it even left Parker's hands.

Or maybe it was just the fact that I was the best wide receiver in all of college football, and when I caught this, the crowd was going to go absolutely fucking wild.

Yeah, it was probably that.

I sprinted downfield, my cleats digging into the ground, my heart pounding like a fucking drum line. The corner was trying to cover me, but I was faster. I always was. I obviously always would be.

Ball in the air. Thirty yards out.

Twenty.

Ten.

It was beautiful. A perfect spiraling bullet heading right for me. I cut hard, shaking my defender, and stretched my arms—

Bam.

Helmet to my ribs.

Pain exploded through my chest as I hit the ground, the wind knocked right out of me. The ball tumbled from my hands, rolling uselessly across the turf.

Motherfucker!

The whistle blew, and I lay there for a second, staring up at the sky, questioning every decision that had led me to this moment. The ref signaled an incomplete pass, and the crowd groaned.

Son of a bitch.

A shadow loomed over me.

"You dead?"

I blinked and found Parker Davis, our golden boy QB, and one of *my* bestilicious bros, smirking down at me.

"Pretty sure I just met Jesus," I wheezed.

Parker held out his hand and yanked me to my feet. I winced, rolling my shoulders. Fucking hell, that hit hurt. "Did you put in a good word for me?" Parker smirked, probably thinking about his little "basement incident" a couple of weeks ago.

"I think you're beyond help," I said, trying to blink away the fact that my lungs had forgotten they were supposed to breathe. Fuck.

"Dude, you had it," Matty said, shaking his head as he joined us. "What happened?"

I glared at him because, obviously, this was the opposite of being a supportive king.

"Oh, I don't know," I shot back, rubbing my ribs. "Maybe it was the linebacker-sized missile that just torpedoed into my lungs."

"Excuses," Parker muttered, jogging back to the huddle.

I flipped him off and followed.

———

Fourth and seven.

Two minutes left.

Down by three.

This was what I lived for. High-pressure moments. Big-time plays.

The chance to be a fucking legend.

Parker called the play, and we broke the huddle, lining up at the snap. The defense was in man coverage, and I snorted. Rookie mistake.

Because no one. And I repeat—no one—could cover me one-on-one.

The ball snapped, and I was *gone*.

I burned past my defender, my legs churning, my lungs on fire. The safety sprinted over to help, but he was too late. The ball was already flying, a perfect deep shot, aimed right at me.

This time . . . I wasn't missing.

I jumped, snagging it right out of the air, my fingers wrapping around the leather like it was made for me. My feet hit the ground, and I was off.

The end zone was ten yards away.

Five.

I dove.

The moment I crossed the goal line, the stadium erupted.

Touchdown.

Game over.

We won.

I rolled onto my back, breathing hard. "You're welcome, bitches," I screamed as Parker sprinted up and yanked me to my feet.

"Way to make that look hard, drama queen," he drawled, pounding a hand against my helmet.

I grinned. "Would've been cooler if I could have done that two plays ago and you hadn't tried getting me killed."

"Details." Parker smirked as we both soaked in the moment.

Matty, my other bestilicious bro, came running up, tackling me back to the ground in his excitement. The rest of the team mobbed us, slamming into me with congratulations, but all I could hear was the roar of the crowd, the fight song blaring, and the announcer yelling my name like it belonged to a hero.

Fucking hell, I loved football.

And I *loved* winning.

———

I leaned back against my locker, tapping out a text while Parker ran a towel over his face. He was trying for a new land speed record to get out of here and through his postgame interviews so he could see his girl, Casey.

"Party at Lucky Strike tonight?" I asked, my eyes suddenly bulging at the boobs that had just shown up on my phone.

"Ah!" I screeched, wondering how a three-nippled woman had managed to get ahold of my phone number. "Someone get this thing off my phone." I tossed it to Matty—obviously. Parker had a no-boobs-but-Casey's rule, and I was all for respecting that.

"What the hell?" Matty said, gawking at the picture as he punched some buttons on my phone. "Is that—"

You might ask me why I had such a problem with three nipples, but I actually didn't.

What I had a problem with, was the fact that I was pretty sure my face had been tattooed around that third nipple. And considering I had no recollection of sleeping with someone with a third nipple, this girl was probably a stalker.

I was stalker-worthy, obviously.

But I actually preferred to be the one *doing* the stalking.

"Deleted," Matty said, grimacing as he handed me my phone back.

"You're a man above men, Matty-kins," I drawled.

"Do you have to call me that?" he asked, *still* grimacing.

"Oh, I'm sorry. Am I annoying you with my *best* friendship?"

"Your *best* friendship?" Parker asked, lifting an eyebrow.

"Yes, my *best* friendship, QB. You guys have qualified for my best, which is very lucky for you, and reminds me . . . I've got one."

They both groaned almost simultaneously, like I wasn't the funniest person they knew. Seriously so rude.

"You mean *another* one," Matty pointed out, obviously remembering my banger of a joke during the game.

"This is a really good one," I told them matter-of-factly.

"Oh, I hear Casey calling my name," Parker said, looking around the locker room as if it were possible to hear anyone through the thick concrete walls. Also rude.

"What do you call a masturbating cow?" I asked them, starting to chuckle a little because I was so damn funny.

"It's weird that you're already laughing. You're setting yourself up for disappointment when you're already laughing."

"Pshh," I said, waving my hand at Matty because I was completely unconcerned about that. "Beef Stroganoff."

Both of them stared at me with blank faces.

"What are you going to do with beef Stroganoff?" Matty finally asked.

"It's the joke. *Beef stroking off*," I said, enunciating it slowly because, obviously, not everyone could have a big brain like I did.

"I still don't get it?" Matty said, surprising me not even a little.

"It's because you interrupt me forty-five million times whenever I *gift* you with a joke. It disrupts the cadence."

"I happen to have incredible *cadence*," Parker drawled.

"When shouting plays to our center, yes. When interrupting my jokes, no, you do not." I grimaced as I removed my shoulder pads because my ribs fucking hurt to move.

I cracked my neck. "Okay, but real talk—am I the best receiver in football, or am I not? And there is only one right answer, so even Matty should be able to get this one right."

Parker snorted, and Matty huffed.

"So braggy for someone who can barely breathe because he got hit so hard," Matty said sarcastically.

"Ah, you're still upset about the one inch," I said wisely, able to see right through the prickly tight end of a lover bean.

Parker laughed, finally accepting how funny I was. But Matty just snarled.

"You can say one inch as much as you want, but it's never going to be true. A quarter of an inch doesn't even round up to one," he hissed, finally showing me a hint of a big brain.

"Proud of you for knowing that, bubs," I told him, ducking at the towel Matty threw at me while simultaneously pulling a clean shirt over my head, even though my bare chest was obviously a gift to mankind.

Matty flung himself down on a bench, scowling at the room. He had the best RBF of anyone I'd ever seen, and somehow it worked for him, the handsome bastard.

"When the fuck do you think our trials are going to start?" Matty asked, his voice pitched low as he wiped a towel through his hair.

Parker, Matty, and I had all been recruited the first week of school by the Sphinx, a shadowy, high-rolling secret society on campus that was apparently supposed to ensure us fame, riches, and power for the rest of our lives if we were lucky enough to join their ranks. Parker had already completed his three initiation trials—with some help from us, of course, but Matty and I were still waiting for ours to start.

Parker lifted a brow at him and took a step closer. "Are you two in a hurry to risk your life? Might I remind you about the little *graveyard* scene you both loved so much?"

Matty shivered, probably picturing all those imaginary ghosts he'd been so afraid of that night. I personally was thinking of the cookies I'd been eating during the event in question—but that was most likely because I was really fucking hungry at the moment.

I shot Parker a grin. "I mean, kinda? If I have to do some insane, life-threatening initiation bullshit, I'd rather get it over with now instead of waiting in constant suspense for some guy in a creepy mask to show up and tell me I have to steal a cop car or something."

Matty snorted. "Please. You're going to wish that was all you had to do. I bet our first trial is gonna be something way worse than anything Golden Boy over here had to do."

I glanced back at Parker, who was watching us, clearly amused. Probably because he was smug in his safeness thanks to the tracker I'd installed in that manly friendship bracelet he had around his wrist. Thanks to me always *gently observing* him, he was guaranteed to have a backup in case anything happened to him.

I was such a good friend.

"It will happen when you least expect it," he said, standing up and tossing his towel onto the bench. "They won't give you any warning."

Matty groaned. "Awesome. Love that for me."

I punched him in the arm. "I love that for you, too, Matty-kins. I know how much you *luvvv* surprises. Especially in the middle of the night . . . with a bag over your head."

Matty looked faintly green at that statement. "Yeah," he croaked, his eyes wide as he probably pictured how they really had stuffed bags over our heads the night we'd been chosen.

Parker shook his head, muttering something ominous that sounded like *Just you wait*, like the drama queen he was, before heading toward the showers.

Matty still had his grumble face on when my phone buzzed, and I pulled it out, seeing it was a congratulations text from my brother, Jagger. He was five years older than me and my favorite brother from the same mother.

Mostly since he was my *only* brother from the same mother. Everything about Jagger was a little sketchy and a lot cool, hence how he was related to me.

> Jagger: There was a lot about that last touchdown celebration that could have been avoided.

> Jagger: I may have a plethora of nieces and nephews in nine months.

> Me: So you agree I'm sexy. Thank you. Not anything I didn't know, but it's always nice to hear.

Jagger: . . .

Me: Excellent use of that.

Me: Parker seems to think that his brother came up with that, but I'm pretty sure the Thatcher brothers were dot-dot-dot people loooong before the Davis boys.

Jagger: I have no idea what you're talking about right now. But I agree, we are much better than them.

Me: So, tell me again how awesome I did in the game.

Jagger: Does anyone really need to do that? Pretty soon your head won't actually fit in your helmet.

Me: What a jokester, Jagger-meister. We really only have to worry about me fitting in my pants.

Jagger: I've told you this before, Jace. I don't want to talk about your dick.

Me: Ugh, what's even worth talking about, then?

Jagger: . . .

Me: See? You're a . . . pro.

Matty stretched out, leaning back on the bench and dragging my attention away from my phone. "So . . . bar?"

I nodded. "Bar."

Because as much as I enjoyed discussing football, my ego, and my excellent dick size . . . right now, I wanted to celebrate.

The Tennessee Tigers were the shit.

CHAPTER 3

RILEY

This was a mistake.

The thought had been whispering in my head since the moment I stepped into the packed bar, but now, standing in the middle of a sea of bodies, shifting uncomfortably in a dress that I was sure looked terrible on me, it was *screaming*.

I tugged at the hem of the tight black dress that I'd forced myself to wear, wishing I'd just stuck with jeans. I wasn't a tight dress person. I wasn't really a bar person. But I was trying, wasn't I? Trying to be normal. Trying to be fun. Trying to be the kind of girl who could leave the library and her dorm room without having a nervous breakdown.

I let out a slow breath, scanning the room for Tasha, the whole reason I was in this situation to begin with. I spotted her near the bar, already draped over a guy in a Tigers baseball cap, giggling at something he was whispering in her ear.

Great.

I wove through the crowd, my heels catching on the sticky floor as I made my way to her. "Hey," I said, trying to get her attention over the pounding bass. She turned, her eyes glassy, and let out a high-pitched squeal. "Riley! You made it!"

"I did," I said, forcing a smile.

"You look hot! Doesn't she look hot?" She turned to the guy next to her, who barely spared my face a glance before his eyes dropped to my boobs.

I resisted the urge to cross my arms over my chest. "Thanks."

Tasha waved a hand. "You need a drink. The drinks are free until ten—" She paused, looking around before frowning. "Oh. I guess not anymore . . ."

I followed her gaze to the sign over the bar: ladies drink free until 10 p.m. . . . but there was a huge red X drawn through it. I sighed. I was really looking forward to those free drinks. That was what finally got me out of my room to come down here after hours of debating myself about it.

I guess that meant I was paying for my own drinks tonight.

Tasha shrugged like it was no big deal, already turning back to the guy, her interest in me fading fast.

I sighed. It didn't seem likely she was going to be introducing me to other girls from her sorority. This was exactly what I'd been afraid of.

I didn't belong here.

The crowd, the heat, the sweaty bodies pressed in too close, the way my heart was already pounding—not from excitement, but from anxiety—it was all too much.

One drink. I'd get one drink, and if the vibes did not improve, I'd leave. One drink was social, right? And that meant progress. A lot of progress, considering how I normally spent my Saturday nights since coming here. I needed to take advantage of the fact that my body was actually cooperating for once.

And being by myself at this bar was better than sitting on my bed while I pretended not to notice my roommate staring at me. Right?

Right.

Walking a little farther down the bar so I wasn't next to Tasha while she tried to eat that guy's tongue, I waved my hand, trying to catch the bartender's attention. He was busy pouring shots with zero urgency, but eventually, his eyes flicked to me.

"What can I get you?"

"Uh . . ." I hesitated, realizing I had no idea what to order. I wasn't a big drinker. And I wasn't about to stand here and google "cocktails that don't taste like rubbing alcohol."

"Screw it," I muttered. "Just make me something. I don't care what."

The bartender gave me a look, but he didn't argue. "Card on file?"

I grimaced, then nodded, sliding my credit card across the counter. I'd have just one. Anything beyond that would break the bank. Turns out, working two campus jobs for minimum wage still took a really, really long time to add up to decent money.

But it was better than the alternative.

A minute later, the bartender placed a dark blue drink in front of me with a lime wedge on the rim. It looked . . . innocent.

I took a sip and immediately regretted everything.

It tasted like cough syrup, chased with a punch to the throat. I forced myself to swallow, plastering on an expression that indicated *Yeah, this is totally fine. I'm not dying.*

The bartender smirked before turning away.

Drink in hand, I wove my way back through the crowd, scanning for literally anyone I recognized. The crush of bodies felt like a trap, every brush of skin making my nerves itch. My stomach twisted. Nope. Not for me.

Five more minutes, and then I was getting the hell out of here.

Jace

The bar was packed.

The bass pounded through my chest, rattling my ribs like it was trying to restart my heart. Beer in hand, I scanned the room, surveying the drunken chaos, the crowd who had come out tonight to celebrate a Tigers win.

I wasn't in the mood for this, which was weird. Because I had definitely been in the mood in the locker room.

I was *always* in the mood to celebrate a win, to have a good time, for a party, for girls in short dresses who wanted a piece of Tennessee's star wide receiver. And they were here, throwing looks my way, biting their lips, giving me every green light possible.

I just wasn't biting back.

My fingers drummed against the neck of my beer bottle as I took a sip, my gaze drifting to where Parker and Casey were tucked in a corner of the bar. She was laughing, pressed against his side, his arm curled around her waist like he'd rather die than let her go.

It was disgusting. It was pathetic. It was *everything* I wanted.

I hated myself a little for it.

I scoffed and turned away, rolling my shoulders like I could shake off the weight settling in my chest. What the fuck was wrong with me?

I had everything.

Football. Friends. The kind of life every guy fucking dreamed about.

But lately, when I actually let myself think for too long, I'd started to get this nagging, empty fucking feeling in my gut. And no matter how many girls threw themselves at me, no matter how many parties I went to, I couldn't shake it.

I was a disappointment to myself was what I was at the moment.

I tipped my beer back, chugging the rest, setting the bottle down with a little too much force.

"You good, Jace-face?" Matty's voice cut through my pity party, amusement laced in his tone as he leaned against the bar next to me.

"Yeah." I exhaled sharply, running a hand through my hair. "Just over . . . everything."

Matty snorted, his eyebrow lifting in mirth because apparently it was *funny* to him that I was undergoing an existential crisis. Either that or an alien had inhabited my body. I wasn't quite sure. The guy didn't know funny when it hit him in the face, but evidently he'd decided I was funny tonight.

Another point in the rude column, thank you very little.

"You? Over a bar filled with girls who would *die* to ride your face?"

I snorted because Matty wasn't funny that often. But that comment actually was.

I grabbed Matty's beer and took a long pull of it without him noticing, my eyes going back to Parker and Casey like they had some kind of tractor beam focused on them.

It wasn't that I was bitter about my best friend being in love.

Parker deserved it.

Casey was good for him. I'd spent enough time watching the guy nearly burn down his own life to get her to know that if *anyone* deserved true love, it was Parkie-Poo based on his insane efforts alone.

But that didn't mean I wasn't a little . . . itchy.

Like something was missing.

Like I was waiting for something—or someone—and I was getting sick of the wait.

I turned back to the bar, giving the girl who had just popped up beside me a lazy smirk when she traced a red manicured hand up my arm.

"You look bored," she purred, pressing closer.

I should've been interested. She was hot. Dark hair, killer curves, wearing a dress that barely qualified as clothing.

But I wasn't.

Not at all.

"Not tonight, darlin'," I said, giving her my best *fake* charming smile before I threw back another sip of beer and turned to face the other way.

Matty was watching me with an arched brow, and I snarled at him. "Why are you looking at me like that? It's creepy."

"Maybe there *is* something wrong with you," he said, smirking. "I don't think I've ever seen you say no to a hot girl before."

"Hey, sometimes I say no," I muttered half-heartedly.

Even though he was right.

Matty choked on his drink. "Name one time?"

I didn't get a chance to answer. As I scanned the bar out of pure habit, I saw her.

My entire body fucking locked up. My chest clenched so tight I thought I was having a fucking heart attack.

I felt it before I even processed what I was looking at. A full-body reaction. Like a fucking punch to the gut.

Everything else disappeared.

The bar. The people. The music.

Gone.

Fuck.

She was standing on the far side of the dance floor, long dark blonde hair cascading down her back, catching in the neon glow of the bar lights. A black dress clung to curves I wanted my hands on immediately. She had this softness about her, an effortless kind of beauty that made my stomach twist.

And her face. Fucking hell.

She looked like something straight out of a dream, like an angel had dropped down in the middle of the bar.

Her beauty gutted me. And her full lips were giving me dirty, dirty images in my mind.

Just looking at her, I knew.

I was ruined.

The hand gripping my chest tightened, like I was trying to physically keep my heart from fucking combusting.

I didn't say a word. I didn't tell Matty what I was doing. I didn't hesitate. I just moved.

Setting Matty's beer bottle down, I started across the dance floor, stalking toward her like a man possessed. Some girl touched my arm, trying to get my attention. I couldn't even look at her.

Another one said my name, trying to pull me toward her. I barely registered them.

All I could see was *her*.

She was fidgeting, shifting from foot to foot, glancing around like she wasn't sure what to do. By the uncomfortable look on her face, she wasn't excited to be here.

And suddenly, that pissed me off.

Who the fuck dragged her here? The goddess in front of me only deserved a lifetime of happiness.

I was pretty sure there was a cereal commercial that claimed to offer that, but I was also pretty sure that I could deliver the goods much better.

I was kind of hyperventilating as I finally made it to her.

"We just found out Grandpa is addicted to Viagra," I told her, stopping just short of invading her space, close enough that she could feel me, but not close enough for her to run. It wasn't my greatest pickup line, but it was all I had in me at the moment. I was surprised I'd been able to form words at all.

Her head snapped up, and the second her wide, honey-colored eyes met mine, something clicked into place inside me. Like the fucking universe had just aligned in my favor. Like I'd been waiting my whole life to meet her.

It was over.

I was done.

She was mine.

She just didn't know it yet.

The angel's lips parted slightly, just enough for me to catch the way she sucked in a breath, her fingers tightening around the full glass she was holding. I liked that. That I had an effect on her. That she was already reacting to me.

She blinked at me, genuine confusion flashing across her face. She glanced behind her, like she thought I was staring at someone else.

But how could anyone else exist?

Alright, so aliens *had* invaded my body. And I was perfectly okay with that.

She blinked up at me. "Um?" Fucking hell, her *voice*. Soft and hesitant, like she wasn't sure what to make of me. Like she hadn't already sunk her claws into my chest and rearranged everything inside.

I smirked. "Nobody is taking it harder than Grandma."

She tilted her head and blinked a few times before she finally snorted in shock . . . or awe. It could have gone either way. "Do I know you?" she asked, like she wasn't sure she'd heard me correctly.

I grinned. Fuck, she was cute.

"No," I admitted. "But you're going to."

Her lips twitched, like she was fighting a smile. I needed to see that smile. I needed to earn it.

"Do you always walk up to random girls and say stuff like that?" she asked, eyeing me like she was trying to figure out my angle.

"Only the one I plan on marrying," I said, dead serious.

She finally laughed. Like a full-body, head-tilted-back-and-giggling kind of laugh.

I felt that shit. Like an electric shock straight to my bloodstream.

"There it is," I murmured, feeling strangely satisfied.

"There what is?" she asked, still smiling.

"The first laugh. The first step toward our inevitable love story."

She rolled her eyes. "Wow. Does that usually work?"

I shrugged. "It's working right now."

She huffed out another laugh and shook her head, finally relaxing a little. She was still hesitant, but she wasn't running.

Yet.

I slid my hands into my pockets, leaning in slightly. "So, what's your name?"

She tilted her head. "What's *yours*?"

"Jace," I said immediately, wanting her to know everything about me. "Jace Thatcher."

She nodded slowly, no hint of recognition in her gaze. That was different.

"Not a big football fan, are you?" I asked, amused.

She shrugged, a light blush hitting her cheeks. "Not exactly."

I fucking grinned. I kind of liked that. "Your name. You were about to tell me that," I pushed.

She hesitated, and I leaned forward, like what she was about to say was the most important thing anyone had ever told me in my life. But then she smirked, taking a sip of her drink, and said, "I'd rather not say."

I blinked. "Excuse me?"

She shrugged, eyes dancing with mischief. "You don't need to know. You're a *stranger*."

The smile that I'd had since the moment I saw her face only widened. "I'm pretty sure everyone starts out a stranger in college," I noted. "But, once you tell me your name, we won't be strangers anymore. So, the whole stranger thing is a pretty easy problem to solve."

She shook her head again, taking an exaggerated sip of her drink and pretending like she was suddenly fascinated by the crowd around us.

I laughed, shaking my head. "Okay, little firecracker. Do you plan on giving me *anything* to work with here?"

She pursed her lips, pretending to think about it. "Hmm. No."

"Fuck." I let out a dramatic sigh. "Guess I'll just have to steal your wallet when you're not looking."

She snorted again. "Good luck with that."

I leaned in closer, my voice dropping. "Why won't you tell me your name?"

She blushed. Just a little. Just enough. But I saw it, and I fucking *thrived* on it.

Huffing, she crossed her arms. "You don't even know if I have a boyfriend or not."

I smirked. "I know."

She narrowed her eyes. "Oh? How's that?"

"Because if you were with someone, they'd be glued to your side. Making sure that no one else could swoop in and steal all that perfection."

Her mouth opened in that perfect little O again, the one that made me want to stuff my dick down her throat.

Whoops. Any more thoughts like that, and lil Jace was going to be making a major appearance at the party.

And that could make her run. He tended to be a little . . . intimidating.

Probably because of that extra inch.

I reached out, barely skimming my fingers along her forearm. Her breath hitched, just enough for me to hear it.

"There's also this, though," I murmured, my voice rough, because it had rearranged my insides just touching her smooth skin. "If you had a boyfriend, you wouldn't sound like that I'm thinking . . . you wouldn't be looking at me like that, either."

Her eyes widened.

Got her.

She pulled back, guzzling more of her drink, before starting to cough, a pained expression on her face because whatever she was drinking evidently tasted awful.

I grinned. "So, do you want me to buy you another drink, or are you still pretending you don't like me?"

She hesitated, and for a second, I thought she might say no.

But then she lifted her still very full glass and tilted her head. "I wouldn't say no to something that actually tastes good."

I fucking beamed. Sign the marriage license. I was gone.

She wanted me.

I could see it in the way her pulse fluttered at her throat. The way she kept tucking that long, thick blonde hair behind her ear, like she needed something to do with her hands.

Without a word, I reached out, taking her hand. The second my fingers closed around hers, my world tilted. Her hand was small and delicate, fitting perfectly in mine, and yet it sent a shock wave through my body like I'd grabbed on to a live wire. My heart slammed against my ribs, my skin burning where we touched. It was just her palm against mine, her fingers curled slightly, hesitant, uncertain.

But I felt it.

I felt her warmth seep into me, felt the way her fingers twitched like she wasn't sure if she wanted to pull away or hold on tighter.

Hold on tighter, baby.

I barely kept myself from saying it out loud, from tightening my grip, from lacing our fingers together just to claim her. To stitching her to my side. She had no idea what she'd just done.

She had no idea how fucking gone I already was.

I swallowed hard, my throat tight as I glanced at her out of the corner of my eye. She was looking ahead, her lips slightly parted, her breathing just a little too shallow. Like she felt it, too.

My chest clenched, something heavy settling deep inside me. I was never going to let this go.

Never.

Not if it felt like this.

I led her through the crowd, the insane urge to rip everyone's eyeballs out riding me hard. I didn't want them to look at her. I wanted her all to myself.

Probably wouldn't be good this early in the relationship to lock us in a room, though. Parker had shown me that.

She was already giving me trouble, and we hadn't even reached the bar yet. "I already have a card on file—Jace—"

Fuck.

The way she said my name. I felt it in my chest.

It was the first time she'd said it, and I fucking *loved* it. I grinned. "Say it again."

"What?"

"My name."

She rolled her eyes, but her cheeks were pink again.

I turned around and kept walking, bringing her to the bar. I didn't want to let go of her hand until I had to.

The bartender looked up, his gaze dragging up and down her body. "What can I get you?" he asked her, like I wasn't standing there holding her hand.

Alright, that whole locked-room scenario was sounding more and more like a great idea.

"My lady needs a drink," I said, dropping my arm onto the counter and tilting my head toward my soulmate. "Something fruity."

Her brows shot up. "You don't even know what I like."

"Okay, tell me what you like, then," I told her, getting so close I could inhale her breaths.

Like a psycho.

She huffed, and I tried not to be completely obvious that I was sucking it in like a crack addict. "Something fruity," she finally mumbled . . . complete with an adorable eye roll.

I held in my snicker like a gentleman.

The bartender chuckled and threw a few things in a glass before sliding it over to her. "That'll do it."

She narrowed her eyes at the bright pink cocktail with a pineapple wedge and a tiny umbrella on top.

I grinned, grabbing the drink and plucking the umbrella out and tucking it behind her ear.

She froze, and then she smiled. A small, secretive kind of smile. Like I'd done something unexpectedly right. Her fingers brushed against mine as she took the glass from me, sending a sharp jolt of heat through my body. Holding my gaze, she took a tentative sip and then licked her lips.

I almost groaned, my gaze caught on her pink tongue gliding across her mouth, watching the way her lips pressed against the glass, a wave of pure, unfiltered possessiveness slamming into my chest.

Fuck.

"Okay," she admitted. "That's pretty good."

I took the opportunity to lean in close again. "Told you," I murmured. "Now, tell me your name."

She hesitated. "I'm still not giving you that."

I grinned. "Not even if I guess?"

She set her glass down on the bar and crossed her arms in front of her as her lips twitched like she was fighting a smile. "You're not going to guess."

I tapped my chin, pretending to think. "Hmm. Angel?" She rolled her eyes.

"Sweetheart?"

"Original."

"Sugarplum?"

She laughed—really laughed, her face lighting up with it, and it felt like a punch to the ribs.

I exhaled, raking a hand through my long hair, trying to compose myself. Her gaze followed my hand, her eyes narrowing slightly. "So . . . the hair," she said, crossing her arms. "That a phase or something?"

I smirked. "It's sexy, isn't it?"

She blinked, clearly not expecting that. "I—"

"Be honest." I cut in, leaning against the bar. "You were already imagining running your fingers through it."

Her jaw dropped slightly. "I—was not."

"You were." I winked. "It's okay. Happens all the time. It can't be helped."

She scoffed. "And let me guess—there's some ridiculous reason you refuse to cut it?"

"Obviously," I said as if that were common knowledge.

She exhaled. "Of course there is."

I leaned in close, enjoying the way her breath hitched when my lips *accidentally* caressed her ear. "It has magical powers."

She stared at me, another one of those small, secretive smiles sliding across her lips.

I nodded solemnly. "I can't cut it. It's part of the deal."

She barked out a laugh. "What deal?"

"The one where I keep it long and, in return, I remain devastatingly handsome, *irresistible*, and completely undefeated in every battle."

She tilted her head. "You're comparing yourself to . . . what, Samson?"

"Brad Pitt in *Troy*," I corrected.

Her lips parted slightly, her gaze flicking down my frame as if she were suddenly reevaluating.

I grinned. She was *so* checking me out.

She shook her head. "I'm not seeing the resemblance."

"Are you sure?"

"You think you look like Brad Pitt?"

"I think Brad Pitt wishes he looked like me."

She let out another laugh, shaking her head again as she went to reach for her drink.

"Here." I grabbed the glass again and handed it to her, just so her fingers had to brush against mine for another moment.

I swear she shivered when we touched this time, and her body swayed toward me like it was as desperate for my attention as I was for hers.

I set the beer I'd ordered down on the bar, completely untouched. Who needed alcohol when she was around? I literally felt drunk just breathing in her same air.

"So, tell me, Mystery Girl . . . what brought you out tonight?"

She blinked. "What do you mean?"

I gestured around us. "You didn't seem to be having a good time before I saved you."

Her lips parted, a little huff of indignation slipping out. "Saved me, huh?"

I grinned. "Definitely. Like the guy in *Troy*. Except without the heel thing," I corrected, reaching out to twist a strand of her long dark blonde hair between my fingers. Soft. Silky. Fucking perfect. "Just an observation, though. You kind of looked like you were waiting to be found."

I leaned in again, because at this point, I couldn't help myself, inhaling the faintest hint of vanilla and something warm and sweet clinging to her skin.

She scoffed, but I caught the flicker of hesitation behind it.

Maybe I wasn't wrong. Maybe my girl *had* been waiting to be found.

I let the strand of her hair slip from my fingers, watching the way her breath caught when my knuckles brushed her collarbone.

Fuck.

"Dance with me." The words blurted out. I didn't usually ask girls to dance. I was pretty good at it, and it could be intimidating to mere mortals, obviously. But I had a feeling she could handle it.

She made a face, biting down on her bottom lip like I'd suggested sawing off her left leg instead of rubbing up against me as "Pink Pony Club" blasted.

"I don't dance," she finally said shyly.

"You do now."

She looked at my hand, hesitant. But I could see the curiosity. The interest. The way her fingers twitched at her side like she was considering it. I didn't give her a chance to say no.

I grabbed her hand, pulled her away from the bar, and led her straight to the dance floor.

The second we stepped into the crowd, the bass pulsed through my bones.

Bodies pressed together, moving in time with the music as I turned to face her. She looked stunning—flushed cheeks glowing under the neon lights, her hair falling over her shoulder.

She was tense at first, unsure. So I did what I do best.

I took control.

I set my hands on her waist, slow and deliberate, tugging her just close enough for her to feel my body heat. She let out the smallest breath. And then she moved. Not much. Just enough for me to feel her.

I dragged my hands over the curve of her hips, bringing her flush against me, rolling my body into hers, enjoying the gasp that fell from her lips when she felt my dick.

I leaned down, brushing my lips against the shell of her ear. "Relax, babycakes," I purred. "Just pretend he's not there."

"He?" she asked, looking adorably confused. I pressed a little closer so she knew what I was talking about, and her cheeks took on the reddest hue of the night.

Perfection.

Her fingers curled into the front of my shirt, and I felt every breath she took . . . every tiny movement.

I became obsessed with watching her let herself go, just a little at a time.

The music pulsed, slow and thick, curling through the air like a whispered promise. She moved with me, her body fitting against mine as if she were made for it. She followed my lead, letting me guide her with the firm press of my hands, my touch lingering, teasing as I turned her around.

I slid an arm around her waist, pulling her back against my chest, wondering how it felt like this was where she belonged. My palm splayed over her stomach, holding her there, keeping her exactly where I wanted her. She didn't resist. Instead, she arched—just enough, just barely—but I felt it.

All of it.

She was so fucking soft. So impossibly perfect against me that my breath came slower, heavier.

I let my lips skim along her jawline, a ghost of a touch, just enough for my breath to dance over her skin. I heard it then—the way her breathing hitched, the barely there whimper that slipped from her lips. Her fingers curled around my arm, nails digging in just enough to send a pulse of heat straight through me.

She was breathless. Flushed. Mine.

I turned her in my arms, not breaking the contact, not letting her slip even an inch away. Her gaze lifted to mine, pupils blown wide, lips parted, chest rising and falling in uneven, shallow breaths.

She wanted me.

And I was going to make damn sure she knew just how badly I wanted her, too.

I leaned in. "You ready to admit it yet?"

Her breath shuddered. "Admit what?"

"That you want me."

She swallowed. "I barely know you."

I smirked. "You will. You're going to know me better than anyone ever has in my entire life."

Her eyes darkened, a flicker of something reckless sparking to life—like she already knew she was about to make a bad decision and wanted to make it anyway.

I reached out, wrapping my fingers around hers before she could even think about pulling away. My grip was firm, possessive, leaving no room for hesitation. She stiffened for half a second, her lips parting, her breath catching, and then—

"What are you doing?" Her voice was laced with something between a laugh and a warning, like she wasn't sure if she should be amused or afraid of where this was going.

I didn't answer. Didn't give her time to think.

I just walked.

Straight through the crowd. Straight toward the back hallway. Straight toward the bathrooms. And she didn't resist.

Didn't tug her hand away. Didn't stop me. Didn't say no.

She followed.

Every step she took, every second she stayed close, sent a surge of fire racing through my veins. I could feel the tension winding tighter between us, heavy and crackling, the air charged with something too sharp to ignore.

She wanted this. Even if she didn't want to admit it yet.

And I was going to make sure she did.

CHAPTER 4

JACE

The door to the bathroom banged shut behind us, the thud drowned out by the pulse of music seeping through the walls. It was a single bathroom, thank fuck, and my back had barely hit the door before her hands were on me and mine were all over her, gripping, pulling, taking.

Her mouth was soft and demanding, kissing me like she needed me to breathe, like she couldn't last a second more without my taste. The dim lighting cast shadows over her face, flickering with every movement, making the moment feel even more intoxicating—like we were the only two people in the world, lost in the dark, lost in each other.

I was drowning in her. In the way she fit against me, in the way her body arched when I ran my hands up her spine. In the soft, desperate sounds she made when my tongue teased hers. My fingers found the hem of her dress and pushed it up, bunching the fabric in my hands as I traced my fingertips along her smooth, bare thighs.

Her nails dug into my shoulders, tugging me closer, as if I weren't already pressed against her, as if there were still space left between us to close.

"Jace, I don't do this kind of thing," she said breathily against my mouth, and fuck if my name didn't sound like a plea coming from her lips. I was vaguely aware of the fact that she still hadn't given me hers. But I wasn't too worried about it right now. Fate would figure it out.

There was no world where this girl wasn't mine.

"There's a first time for everything, then, I guess."

I spun her around, hands pressing firmly against her stomach as I pulled her flush against me. She gasped, bracing herself on the sink as I bent my head to press my lips against the curve of her neck. I wanted to mark her, wanted her walking out of here with reminders of me all over her skin. She tilted her head, granting me access, and I groaned, my fingers skimming up, grazing the curve of her breast before dipping lower.

"Tell me you want this," I murmured against her skin. I needed to hear her say it.

She turned her head slightly, her lips ghosting over mine, teasing me. "I want this."

Fuck. My grip tightened, my self-control slipping like sand through my fingers. I yanked her dress up farther, sliding my hands over her ass as I pushed her forward until her hips pressed into the counter. My palm flattened against her stomach, holding her there as I ground against her, both of us gasping at the contact.

Her breath was ragged, and mine wasn't much better. I could feel the tension coiled in her back, the slight tremors running through her muscles beneath my hands. My fingers dipped even lower, teasing, circling, feeling her heat.

I lifted her, turning her around as her legs instinctively wrapped around my waist. The lock clicked as someone tried to get into the room, but I barely registered the sound over the blood roaring in my ears, over the way she arched into me like she'd been waiting for this just as much as I had.

Like maybe—just maybe—she felt this thing crackling between us, too.

"You're unbelievable," I murmured against her lips, my breath shaky.

She let out a choked laugh, her teeth grazing my lower lip before pulling back just enough to meet my gaze. "You say that now," she whispered.

I didn't understand what she was saying, but it was hard to concentrate on deeper meanings when her lips were swollen from my kiss and she looked like she might die if I didn't get inside her. I swore I felt something snap inside my chest when she locked eyes with me, something visceral and dark and possessive.

"I don't need your name to know this is something special," I rasped, rolling my hips into hers, feeling the way she shuddered at the contact. "Something once in a lifetime. Do you feel it, too?"

Her lips parted, her breath catching as her nails scraped against the back of my neck. Her body responded before her words could catch up, grinding against me, chasing the friction, the heat. I gritted my teeth, pressing my forehead to hers. "Yes," she finally whispered.

"I'm going to ruin you for all other men," I told her, a challenge in my voice like I was daring her to argue with me.

A sharp inhale. "Then do it," she answered.

I didn't need more of an invitation than that.

I spun, setting her down on the edge of the counter, knocking over a soap dispenser in the process, but neither of us cared. My hands gripped her thighs as I stepped between them. She grabbed my belt, yanking it loose, and I swore under my breath as her hands dipped lower, fingers skimming over me.

I was already hard. Already aching. Already so fucking gone for her, it didn't make sense.

She dragged her lips over my jaw, her tongue flicking out to tease just beneath my ear, and my control slipped another inch. My fingers slipped under the hem of her dress, pushing her panties aside, and she gasped as I ran my knuckles along her inner thigh.

"Holy fuck," I muttered, feeling just how wet she was.

Her head fell back against the mirror, her lashes fluttering. "Are you just going to stand there and admire the view?" she teased, her voice breathy, wrecked.

A low growl rumbled from my throat as I grabbed her chin, forcing her to look at me. "I want to see your face when I'm inside you."

Her breath stalled for a second before she nodded, her lips parting like she wanted to say something. But I didn't let her.

I growled against her mouth, nipping at her bottom lip, tasting the heat of her, the faint tang of her sweat as her fingers tangled in my hair, pulling hard, demanding more. She made a soft sound, half sigh, half moan, that sent fire ripping through me, my cock throbbing against her thigh like it had a mind of its own. I shoved my jeans down, my hands shaking with need as I pulled her closer until her ass barely clung to the counter's edge.

I could see everything with her flimsy dress bunched up around her hips like that—her soaked panties shoved aside, her heat glistening, dripping for me.

"Beg me to fuck you. Let me hear how bad you're dying for it," I murmured against her skin, my voice low, rough, my lips brushing her jaw, teasing her until she squirmed. I needed her to say it; I needed those words to snap the last thread holding me back.

She turned her head, lips ghosting over mine, teasing me right back, her breath hot against my skin. "I want you to fuck me," she said, a dare wrapped in a plea.

I gripped myself, gliding the tip along her folds, teasing, feeling her slickness coat me, and she gasped, sharp and ragged, her nails digging into my scalp, tugging me closer.

"Jace—please," she breathed in a dark and wild voice, her hips rocking up, chasing me.

I loved the sound of her desperation. I needed her to feel this, this ache . . . this crushing desire, like her body was unraveling by the second and only I could put it back together.

I pressed in—just the tip, slow as hell, stretching her tight heat—and she moaned, the sound almost like a sob as her head tipped back against the mirror, the glass above her head fogging from her breath.

"Say it," I growled, voice low, thick with need, pushing in an inch more, feeling her clench around me, hot and perfect, my restraint hanging by a thread. There was still quite a bit of me to go, but I wasn't going to bring her attention to that. If she went off screaming right now, I'd probably die.

"Tell me you want me—tell me you're mine," I growled.

She wouldn't understand right now what was happening, how she was sealing our fate in stone. But *I* knew what those words would mean. I knew what would happen as soon as they came out of her mouth.

Her eyes snapped to mine, honey colored and blazing, her lips swollen from my kisses. "I want you. Fuck, I'm yours," she gasped in a breaking voice, her hands sliding down my neck, nails scraping, leaving red trails I'd wear like a badge. That was it—I thrust in—hard, deep, all the way, burying myself in her until our hips slammed together, the counter rattling under us.

"I own every damn inch of you, sweetheart. I'm gonna fuck you until I'm carved in your bones."

A hitched sob burst from her mouth, and she froze, her breath stuttering as she blinked at me, obviously dealing with the consequences of having . . . a lot . . . stuffed inside her at the moment.

"Fuck. Yes," I groaned, loud and raw, my hands gripping her thighs, fingers bruising as I held her there, feeling her pulse around me, tight and wet and mine. She cried out my name again, a jagged sound that echoed off the tiles, her legs wrapping tighter around my waist, heels digging into my ass, pulling me deeper like she couldn't get enough. "You're so fuckin' perfect," I muttered roughly, kissing her hard . . . messy. Our tongues clashed together as I started moving—slow at first, dragging out every inch, feeling her tremble, then slamming back in, hard and fast, the rhythm wild and primal.

Her hands moved back under my shirt, clawing at my skin as she rocked with me, meeting every thrust, her moans spilling out, loud, unrestrained, bouncing off the walls.

"So good." She gasped, her voice breaking, her head falling back again, hair sticking to the mirror, wild and tangled, and I grinned smugly, loving how she was unraveling under me, how she was giving it all up for me.

"You're so fuckin' hot, taking me like this, all mine," I growled, my voice thick, possessive, one hand sliding up her stomach, under her dress, shoving it higher until her bra peeked out . . . black lace that barely held her in.

I yanked it down, her breasts spilling free, her nipples hard and pink, and I ducked, sucking one into my mouth, my tongue flicking, teeth grazing just enough to make her arch, a high whine tearing from her throat. "Nobody else. Say it, baby," I muttered against her skin, thrusting deeper, the counter creaking as we moved.

"Yours. Fuck. Yours," she moaned in a shattered voice, her hips bucking against me as she chased her pleasure, her hands fisting my hair, pulling hard enough to sting. I groaned into her skin, sucking harder, leaving a red mark as my fingers found her clit. It was wet and swollen as I rubbed fast, tight circles that made her shake.

"Please, please, please," she cried, loud and desperate, her body clenching around me, so tight and hot I might die of pleasure.

The handle rattled again, more insistent this time, like whoever was on the other side wasn't planning on giving up anytime soon. I clenched my jaw, every muscle in my body wound tight.

I dragged my lips up the column of her neck, my own breath shaky. "You gotta be quieter, babycakes," I murmured, trying for a warning but landing somewhere between desperate and amused.

She nodded, but then I shifted my hips, and she let out this quiet little gasp that went straight to my fucking head.

I growled, thrusting deeper, the counter rocking, her ass sliding with every hit, her breath hitching as she broke—hard, loud—her orgasm squeezing me so tight I nearly lost it.

Her head thrashed, banging the mirror, her moans echoing rawly around us. I kept thrusting, dragging it out, feeling her tremble, her thighs quaking around me. "That's it, baby, come again for me," I rasped in a rough voice as I kissed her neck, licking the sweat off her pulse, my fingers relentless as I continued to push her higher.

She gasped my name again, her hands slipping, scratching down my back, leaving more marks I'd no doubt feel tomorrow, and the only word that could describe me at the moment was . . . feral. Her breath hitched, a second wave building, and I could feel it—her tightening, her moans turning to whimpers, high and needy.

"Such a sweet, tight pussy," I purred, as I sucked another mark. My fingers were relentless, pushing her higher, her moans turning to whimpers, oversensitive and perfect.

"Jace," she begged, her hips grinding against me, and I smirked, gripping her tighter as I squeezed her ass, lifting her just enough to angle deeper. Hitting that spot that made her eyes roll back.

"Yes. Right there." She gasped, loud and ragged, her nails finally digging in enough to draw blood. I groaned, low and guttural, the sting mixing with the heat and driving me wild.

"Look at you," I rasped thickly, watching her—dress rucked up, bra shoved down, skin flushed and slick—taking me like she was born for it. "So fucking sexy."

I thrust harder, slow and deep, then fast, relentless, her moans a melody I'd kill to keep, her body trembling, clenching, pulling me in tight. My hand slid up her spine, and I gripped her hair, pulling her head back until her throat was bared, kissing it and sucking hard, marking her again so she was red, raw . . . mine.

Her cries echoed around the room, her body shaking, a second orgasm crashing through her, harder, louder, her thighs clamping around me, squeezing so tight I could barely move. "That's it, give it to me *again*," I growled, thrusting through it, feeling her pulse around me, wet and hot, dragging it out until she was whimpering, oversensitive, her hands slipping on my shoulders.

Her second climax had been even greater; I groaned, feeling her pulse around me, and my rhythm faltered. My balls tightened as the heat coiled fast. I slammed in one last time, spilling inside her, hot and thick, my groan bouncing off the tiles, my hands clutching her hips until my knuckles ached, marking her with every pulse . . . every shudder.

We stayed there, panting, tangled, sweat dripping, the counter creaking under us, the bathroom thick with heat—her scent, mine, and sex. I pulled out in a slow, wet glide, and she gasped, soft and wrecked, her legs still trembling around me. I tilted her chin up, giving her another messy, hard, possessive kiss, claiming every inch of her mouth.

"You're mine," I muttered again roughly, smiling against her lips because I'd never felt happier in my entire life.

My hands roamed over her hips, her ass, pulling her against me, the counter digging into her thighs. Her dress was a wreck, bunched up, her bra half off, and her breasts bare. I was still half hard, still wanting, and I cupped her breast, my thumb brushing her nipple until she whimpered, soft and needy.

I slid two fingers inside her, unable to stop myself. Loving the feel of my cum mixed with hers, how she clenched around my fingers . . . how her moan vibrated through me. She gripped my shoulders, her breath hitching as I curled my fingers, hitting that spot again relentlessly.

"I can't—" She gasped rawly, her head falling forward until her forehead was pressed to mine, her breath hot on my lips as she broke again, a soft, sharp, third wave.

Her moan was a whisper now, wrecked and *mine*. I grinned, kissing her slow and deep, tasting her gasps. My fingers were still lazily sliding in and out of her slick, warm heat, smearing her thigh as I held her there, pinned against the counter, the bathroom a haze of heat and *us*.

I hadn't even buttoned my jeans yet when she said it.

"I need to go."

I blinked, still in a postorgasmic haze, my brain taking a solid three seconds to catch up. "What?"

But she was already moving. Fast.

She shimmied her dress back down, fixed her bra, and smoothed her hair. Then grabbed the door handle like she was escaping a crime scene.

I lunged for her wrist. And missed.

"Hey—wait a second."

Spoiler alert. She didn't wait. She bolted. She slipped right past the door and disappeared into the crowded bar before I could even breathe.

I stood there, my jeans half zipped, completely fucking *stunned*. Had I imagined that?

That insane, mind-blowing, earth-shattering sex?

Had I hallucinated the way she'd gasped my name like it was a fucking prayer?

I ran a hand through my hair, tugging at the strands as I tried to shake off the whiplash. What the fuck just happened?

I stared at the door, still swinging slightly from her rush to get the hell away from me. No. No way. That was not how this ended.

I was still reeling, still feeling her nails on my back, still aching to kiss every inch of her all over again, and she just ran?

I hurriedly finished zipping up my jeans and shoved open the door.

The bar was a blur of bodies and music, the bass vibrating under my feet as I scanned the room, searching for that flash of dark blonde hair.

There was no sign of her.

I cursed under my breath, shoving a hand through my hair as I spun on my heel and bolted for the front door. My pulse pounded like the relentless bass line threatening to drive me insane as I yanked the door open and stepped outside.

I scanned the street, searching, but she was nowhere. Just a bunch of people milling around, giving me weird looks—probably because I looked like I'd just gone three rounds with a wildcat.

I exhaled sharply, jaw clenching as frustration clawed up my spine.

Where the hell did she go?

I lingered for another second, half expecting to see her slipping around a corner or ducking into a car. But there was nothing—no trace of her at all.

With a muttered curse, I stepped back inside, the door shutting with a thud behind me.

I exhaled through my nose, dragging my hands down my face before heading back to the bar.

I barely made it back before my legs gave out, and I collapsed onto the stool like I'd just gotten off a damn roller coaster.

Holy. Fucking. Shit. I was wrecked. I'd said I was going to ruin her.

But I was the one who'd been ruined. Shaken to my fucking core.

My shirt was half untucked, my collar pulled so wide it looked like I'd been in a fight. My hair? A total disaster thanks to her fingers having tugged at it. My face burned from the heat still running through my veins, my skin buzzing like it had been permanently marked by her touch. I could still smell her on me.

And my chest hurt. Like, actually ached, and I had no idea what the hell to do with that.

I sat there, staring at nothing, trying to catch my breath, and then—

"What's wrong with you?"

Parker's voice cut through my daze, and I looked up to see him and Matty staring at me, both fully entertained at whatever mess I must've looked like.

Matty smirked, eyes glinting. "And what—or rather, who—did you just do?"

I opened my mouth. Paused. How the hell was I supposed to explain this? I swallowed, rubbing at my chest again, because seriously, what the fuck was this feeling?

"You're never going to believe this."

Matty raised a brow. "You got funny since you went to the bathroom? Yeah, I'm probably not going to believe that."

I ignored him, my mind still spinning, still trying to process whatever the hell had just happened back there.

I licked my lips. "I just . . . I just found the love of my life."

Matty and Parker stared at me for a second—before losing their shit.

Parker actually choked on his drink, coughing through his laugh, while Matty was practically bent over, his shoulders shaking.

"Where?" Matty managed. "In the bathroom?"

"No, man," I said seriously, jabbing a finger toward the dance floor. "She was out there. We were dancing, and then . . . well, you know."

Parker was still laughing as he wiped his mouth. "Wait, you did that just now—"

"Yep. Right out back."

Matty whistled. "That good, huh?"

"Best fifteen minutes of my life—and don't give me a hard time about fifteen minutes. I had to work my ass off to even last *that* long." I sighed, still feeling wrecked, still feeling like I'd been hit by a fucking truck. I leaned forward, bracing my elbows on the bar, my mind still back there, still with her.

"She was perfect," I murmured.

Matty snorted. "Okay . . . so where is she? What's her name?"

I froze.

My stomach dropped.

Oh. Shit.

I sat back, rubbing my face, fully panicking as my brain caught up. "She left," I admitted, my voice tight. "And . . . I don't know her name. She wouldn't give it to me. Fuck. I don't know her name. What the fuck am I going to do?"

Silence.

Matty absolutely lost it. Again.

Parker was grinning, shaking his head, while Matty was practically doubled over, wheezing.

"Let me get this straight," Matty said between gasps of laughter. "You think you met the 'love of your life,' and she wouldn't even give you her name?"

I groaned, gripping my chest, because fuck. It was still hurting.

What the hell was wrong with me?

Just then, the bartender appeared in front of us, setting a card down on the bar. "Hey, man," he said, looking at me. "That blonde you came up to the bar with—was that your girlfriend?"

My head snapped up.

I sat up so fast that my stool nearly tipped over.

"Yeah," I said quickly, voice way too high. I cleared my throat, forcing casual. "Yeah. Why?"

"She left her credit card behind. Figured you might want it back."

He pushed it toward me. I stared at it. The shiny black card, the little gold chip in the corner. The *name* printed across the front.

"Thanks." I reached for it, my fingers shaking, my pulse racing.

Riley St. James.

I knew her name now. I finally fucking knew her name. My grin was so wide it hurt.

"Gentlemen," I said, holding up the card like I'd just won the fucking lottery. "Do you know what this is?"

Parker and Matty both stared at me for what seemed like the hundredth time.

"What?" they both asked at the same time. Parker raised a brow.

Matty leaned in. "A credit card?"

I laughed, because oh, they had no idea. My whole body was thrumming with victory.

"This—this is a sign."

Matty rolled his eyes, clapping me on the back. "Or it's just her credit card, man. Either way, let's get you another drink before you have another revelation about your future wife."

But I didn't need another drink. Because I had what I needed.

I had her name. And now?

Now, she was never getting away from me again.

CHAPTER 5

RILEY

I woke up gasping for air.

My body ached, a delicious soreness lingering in places I hadn't felt in a long time, and for a moment, I was warm. Safe. My mind drifted back, memories of his hands gripping my waist, his mouth branding my skin, his deep, husky laughter vibrating through my chest as he teased me, his eyes locking onto mine as he buried himself inside me.

Jace.

I shuddered and squeezed my eyes shut, willing the memories away, but they didn't leave. I could still feel him. The way he watched me, like I was the only thing in the room, the way he touched me like he had every right to, and the way his voice had wrapped around my throat like a velvet noose every time he called me sweetheart or babycakes or any of the other names he'd said.

No. No. No.

I sat up too fast, and my head pounded in protest. A rush of nausea rolled through me, the aftermath of too much alcohol and even more regret.

I needed water. I needed coffee. I needed to pretend last night had never happened.

Groaning, I covered my face, and that's when I felt it—my bare skin.

I ripped my hands away and looked down at myself.

Shit.

I was completely naked under my covers.

Panic shot through me like a struck match. Had I even locked the door last night? Had anyone seen me like this? I grabbed my sheets and clutched them to my chest like they could erase the memory of what I'd done.

This wasn't me.

I wasn't the kind of girl who had a one-night stand in a bathroom. I wasn't the kind of girl who let a stranger unravel her so easily, who let herself get lost in someone else.

I wasn't. I knew better than that.

Callum had taught me better than that.

So why was I still thinking about Jace?

I dragged a shaking hand through my hair, forcing myself to get it together.

And that's when I saw her.

My roommate, Emma, was sitting at her desk.

Staring.

I froze.

She wasn't doing anything—not studying, not scrolling through her phone, not even pretending to look busy.

Just . . . watching.

My stomach turned.

"Uh, morning," I said hoarsely.

She didn't respond. Didn't even blink.

She just tilted her head slightly, her gaze locked onto me like I was a lab experiment she was studying.

Okay. Nope. Nope. Nope.

I kept a sheet wrapped around me while I scrambled to grab my discarded sweatshirt from the floor, yanking it over my head.

"You okay?" I asked hesitantly, my heart pounding.

Nothing.

Fucking fantastic.

I grabbed my leggings, hopping on one foot as I pulled them up. Emma still didn't move. She just kept watching me, silently, like some kind of horror movie ghost girl.

I yanked open my drawer for socks and caught her slight flinch at the sudden movement.

What the hell was wrong with her?

Slamming the drawer shut, I forced a fake smile as I slid on my shoes and then grabbed my bag and slung it over my shoulder. "Well. This has been fun. Super normal. Can't wait to do it again tomorrow."

Still, nothing.

I backed toward the door, keeping my eyes on her, half expecting her to start crawling toward me like a demon from *The Ring*.

The second my hand hit the doorknob, I yanked it open and slipped out, gulping in the fresh air.

Holy shit.

I stood in the hallway for a moment, my heart pounding, debating whether I should request a room transfer.

But I knew how that would go.

What was I supposed to say? *Hey, my roommate just exists too quietly, and I think she might be possessed by a Victorian ghost?*

Yeah. That would go over well.

I shook my head, exhaling sharply.

I had bigger problems than my roommate from hell.

Like the fact that I had left my credit card at the bar.

And, oh yeah—the fact that I had slept with Jace Thatcher.

The fact that I'd had *unprotected* sex with Jace Fucking Thatcher. The birth control I was on would prevent a baby . . . but it wouldn't stop anything else.

A guy who looked like that . . . aka the hottest man that I'd ever seen in my life.

Fuck. He could have any number of things on that giant dick of his.

If he could do that so easily—if he could pull me onto the dance floor, move with me like we'd been doing it forever, then drag me into that bathroom like he needed me more than his next breath—then how many times had he done it before?

Because it had felt effortless for him. Natural. Like a well-practiced routine.

I wasn't special. I wasn't different.

I groaned, rubbing my hands over my face.

I needed coffee. And a redo on life choices.

Maybe, if I was really lucky, I'd never have to see him again.

But who was I kidding? I was *never* lucky.

———

The campus eatery was mercifully mostly empty.

I stood in line, shifting from foot to foot, my head still pounding from I wrapped the large, scalding cup in my hands, willing the heat to burn away the memory of what I had done. Of *who* I had done.

I groaned internally.

I needed to forget that guy existed.

But my body had other plans.

Because despite my very real, very justified panic, my lady bits were still basking in the afterglow, completely unbothered by my emotional crisis. The traitors. They didn't care that Jace Thatcher was probably the most reckless, insufferable, womanizing disaster to ever exist. They only cared about the way he had touched me—like he had every right to. Like he had been waiting. Like he *knew* me in a way no one else ever had.

My thighs clenched involuntarily, a deep, traitorous ache pulsing in my core.

No. No, no, no.

I squeezed my eyes shut and took a careful sip of my coffee, hoping the heat would shock some sense into me.

Turning toward the seating area, I scanned the room for an empty booth when I spotted her—Tasha.

She was slumped at a table, wearing oversized sunglasses indoors like a Z-list celebrity pretending to be avoiding the nonexistent paparazzi following her. A barely touched croissant sat on a napkin, and she had two iced coffees in front of her—one half gone, the other untouched.

I debated walking past her, but her head tilted up slightly, like she had some kind of sixth sense for drama, and she waved me over.

I sighed, gripping my coffee like it could physically anchor me, and walked toward her.

Tasha groaned as I slid into the seat across from her. "Too early," she muttered. "Too bright."

I raised an eyebrow. "You're wearing sunglasses."

She just groaned louder, resting her forehead against the table for a moment before snapping her head up. "Wait." Her head tilted slightly, assessing me from behind the dark lenses. "You didn't go home early last night, did you?"

My stomach dropped, but I forced a casual shrug. "I—uh—yeah, I mean. Kinda. I left."

Her lips curled into a slow, knowing smirk.

Shit.

I cleared my throat and took a deliberate sip of my coffee. "I—um—talked to someone for a second, but that's it."

Tasha perked up instantly, shoving her sunglasses to the top of her head. "Talked?" She grinned, too wide, too smug. "That's all?"

I swallowed hard, keeping my face neutral. "Yeah."

She hummed, tapping her fingers against the table, unconvinced. "That's funny."

I narrowed my eyes. "What's funny?"

She stretched, rolling her neck like she was settling in for a long interrogation. "Because I could have sworn I saw you dancing with Jace Thatcher last night."

My blood turned to ice.

I fought to keep my expression impassive, but my grip on my coffee tightened just a little too much. "Oh," I said, forcing nonchalance. "Yeah. I guess I did."

Tasha's grin was positively evil. "You guess?"

I shrugged, looking at my coffee like it had suddenly become the most fascinating thing in the world. "It was just for a second."

Tasha leaned forward, her glassy, hungover eyes still way too sharp. "Just a second?"

I nodded.

She smirked. "Just a second with Jace Fucking Thatcher?"

I groaned, slumping into my seat. "Why are you saying his name like that?"

She ignored my question entirely. "Do you know who he is?"

I shifted uncomfortably. "I—"

Tasha grinned. "Jace. Thatcher," she said his name again, slow and deliberate, like I was missing something massive.

I rolled my eyes. "I get it. You're very impressed."

She let out a high-pitched laugh, shaking her head. "Oh, babe. You really don't get it."

I exhaled sharply, already exhausted. "Okay. Enlighten me."

She gestured wildly, like it should have been obvious. "He's only *the* Jace Thatcher. Wide receiver. Star player. Campus fucking royalty." She leaned in conspiratorially. "Rumor is he's a Sphinx recruit, too. He could literally say he wants someone, and they'd drop their panties on the spot."

My stomach twisted. I didn't know what the Sphinx was. But I did have personal experience with that last part of her statement.

He had wanted me.

And I had definitely dropped my panties for him.

I forced a tight smile. "Well, good for him."

Tasha snorted. "Oh, honey. He's good for everyone."

I frowned. "What does that mean?"

She took a lazy sip of her coffee, her smirk widening. "I mean, he doesn't really do relationships. Like, ever. The guy has more hookups than I have shoes. He can have anyone."

My stomach dropped.

I don't know why it made me feel like shit.

I wasn't looking for a relationship. I wasn't even looking for a hookup. Last night was a mistake, something I'd never done before, something I wouldn't do again.

I had no right to feel . . . disappointed.

But I did.

Because last night, Jace Thatcher hadn't looked at me like I was just another girl at a bar.

He had looked at me like I was the only thing in the world.

I remembered the way his eyes had locked onto mine, how they had darkened with something intense and undeniable. I remembered the way he had spoken, the way he had moved, the way he had whispered filth into my ear like he couldn't help himself.

And the way I had felt—not like a nameless, forgettable one-night stand, but like I was his.

That thought alone should've terrified me. Should've sent me into full-blown panic mode. But instead, something else settled in my chest—something strange, something dangerously close to relief.

Because no matter how complicated this was, no matter how reckless, I had still taken a major step.

Callum was no longer the only man who had touched me.

My fingers tightened around the coffee cup as I inhaled sharply, and I swallowed hard, forcing my thoughts away from that.

Tasha was still talking, still rambling about how many girls Jace had been with, how he was the campus legend, how she was so jealous of me.

I nodded along, pretending it didn't matter. Pretending I wasn't still tangled in the feeling of him—his hands, his voice, the way he looked at me like he already knew I'd give in.

Like I hadn't spent the entire night haunted by him, trapped in dreams that felt too real, too consuming.

Like I wasn't still shaking from the weight of it, from the way my body betrayed me, from the way I wanted something I had no business wanting.

I told myself I was fine. That I was stronger than this. That it was just a moment, a mistake, something I could walk away from.

But deep down, I knew the truth.

If I ever saw him again . . . and he looked at me like what happened between us had meant nothing?

Like *I* was nothing?

I wasn't sure I'd survive it.

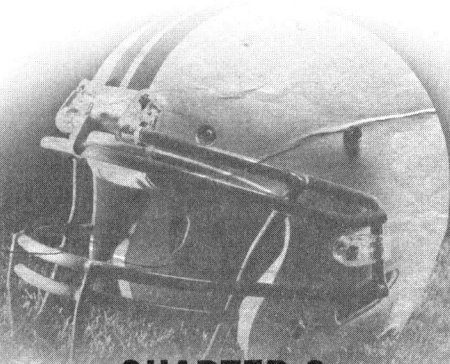

CHAPTER 6

RILEY

I was late.

Again.

I bolted down the hall, my bag slamming against my hip as I turned the corner toward my Intro to Ethics lecture. It wasn't my favorite class, but it was an easy A—or it was supposed to be, if I wasn't constantly behind and exhausted and too distracted by my own life crumbling around me to actually focus.

Tasha's words were still running through my head as I reached the door.

The guy has more hookups than I have shoes.

He can have anyone.

He was probably already on to the next girl.

I shook off the irrational stab of disappointment, pulling open the heavy wooden door as quietly as possible. The professor wasn't here yet—thank God—but the lecture hall was already packed, students filling the rows, voices a low murmur as they whispered and gossiped about something I wasn't paying attention to. I raced down an aisle, breathing a sigh of relief when I saw an empty chair and could put down my stuff.

"How do you tell the difference between a frog and a horny toad?"

My stomach dropped.

I turned my head slowly, my entire body locking up as my eyes met his.

Jace Thatcher.

In the daylight.

And holy hell, he still looked just as good—*better*—without the haze of alcohol and dim bar lighting softening the perfect angles of his face.

His long blonde hair was slightly tousled, like he'd rolled out of bed looking that effortlessly flawless. His golden skin still held a lingering summer tan, his strong jawline sharp enough to cut glass. And then there were his brown eyes—piercing, mischievous—locked onto me with a smug intensity that sent heat rushing to my cheeks.

He was leaning back in his chair like he owned the place, one arm slung over the empty seat next to him, his legs spread wide like he didn't have a single worry in the world.

And me?

I looked like I'd been dragged through a dumpster at the moment.

Oversized sweatshirt, leggings, tangled mess of hair that I hadn't bothered to brush, last night's makeup . . . and oh yeah, probably still smelling like him.

I was again regretting every decision I'd ever made up to now and hating my roommate for making me flee the room.

His smirk deepened. Why did he have to look so hot doing it? It was annoying.

"A frog says, 'Ribbit, ribbit,' and a horny toad says, 'Rub it, rub it,'" he finished, looking absurdly proud of himself.

I gaped at him, and he beamed like I'd paid him some sort of huge compliment.

An embarrassing choking sound came out of my throat.

"The bartender thought you were my girlfriend."

My eyes widened in confusion.

He tilted his head, studying me with *way* too much interest.

"Are you?"

I choked. "What?"

He leaned in slightly, his cocky expression never wavering. "Are you my girlfriend, *Riley*?"

My stomach twisted at the way he said my name. Like he was tasting it, savoring it.

"How do you even—"

Jace laughed, completely unbothered. "There was no way I wasn't going to find you."

I blinked at him, and his grin spread. "You left something behind, babycakes," he murmured.

Before I could react, he reached forward, grabbing my wrist, flipping my palm face up, and dropped something into it.

I looked down.

My credit card.

I stared at it like it was a bomb about to explode.

"You—" My mouth opened, then closed, then opened again.

Jace just grinned.

I snatched my card up, fingers tightening around the plastic, staring at him as I tried to process what was happening.

I had been going to this class for months. He wasn't in this class.

Which meant . . .

"You transferred in," I blurted, heart pounding.

He shrugged, like it was nothing. "Turns out I had some free time in my schedule."

"Jace," someone hissed from a few seats away. I turned and saw a guy with a baseball cap shaking his head, holding a notebook full of nothing but doodles of dicks. "Dude. Why the hell are you even here? You're a junior. This is a freshman class."

I turned back to Jace, waiting for his answer.

His eyes never left mine. His lips twitched, like he was holding back a laugh.

"What, can't a guy expand his academic horizons?"

I narrowed my eyes.

"You're stalking me," I accused.

Jace's smirk grew impossibly wider.

"That depends," he said, his voice low . . . intimate. "Would you be into that?"

I flushed, hating that I felt warm all over.

I scanned the classroom, searching for another open seat—one that wouldn't come with a cocky, insufferable, six-foot-four football player attached to it. My eyes landed on one near the middle of the room, a desk flanked by two already occupied chairs. Perfect. No room for him to slide in beside me.

Keeping my expression neutral, I strode toward it, setting my bag down as I pulled the chair out. But before I could sit, a shadow loomed in front of me.

Jace.

Standing directly in front of the person next to the empty seat, his broad shoulders squared, his stance casual but somehow . . . menacing.

The poor guy barely hesitated before gathering his things and scrambling out of the seat like it had just burst into flames.

I gawked at Jace. "You're ridiculous," I muttered, stepping around him toward the desk, pretending like my heart wasn't slamming against my ribs.

He turned his head, tracking my every move with that knowing smirk.

"I'll take that as a maybe."

I dropped into my chair, gritting my teeth. "You're joking, right?"

Jace winked, sliding effortlessly into the now empty seat beside me. "Sure, Riley. Whatever helps you sleep at night."

I was about to come up with a scathing retort—maybe even make another escape attempt—but before I could, the professor walked in, effectively trapping me in place.

Jace leaned back in his chair, all smug satisfaction, like he'd just won some kind of game.

I let out a breath, wishing I had something on under this sweatshirt because I was suddenly boiling. I tried to focus on the professor as he set down his books and started rambling about the foundations of moral philosophy.

I was determined to pay attention.

But Jace?

Jace had other plans.

Halfway through the lecture, I felt it—his fingers brushing against the back of my arm.

I froze, resisting the urge to whip my head around. The contact was light, barely there, but it sent a rush through my entire body. I clenched my jaw, staring straight ahead, trying to pretend like I wasn't hyperaware of him.

Then his fingers traced down, skating over my elbow. I shivered, my entire body going rigid.

I heard him exhale a quiet laugh, and I decided right then and there that I hated him.

Alright, that might have been a lie, but I at least *hated* that my body was reacting. Even through my freaking sweatshirt.

It was official. I was swearing off men. All men.

I tried to ignore him and focus on the lecture. It didn't work.

His touch was slow, teasing, like he had all the time in the world to drive me insane.

Every time he touched me, my stomach tightened and my breath hitched. I was utterly unprepared for him.

The attention. The heat. The way he leaned in close, his breath warm against my skin, like he was waiting for me to do something—anything—to acknowledge what was happening between us. How it seemed like he wasn't just looking at me . . . but *seeing* me.

I didn't know how to handle that.

His touch lingered, soft yet possessive, like he had every right to touch me.

I swallowed hard, keeping my eyes glued to the professor, but I wasn't hearing a single word being said.

I shifted in my chair, trying to put a few inches of space between us, but the moment I moved, Jace chuckled under his breath.

"Where you goin', babycakes?"

My pulse spiked. "Nowhere."

"Sure about that?" He held something up between his fingers, the glow of the screen catching my eye. My phone. Unlocked still from my earlier mindless scrolling.

I stiffened. "Jace."

"Riley." His lips quirked like he was enjoying this far too much.

I snatched it from his grip, my fingers brushing against his, and I swore I heard the sharp exhale he let out at the contact.

I glanced at my screen. The message app was still open. A new number was already saved under *Hottie of my Body.*

I shot him an annoyed glare, and he leaned in, dropping his voice to a whisper, his words ghosting over my skin like a promise.

"Now I've got your number. And you've got mine, too. Buckle up, buttercup, because it's about to get fun."

I scoffed as Jace's fingers traced a slow, lazy pattern along my hip, where my sweatshirt had ridden up and exposed a sliver of skin. My body completely betrayed me by shivering again under his touch. I should have pulled away. I should have moved.

But I didn't.

I just sat there, heart pounding, cheeks burning, completely trapped in the moment—

Until it hit me.

Another touch.

Another man.

Another time.

I sat stiffly on the couch, pulling the sleeves of my sweater over my hands as Callum poured himself a glass of whiskey.

"You're too tense, darling," he murmured, swirling the amber liquid in his glass before taking a slow sip. He was always drinking. Always watching me over the rim of his glass with those knowing eyes.

I swallowed hard, forcing a smile, trying to please him because it was easier than the alternative.

"I just . . ." I hesitated, my fingers twisting in the fabric of my sweater. "I was looking at some other programs, maybe a veterinary program?"

His lips curved into a mocking smile. "Riley," he chided, setting his glass down on the coffee table before turning to face me. "We've talked about this."

My stomach clenched at his words.

He'd helped me with exactly one application. The only one I'd actually been able to submit. At the university where he taught—Chapel Hill.

"Besides, you'd never be able to keep up with that rigorous of a program."

"Well . . . I mean, maybe I could," I murmured, knowing it was the wrong thing to say.

His expression darkened, his fingers curling around my chin, tilting my face up to meet his gaze. "Are you doubting me?"

My throat felt tight.

I shook my head quickly. "No. Of course not."

His thumb brushed my lower lip, a quiet chuckle escaping him as he leaned in, his voice dropping to that low, velvety tone that always made my stomach turn.

"Good girl," he murmured.

Then his lips were on mine.

I froze.

I always froze.

It wasn't that he was a bad kisser.

It was that I never had a choice.

His hands were already moving, gripping my waist, pulling me closer, fingers digging in.

He always kissed me like he was sealing a deal, his mouth a contract I had no say in. Like he wasn't just claiming me—he was reminding me he wasn't optional. His hands never allowed space, never let me pull away, always holding, always directing, controlling, demanding submission without a single word. It wasn't about passion. It was about possession.

His lips trailed down to my jaw, my neck.

"I'm all you've got," he whispered. "No one will ever want you the way I do. No one will ever love you the way I do."

I squeezed my eyes shut, trying to convince myself that I should feel grateful.

That Callum loved me.

That he was taking care of me.

That I was lucky.

Because like he said—who else would want me?

Sick.

Exhausting.

Naïve.

Too much to deal with.

He had told me so many times.

I felt the weight of him, the pressure, the power in his grip.

A tear slipped down my cheek, and when he pulled back, he smiled like he'd won something.

Like I was his, no matter what.

I jerked away from Jace's touch like I'd been burned, my chest heaving as I tried to breathe past the sudden wave of panic.

I could feel his eyes on me, sharp and focused. He knew something was wrong.

I forced my gaze to the front of the room, gripping the edge of my desk until my knuckles turned white, willing the memory away, willing the panic down.

Breathe.

Just breathe.

By the time class ended, my pulse had finally slowed to something almost normal.

But my decision had already been made.

I needed to stay away from Jace Thatcher.

As the students around us started gathering their things, Jace leaned toward me again, completely at ease.

"What just happened, Riley-girl?"

I stood up fast, clutching my bag against my chest like it was a shield.

"I don't know what you're up to," I said, my voice steady despite the lingering panic in my veins.

Jace arched a brow, the corner of his lips tugging up like he found me amusing. "Up to?"

I swallowed.

"You transferred into this class. You're following me around. You—" I gestured vaguely, my fingers curling into fists. "I'm not interested."

His expression didn't change. His eyes stayed on mine, assessing, calculating.

And then he smiled.

A slow, knowing smile that sent butterflies shooting around in my stomach.

"Not yet," he murmured.

I took a step back, forcing space between us. "Leave me alone, Jace."

For a moment, he just watched me, like he was deciding whether or not to listen.

Then, finally, he lifted his hands, palms up.

"Whatever you say, Riley-girl."

I didn't wait for anything else.

I turned and walked away, forcing my legs not to shake, forcing my heart not to pound, forcing myself not to think about how good it had felt when he touched me.

Jace Thatcher was dangerous.

I'd already been burned by one fire.

I wasn't going to get burned by another.

Jace

Riley ran.

Again.

And I let her—for now. But if she thought that meant I was letting her go? Adorable. Truly.

I leaned back in my desk chair, biting into the Costco corn dog I'd just heated up—because my body was a temple, obviously—as I stared at my laptop screen, my fingers twitching with anticipation.

She thought she could walk away, that she could just pretend like last night never happened.

She thought she could run from me . . .

Precious.

Her name was bold at the top of the page. Riley St. James.

Mine.

I wasn't good at school—not in the traditional sense, anyway. Classes, tests, actually *studying*? No, thanks. The only reason I was even here was because of football. But computers?

That was different.

It started when I was a kid—messing around on an old laptop that barely functioned, figuring out how things worked, breaking them down, and building them back up. By the time I was thirteen, I had figured out how to hack into my middle school's grade system. Turns out if you changed your grade by one point every other week, no one noticed.

From there, I started messing with stocks.

At first, it was just a game. I ran simulations, learned the system, and read the trends. By the time I turned sixteen, I was making actual money. My friends in high school spent the paychecks from their part-time jobs on specialty Nike sneakers and video games. Meanwhile, I was reinvesting mine, building accounts in fake names, keeping things quiet.

I managed Parker's and Matty's money now, too.

Not that they really knew what I was doing with it. They just knew it was growing.

"Dude, should we be concerned that you're handling all our investments?" Matty had asked once.

"Not unless you want to be poor," I'd answered.

That had shut him up. Matty had grown up poor—like his dog had to lean against the fence to bark kind of poor—his words not mine, since I didn't even know what that meant. It was probably supposed to be funny, but since Matty wasn't funny, it just made no sense.

But I digress . . .

Hacking, tracking, reading numbers—it all came naturally. And right now, all those skills were being put to good use.

Because Riley St. James?

I was learning everything about her.

I pulled up her credit card statement, scrolling through her transactions. My girl did not have my spending habits. She spent almost . . . nothing.

Riley was on the base plan for the campus dining hall, which meant she got two meals a day of their cheapest meal option, and her last grocery store trip had been almost three weeks ago. The receipt showed protein bars, soup, electrolyte drinks—shit you bought when you weren't feeling well—or you couldn't afford anything else and were just trying to get the most bang for your buck.

Was she sick? Because the money problems didn't make sense. I'd found her birth certificate . . . and then her parents. And they were rich, North Carolina high-society people.

Unless they'd cut her off for some reason.

But why would they have cut off the most perfect little angel baby on earth?

I frowned again because I didn't like when I couldn't figure things out, and I especially didn't like that I couldn't find out everything I wanted to know about my future wife.

I pulled up her medical history—nothing easy to find, of course, but I had my ways. *Chronic fatigue syndrome. Periodic flare-ups.*

The words sat heavy in my chest. I didn't know much about her yet, obviously—I hadn't been watching her long enough to notice anything was off—but this? This changed things.

Chronic meant long-term. It meant this wasn't just some temporary thing she'd get over.

I clenched my jaw.

That explained the transaction gaps, the lack of social charges. She wasn't just avoiding people—she probably *couldn't* go out sometimes.

Fuck.

I didn't like not knowing what I was dealing with. I didn't like that I'd just assumed she was *fine* when, clearly, she wasn't. Had I missed a sign last night? Had she seemed tired when we were talking? Was this something that made her life harder every day, or only sometimes?

I had no idea.

And I hated that.

I leaned back, tapping my fingers against my desk, already pulling up articles, medical journals, anything I could get my hands on. I needed to know what this meant, how bad it could get, what I was supposed to do with this information.

Because if she was sick, if she was dealing with this every day and pretending like she wasn't, then I needed to catch up. Fast.

I needed to know how much she could handle, how much I could push, what she'd need from me—whether she wanted my help or not.

I leaned back, running a hand down my face.

I didn't know much about Riley yet.

But I knew one thing.

She was mine now. And I took care of what was mine.

My phone buzzed.

> Matty: So . . .

This was going to be good.

> Me: Yes, Matty? It seems like you have something you want to say.

> Matty: Well, it seems like maybe you have something you want to say.

> Parker: Spit it out, Matty. You've summoned us, now tell us why.

> Me: That was very magnanimous of you, Big Brain.

> Matty: Just once I would like to be called Big Brain.

Me: Well, we're definitely not going to call you Big Dick.

Matty: It's a quarter of an inch. You can still have a big dick and be a quarter of an inch smaller compared to another big dick.

Me: I'm just saying.

Parker: Can we talk about the other thing?

Matty: Like the fact that Jace transferred into a freshman class and forgot to tell us. Yes, let's talk about that.

I smirked, leaning back in my chair. Here we go.

Me: What's wrong with expanding my horizons?

Me: Maybe I wanted to develop a deeper appreciation for classic literature.

Parker: Classic literature, huh?

Matty: You do realize you transferred into Intro to Ethics?

Oh. I probably should remember that.

Me: . . .

Parker: You barely read our playbook, and that's got pictures. So, forgive me if I have trouble imagining that you have a desire to appreciate ethics.

Me: You're forgiven.

Matty: Plus . . .

Me: Yes?

Matty: I'm not exactly sure you or QB over there appreciate the finer point of . . . ethics.

Me: I'm perfectly ethical.

Parker: He's not talking about how good you are with your tongue. You know that, right?

Me: . . .

Matty: This has to do with the girl, doesn't it?

I didn't respond right away.

Because yeah. It did. But I also liked to keep them on their toes. Can't have them getting too complacent in this best friendship.

Me: . . .

Parker: You're stalking her, aren't you?

Me: I prefer to call it strategically placing myself in her orbit.

Matty: You say that like it sounds less insane.

Parker: I don't think it sounds insane at all.

Matty: You wouldn't, Mr. I Like to Watch Casey While She Sleeps.

Parker: At least I'm not watching you while you sleep.

Me: Hey, that was one time. And I was just curious. And in case you were wondering, Matty looks like an angel when he's asleep.

Matty: . . .

Matty: The thing about you being curious is it's probably going to mean you hacking her student email. Stealing her panties. Wearing some of her blood around your neck.

I snorted, contemplating such a necklace for a moment before deciding that was a little too vampire for my taste.

Me: Is that a thing?

Parker: Yeah, that seems a little out there. Is that something you've done?

Me: He's probably planning on doing that for his stalker.

Matty: Why would I do it for my stalker? I'm trying to get her to not stalk me.

Me: Don't get embarrassed, Matthew. We're all besties here.

Matty: . . .

Me: Relaaaax. I'm just making sure she's doing okay.

Me: You know, looking out for her. Hacking into her medical records. Paying off her credit card. Things like that.

Matty: YOU PAID OFF HER CREDIT CARD?!

Me: Fiscal responsibility is important, sir.

Matty: OMG!

Me: See. Not a stalker. More like a benefactor who secretly watches over her.

Parker: ☺

Matty: ⚐⚐⚐⚐⚐⚐⚐⚐⚐

Me: Parkie-Poo gets me.

Parker: Of course I do. A man protects what's his.

Me: Exactly.

Me: I'm making sure she's taken care of.

Matty: This is all EXACTLY what a stalker would say.

Me: It's called being a devoted boyfriend.

Matty: You're not her boyfriend.

Me: Yet.

Parker: Yet.

I tossed my phone onto the desk, grinning as I stared back at her name on the screen.

Matty didn't get it. But Riley would.

Soon enough, she'd understand—there was no running, no hiding, no pretending this wasn't real.

And when she did?

She'd never want to escape me again.

CHAPTER 7

RILEY

There were a lot of things I hated about my job at the campus bookstore, but three stood out above the rest.

First, no matter how many hours I worked there or at the campus coffee shop, I was always scraping by. And with my condition, sometimes I couldn't push myself as hard as I needed to—something my manager didn't exactly sympathize with. I was constantly worried that one bad flare-up, one missed shift, would be enough to get me fired.

Second, Eddie—one of my coworkers—did not understand the meaning of *no*. He lingered too long, stood too close, and always managed to brush up against me in ways that made my skin crawl.

And third—something that shouldn't have been a big deal—I hadn't made a single friend.

That was by design, obviously.

I kept to myself. I didn't make connections, I didn't let people ask too many questions. It was safer that way. If people didn't know me, they couldn't pry. They couldn't ask where I was from, what I had left behind, or why I never mentioned my family.

Not that there was much to say.

I had to get a prepaid phone once I decided to leave, too afraid that Callum would use my phone to try and find me.

The one time I called my parents when I got here, they'd immediately started in on a lecture that I was a fool for giving up Chapel Hill. That my actions obviously showed I wasn't ready to make my own decisions. And then I'd heard Callum's voice in the background agreeing with them that I should come home.

And that was it; I hadn't called again.

I wasn't sure if it was freeing to completely cut them off, or if it just made me want to cry.

Either way, I was on my own, and I was determined to make it work.

It was a lonely way to live, but loneliness was nothing new.

I was determined to survive.

Which meant I was currently standing behind the register, checking out a customer while Eddie stood beside me, leaning in too close with his usual half-assed flirting attempt.

Eddie was one of those guys.

The kind who thought he was charming but actually just made you want to walk into traffic.

Medium height, shaggy brown hair, with the kind of douchey grin that made my entire body recoil whenever he turned it on me.

And to top it all off? No shame.

None.

Not a speck.

Because no matter how many times I rejected him, he still found ways to wiggle back into my personal space and waste my time with pickup lines that were about as effective as a wet napkin in a hurricane.

"Come on, Riley, just one drink."

I sighed, not looking up as I rang up the last item. "Still not interested, Eddie."

"Why not?"

I shot him a look and deadpanned, "Because I don't want to."

The customer grabbed their bag and hightailed it out of there, eyes wide like they had just walked in on something deeply uncomfortable.

Eddie smirked, undeterred. "Fine. No drinks. What about coffee?"

"No."

"Lunch?"

"Eddie."

He held his hands up in mock surrender. "Alright, Alright. But one of these days, you're gonna give in."

I let out a slow breath, pressing my fingers into my temples. I really needed a different job.

I glanced at the clock; my shift was almost over. Almost. Just a few more customers, and then I could go home and—

It started as a low rumble.

At first, I thought it was just my imagination—some lingering headache from dealing with Eddie's *third* dinner invitation of the week. But then it got louder.

And louder. Until suddenly—

The entire bookstore went *silent*.

I froze, fingers hovering over the register as my latest customer turned toward the entrance with wide eyes. Eddie, standing way too close beside me, stiffened. "What the hell?" he muttered.

I turned my head slowly and immediately blinked a few times, unsure if I was dreaming or not. Barreling through the entrance, taking up the *entire* entrance to the bookstore, was a *horde* of massive men.

Men who looked vaguely familiar thanks to the fact that I *may* have looked up the school's football roster after my run-in with Jace.

The men were built like walking refrigerators, with arms the size of small tree trunks and bellies that could double as beer kegs. One guy's stomach jiggled with every movement, his entire torso covered in chest hair that I could *see* because—oh yeah—*they were all shirtless.*

They were all singing, and not just singing—absolutely *butchering* Taylor Swift's "You Belong With Me."

It was *horrendous.*

It was *incredible.*

Everyone *stopped* in their tracks.

A woman in the self-help aisle clutched her chest like she'd just been *shot*.

The girl in front of the counter looked at me like I had personally orchestrated this disaster and demanded, "What's going on?"

Like I was supposed to know.

The linemen, who I could only assume were linemen because I didn't think most athletes were built like that, stood in a perfect formation, arms slung over one another's enormous shoulders, swaying like they were drunk on a rocking boat.

And then—like the gates of hell had opened and Lucifer himself had decided to ruin my life . . .

The linemen parted down the middle, their giant bodies shifting like the Red Sea making way for the world's most obnoxious golden god.

Jace. Freaking. Thatcher.

Striding into the bookstore like he owned it.

Shirtless. With my name painted boldly in bright red letters across his obscenely muscular chest. The smuggest, sexiest smirk I had ever seen stretched across his perfect, infuriating face. His ridiculous, Trojan-era, golden-blond hair flowed behind him like he was some kind of Grecian war hero.

I forgot how to breathe.

Because he wasn't just shirtless. He was tan, all perfect flexing abs, walking like he was about to take over the world, and he had . . . props. A gold microphone—because why wouldn't he?!

His insufferable smirk only got wider as he lifted the mic and growled out the next part of the song like he was performing in a sold-out arena.

"Meeeee!" he finished as he threw the microphone over his shoulder, dropped low like he was about to start a whole strip routine, and rolled his hips.

I. Wanted. To. Die.

College coeds in the store literally screamed as they recorded him. One girl dropped her iced coffee and let out an excited sob. Rachel, my other coworker, was openly fanning herself, while Eddie looked like he was about to have a stroke.

Jace didn't take his eyes off me. He dragged his hands down his abs, flexing obscenely before popping back up and pointing directly at me.

The bookstore erupted into even more chaos, and I was a little afraid there was about to be a stampede of screaming fans.

Jace spread his arms wide and grinned at me like he had just won something. "So, Riley-girl, what do you say?"

For a long, excruciating moment I just *stared* at him.

At the cocky tilt of his head. The golden glow of his skin under the fluorescent lights. The way his entire body looked like it had been sculpted by some higher power with an unnecessary attention to detail.

At my *name* painted across his bare chest like a brand.

Jace didn't move. Didn't speak.

He just watched me.

And something in his expression—something dark, knowing, *certain*—sent a surge of panic straight through me.

I turned on my heel and sprinted out the back of the bookstore.

My heart beat against my ribs as I shoved past shelves, darting into the dimly lit hallway that led to the only possible escape—the elevator. Waiting with its doors open like my saving grace.

My fingers were shaking as I slammed the button, my pulse thundering in my ears. *Come on, come on, come on.*

The doors started to slide shut, and I exhaled, pressing my back against the wall, closing my eyes. Okay. Deep breaths. Everything was going to be alright. I'd get to the lobby, slip out the side entrance, and by the time I got to my dorm, this would all be a bad—

A foot slipped through the gap of the elevator doors.

A strong, muscled arm followed.

And then, before I could process what was happening, Jace was inside the elevator with me.

I froze, my entire body locking up as the doors sealed shut behind him, trapping us together in the too-small, airless metal box.

He didn't say a word. He just leaned against the opposite wall, shirtless and grinning, his golden-blonde hair still unnaturally perfect and flowy like I'd stepped into a shampoo commercial. His abs flexed with every slow, easy breath he took.

Ugh. How was it possible I was already taking in hits of his scent, like I was in one of my omegaverse books or something?

The elevator lurched.

I grabbed onto the railing, my stomach flipping as it gave another violent shudder—then stopped.

The lights flickered, and my heart shot straight into my throat.

No. No. No. This was not happening. Why the fuck hadn't I used the stairs?

I turned, uselessly slamming my fingers against the buttons. "Lobby. Lobby. *Lobby.*"

Nothing.

"Oh, you've got to be *fucking* kidding me."

A soft chuckle came from behind me, and I whipped around.

Jace was still leaning casually against the wall, a slow, lazy smirk tugging at his lips that made me want to kick him.

He lifted one shoulder in an infuriating half shrug. "Looks like fate wants us to spend a little more time together, babycakes."

I pressed my back against the opposite wall, very aware of how small the elevator was. How there was nowhere to go.

"This isn't fate," I muttered, willing my voice to sound steadier than I felt. "This is an old building with shitty maintenance."

Jace shrugged. "You can believe that if it makes you feel better. It doesn't make it true."

My breath came faster as I pressed the emergency call button. Static crackled, followed by a distorted voice.

"Campus maintenance."

"Hi," I said, exhaling in relief. "The elevator in the bookstore is stuck. There's two of us inside."

"We're aware of the issue. Techs are on their way."

"How long?" I asked, already dreading the answer.

"Could be twenty minutes. Could be an hour."

An hour?

The line cut off before I could demand a more specific time frame. I turned back to Jace, who looked entirely too pleased about this development. He was too big for this elevator. His presence filled every inch of it, swallowing up the air, making it impossible to not look at him. To not notice the sweat glistening on his skin. The ridges of his abs. How my name was painted on those abs. And the way his gray sweatpants sat *way* too low on his hips.

"An hour, huh?" His smirk deepened as he pushed off the wall.

I swallowed hard. "Don't even think about it."

"Think about what?" His tone was all mock innocence. "All I'm doing is standing here. With you. In a tiny, enclosed space. Where no one can interrupt us."

Jace tilted his head slightly, studying me like I was something to unravel. "Why do you keep running from me?"

I blinked. "Excuse me?"

He came toward me, his movements slow, predatory. His long legs ate up the space between us, and I could do nothing but stand there, frozen, as he stopped just inches away.

"Every time I get close, you bolt," he murmured, his voice like smoke and silk. "Why is that?"

Because you're dangerous.

Because you make me feel things I don't want to feel.

Because the last time a man gave me this kind of attention, it nearly destroyed me.

I lifted my chin, trying to act unaffected. "Maybe I don't like you."

His grin deepened, feral and knowing. "Riley-girl, we both know that's not true."

I scowled, heat licking at my skin. "It could be."

His hand lifted, and I sucked in a breath as he traced the curve of my jaw with the back of his knuckles, his touch featherlight but devastating. My pulse pounded so hard I felt dizzy.

His voice dipped lower, rough with amusement. "And yet, you can't stop looking at me."

I tore my gaze away, jaw clenching. "You're literally half naked in a confined space, Jace. It's called human instinct."

He hummed, pretending to consider. "Hmm. I think it's something else." The air between us felt thick, charged. My skin tingled, my body betraying me in every possible way. I was hot, flushed, completely wound up—and he knew it.

His fingers traveled down my throat, skimming my collarbone before they traced the delicate strap of my dress. His touch left goose bumps in its wake.

"You can't stop looking at me," he murmured, his lips inches from mine. "And I can't stop thinking about you."

Something snapped.

Before I could stop myself, my hands were on his bare shoulders, and then I was kissing him.

Hard.

Jace didn't hesitate.

He groaned against my lips, his hands gripping my waist, pulling me against him like he wanted to fuse us together. My fingers dug into his skin, and I felt every inch of him—his strength, his heat, the raw, electric energy humming between us.

His lips moved against mine with deliberate hunger, his tongue sweeping inside my mouth, stealing my breath. He kissed me like he wanted to own me, wreck me, ruin me for anyone else.

And I let him.

Because, God help me, I wanted to be ruined.

One of his hands slid into my hair, tilting my head back so he could kiss me deeper. His other hand dragged down my spine, past my waist, gripping the back of my thigh. With one swift movement, he lifted me, pressing me against the cool elevator wall.

I gasped into his mouth, and he swallowed the sound, his grip tightening, his body pressed flush against mine. I could feel him—hot, hard, and completely unashamed.

"Fuck," he muttered, his breath ragged. "You feel so fucking good."

His mouth moved down my jaw, my neck, licking and teasing, his teeth grazing my skin. I gasped as his lips found the hollow of my throat and he sucked gently. A sound left me that was utterly humiliating, and he smirked against my skin.

His fingers gripped my hips, grinding me against him, and I let out a desperate, breathy moan, my head falling back against the wall.

"Jace—"

"I know, sweetheart," he murmured. "I know."

I shuddered. "Jace . . ."

He lifted his head, eyes blazing, his pupils blown wide.

"I got you," he promised, his voice softer now, filled with something real. "Let me take care of you."

And then he set me back on my feet and dropped to his knees. His big hands ran down my legs before gripping my thighs, spreading them as he stared up at me with a smirk that was pure sin.

"You're gonna wish this elevator never gets fixed," he growled as he shoved the skirt of my dress up with zero hesitation. The fabric bunched around my hips, exposing me, and my heart slammed against my ribs, panic and heat twisting into a knot I couldn't unravel.

"Relax, Riley-girl," he murmured, his voice low, a gravelly edge that sent a shiver racing down my spine. His fingers hooked into my panties, tugging them aside, and before I could protest—before I could even think—his mouth was on me, hot and relentless. I gasped, head tipping back again as his tongue slid through my folds, and then flicked against me, bold and precise. My knees buckled, only the wall keeping me upright.

"Jace—no," I choked out, not meaning it at all. My hands shot to his head, fingers tangling in his hair, tugging hard, not to pull him away, but to hold on, because holy shit, he was good. Incredible, in fact. His lips closed around my clit, sucking lightly, and a moan ripped out of me, raw and unbidden, echoing in the tight space. He groaned against me, the vibration sinking into my core, and I felt my resolve crumbling, piece by jagged piece.

He pulled back just enough to look up at me with glistening lips, his eyes dark with hunger. "You don't want me to stop," he said roughly, a challenge laced through his voice. "You've been running from this, from me, and I'm done with it."

He licked into me again. "Time's up, Riley-girl."

I glared down at him, my chest heaving, my thighs trembling under his grip. "This doesn't mean anything," I spat, but it lacked bite, and he knew it. His smirk widened, and then he was back on me, tongue diving in, circling my clit with a rhythm that made my vision blur. My hips jerked, chasing the heat, and I cursed under my breath, hating how much I wanted this, wanted him, no matter how much I fought it.

He gripped my ass, spreading my cheeks apart as he pulled me closer. I couldn't stop the sounds spilling out—gasps, moans, little whimpers I'd never admit to later. He ate me out like he was starving, relentless and messy, his stubble scraping my inner thighs, adding a sting that only sharpened the pleasure. My fingers tightened in his hair, pulling harder, and he growled, the sound vibrating through me, pushing me closer to the edge.

"Yes, yes, yes," I panted, my head slamming back against the wall, the cold metal a stark contrast to the fire building low in my belly. I was so close, and he seemed to sense it. He doubled down, sucking hard, and I shattered, my orgasm crashing through me like a wave, intense and overwhelming. My knees gave out, but he held me up, pinning me against the wall as I rode it out, trembling, gasping, his name a broken chant on my lips.

He didn't stop, not really. He just eased off enough to let me breathe, his tongue tracing slow, lazy circles over my clit as I came down, oversensitive and shaking. I shoved at his head, weak and half-hearted, my voice a wreck. "Enough, Jace—"

He pulled back, licking his lips like he couldn't get enough of the taste, and then stood, towering over me again. His hands braced on either side of my head, caging me in, and I couldn't look away from those eyes—dark, wild, burning with a need that matched the pulse still throbbing between my legs. "Not even close to enough. I want to eat your sweet cunt until my dying breath," he said in a low voice, a promise wrapped in a threat. "You're not getting off that easy."

I swallowed hard, my chest tight, the air between us humming with tension. "The elevator could start working at any time," I snapped, trying to claw back some control, but it sounded weak, and he just grinned, slow and dangerous.

"But it's not working yet, my Riley-girl," he said, leaning in, his breath hot against my ear. "Which means you still can't run . . ."

Before I could argue, his mouth was on mine, hard and demanding, tasting of me and him and some kind of magic I couldn't name. My hands fisted the waistband of his sweats, pulling him closer even as I cursed myself for it, and he groaned into the kiss, pressing his body against mine. I felt him—hard, insistent—through his sweatpants, grinding into me, and a fresh wave of heat surged low, reigniting the ache he'd just sated.

He broke the kiss, panting, his forehead pressed to mine. "Tell me you don't want this," he growled, daring me to lie. "Tell me, and I'll stop."

I opened my mouth, but nothing came out—because I couldn't. I wanted him. Since the second I saw him walking toward me in the bar, since the second any words had come out of his mouth.

I didn't want to want him.

I didn't want to feel the heat curling in my stomach, the sharp pull in my chest every time he looked at me like I was something he'd already won.

I didn't want to notice the way his presence filled a space, the way his voice wrapped around my name like a claim, the way his touch lingered long after he was gone.

But I did.

And I hated myself for it.

Because wanting him meant stepping into something I couldn't control. Something reckless. Something dangerous.

And I was *so tired* of danger.

But standing here, trapped with him, his scent in my lungs, his voice sinking into my skin, his body so close I could feel the heat radiating from it—

I was terrified.

Because it was too late.

Because maybe, despite everything . . .

I already *belonged* to him.

"That's what I thought," he murmured, and then his hands were on me again, yanking my dress all the way up, pushing my bra down. My breasts spilled free, and he groaned, low and guttural, his mouth dropping to my nipple, sucking hard. I arched into him, a cry tearing out, my hands scrambling for purchase, one gripping his shoulder, the other slamming against the wall.

"Jace—" I gasped, but he didn't let up, his tongue flicking over me, teeth grazing just enough to sting. His other hand slid down, tugging my panties all the way off, leaving me bare. I should've felt exposed, vulnerable, but all I felt was heat—his heat, my heat . . . the suffocating pull of him.

He straightened, eyes locked on mine, and pushed down his sweatpants with one hand, shoving them down just enough to free himself. My breath caught. He was thick, straining, and the sight of his huge dick had my core gushing even more. He stepped closer, pinning me tighter against the wall, one hand gripping my thigh, hitching it over his hip.

"Hold on," he said roughly, a command I couldn't ignore. My arms looped around his neck, fingers digging into his shoulders, and then he was pushing into me, slow at first, stretching me, filling me until I couldn't breathe. I moaned, loud and unfiltered, the sound bouncing off the walls, and he smirked, thrusting deeper, harder, setting a rhythm that had me gasping.

"Fuck, Riley-girl," he growled as he licked down my neck, biting down as he moved, each stroke a claim, a punishment, a plea. "You feel so good— so fucking *mine*."

I couldn't argue, I couldn't think . . . I could only feel him. Feel the relentless drive of his hips, the way he hit every spot that made me unravel.

I bit down on his chest, and he hissed, the bite of pain seeming to spur him on faster. The elevator creaked, a faint groan of metal, but neither of us cared—too lost, too tangled in the heat and the need.

"I'm so close," I panted, my head tipping back, his mouth finding my throat again, sucking a mark that would linger for days. I was almost there again, the pressure building fast, and he knew it—he could feel it in the way I tightened around him, the way my breaths hitched.

"Come for me," he snarled, his hand slipping between us, fingers finding my clit, rubbing hard. I shattered, my orgasm ripping through me, sharp and blinding, my cry echoing in the tight space. He didn't stop, he kept thrusting, dragging it out, pushing me through the waves until I was trembling, clinging to him as he pressed against my body.

Jace's rhythm faltered, his hips jerking, and then he groaned, low and guttural, spilling hot cum inside me that then dripped down my thighs. His weight pinned me to the wall, both of us panting, sweat-slick and wrecked, the air thick with the scent of us. For a moment, neither of us moved.

We just breathed.

His forehead pressed to mine, his hands still gripping my thighs.

"Why don't I mow the lawn naked?" he suddenly asked, and I blinked at him, gasping when he slid a few inches out of me.

"The grass isn't the only thing that would get a trim."

It took me a second, and then the most unsexy snort known to man came out of my mouth, and his answering smile was so blinding that I lost my breath for a second.

"Still think you can run, Riley-girl?" he murmured, his forehead still against mine.

I glared at him, my chest heaving, my body still humming from everything we'd just done. "I should," I muttered, but it lacked the necessary emphasis that such a statement required to be taken seriously.

"Yeah," he said, grinning as he brushed a damp strand of hair off my face. "But you're stuck with me now."

The elevator jolted violently, the lights flickering back to life, yanking me from the haze of heat and reckless desire. My heart slammed against my ribs as reality came crashing in like a tidal wave.

Jace pulled all the way out of me, adjusting his monster of a dick back into his sweatpants with the lazy confidence of a man completely unbothered—his bare chest still heaving, my name smeared across his skin. A maddeningly smug smirk stretched across his face.

Meanwhile, I was scrambling, fixing my bra, tugging my dress down . . . freaking out about the fact that paint was now smeared all over me . . . and there was cum dripping down my thighs. I straightened everything with frantic hands, my breath coming too fast, my entire body still thrumming from the way he had just *wrecked* me.

I reached down to grab my panties, but . . . Jace was faster. His fingers closed around the fabric before I could even process what was happening, and instead of handing them back like a *sane* person, he lifted them, twirling them around one finger with a knowing look.

"Jace," I hissed, reaching for them, but he smoothly tucked them into the pocket of his sweatpants, patting it like he had just stored away some kind of prize.

My stomach flipped. "Give them back."

He winked. "Finders keepers, babycakes."

The elevator dinged, and the doors slid open.

I made a move to dart out, to put as much space between me and the disaster that had just occurred in this elevator, but Jace was once again quicker. His hand wrapped around mine, strong and sure . . . and perfect. And before I could even think about bolting, he tugged me forward, stepping into the hallway like he hadn't just fucked me silly.

"I—" I started, my voice still breathless, still shaky.

He turned his head slightly, his lips brushing against my ear as he murmured, "Relax, baby. You're walking out of here looking thoroughly fucked and glowing and hot. *You're welcome.*"

Heat flooded my face. I nearly stumbled over my own feet. "Jace!"

He just grinned, gripping my hand tighter. "Come on, Riley-girl. Let's get you home."

And then he was leading me down the hallway, like he hadn't just stolen my underwear, my self-control, and possibly . . . the last shred of my resistance.

Because that was the hottest thing I'd ever experienced in my life.

———————

Jace led me through the hallway, his grip firm, and every step felt surreal, the haze of what had just happened in the elevator wrapping around me like a dream I hadn't fully woken from. The air between us crackled, a residual charge left behind from the way he had touched me, the way he had looked at me like I was the only thing that had ever mattered.

I was lost in my head as we walked outside and down the sidewalk, jumping however long later when he stopped, and I realized we were standing outside my dorm—a dorm name I hadn't given him, as a matter of fact. But why was that not surprising to me anymore? He'd figured out my name, got my credit card, transferred to my class, and found out where I worked. And every time I was in an enclosed space with him, I practically jumped him. My cheeks heated.

Jace turned to face me, his fingers still loosely wrapped around mine. His other hand came up, knuckles grazing along my jaw, tilting my face up until I was staring into those warm, knowing brown eyes.

"You can run, you know," he murmured in a teasing voice. "You can pretend all you want. But the thing about fate is, it doesn't take no for an answer." His smirk softened, just a little, replaced by something quieter, something deeper. "You feel it, too, don't you?" It was a question he'd asked me before, but now there was an edge of vulnerability in his voice, like I had the power to break his heart with my answer.

My breath hitched, but I couldn't answer. I didn't trust my voice, I didn't trust the way my body was still shaking from him, from everything. I hated how much I wanted to believe him, how much I wanted to lose myself in the comfort of his words.

And then . . . he ruined it.

"Be a good girl for me, darlin'," he murmured, his thumb brushing against my lower lip as he leaned down for a kiss.

The ground beneath me vanished.

I was in a cold bedroom. Silk sheets against my skin. Callum's voice, low and amused as he dragged a finger down my arm.

"Be a good girl for me, darling," he whispered, his lips barely brushing my ear as his fingers traced the bruises on my wrists. "You don't want me to be disappointed in you, do you?"

I shook my head, my throat too tight, my heart too frantic. Because disappointment led to worse things. Disappointment meant I had failed him. And failing him meant I didn't deserve to be seen, didn't deserve to be touched.

Didn't deserve anything at all.

I yanked my hand away from Jace's like I had been burned, my breath coming in shallow, ragged gasps. My vision blurred, my body locked in place, frozen in a past I couldn't outrun.

Jace frowned, the playful ease on his face disappearing in an instant. "Riley?" His voice was different now—concerned, cautious. He reached for me again, but I flinched.

His jaw clenched. "What just happened?"

I shook my head, not trusting myself to speak, willing the trembling in my limbs to stop. I wasn't there. I wasn't *back* there.

But in that moment, it didn't feel like Jace was standing in front of me. It felt like Callum had never let me go.

My throat was tight, air refusing to come in full breaths, like I was being squeezed by invisible hands.

I had to get out of here.

"I—I can't," I whispered, my voice breaking over the words.

Jace stilled, his whole body locked in place, his grip hovering like he wasn't sure if he should reach for me again. His jaw clenched, that sharp, unreadable stare flickering between my face and my shaking hands.

I turned before I could see his expression fall, before I could second-guess myself. My legs felt weak as I ran inside the building, the door clicking shut behind me. I didn't stop until I was inside my thankfully empty dorm room, and I could sag against the door, pressing a hand over my mouth to silence the jagged breath that tore from my throat.

I shouldn't have let it get this far. Because Jace *wasn't* Callum.

But that didn't stop the past from sinking its claws into me, dragging me back into the dark.

CHAPTER 8

JACE

I was almost inside my house when Jagger texted me.

> Jagger: I need a favor.

Sigh. It was hard being the cooler, more capable brother.

> Me: It's going to cost you.

> Jagger: Obviously. You can have 10% more of the investments you do for me.

> Me: 10%. What the fuck do you need? Because you must be desperate.

> Jagger : If Mom and Dad ask, tell them the blow-up doll in my house was yours.

> Me: . . .

> Me: You know what, I was going to ask for context, but I feel like it's better if I don't.

> Jagger: It is. Just do it.

Me: No.

Jagger: Jace.

Me: Jagger.

Jagger: Do you want them thinking their firstborn son is a pervert?

Me: Firstborn son. You do realize that if I claim the doll is mine, then they will think I'm the pervert.

Me: Seriously. I feel bad for you that you weren't born with the big brain.

Jagger: I need the blow-up doll to distract them.

Me: Distract them from what?!

Jagger: Unimportant.

Me: NOT TO ME.

Me: Wait.

Me: Wait.

Me: DID THEY FIND A BODY?!

Jagger: This is why I didn't want to tell you. You'll get all dramatic. Like a drama llama.

Me: It's No Drama Llamas, actually. But don't distract me.

Me: THEY FOUND A BODY.

Jagger: Stop yelling.

Me: IN YOUR HOUSE?!

Jagger: Look, it was technically in the garage.

Me: Jagger. I can't tell if you're kidding.

Jagger: It wasn't my fault!

Me: THAT'S EXACTLY WHAT SOMEONE WHOSE FAULT IT WAS WOULD SAY.

Jagger: Anyway, I need you to go along with the doll thing.

Me: I am not taking the fall for your blow-up girl-friend/dead body.

Jagger: Then they'll keep asking questions about the dead guy.

Me: I'M ASKING QUESTIONS ABOUT THE DEAD GUY.

Jagger: Again. Unimportant.

Me: I need more information before I can agree to this.

Jagger: No, you don't.

Me: Yes, I do.

Me: Did you kill him?

Jagger: No.

Me: Did you want to kill him?

Jagger: . . .

Jagger: Not the point.

Me: Uh-huh. So, what did this guy do?

Jagger: Again. Not the point.

Me: Jagger, did you take out a hitman and forget to cancel the appointment?

Jagger: No.

Me: Did the guy insult Mom's cooking?

Jagger: You think I'd unalive someone for doing that? Did we grow up in the same house? We both know Mom's a terrible cook.

Me: So you did unalive someone.

Jagger: NO!

Me: Was he a tax fraud investigator?

Jagger: Why would that be a guess?

Me: I don't know your life, Jagger. Maybe you've been evading the IRS.

Jagger: For the last time, I did not kill him.

Me: Okay, so he just happened to be dead in your garage?

Jagger: Technically, he died somewhere else.

Me: WHY DOES THAT MAKE IT WORSE?

Me: Is this an organ trafficking thing?

Jagger: Jace.

Me: What about a former Russian spy?

Jagger: Stop.

Me: A parking ticket enforcer?

Jagger: . . .

Me: OMG. IT WAS.

Jagger: IT WAS NOT.

Me: JUST ADMIT IT. You finally snapped after too many unpaid parking tickets.

Jagger: Jace.

Me: THEY BOOTED YOUR CAR ONE TOO MANY TIMES, DIDN'T THEY?

Jagger: . . .

Me: HOLY SHIT.

Jagger: I did not kill a parking ticket enforcer.

Me: . . .

Me: Jagger, I need to know if I should be looking into extradition laws.

Jagger: No.

Me: Was he a rival blow-up doll distributor, and you had to take him out?

Jagger: STOP.

Me: I'm just trying to understand what kind of dead-person scenario we're dealing with here.

Jagger : If I tell you, will you just go along with the doll excuse?

Me: . . .

Me: Maybe.

Jagger: Forget it.

Me: So it was a parking ticket guy.

Jagger: I'M DONE.

Me: Did they believe that the doll was yours? Because Mom has that weird lie detector thing.

Jagger: I told them you were lonely.

Me: I HAVE A GIRLFRIEND.

Jagger: No, you don't. I asked Matty last time you made that claim. And it was a lie.

Me: It's not a lie.

Jagger: Focus. Is that a yes?

Me: . . .

Me: Fine.

Me: But I'm telling them it was just a joke. And, if another corpse shows up, I'm telling Mom.

Jagger: Deal.

Jagger: You're the best, Jace-face.

Me: . . .

It was a little concerning that I could never tell if Jagger was kidding when we had these conversations. I was always *pretty* sure he was kidding . . . but there was still a part of me that wasn't *quite* sure.

I was still pondering the mystery that was Jagger as I walked into my bedroom and saw a crisp red envelope sealed with a familiar-looking red wax seal sitting on my bed. I stared at it for a second before picking it up and tearing it open. Inside, nestled between the folds of paper, was a small black card emblazoned with a Sphinx symbol. Beneath it sat several neatly stacked bundles of cash, pristine and untouched, like they had just come straight from a vault. No name. No return address. Just a single, bold *ten thirty p.m.* and an address printed on the inside.

Very spooky-like and completely meeting my expectations for how this secret society thing was supposed to work. I grinned.

Looked like my Sphinx trials were finally going to begin. A welcome distraction for the fact that Riley had once again decided I was the worst person on earth.

I needed to prepare.

I walked out to the main room where Matty was watching the Colorado/Baylor game on the big screen we had in our living room.

"Hand me your phone," I ordered.

He took his time flicking his attention from the TV to my face. "Pardon?"

"I need your phone to install an app."

Matty eyed me suspiciously. "The last time you installed an app it was to track a sea turtle's migration that I had absolutely no interest in."

I scoffed indignantly. "Oh, I'm sorry that I care about endangered species, Matty. That must be so terrible having such a Good Samaritan in your life."

"It was a monthly five-hundred-dollar charge that you 'forgot' to tell me about. And you know what it said on the bill for what it was for?"

"Sea turtles," I answered, thinking that was a dumb question.

"Wrong. It was for Earth," Matty said snarkily as he shoved some beef jerky in his mouth. "What does that even mean?"

"A worthy endeavor is what it means," I told him, reaching out to grab his phone. He yanked it away.

"When I tried to cancel it, the price went up to a thousand dollars!"

"Well, this isn't for Earth," I said as patiently as I could—which actually wasn't patient at all. "This is for me. So you can track me properly."

Matty's eyebrows got so high they disappeared under his hair. "I don't want to track you properly," he said slowly.

I scoffed and waved him off as I finally secured his phone, quickly downloading Find My Friends and connecting it to my phone. "Of course you want to track me properly," I mused, putting in his password.

"Hey! How do you know my password?" he snarled, making a grabby motion at the phone.

There was a lot of scoffing happening in this conversation on my end. Because it was frankly insulting that he assumed I wouldn't have his passwords. All of them. If he were a better bestie, he'd have all of mine as well.

"Why are we doing this? I'm okay with not knowing where you are at all times," he said pointedly, finally giving up his fruitless endeavor to get his phone back.

"This is in case I disappear," I told him vaguely, ignoring the part where he pretended he didn't care about my whereabouts because it was rude to call your besties liars.

That explanation finally got his attention. "Why are you going to disappear, exactly?"

I grinned at him. "The Sphinx has called."

Matty straightened up, a piece of beef jerky falling into his lap. "Oh cool, I get to track your lifeless body. Love that for me," he tried to joke, but his eyes were doing that wild, shifty thing that they did when he was nervous.

"Wish me luck," I said, tossing him his phone and heading toward the door.

"Don't die," he called out behind me, and I gave him a thumbs-up. "Wait, how do I use this app?" he added, a little panic in his voice as I walked out of the house.

"I have faith in you, Matthew," I told him, hoping that the use of his full name would inspire him to reach new heights.

Of the three of us, Matty was the worst at technology, so if I really had to depend on him not to die . . . it could get tricky. Parker was probably balls deep in Casey, though—or he had her in that basement again. So, I really needed Matty to come through.

I hopped into my Jeep Gladiator, plugged in the address, and blasted Olivia Rodrigo as I drove. Because if that didn't get you amped up to conquer your first trial, I didn't know what would.

As Parker would say—or as I'd first said to Parker, and now he copies it, and everyone thinks it's his saying even though I got it from a certain NFL GOAT—LFG.

The warehouse sat at the edge of the city, surrounded by crumbling brick buildings and chain-link fences topped with razor wire. The streetlights flickered, casting long shadows over the cracked pavement. Someone was going to steal my tires. Or my Jeep.

I glanced at the few cars parked haphazardly along the broken curb. Judging by the thick layer of dirt on them, their owners had not been in them for a long time.

Kind of made you wonder if the owners were still alive.

The street was silent except for the occasional rustle of wind through broken window glass. My steps echoed as I walked, an ominous drumbeat. Matty better be tracking me right fucking now. This was definitely the kind of place where people died. And he and Parker definitely couldn't live without me.

The building itself looked like it had once been something legitimate— maybe a shipping hub or an old factory—but now rust crawled up its sides, and the windows were covered in thick grime. A dented metal door stood beneath a single buzzing light, where a man who was a cross between a linebacker and a brick shithouse leaned against the wall, his tattooed arms folded over his chest.

Oh, was that a tattoo of a man eating someone's heart?

Lovely.

The guy had the kind of face that looked like it had been broken and put back together a few too many times. And the barely concealed holster under his jacket told me he wasn't here to hand out welcome drinks.

Although, that would be delicious right now. If the Sphinx had a survey after this, I would definitely be recommending something like that. It would really help offset the "you're going to die" ambience this place had going on if they served me one of those drinks with the pink umbrellas.

Ugh, don't think about pink umbrellas, Jace. That will make you think about Riley.

As I stepped up, his eyes dragged over me with the warmth of a dead fish. We both stood there until I realized he seemed to be waiting for something. The Sphinx really needed to come with some sort of instruction manual. I pulled the black card from my pocket and held it up between two fingers, hoping that was what he was waiting for. His gaze flicked to it, then back to me, and with a grunt, he took it from my hand. "Weapons?" he demanded.

Hmm, should I joke about my fists? Decisions, decisions.

Better not.

"Spread 'em," he growled impatiently when I didn't answer right away, his voice like gravel underfoot. I complied, and he began frisking me with the gentleness of a gorilla looking for lice.

"Hey, hey," I told him when he got a little close to the family jewels. I was a shower, not a grower, so lil Jace, aka the Anaconda, aka Sir Humps-a-Lot, hung down low.

The guy snorted like I'd said something funny, obviously not realizing he'd been an inch away from being traumatized for the rest of his life with insecurity about the size of his dick compared to mine. I'm just saying . . . it was a close call.

"Clean," he muttered, handing me back the black card and stepping aside to reveal a steel door that looked like it belonged to a fucking vault.

I wiped imaginary dust off my shirt and pushed the door open, the smell of oil and metal assaulting my nostrils. Lights flickered overhead, casting long shadows across the concrete floor, and my pulse kicked up. Yep, if murder had a zip code . . . it'd be here.

I was pretty sure that was a bloodstain on the floor over there.

The hallway ahead of me was narrow and dimly lit, the concrete walls lined with pipes that dripped condensation. My footsteps echoed as I moved forward, the floor uneven beneath my shoes.

Another door waited at the end, this one manned by a second guy—leaner than the first but just as unfriendly. His suit was pristine, his posture relaxed, but there was no mistaking the weight of the gun on his hip. He didn't speak. Just looked me and the black card over with a sneer like my gloriousness offended him, and then he pulled open the door and stepped aside.

The moment I entered, the atmosphere changed. The air was thick, hazy with cigar smoke, the scent of whiskey sharp against the stale air. Low murmurs filled the room, the quiet shuffle of playing cards against felt, the occasional clink of chips being stacked.

It took me a second to see who else was in the room. Dozens of people were seated at round tables, heads bowed over hands of cards, faces unreadable beneath the dim hanging lights. A chandelier flickered overhead, casting a dull glow over the scene and making the shadows dance along the cracked walls.

A poker game.

My lips curled into a relieved smirk. I could play poker.

A woman in a sultry red cocktail dress appeared from the shadows, her perfume cutting through the haze. "Follow me," she said, her voice smooth, practiced.

Her heels clicked against the floor as she led me through the room, weaving between tables stacked with cash, liquor bottles, and more than a few knives. When we reached the main table, she gestured for me to sit before slipping away, disappearing into the crowd like a ghost.

I took my seat, eyeing the men around me.

Slicked-back hair and a scar across his jaw—Scar Jaw, I decided. He probably collected debts with a crowbar.

To his right, there was a guy with yellowed teeth and fingers stained with nicotine. He grinned, revealing more gums than I needed to see. If we became friends, I was definitely going to give him my dentist's number. Although, he looked like the kind of guy who knew how to make people disappear. So maybe not.

Next to him was a guy who was all muscle—I was going to call him Neck Tattoo on account of the skeleton hand gripping his throat. He cracked his knuckles every few seconds like he was debating whether breaking bones or winning money was a better use of his time.

And finally, next to him, Dead Eyes. His face was unreadable, his suit too perfect. He watched me like I was already a corpse waiting to drop. I liked him the least, I decided. If anyone was going to kill me, it was going to be him.

Man, these secret society people took their membership trials seriously. Scar Jaw gave me a lazy grin as I took my seat. "Hope you're better at cards than you look."

Offensive. I'd been told by many a person—mostly women—that I looked very capable. They might have been talking about my skills in the bedroom, but I was going to not think about that at the moment because this man had just insulted me. He was going in my burn book. Probably would never enact my revenge because he looked like he could eat me, but he was going in the book anyway.

Yellow Teeth shuffled his chips and sneered. "You got a name, or should we just call you Fresh Meat?"

I met his gaze, letting a slow smirk of my own creep onto my face. "Call me whatever you want," I said.

The dealer flicked cards out in smooth, precise motions. "Spoken like someone who doesn't know who he's playing against."

In the center of the table sat a pile that would make a lesser man sweat. Bundles of cash, some still bound with foreign bank seals, stacks of gold coins, and an assortment of glittering jewels—rings, necklaces, even a diamond-encrusted watch that probably belonged to someone who wasn't alive to miss it. A single silver briefcase sat on top, latched shut, the kind of thing that in any movie would be filled with either more money or something significantly worse.

I took it all in. Alright, I was going to assume that the Sphinx wanted me to win all of that. Or if they didn't, I would hope some kind of sign would appear, because I wasn't a fucking mind reader.

The first few hands were a disaster. I played cautiously, testing the waters. But it didn't matter—bad cards, bad luck, and a table full of men who had no problem taking my money made sure of that. The cockiness around me widened as my stack dwindled, and Scar Jaw chuckled under his breath.

"Tough luck, Fresh Meat," Yellow Teeth taunted, stacking his winnings. "Maybe you should stick to the kiddie tables."

I shrugged, pretending to brush it off. "Just warming up," I told them with a small grin, ignoring the bead of sweat sliding down my spine as he picked his teeth with what may have been a human bone.

A few more rounds, and I realized something was off. The guy to my left was dealing himself better hands than probability should allow, and the man across from me had a habit of adjusting his sleeve right before a good hand came his way. They were cheating.

Of course they were.

I pretended not to notice, letting them think I was just another sucker out of his depth. Meanwhile, I memorized their tells, their tricks. The way Scar Jaw flicked his index finger when he bluffed. The way Yellow Teeth smirked half a second too soon when he had a sure thing. On my next hand, I won. A full house—aces over kings. Wasn't sure how I'd gotten that hand with the Cheater-McCheaters at the table. But I'd take it.

The shift around the table was immediate. A few eyes flickered toward me with new interest. Scar Jaw raised an eyebrow, smirking. "Beginner's luck," he mused, taking a slow sip of whiskey. I mean, I wasn't sure that losing five hands in a row and then winning one was "beginner's luck," but I wasn't going to argue with the man.

There was a full tumbler of whiskey in front of me, but I wasn't taking slow sips . . . or any sips at all. There was a 99 percent chance it was drugged, so I wasn't going to take that risk.

Yellow Teeth scoffed, shaking his head. "Yeah, let's see if it holds."

Let's see if those teeth last the game, I was thinking, but at least my inside thoughts were staying that way. That wasn't always a sure thing with me.

Smelling money, a few women began drifting over to the table, draping themselves over the men like expensive fur coats. One slid into Scar Jaw's lap, her red nails trailing down his chest as she whispered something in his ear. Another wrapped her arms around Neck Tattoo, giggling as she toyed with his shirt.

Across from me, one of the players leaned back as a brunette in a skin-tight dress perched herself on the edge of the table, giving him an eyeful of boobs. Without missing a beat, he pulled a tiny glass vial from his jacket, tapped out a line of fine white powder onto the curve of her very fake breast, and snorted it in one quick motion.

She giggled, raking her fingers through his oiled-up hair . . . and then slowly sank to her knees so only the top of her head was visible.

Oh boy, I was pretty sure I was about to witness something that not even bleach was going to be able to erase from my mind.

The dealer didn't even blink. He just kept shuffling, kept dealing.

I'm just saying, I was quite sure that Parker's trials were infinitely better than mine. I'd take a corpse over this scene, *thank you very much.*

I exhaled slowly, trying to keep my features blank as her head started to bob up and down in his lap. At the same time, I had to work on not choking on how thick the smoke was in the room. These people obviously hadn't had D.A.R.E. as kids, and it showed. This wasn't just a poker game. It was a fucking circus.

Play continued, and every time I won, the strain in the room grew. The Sphinx better not have my death as the outcome they were aiming for, because One: It was going to take a miracle to get me out of this alive, I was pretty sure, and Two: I would make sure to haunt their asses for the rest of time if this was the end.

This place was far too smelly for it to be where my magnificence ended.

The man beside me had also won his fair share—only because I'd let him, obviously—and he was getting cockier with each round, tossing back whiskey like it was water and raking in chips with a greedy smirk. But he was playing too fast, too loose, and that was a mistake in a room like this.

I saw it happen a second before it did. He reached for a stack that wasn't his, sliding an extra pile of chips into his own with a sleight of hand that might've worked at a lesser table. But not here. Scar Jaw caught it immediately.

"That was a mistake," he murmured, setting his cards down slowly. The room stilled, the air thick with the kind of tension that felt like it could snap a neck.

The guy beside me swallowed, his bravado cracking. "Just a mistake," he said nervously.

A loud crack split the air, and the man beside me jerked, his breath leaving in a wheeze. Blood bloomed across his shirt. He slumped forward, face hitting the felt, chips scattering.

No one moved.

No one reacted as Scar Jaw tucked the gun back beneath his jacket.

The dealer calmly reached across the table and pushed the dead man's cards aside. "Next hand."

Scar Jaw leaned forward, steepling his fingers like I was in some low-budget mafia film where literally only the worst actors had been available. "See, the thing about this game is . . . some people don't leave with all their parts intact. Hope you're smart enough to know when to walk away."

I glanced down at my cards, then back at him. He was watching me closely, a knowing smirk tugging at his lips.

I returned the smirk, rolling my shoulders. "You know, Scar Jaw, if I needed a lesson in subtlety, you wouldn't be the guy I'd call."

His face darkened instantly.

Oops. I'd said that name out loud. So much for my inside thoughts . . .

His hand came up, tracing the jagged scar along his jawline, his fingers twitching slightly as if resisting the urge to reach for something more dangerous. The veins in his neck pulsed, his nostrils flaring as he gave me a slow, measured look.

"Careful, rookie," he murmured, his voice like gravel. "Mouths that run too much tend to get sewn shut around here."

Well, that was a delightful piece of imagery. I hoped the world never had to experience the darkness that would exist without my mouth running too much.

I'd save that thought for a more . . . welcoming crowd. Something told me they wouldn't be quite as appreciative as I would've liked.

I leaned forward, sliding my next bet onto the pile, meeting Scar Jaw's furious glare with a grin that hopefully rode that fine line between *confidence* and *getting a bullet through your head*. I'd never had to have that thought before, but here we were.

Someone came and dragged the dead body away, and then the next round was dealt, the tension so thick it felt like the air itself had weight. The pot had grown beyond ridiculous. Stacks of cash, watches that looked like they belonged on the wrists of Fortune 500 CEOs, diamond-studded cuff links, and a set of car keys that might've belonged to a sports car or a getaway vehicle. Even a deed to a property had been thrown in, written in precise, looping handwriting. Someone was either desperate or very, very stupid.

The guy next to me—my new neighbor since my last one had . . . vacated—was sweating bullets. His collar was damp, his fingers trembling as he drummed against the table. I could practically hear his thoughts screaming. He had too much in the pot, and he knew it. He kept licking his lips, stealing glances at Scar Jaw, who had been watching him like a predator sizing up its next meal.

I resisted the urge to lean over and tell him, *Buddy, if you're sweating this much, you should've folded three hands ago*.

The dealer flicked out the cards, his expression unreadable. My hand—a decent pair, but nothing game-changing. The others tossed in their bets, the clink of chips echoing in the heavy silence.

Yellow Teeth leaned back, grinning. "Let's up the stakes. Make this more . . . interesting."

Any more interesting, and I'd have a heart attack. But, what the hell. Let's do it.

A man across the table produced a thick gold ring from his pocket and set it on the pile. Someone else threw in one of those ornate gold keys that usually belonged to real-live treasure chests. The small mountain of cash, jewels, and possessions in the center of the table grew, the air thick with greed and challenge.

"Hope you got more than just beginner's luck," Neck Tattoo muttered, rolling a chip between his fingers.

Scar Jaw, still glaring, laid his cards down first—three kings. Strong. He smirked, already reaching toward the pot like he was about to collect. Yellow Teeth leaned back in his chair, rubbing his fingers together.

I wasn't done yet, though. The room hummed with anticipation. The others revealed their hands, each one a calculated risk. I was last.

I took my time, letting the moment stretch before laying my cards down—four jacks.

The sweat-drenched guy next to me made a choked sound, somewhere between a whimper and a swear. His eyes darted between me and Scar Jaw like he was waiting for an explosion.

Silence.

Until Dead Eyes let out a slow, measured chuckle that kind of sounded like he was laughing at my impending death.

Scar Jaw's expression darkened further, his fingers twitching toward his whiskey glass. The guy next to me tensed like he was expecting the table to flip, and honestly, so was I.

I kept my eye on him as I dragged my winnings toward me, and Scar Jaw's glare deepened. For a split second, I thought he was about to lunge across the table. Instead, a chair scraped against the concrete as someone stood up too fast. A hand went to a jacket—metal glinted. A gun was drawn.

The room tensed, the weight of atmosphere pressing against my shoulders like a loaded trigger.

"Bad move, kid," Yellow Teeth muttered, shaking his head. "Should've known when to cash out."

Before anything could escalate, a single sharp clap echoed through the room.

Everyone froze.

A masked man stood in the doorway, dressed in black, his face obscured except for his piercing, calculating eyes. He clapped again, slow and deliberate.

As if a silent command had been issued, the entire room shifted. The gun disappeared. The tension dissolved into something eerily normal. One by one, the spectators drifted away, returning to their tables, their games, their drinks—like nothing had happened at all.

Scar Jaw exhaled heavily, his jaw tight as he glanced between me and the masked man. "Looks like you've got friends in high places, rookie."

I didn't reply. Didn't dare take my eyes off the masked figure as he gave a final nod, then vanished into the hallway like a ghost.

I let out a slow breath before gripping the stacks of cash and other goodies and shoving them into my jacket. "Damn it," I muttered under my breath. "He could've at least let me enjoy the win."

No one stopped me as I stood up and strode toward the exit, my pulse still thrumming, my mind turning over what the hell had just happened.

I hustled out of the room while trying not to look like I was rushing and pushed open the exit door, stepping out into the cold night air, my pulse still hammering in my ears. The metallic scent of blood and stale cigar smoke clung to my clothes, and my fingers tightened around the wads of cash stuffed into my jacket pocket.

A man in another mask stood stationed just outside the door, leaning casually against the wall, arms crossed like he'd been waiting for me. His face was completely obscured, but when he spoke, his voice was low and smooth. "The Sphinx sends its regards."

Then he was gone, slipping into the darkness as if he had never been there at all.

I stood there for a moment, inhaling deep, trying to ground myself. My brain was still spinning from everything that had just gone down. I had played a rigged game, outplayed criminals who had no problem murdering in front of an audience, and somehow walked away in one piece.

Parker had definitely gotten off easy. At this rate, my next task was going to be proving my bravery by swimming across a crocodile-infested river or something equally traumatizing. I'd probably get my McSnuffles bitten off and be forced to spend my days dickless and sad all because I was an incredible man above men who had caught the eye of a random secret society.

I'd better be getting a whole lot of something from this organization after I was officially inducted because this fucking sucked.

I was halfway back to my Jeep when the screech of tires ripped through the night.

A familiar black car came skidding to a halt in front of me. The driver's door flew open, and Matty practically launched himself out.

"What the actual fuck, dude," he shouted, his eyes wide and crazy, arms flailing like he was trying to swat bees.

"Oh hey, what are you doing here?" I asked, trying to play it cool like I hadn't just almost died over the last however many hours.

"What am I doing here?" He gaped at me even more, his eyes bugging out. I kind of wanted to reach out and push them back in just in case they were in danger of popping out.

"Your last words to me were basically 'I hope I don't die,' and then you disappeared. I texted you fifteen times, Jace Thatcher. Do you know what happens when you tell someone 'I hope I don't die,' and then you go radio silent for hours? I had two options: call the cops and ruin this whole Sphinx thing, or find your dumb ass myself. Guess which one I picked?"

I blinked at him. The fifteen times was serious. I was known for responding back within seconds—because it was rude to keep people waiting. My blinking slowly turned into a grin.

"You tracked me," I declared triumphantly. Because tracking was caring. Everyone knew that.

His face turned a weird gray color, and his eyes were still bugging out. "Yep, I tracked you," he answered quickly.

Huh, that was a little . . . suspicious.

"Whatcha hiding there, Matty-boy?" I asked, crossing my arms in front of me and feeling much better about the fact that I'd almost died trying to join an organization of a bunch of people who wore Halloween masks for fun.

"I'm not hiding anything," he said.

"You look suspicious," I countered.

"How does someone *look* suspicious?" he huffed . . . still looking suspicious.

"Did you have any trouble figuring out the tracking app?" I asked innocently.

His face paled even further, and he literally gulped.

"Matty . . . you know I'll find out eventually, so you should just fess up now—so I don't have to waste my precious new lease on life finding out what you're hiding from me."

"So, you *did* almost die!" He looked around like Yellow Teeth was about to pop out from behind a bush—or a piece of trash, since there weren't a whole lot of bushes around here.

"Answer the question," I pressed, opening up his passenger door so I could find some snacks. Almost dying made me hungry.

"That's been there for like three months," he commented when I found some crackers and ripped open the package, biting into the cheesy goodness like a shark.

"Pretty sure these preservatives were built to last." I groaned as the artificial flavoring hit my tongue. Sure, one could say they were a little stale.

But there'd been a few moments there where I thought I'd never have food again.

"Okay, proceed," I said with a full mouth. Matty looked a little grossed out by the crumbs spraying out of my mouth, but then he must have remembered what he was hiding from me, and his face resumed that blank, grayish pallor he had going.

"So, obviously, the app was intended for people with doctorates in technology," he began.

"Or someone who possesses basic phone capabilities," I inserted helpfully.

He scowled at me. "When the fifteen texts went unanswered, I may have freaked out. And then I may have had to get help."

"You didn't!" I gasped in horror as I realized where he was going with this.

"I had to do it. You could have been dead," he snapped, waving his hands around all crazy-like again.

"I went to Darla's house and . . ."

This was too good. I was glad I hadn't died. Just for this moment.

Darla was our next-door neighbor, and the kind of person you tried to avoid making direct eye contact with because you just *knew* she had a collection of teeth that didn't belong to her.

Supposedly, she'd lived in that house for as long as anyone could remember—which was weird because this was student housing, and I had no idea if she was even registered. She was somewhere between twenty and forty, had a wardrobe that consisted entirely of aggressively clashing patterns, and smelled like patchouli, burnt toast, and what I could only describe as *bad vibes*.

"Wow, you really like me," I interrupted. "You totally let her give you a blowjob in exchange for figuring out the app, didn't you?" I doubled over, choking on my laughter. "You *literally* let Darla Pinswallow . . ." More gasps for breath. "Swallow your—"

"Why would that be the first thing you think of?" Matty gasped, sounding horrified. "Of course I didn't let her give me a blowjob!"

I wheezed out a breath. "This is the best thing that's ever happened to me."

"You disappeared into an abyss. The therapy I'm going to need for the next hundred years is on you—and Parker! But I did *not* let her give me a blowjob."

"So what did you do, then?" I asked, not actually believing him.

"Well, not that."

"Matty . . ."

"I was in a rush, okay? She put me on the spot. She might have asked me to wear a cowboy hat."

I was laughing so hard, this could've been the thing that actually killed me. Lack of oxygen. "You stripped down, didn't you! Butt naked."

"I wasn't nude! I had my briefs on!"

I continued to die of laughter.

"She took pictures, Jace. This is *your* fault."

"That could be considered *art* in some places," I noted. "*A lot* of places, probably!"

Matty made some sort of gassy elephant sound. "I suffered trying to save you! I made a sacrifice that will haunt me until my dying day." He pointed at me. "You and Davis owe me for the rest of your existences. I probably need an exorcism now."

I ran a hand through my hair, feeling decidedly more chipper after my snack and my bestie's act of sacrifice that I would be able to relive in my darkest moments. "Well, I'm fine if that makes you feel any better."

"Oh yeah?" Matty gestured wildly at my clothes. "Then explain why you look like you just crawled out of a mob movie and smell like a liquor store on fire."

I smirked. "Would you believe me if I said I just played a really intense game of Go Fish?"

Matty groaned, dragging a hand down his face. "Get in the car before I kill you myself."

"That app really is easy," I told him as he threw himself into the driver's seat and started driving me to my Jeep . . . which was still there, surprisingly, because apparently Lady Luck loved me today.

"I'd wash your dick," I told him seriously as I got out of the car, and he growled at me like a wild animal, even though I'd just given him very useful information.

He looked a little angry at that comment, so I gave him some love. "Thank you for endangering your chance of having future children to track me. ILY. Also, I'll teach you how to use your phone like a normal person so you're never in this situation again."

I narrowly avoided a soda can to the head because he was apparently feral, and then I closed the door, laughing as he sped away.

Trial number one: check.

Time to get back to convincing Riley I was the love of her life.

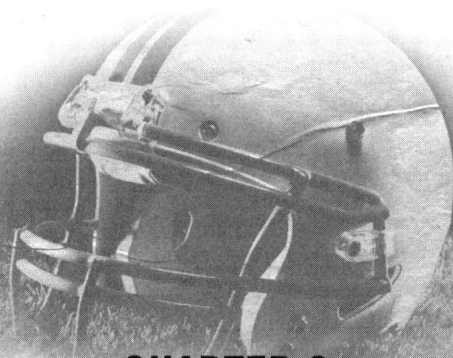

CHAPTER 9

RILEY

I wasn't going for him.

That's what I kept telling myself as I stood in front of my mirror, tugging at the hem of my black tee for the hundredth time, like it'd magically turn me into someone who wasn't full of shit. My reflection stared back—messy blonde hair spilling over my shoulders, my hazel eyes too wide, too jittery, like I was about to bolt. I yanked my fingers through a tangle, cursing under my breath, trying to shake the nerves buzzing under my skin like a swarm of pissed-off bees.

I was going for me. Not Jace. Not the guy who'd been haunting my head for two days straight, ever since I'd run away from him, my chest tight, throat burning . . . telling myself it was done. Tasha had invited me to the game after she'd found me hiding out in the library again—another sorority recruiting event, apparently. And while I was pretty sure sorority life wasn't for me and Tasha had not shown me the sisterhood that supposedly went with it . . . I hadn't said no.

The fact that Emma had done something weird again had also been motivating in accepting any excuse to get out of the room.

Yesterday morning, I had woken up to find her sitting cross-legged in the middle of the floor, completely still, just staring at me again. Not blinking. Not moving. Just watching.

When I finally sat up, groggy and thoroughly creeped out, she smiled—an eerie, slow stretch of her lips—and whispered, "I counted how many times you stopped breathing in your sleep."

I had bolted out of bed so fast I nearly tripped.

So yeah, maybe I didn't have a future as a sorority girl, but getting out of my dorm, away from Emma and her unsettling midnight activities, seemed like the right call.

If I was honest with myself, though . . .

I wanted to see him. Even from far off. It had been two days, but no amount of reasoning, no stern self-lectures, had made the ache in my chest go away.

Two days since his brown eyes had locked on mine, all heat and fight, since his voice, low and rough, had cut through me like a blade. Two days since I'd let the past dictate my future.

Two days . . .

And now? Now, I was craving him, like a starving woman desperate for a taste, even though I knew how it would end. It was pathetic. Stalker-ish, even. I'd been the one to run, and here I was, creeping back for a peek through the crack.

I groaned, loud and dramatic, grabbing my small purse off the bed and storming out before I could talk myself into staying. The air outside hit me cool and sharp, late October crispness cutting through the humidity, and I shoved my hands in my jeans pockets, trudging toward the stadium. My sneakers scuffed the pavement, each step a little heavier, my stomach twisting tighter the closer I got. I could hear the crowd already—distant roars, chants bleeding through the trees—and my pulse kicked up, a quick *thud* against my ribs.

Tasha was waiting by the gate, bouncing on her toes like a cheerleader, her dark ponytail swinging and an orange T on her cheek as she waved me over. "I thought you were gonna flake again, St. James," she teased, linking her arm through mine before I could dodge, her grip firm and her demeanor annoyingly chipper.

"I almost did," I admitted, letting her pull me toward the entrance, my sneakers dragging like I could slow this whole thing down. My eyes darted around—orange jerseys everywhere, drunk guys yelling, girls in glittery makeup giggling past us—and once again I felt like a fish out of water, flopping in the chaos.

Tasha laughed, bright and unbothered, her eyes glinting with that sorority-girl shine I'd never get. "That's 'cause you don't know how good these games are yet. You're gonna love it—promise. But first—" She stopped, digging into the little pouch slung over her shoulder, pulling out a sponge and a tube of thick orange paint. "Face paint."

I blinked, stepping back like she'd pulled a knife. "Wait—what?"

"For school spirit, duh," she said, already dabbing the sponge into the paint, the stuff oozing like tar. She gestured for me to lean down, her grin wide and relentless. "C'mon, sweetcheeks—don't be a buzzkill." Her calling me something ridiculous reminded me of Jace. Ugh.

I sighed loudly but bent anyway, feeling the cool, wet stroke of the sponge as she pressed it to my left cheek. It tickled, the paint cold against my skin, and I scrunched my nose, holding still while she worked. "What are you putting on me?" I mumbled.

"Perfection," she said vaguely, stepping back, admiring her work like I was a canvas instead of a human being. She held up her phone to show me the sorority symbol—a swoopy theta thing—staring back at me from her camera. Then she winked . . . suspiciously and said, "One more thing."

Before I could open my mouth to protest, she was at it again, the sponge swiping across my right cheek, quick and deliberate. Her grin turned smug, all too pleased with herself, and my stomach did a slow, uneasy flip. "Tasha," I said, voice low, warning, "what are you doing?"

She smirked, flipping her phone around again, the front camera flashing my reflection back at me.

I nearly choked. There—clear as day, bold and orange—was Jace's number. The 77 scrawled across my right cheek was like a neon sign screaming my stupid, secret obsession.

"Tasha—" I started, my voice climbing as my hand flew up to scrub it off. The paint was already drying, though, sticking like glue.

"Relax," she giggled, grabbing my wrist to stop me, her nails digging in just enough to hold me still. "It's just a number. Besides, you like him."

"I do not—" I spluttered, heat rushing to my face, my free hand flapping like I could wave the lie away. "That's not—I'm not—"

"Then why are you here?" she cut in, arching a brow, her voice all-knowing, like she'd caught me red-handed.

I opened my mouth. Shut it. Opened it again, fumbling for something—anything—that wasn't the truth. "I—I'm checking out your sisterhood thing," I finally said lamely, crossing my arms tight over my chest, glaring at her like it'd make her drop it.

"Uh-huh," she said, smirking wider, dragging me through the gate before I could bolt. "Sure, Riley. It's fine—no one'll even notice."

For a dumb, fleeting second, I let myself buy it. I told myself one little number didn't mean anything, that I could slip into the crowd, watch from a safe distance, get my fix of Jace without him even knowing I was there. Just a glimpse—his broad shoulders under the pads, that cocky grin flashing through the helmet—then I'd be gone, back to my room, back to pretending I didn't care.

Until we got to our seats.

Tasha tugged me down the steps, chattering about tailgates and some sorority mixer after, her voice a blur as my eyes darted around, taking it in. The stands were packed—orange and white bleeding together, flags waving, the air thick with beer and sweat and that electric hum of a game day. She stopped, plopping down, and I sank into the seat next to her, my bag thudding to the concrete under my feet. Then I looked up—really looked—and my stomach dropped like a rock.

Front row. Practically on the freaking field. So close I could see the scuff marks on the sideline, the sweat on the referees' foreheads as they jogged past, the field passes on some of the people wandering around. My breath caught, a sharp hitch in my chest, and I slouched lower, tugging my hair forward like it'd hide me. "Tasha," I hissed, voice tight. "You didn't say we'd be this close."

She grinned, popping a piece of gum in her mouth, completely unfazed. "Best seats in the house—sorority perks. You're welcome."

"I'm not thanking you for this," I muttered, my hands twisting in my lap, nails digging into my palms. The 77 on my cheek felt like it was glowing, burning, like every eye in the stadium could see it, could see me, sitting here like some desperate groupie stalking the guy I'd pushed away. I'd told him no—told myself no—and now here I was, painted up like his biggest fan, heart hammering so loudly I swore it'd drown out the crowd.

The field was still empty, and I let out a shaky breath, trying to calm down. He wouldn't notice. There were thousands of people here, and he'd be concentrating on the game. Maybe I could keep my head down, blend in with the crowd, sneak my glimpse and get out before he ever—

The *roar* hit first, a wave of noise crashing over the stands as the team burst from the tunnel, their helmets glinting under the lights. My eyes snapped up, traitor that I was, as I desperately scanned the pack of broad shoulders in orange jerseys.

And then, there he was.

He was jogging out with his helmet tucked under one arm, his long hair flowing behind him. His stupid, cocky . . . incredibly gorgeous grin tugging at his lips like the roar of screaming fans was no different than any other day, and he was king of it all. My chest tightened, a quick, sharp squeeze, and I slouched lower, heat flooding my face, the 77 prickling like a brand.

Jace moved like he always did when I saw him—loose, easy, all swagger and muscle. His pads shifted with every step, and I watched in awe at the sight of his biceps flexing as he slid on his helmet. I couldn't look away.

I didn't want to.

My breath was shallow as I stared, my hands clammy against my jeans. Two days without him, and it hit me like a freight train—how much I missed him . . . and how much I hated myself for it. I'd pushed him away, and now I was here, creeping like some lovesick idiot, desperate for just one look.

Then it happened. His head turned, casual at first, scanning the crowd, and his eyes found me. Instantly. Like he'd known exactly where I'd be. His piercing brown eyes locked on me, cutting through the chaos like a laser, and my heart stopped, a dead thud in my chest. His grin faltered, just for a second, then stretched wider—smug, knowing, a little dangerous—and I froze, my face on fire, the 77 screaming my guilt louder than the crowd ever could.

But then I saw it—something on his cheek, a smudge of black under the stadium lights. I squinted, leaning forward despite myself, my breath catching as it came into focus.

Riley St. James. My name. Scrawled across each cheek in bold, messy paint, right there for the world to see.

Shock hit me like a slap, my jaw dropping, a choked sound slipping out before I could stop it. "What the—" I whispered, my hands gripping the seat . . . my brain short-circuiting. He'd painted my name on his face . . . my name. Like some kind of claim, like a mirror to the 77 Tasha had slapped on me. My stomach flipped, a wild, dizzy lurch, and I sank back, my pulse roaring as his gaze held mine, way too long and intense, before he turned back to the field, jogging off with that same damn swagger.

"Shit," I breathed in a shaking voice. Tasha nudged me with a giggle I barely registered. He'd seen me. He'd seen the number. And now, I'd seen my name on him—Riley, right there, like he'd marked himself with me.

I loved it.

Jace

The stadium roared as we took the field, the noise shaking the ground as we ran, but it barely hit me. My head was somewhere else—locked on one thing, one person, like a missile with a target painted in neon. *Her.*

Helmet tucked under my arm, I stood on the field, sweat already beading down my neck from warm-ups, my eyes scanning the stands like a predator sniffing out prey. Even if I hadn't given the tickets to that sorority chick so I could make sure Riley was here, it wouldn't have taken long to find her—it never did. I had a built-in radar for Riley St. James, some fucked-up homing device wired into my bones. I hadn't asked for it; it would have been easier without it, but hell if I was turning it off now.

There she was—front row, smack in the middle of a few sorority girls. Her blonde hair was a wild mess over her shoulders, catching the stadium lights like some kind of golden beacon. And those hazel eyes . . . I could feel them from here; even if she was doing her best I-don't-see-Jace-Thatcher act.

Then I saw it.

My number.

Big, bold, *mine.*

An orange, inked-up 77 scrawled across her cheek. Holy fuck . . .

"What the hell is wrong with you?" Matty hissed, his gaze weirdly directed toward the sky.

"What's wrong with *you*?" I growled back, because something primal had risen in my chest when I saw my number on her skin, and I kind of felt like a grizzly bear . . . or a lion. That was cooler. But seriously . . . how the fuck was I going to react when I got her to wear my jersey if this was how I was acting now?

One thing was for sure, I was definitely winning today, and the game hadn't even kicked off yet.

"Why are you . . ." Matty continued, waving down at my . . . crotch?

Oh . . . the Anaconda was currently in striking position. Apparently, seeing my number on my lady was cause for him to celebrate. *Down boy . . .* That would not be pleasant if I got hit in this condition. I turned toward my bestie, hoping changing my viewpoint would help me to settle. "It's okay, Matty. That extra inch won't bite," I told him assuredly.

He huffed and eyed my face paint, because evidently he'd decided to be Judgy McJudgster today. My lips twitched, stretching into a slow, smug smirk as I smeared my eye black under my eyes just to fuck with him. At some point in this game I was obviously going to score, and then the cameras would catch me. And when they zoomed in, the whole world was gonna see what I'd painted on my own cheeks. Riley St. James scratched in black, a little messy but clear as hell. Just another way I was hoping to nudge Riley to figure out she wasn't just some girl . . . she was mine—signed, sealed, and about to be delivered.

We lined up at the twenty-yard line, second and five, clock ticking down in the first quarter. I adjusted my gloves, fingers flexing, digging my cleats into the turf until I felt the bite through my soles. My eyes flicked across the defense—the linebackers creeping up, the corners pressing tight . . . obviously expecting some short-yardage play.

"Hey, Thatcher, your dick's the size of a Tic Tac," Clayton, one of the aforementioned corners, taunted.

"That's why your mom's breath smells so good," I told him, enjoying the weird red color that crept up his neck.

Parker's cadence cut through the noise, sounding suspiciously like he was struggling not to laugh. "Set! Hut!"

I exploded off the line, legs pumping, faking a quick inside slant before cutting hard to the outside, my cleats tearing into the field. The cornerback bit like a dumbass, his feet tripping over each other as he scrambled to recover, his arms flailing.

Parker read it like the god he was, and the ball was already soaring—a perfect spiral slicing through the stadium lights, glinting as it arced toward me. I stretched out, fingers brushing the laces, then hauled it in, yanking it tight against my chest, my heart slamming like a jackhammer. A safety charged in, and I lowered my shoulder and plowed through, slamming into him like a truck, dragging his ass a few extra yards, his grunt loud in my ear as we hit the turf hard.

First down. I popped up, the ball still locked in my grip, adrenaline buzzing through me, and my pulse thundering in my chest. Every yard, every route, every hit—I was playing for her. Knowing Riley was up there watching, those honey angel eyes tracking me, was like pure, uncut dope pumping through my veins. Superman? Fuck that—I was better, stronger, running on her like she was my own personal fuel.

We didn't slow down. We kept the tempo hot, snapping the ball fast. The next play, I ran a quick hitch, letting Turner take the spotlight. Parker fired it out—an out route, crisp and low—and Turner caught it clean, turned upfield, and took off. The crowd lost their shit, screaming as he juked one defender, then spun past another, cutting through them like a magician pulling tricks before a linebacker finally snagged him at the knees, dragging him down. Fifteen yards, easy. We were marching—eating up the field—and the anticipation of scoring and getting in front of those cameras was making me giddy.

"Why do you have that look on your face?" Parker muttered as I jogged past him to line up.

"It's my face, Parkie-Poo. It's just pretty like that."

Third and goal. Red zone flashing under the lights, the kill zone—where games got won, where legacies got carved into stone, and where gods like me loved to live. I lined up wide, rolling my shoulders, shaking out my hands, my gloves tacky with sweat and turf.

And then I looked. *I couldn't help it.*

Riley.

Front row, arms wrapped tight around herself, her hair falling in her face like she thought that'd be enough to keep me from seeing her. *Fat chance.* I felt her watching—like static in my veins, that undeniable charge between us. She was definitely nervous about the play, judging by the way she was biting down on her lip like she wanted to chomp it off.

I wanted to bite that lip.

Focus, Jace. Now's not the time to pop another woody.

Parker clapped his hands, voice sharp over the line. "Hut!"

The second the ball was snapped, my body ignited. Instinct took over. I exploded off the line, cutting straight through the defense. The red zone was tight—less space to work with, less time to react—but I knew where I was going before the defense even realized it.

Footsteps thundered behind me. I felt the safety closing in, felt his presence like a storm at my back. But I was already there—already two steps ahead, already reading Parker's eyes as he scanned the field.

A beat. A breath.

Then—release.

The ball spiraled through the air, cutting clean through the stadium lights, headed exactly where I needed it to be. I turned, extending my hands, fingers tightening around the leather just as a linebacker lunged for me.

Too late.

I planted my foot and twisted, breaking past his outstretched arms. The moment my cleats hit the end zone, I tucked the ball tight against my chest, grinning as the roar of the stadium crashed over me.

Touchdown.

Jogging toward the nearest camera, sweat sliding down my face, my chest heaving under my pads, I waited for the lens to find me—which it obviously would . . . because I was the fucking *money shot.*

And when it did?

I tapped my fingers against both cheeks, right where *her* name was smeared in black ink.

Then I turned, slow. Deliberate.

And locked eyes with *her.*

I was too far away to catch every detail, unfortunately—there was no way to see if her face went white, if her lips popped open, if her whole body locked up when she saw what I was doing. But I knew they had. I felt it, deep and sure, like I could reach out and touch her from fifty yards away.

Those honey-colored eyes were burning into me—I'd bet my left nut on it—wide and shocked, pinned on me like I'd just ripped the ground out from under her.

My Riley-girl thought she could run. She thought she could hide, push me off, bury whatever this was under two days of silence. But there was no escaping this—no ducking me, no dodging what I'd carved into my skin for her to see. She'd painted my number on her cheek—willingly or not, it didn't matter—and I'd answered with her name on mine. Checkmate, baby llama.

We wouldn't address the fact that I'd been stalking her across campus the last two days whenever I wasn't in class or at practice. Because, obviously, I couldn't go two days without seeing her.

That would've just been crazy.

The ref's whistle cut through, signaling the extra point, and I jogged back to the sideline, giving Parker the hip thrust I usually did in the end zone because I knew he would be missing it. He rolled his eyes, grinning like a jackass, and slapped my shoulder. "I thought you were trying to stop her from running," he said, his voice rough with a laugh.

"It's all in my master plan," I shot back, wiping sweat off my forehead, my eyes flicking up to her again. She was still there, standing stiff, like she was caught in my crosshairs and didn't know how to break free.

Good. Let her squirm. Let her feel it, the weight of my number on her, her name on me, this thing between us she couldn't outrun.

Halftime came eventually with the score seventeen to seven, us in the lead, of course, and I jogged to the tunnel, peeling off my helmet, sweat dripping down my neck and soaking my jersey.

The boys were loud—Parker yapping about the drive, Matty cackling about some hit—but I tuned them out, my gaze flicking back to the stands one last time. Riley was still there, rooted, that 77 bold on her cheek, her arms crossed tighter now, like she could shield herself from me.

I tapped my cheek again, even though she couldn't see me, my cock twitching just looking at her. I grinned, slow and determined, already picturing it—another image coming to mind . . . of me smearing that paint across her skin, dragging it over her lips, down her jaw, making her messy with *me*.

I'd paint her in my cum, inside and out, until she couldn't breathe without tasting me.

She thought she could ditch me two days ago—she thought she could wash me off.

Nah, babycakes.

Riley St. James was *fucked*. 'Cause I wasn't letting her go—ever.

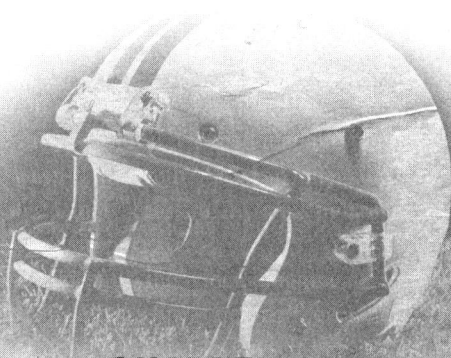

CHAPTER 10

RILEY

S tats class was another version of hell. Math had always been my weakest subject, and taking a year off between high school and college . . . and then missing time at the beginning of the semester from being sick . . . hadn't exactly improved my skills. I sat near the back, doodling in the margins of my notebook while Professor Lang droned on about probability distributions.

My phone buzzed in my pocket, and since I didn't talk to anyone and it was unlikely that one of my coworkers had decided to start up a conversation . . . it was probably another text from Jace.

I ignored it, just as I'd ignored him all week as he popped up everywhere I was. Both my jobs, outside my classes, and in the dining hall, even though I knew the athletes had a special dining hall just for them.

His tongue, his hands . . . him. It felt like he was burned into me.

But I couldn't cave. Even though I wanted to.

Callum had sent an email to my personal email address yesterday. Telling me how much he missed me and how everything was going to be different when we were reunited. *When.* Not *if.*

The shock of seeing his email had reminded me why beautiful boys—and men—were the most dangerous.

And why I should be avoiding Jace at all costs.

"Riley?" A quiet voice cut through my haze, and I glanced up to see a guy hovering by my desk. Danny, that was his name. He had an easy smile and tousled brown hair. He looked kind of like a guy who'd stepped out of a J.Crew catalog, with sharp cheekbones, blue eyes, and a navy sweater that hugged his lean frame just right. He was nice looking, sure, but safe. Predictable. The opposite of Jace's walking chaos.

And why was I comparing him to Jace right now?

"Do you have a second after class?"

I blinked, my pencil stalling mid-scrawl. "Sure," I said, wary but curious. Hopefully he wasn't trying to ask for help in this class; I was more likely to help him fail than improve on any of his skills.

Class dragged on, but when the bell finally rang, I shoved my stuff into my bag and followed Danny into the hall. He stopped near the vending machines set up against the wall, shifting his weight like he was debating bolting. "So, um," he started, rubbing the back of his neck. "I was wondering if you wanted to grab dinner or something. Friday night . . . if you're not already busy, of course," he added quickly.

I stared at him, caught off guard. My brain short-circuited for a second, Jace's face flashing through it . . . but I shoved it down, glancing at Danny closer than I ever had before. He was handsome enough, pleasing to the eye when you looked, but not enough to actually make you look in the first place. He had kind eyes, if that was a thing. He was . . . safe. A guy who wouldn't follow me into elevators, leave me a trembling mess, and then stalk me across campus.

A guy who wouldn't break my heart.

If I went out with him, maybe Jace would know I was serious about not getting involved . . . since his number on my cheek at the game had definitely sent mixed signals.

"Yeah," I said, forcing a smile. "That sounds nice. Friday works."

His face lit up, a wide grin breaking through his nerves, making him nicer-looking in a wholesome, golden retriever kind of way. "Awesome, I'll pick you up at seven, and we can go to that Italian restaurant on Elm— Giovanni's? Well—if you even like Italian?" he asked awkwardly.

"Italian's great," I murmured, trying to ignore the weird twist in my gut. Danny was a palate cleanser, a reset. This would be good for me. "See you then?"

"Great," he said, backing away, flashing that smile again—bright and uncomplicated. "Oh, what dorm are you?" he asked.

Right, because it wasn't normal for someone to just know everything about you without you telling them . . . Another way he was safer than Jace.

"Carrick Hall," I said, immediately wishing that I'd just told him I'd meet him at the restaurant.

He nodded. "See you, Riley." He left, and I stood there, staring at the humming vending machine, wondering why "safe" felt so wrong.

Friday night crept up, and I stood in front of my mirror, fussing with the hem of my soft gray sweater. I'd paired it with dark wide-leg jeans and ankle boots. Simple, comfy, not trying too hard. Danny didn't strike me as the type to care about plunging necklines or stilettos, and I wasn't in the mood to play vixen anyway. My hair fell in loose waves, brushing my shoulders, and I swiped on some gloss, the faint berry scent clinging to my lips. I grabbed my purse, checked the clock—six fifty—and hesitated, my phone sitting dark on the dresser.

I shouldn't have looked. I should've just walked out. But my hand moved anyway, unlocking the screen, and there it was: a text from Jace, time-stamped ten minutes ago. No words, just a selfie—him shirtless in a bathroom, leaning against the wall, one hand raking through his long blonde hair, the other snapping the pic. His abs were on full display, all ridges and shadows, sweat gleaming from a workout, that V-line dipping into his low-slung sweats like a freaking invitation. His smirk was pure sin, his eyes glinting with that cocky, I-know-you-want-me stare, and lust hit me like a freight train, hot and sudden, pooling low in my belly.

"Fuck," I muttered, gripping the dresser, my thighs clenching as I stared at the screen. My pulse raced, heat flushing my face, and I could almost feel him—his breath on my neck, his hands pinning me, that elevator moment replaying in vivid, torturous detail. I should just delete the picture, but my fingers seemed to have a mind of their own, traitorously tempted to zoom in on those abs.

I forced myself to shut the phone off, shoving it into my purse.

But the image stayed burned into my vision, an itch I couldn't scratch as I forced myself out the door.

Danny was waiting outside, leaning against a black Honda, his hands in his pockets. He looked good in his crisp white polo, his dark jeans that fit just right. His hair was swept back from his face, and when he saw me, he smiled, all warmth and no edge. "Hey, Riley," he said, opening the passenger door. "You look great."

"Thanks," I said, sliding inside. "You too," I added. My voice was steady, but my skin was buzzing, Jace's selfie still simmering in my veins. I did my best to shove it down, focusing on Danny as he climbed in, the car smelling faintly of an ocean-scented air freshener.

The drive to Giovanni's was quick. Danny was chatting about one of his classes, a project he was stressed over, and I nodded along, half listening, the city lights smearing gold and red across the windshield.

The restaurant glowed ahead, all warm brick and ivy curling up the walls. We parked and walked inside, the scent of garlic and basil immediately surrounding me. The dining room was cozy, with its dim lights, red-checkered tablecloths, and candles flickering in little glass holders. A hostess led us to a booth, and I sank into the cushioned bench, the murmur of voices and clink of dishes wrapping around us.

The hostess handed us our menus and stepped away. "Ever been here?" he asked, scanning his own.

"Nope," I said, flipping mine open, the list of pastas and wines blurring as Jace's abs flashed through my head again. I blinked. Hard. Trying to focus. Danny said something about carbonara, and I nodded.

Crap. *Why had I looked at that picture?*

"I'm leaning toward the lasagna," he said, setting his menu down. "Mama makes it all the time—hers is killer."

"Yum," I said lamely.

Danny started talking about his "mama," and while charming when mentioned once . . . it was obvious that he was a *huge* mama's boy. I couldn't relate to him about that, obviously, so all I could do was hum along like I was interested.

The waiter swung by, and I ordered the carbonara while Danny ordered the lasagna plus a glass of water for each of us. The restaurant thrummed with life, couples chatting over plates of ravioli, a kid giggling two tables over, spilling spaghetti on his shirt. I sipped my water, letting it settle me, trying to drown the heat Jace had sparked.

Our pasta arrived in fat, steaming plates. My carbonara glistened, rich with pancetta and cream, and Danny's lasagna was a gooey stack of cheese and meat. "This is unreal," he said, digging in, his fork scraping the plate. "Mama might be dethroned."

I twirled a bite, the sauce coating my tongue, and nodded. "Yeah, this is delicious." He smiled, and I relaxed a bit more, the food warming my chest, the night almost . . . normal. Almost good.

We talked—small stuff, stats class, his dog back home (a golden retriever named Spot, because of course he would have a dog named that) and I let myself sink into it. The candlelight softened his features, making him look even better. His eyes crinkled when he smiled, and his laugh was light, unforced. "So," he said, sipping his water. "Are you into football? I saw you at Saturday's game."

I froze mid-bite, Jace's smirking face slamming back into me. "Uh, yeah," I said, swallowing hard. "It's . . . fun, I guess." My voice sounded off, and I cursed myself, shoving another bite in to cover it.

"Fun's right," he said, grinning. "Davis and Thatcher? Those guys are beasts. You see that last play?"

My stomach twisted, Jace's name dropping like a bomb. "Yeah," I muttered, forcing a smile. "They're . . . something." *Beast* didn't cover it—Jace was wild, unhinged; mine in ways I couldn't admit. I took a bigger sip of water, suddenly wishing it was wine, and I tried to focus on Danny's next story—something about his sister's cooking fails—but my skin prickled restlessly, Jace haunting me like a freaking ghost.

The door swung open, the chime slicing through the restaurant's hum. I happened to glance over, only to drop my fork with a loud *clank*.

"Riley?" Danny asked, but I couldn't look at him.

I was too busy staring at Jace, standing there at the hostess stand, his hair mussed from the wind, his brown eyes locked on me, glinting with mischief . . . and something feral.

How was he here right now?

Danny was trying to talk to me, but I was stumbling over my words, watching as the hostess led Jace into the spot right behind Danny. He slid into the booth, sitting so he was facing me, his back to the wall. His smirk was a weapon, sharp and knowing, and his eyes bore into mine over Danny's shoulder. My heart kicked into overdrive, my palms sweating as I picked my fork back up and gripped it tight.

Danny was back to talking about his mom again. "So, she forgot the oven was on, and the whole kitchen—"

"Sounds like a real tragedy," Jace cut in, his voice loud and dripping with sarcasm, his gaze never leaving me. "I'm riveted, man. Keep going."

Danny faltered, turning slightly, confusion creasing his brow. "Uh—"

"Just ignore him," I snapped, confusing Danny even more.

Jace grinned, predatory and knowing. His arms stretched along the back of his booth, all lazy confidence.

Danny shifted, eyeing Jace over his shoulder. "Oh, you're Jace Thatcher!" he said excitedly . . . because, of course, he recognized him instantly. "We were just talking about you!"

Jace's gaze glimmered with something that should have sent Danny running—but Danny obviously wasn't good at reading signs.

I'd blame his *mama* for that.

"Do you know each other?" Danny asked, his eyes shifting between the two of us.

Jace snagged a breadstick from a passing waiter's tray. "I do know Riley. Intimately, in fact. Right, buttercup?"

My face burned, and Danny's face finally started to show a touch of unease.

"So, uh," Danny tried, turning back to me. "Anyway, my mama—"

"We get it. She's a fantastic cook and the greatest lady you've ever met," Jace interrupted again, biting into the breadstick, chewing loudly . . . and obnoxiously. "But let's be real here, Casanova, your date couldn't care less about the fact that you dream about your mama when you're yanking your dick."

"Jace, stop," I said, my voice low and as venomous as I could make it. But he just winked, leaning forward.

"Stop what?" he asked, his voice teasing, eyes glinting. "Pointing out the obvious? That he's completely fucking up this date? That you're completely bored. Oh . . . should I tell him about what you're really thinking about right now?"

"Don't you dare," I hissed.

Danny's shoulders had stiffened, and he set his fork down, glancing at me. "I feel like I'm missing something. Um . . ."

"No, you're not missing anything," I said quickly, shoving my plate aside since my appetite was nowhere to be found. "He's just an asshole who doesn't know boundaries."

"Boundaries?" Jace laughed, low and rough, leaning forward. I was pretty sure Danny could feel Jace's anger on the back of his neck. "Baby-cakes, I crossed those in the elevator last week—remember? You didn't mind then."

Danny's face went pink, then pale, his hands fumbling with his napkin. "I—I don't—"

"Feeling overwhelmed yet? Like you've made a terrible . . . possibly a dangerous mistake?" Jace asked, smirking over Danny's shoulder, his eyes still locked on mine. "Feeling like she belongs to someone else?"

"Jace, I swear—" I started, but he cut me off, his voice dropping, all silk and menace.

"Swear what, Riley-girl? That you're not mine? Go on, tell him. Tell him you didn't cream over my abs right before you walked out to meet him."

My jaw dropped, heat flooding my cheeks.

Danny's eyes widened, and he practically leapt out of the booth. "I think—uh—I should go—"

"No, stay," I said desperately, reaching out for his arm like a woman possessed. Jace laughed, standing now, towering over the booth.

"Let him run, Riley," he said, stepping around to loom in front of Danny, his grin dark. "He knows what's good for him. He knows when he's out of his league." He leaned down until he was right in front of Danny's terrified-looking face. "*And* he knows that he should never have gotten close to what's *mine*."

Danny literally squeaked. He grabbed his jacket and bolted for the door, the chime filling the restaurant as he fled.

Jace slid into Danny's empty seat across from me, leaning back like he'd won.

"You're a bastard," I snapped, grabbing my water glass and throwing the rest of it back. My pulse was racing, heat pooling low despite my fury. "What the hell is wrong with you?"

"You're what's wrong with me," he said, grinning, unrepentant as he reached across to snag a bite of my discarded carbonara. "And you love it."

"You scared him off like a psycho. Why can't you just take the hint? I'm not going out with you!" My voice was shaking, and his presence was overwhelming me, like the table between us didn't even exist. His knee brushed mine.

"A psycho?" He smirked, leaning in, his hand sliding to my thigh, firm and possessive. "You haven't even *seen* psycho yet." His smile dropped. "Danny was lucky. If something like that ever happens again . . ." His voice trailed off for a moment, and it was like a mask had slipped from his face. His fingers squeezed, and I sucked in a breath, caught between shoving him off and pulling him closer.

"Jace . . ." I started, but he stood, tugging me up, his grip unrelenting.

"Let's go," he said roughly, his eyes burning as he threw cash on the table. "We're done here."

I should've fought, I should've yanked free, but my body betrayed me, following him out into the night, the cool air hitting my flushed skin as he hauled me to his Jeep parked across the street. The restaurant's warm glow faded behind us, but all I could feel was him, his heat, his pull, his stupid, obsessive need that I couldn't escape.

————————

Jace sat me in the back seat of his Jeep, the door slamming shut with a *bang* that echoed in the lot. I barely caught my breath when the opposite door was yanked open and Jace was in the back seat with me, all muscle and hunger.

The air was thick, heavy with the scent of his woodsy cologne, sweat from practice, and the faint tang of turf clinging to his skin. His hands were everywhere, gripping my hips, yanking my sweater up and tossing it aside. His fingers, rough and calloused from football, scraped across my stomach, igniting every nerve, and I gasped as I gripped his shirt, the hard planes of him unyielding under my palms.

"Jace, wait. We should talk about this!" I tried to reason with him. He just smirked, catching my wrists and pinning them above my head with one hand, the leather creaking under me as I squirmed. His other hand shoved my bra up, baring my breasts, my nipples tightening in the cool air. He groaned, low and guttural, his mouth dropping to one nipple as he sucked hard. The wet heat of his tongue flicked over me, his teeth grazing just enough to sting, and my back arched into him despite my protests.

I could complain all I wanted, but one thing was absolutely true. My body fucking loved this.

"Yeah, let's talk about this," he growled against my skin, his voice rough as he bit down lightly, then sucked again, harder, pulling a moan from my throat. "Let's talk about how you went on this date just to try and push me away. Again. Let's talk about what an asswipe that guy was. How you couldn't stop thinking about me the entire time. Let's talk about how there's not a replacement for me. For *us*." His voice bounced off the Jeep's fogging windows. "Let's talk about it, Riley-girl. Whatcha have for me?"

I writhed against him, my shoes scraping the seat, the leather starting to get slick with our combined heat. "You're right. About all of it," I panted, but my hands, freed now, fisted his shirt, yanking it up and over his head. My nails raked down his back, digging into the taut muscle, tracing the lines of his spine. He hissed, his head lifting up. I followed the bend of his throat. His sweat-slicked skin . . . his perfect abs that had ruined today in the first place. It felt like I was burning alive. "But you're still insane."

"I'm insane for you," he muttered as his mouth moved to my other breast, licking and biting, leaving a trail of red marks across my chest like a map of his claim. His tongue swirled, teasing, then plunged lower, licking a slow, deliberate line down my sternum, tasting the salt of my skin. I moaned again, my head tipping back, thudding against the window, the glass cool against my scalp as his hands slid to my jeans, popping the button with a flick of his thumb.

"Jace," I whimpered, my hips jerking as he shoved them down my thighs, taking my panties with them in one rough, impatient pull. I kicked them down my legs, the denim tangling around my boots for a second before I shook them both off. I was almost naked, sprawled out in the cramped back seat. The air inside the cab was muggy, and his body was a furnace, pinning me, his knees spreading my legs wide, exposing me completely.

He pulled back, his eyes raking over me, and I could only imagine what I looked like right now, flushed, sprawled out for him. His smirk turned feral . . . as if he could read my mind.

"Fuck, look at you," he said hoarsely, his voice thick with need as he undid his jeans, shoving them down just enough for his cock to spring free— thick, hard, glistening at the tip. My breath caught, my thighs clenching as I stared, the sight releasing every dirty thought I'd had since that picture he'd sent me.

"You look a little hungry, Riley-girl," he taunted, gripping my hips, his thumbs digging into the soft flesh as he pulled me under him with a possessive yank.

"Asshole," I muttered, but my voice was a wreck. I wrapped my legs around him as I urged him closer. His lips curled as he dragged his cock along my inner thigh, teasing, the slick heat of him brushing my skin, leaving a trail of precum that made me squirm.

"Please," I begged, my hands sliding to his shoulders as I tried to pull him down. He laughed, low and dark, positioning himself, the head of him nudging against me, hot and insistent.

He locked eyes with me as he thrust in . . . slow at first, stretching me inch by agonizing inch, filling me until I couldn't breathe, couldn't think. I cried out, sharp and desperate, the sound echoing off the foggy glass, and he groaned, burying his face in my neck.

His breath scorched my skin, the heat of him searing me from the inside out. Every slow, deliberate thrust sent another wave of pleasure crashing through me, my body arching instinctively, needing more—needing him.

Jace groaned, his hands gripping my hips, holding me exactly where he wanted. "Tell me," he rasped, his voice thick with something darker, something possessive. "Tell me you didn't want to be there with him."

I gasped as he thrust deeper, my nails digging into his shoulders, but I didn't answer.

I didn't want to.

Because I had spent the entire night trying to convince myself that I did. That I wanted Danny, that I wanted normal, that I wanted any of this to make sense.

But Jace saw through it. Through me.

He pulled back, just enough to make me feel the loss; his eyes locked onto mine in the dim glow of the streetlights coming in through the windows. "Say it, babycakes," he murmured, his tone like silk wrapped around steel. "Say you didn't want him. Say you wanted *me* instead."

I swallowed hard, shaking my head. "Jace—"

"Say it." His fingers tightened, his hips pressing forward just enough to tease, enough to drive me insane. "Or I stop."

A whimper slipped out before I could catch it. The threat was real—Jace Thatcher never bluffed. And my body? My body wasn't built to be deprived of him.

I clenched my jaw, hating how much control he had over me. Hating that I had spent all this time running, denying what had been so painfully obvious.

I inhaled shakily, my resolve splintering beneath the intensity in his gaze. "I didn't want to be there with him." My voice was a whisper, barely audible over our strained breaths, but it was enough.

Jace's smirk was slow, triumphant. "That's my girl."

And then he was moving again, pushing deep, stealing my next breath as his lips crashed into mine.

But he wasn't finished.

His mouth trailed to my ear, his voice low and devastating. "Did you think about me while you were with him?"

I stiffened. Heat bloomed up my neck, pooling between my thighs, because—fuck. Of course I had. I had spent every second of that stupid date comparing Danny to Jace, every word, every smile, every insignificant moment failing to match the way Jace made me feel with just a look.

Silence stretched between us, but Jace wasn't letting me get away with it. His hand slid down my thigh, slow, teasing, until he was gripping my knee, pushing it higher, opening me wider.

"I'll take that as a yes," he murmured, his voice a taunt, thick with satisfaction.

I clenched around him involuntarily, my body betraying me, and he groaned, his forehead dropping to mine. "Fuck, Riley," he whispered, voice unraveling. "You're just as addicted to this as I am."

He wasn't wrong.

I just wasn't sure I'd survive admitting it.

"Fuck, you're tight," he growled, his voice breaking as he moved, pulling back slow, then slamming in hard, deep, each stroke a claim that rattled the Jeep, the suspension creaking under us. His hands gripped my hips tighter, fingers bruising, angling me to take him deeper, and I moaned, loud and unfiltered, my body rocking with his rhythm. "You're mine—say it, Riley."

I shook my head, defiant even as my body surrendered, my hips bucking to meet him. "Make me." I gasped, my voice a challenge, and his grin turned savage, his thrusts picking up, relentless, the leather slick with our sweat, the air thick with the scent of sex—musk, salt, and that faint pine scent.

"You should know it's a bad idea to challenge me," he snarled, one hand sliding between us, his fingers easily finding my clit, rubbing fast and rough, circling with a precision that made my vision blur. "I always win."

I shattered, my orgasm ripping through me, sharp and blinding as a scream tore from my throat. It bounced off the windows as my body clenched around him, pulsing, trembling.

He didn't stop. He kept thrusting, dragging it out, his fingers relentless, pushing me through the waves until I was a shaking, oversensitive, mess . . . gasping his name like a prayer.

"Jace—please—" I whimpered, my hands fisting his hair, pulling hard, strands tangling in my fingers as I tried to ground myself. But he just growled, his mouth crashing into mine as he kissed me deep and messy, all teeth and tongue. He tasted like salt and sin, his lips bruising mine, swallowing my moans as he fucked me harder, the Jeep rocking with every slam of his hips.

"I'm not done," he muttered against my mouth, pulling out suddenly, leaving me empty and aching. I whined, a needy sound I'd never admit to, but before I could protest, he flipped me over, his hands gripping my hips as he yanked me onto my knees. My palms slapped the leather as he positioned me, ass up, face down, and I felt the heat of him behind me, his cock brushing my thighs as he teased me once again.

"Yes . . ." I cried as he thrust in, hard and deep, filling me from behind, and I screamed, the angle hitting something inside me that made my whole body quake. His hands slid up my back, rough and possessive, one tangling in my hair, pulling my head back as he pounded into me, relentless, the sound of skin slapping skin filling the tight space.

"You're mine," he growled in a hoarse voice, his free hand snaking around to my front so he could cup my breast. Jace pinched my nipple hard enough to make me cry out again. "Say it, Riley. Fucking say it."

"No," I gasped defiantly, pushing back against him, meeting every thrust even though my body was trembling and slick with sweat, one knee on the seat, one foot on the ground as he pushed into me. He laughed, dark and wild, his hand sliding down, his fingers finding my clit again. He rubbed slowly this time, teasing, dragging me to the edge without letting me fall.

"Stubborn little angel cake," he muttered, his mouth on my shoulder, biting down, sucking a mark that would bruise by morning. "I'll make you scream it. I'll fuck you until you can't remember his name." His thrusts slowed, deliberate now, each one rocking me forward, my hands slipping on the leather, grasping for anything to hold.

"Danny who?" I shot back, breathless, taunting him, and his growl turned feral, his hand tightening in my hair, pulling harder, arching my back as he slammed into me, fast and brutal, the Jeep shaking with the force.

"That's it," he snarled, fingers circling my clit faster, rougher, sending sparks through me. "Say my name. Say you're mine, Riley, or I'll keep you edging until you beg."

"Jace—" I moaned, my body betraying me, trembling on the brink, and he thrust deeper, hitting that spot again relentlessly, his breath frayed against my ear.

"Say it," he demanded, his voice breaking, hips jerking, his rhythm faltering as he chased his own edge, his fingers relentless on my clit, pushing me higher, higher. "You're mine. Fucking say it."

"Yes. Fuck, yes," I sobbed, shattering again as my orgasm crashed through me, sharper, hotter, a tidal wave that left me screaming his name, my body clenching around him, pulsing, shaking. He groaned, low and guttural, thrusting once, twice, then spilling inside me, hot and deep, his weight pinning me as he came, his hands gripping my hips like he'd never let go.

We collapsed, panting, tangled in a sweaty heap, his chest pressed to my back, his breath hot on my neck, the Jeep a sauna of fogged windows and wrecked leather. He stayed inside me, softening but still there, his hands sliding up my sides, tracing every curve like he was memorizing me. My knees ached, my body thrummed, and I couldn't move. Aftershocks were rippling through me as his lips caressed my shoulder, soft now, almost tender.

"I'm pretty sure I know what heaven feels like," he murmured roughly, rolling off me but pulling me with him, flipping me onto my back again. His hands framed my face, his thumbs brushing my cheeks, and he smirked, that smug, infuriating grin back in full force.

I glared, chest heaving, my skin slick and flushed, my body still humming from—three orgasms, maybe four, I'd lost count. "It doesn't mean anything," I said, but it was as weak as it had ever been. He laughed, low and rough, leaning down to kiss me slowly, his tongue sliding against mine, tasting me, claiming me all over again.

"Yeah," he said, pulling back, his lips brushing mine, his voice a dark promise. "I'm pretty sure you're done with that lie."

Jace shifted and tugged me up, his hands roaming my body—my breasts, my hips, my thighs—like he couldn't stop touching me, and I let him, too wrecked to fight. My sweater was gone, my bra shoved up, my jeans a crumpled heap on the floor, and I didn't care. The heat of him, the weight of his stare, it pinned me there, raw and exposed. His fingers traced the marks he'd left, the bites on my neck, the bruises on my hips, and his smirk softened, just a flicker, into something almost . . . worshipful.

"You're perfect," he whispered in a thick voice as he leaned down to kiss my throat, slow and deliberate, sucking another mark over my pulse. I felt the strange urge to cry because not once had anyone ever said that to me before.

I moaned as I tugged lightly on his hair. Jace pressed himself against me again, half hard already, the slick heat of him brushing my thigh.

"Jace, I can't . . ." I panted, but it was a lie, and he knew it, his hand slipping between my legs and the mess that was dripping down my thighs.

His fingers teased my swollen clit, light and maddening. I tensed, over-sensitive, a whimper slipping out, and he grinned as he kissed me again, hungrily swallowing the sound.

"It will never be enough," he said against my lips, his fingers circling slowly, building that heat again as his cock hardened fully now and pressed into me.

I didn't answer him, because if I believed that . . . and it turned out to be a lie . . .

"You're it for me, Riley St. James," he murmured.

I growled at his ridiculous, *thrilling* words, my hands gripped his shoulders, my nails digging in, and he laughed, dark and wild, thrusting in again—slow, deep, filling me until I gasped, my legs wrapping around him tighter, pulling him closer.

"Good girl," he growled, moving now, steady and deliberate, each stroke stoking the fire as his fingers continued to work my clit. "Scream for me one more time; let everyone hear you."

And I did. I screamed his name as another orgasm hit, slow and shattering, my body convulsing around him, and he groaned, following me over, spilling again, his hands clutching my hips, holding me there as we broke apart together. We stayed like that, panting, trembling, his forehead pressed to mine, sweat dripping between us, the Jeep a cocoon of heat and wrecked passion.

He pulled back finally, a soft smile on his lips as he swept a damp strand of hair off my face with a gentleness that didn't match the carnage we'd made. His brown eyes—dark, stormy, endless—held me there, drowning me in something I wasn't sure I could name.

"You ruin me, you know that?" His voice was raw, edged with something dangerously close to awe. "Every time. It doesn't matter what I do, how much I prepare myself—I get near you, and it's game over."

I swallowed hard, my pulse hammering in my throat.

Because I felt the same way.

He pulled back just enough to look at me, his brown eyes burning, stripping me bare. "I don't think you understand, Riley." His thumb swept over my bottom lip, a slow and deliberate caress. "How serious I am."

A shudder rippled through me, and my stomach twisted. "Jace—"

His fingers tightened around mine. "You don't have to say anything. Not yet." His lips quirked, a shadow of a smirk playing there, but there was something softer beneath it. Something *real*. "Just know, Riley—you're the best thing that's ever happened to me."

My heart lurched, my breath stalling in my chest.

"And I would never lose my best thing." His voice dropped lower, his forehead pressing to mine again, our noses brushing. "Not *ever*."

Something inside me cracked wide open.

My lips parted, but nothing came out.

His gaze flicked over my face, taking me in, committing me to memory like I might disappear if he blinked. Then he leaned in, pressing a kiss to my temple, lingering there, like he wasn't just kissing me—he was *claiming* me. A shiver rolled through me, my heart slamming against my ribs, the weight of his words sinking in, curling into the deepest parts of me.

And I knew, with a certainty that terrified me—Jace Thatcher was never letting me go.

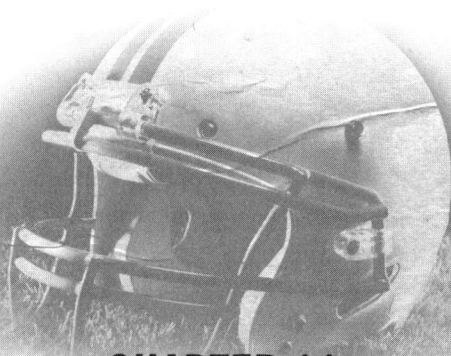

CHAPTER 11

RILEY

The coffee shop smelled like burnt beans and desperation, a bitter haze clinging to my apron as I wiped down the counter for the fifth time in an hour. The thrum of the espresso machine buzzed in my skull, syncing with the dull ache in my legs, my body wrung out from the week's grind—and from *him*.

Jace.

I hated that I couldn't stop thinking about him, that even as exhaustion weighed heavy in my limbs, my skin still hummed from his touch. Every time I closed my eyes, I felt his hands on me, his mouth, the way he *looked* at me, like I was something to be claimed, cherished. It was maddening. Infuriating. And worst of all, it made me ache for more.

But last night, when I had finally closed my eyes, it hadn't been Jace's hands I felt.

It had been *his*.

The nightmare had dragged me under fast—Callum's voice was like a snare, his touch a brand I couldn't escape. I woke up gasping, drenched in sweat, my pulse thrashing against my ribs like I was still trapped in his grasp. And for a long, awful moment, I wasn't sure where I was. If I had really escaped him.

If I was making the same mistakes all over again.

I should've been in my dorm, curled up in my bed—without Emma staring, obviously—cocooned in the kind of silence that let me forget. Instead, I was stuck here, trapped behind the chipped counter at Brewed Awakening, desperately trying to focus on anything *other* than the way Jace had wrecked me yesterday, the way my past was trying to claw its way back into my present.

But my body still remembered. His marks were still on my neck. His fingerprints were still visible on my hips.

And all my thoughts still kept circling back to him.

No amount of coffee or counter-wiping seemed to be enough to make it stop.

It should've been different.

Jace should have been different.

A guy like him wasn't supposed to happen to me—not after everything. Not after Callum. And yet, here he was, persistent and unapologetic in the way he wanted me, in the way he looked at me like I was something worth chasing.

I should have let myself enjoy it. I should have let myself sink into the way he made me feel, the way his touch ignited something in me that had been numb for so long. But instead? I was fighting it. Pushing him away.

Because of Callum.

Because of the way he had twisted the meaning of touch, of love, of trust, until I didn't know how to separate the poison from the pleasure.

Bitterness clawed up my throat, thick and insistent.

Jace was good. Jace was right. He was every fantasy I'd never let myself have—one I should have been drowning in, losing myself in. But I couldn't. Not when the past still had its fingers wrapped around my throat, squeezing every time I started to breathe.

And that was *his* fault.

Callum had taken everything. He had filled my head with ideas about what I was worth, what I was meant for, and even now—even now—I could feel the shadow of his control stretching over me, keeping me from feeling this.

From feeling Jace.

I gritted my teeth, gripping the counter hard enough for my knuckles to ache.

I hated him for that.

For making me doubt every good thing in my life. For making me second-guess the one person who had never given me a reason to.

And yet, I couldn't let it go.

Couldn't let myself be happy.

Because when you spend a year learning that love comes with a price, you start assuming every touch comes with a debt.

Outside, Knoxville pulsed with pregame energy—orange jerseys crowding the sidewalks, the roar of tailgate chatter rolling into the café every time the door opened. A week ago, I didn't get the hype. Football had been nothing more than a game to me, an excuse for people to scream at a TV and paint their faces like war was coming. But now?

Now, I got it.

Because when you were sitting in that stadium, when you felt the ground shake beneath you as thousands of people lost their minds, when you saw a player break free and *run*—unstoppable, untouchable—yeah, you understood.

And one player in particular?

Jace Thatcher.

He wasn't just hype. He played like he was born for it, like he had the world in his hands, and all he had to do was decide what to do with it. I knew nothing about football, but I hadn't been able to take my eyes off him the entire game.

Not that I would be admitting that to him anytime soon. His head was already too big.

Just like another part of him . . .

The bell above the door jangled, snapping me out of my haze, and there he was—prowling toward me like he owned the place, all broad shoulders and messy blonde hair, a Tennessee Tigers shirt stretched tight across his chest. His brown eyes locked on me, glinting with the unshakable certainty that twisted me up inside—half in irritation, half in something I was obsessed with but refused to name. My cheeks blushed automatically, thinking of yesterday's Jeep incident.

Gird your loins, Riley. Your vagina has been a hoochie mama, but that ends now.

I blinked at him as he came up in front of me, taking in how ridiculously gorgeous he was and having a bit of trouble with the whole girding thing.

"Morning, Mrs. Thatcher," he drawled, leaning over the counter and getting way too close to me. My heart ached a little at his grin, and his voice, with its lazy Tennessee lilt, somehow managed to wrap around me like a warm breeze.

Those words, though . . . I wanted nothing to do with them.

"What can I help you with?" I said, trying to keep my tone brisk and businesslike.

He grinned as if he could see right through me. "Although *I* should be the one getting *you* coffee, I would absolutely love a caramel macchiato, extra vanilla cold foam, a sprinkle of cinnamon and pink sugar, and if you could draw that little leaf thing on the top—I'd love that, too."

I gaped at him, my hand freezing mid-reach for a cup. "You want . . . what?" My voice came out a little incredulous, but who could blame me? Jace—who was six feet, four inches of cocky football muscle—had just ordered what might be the girliest drink on the planet.

"You heard me," he said with a wink, propping an elbow on the counter in a way that had me automatically admiring his bulging bicep . . . a real problem for sure. "I'm very secure in my masculinity, and it's a known fact that everything is better with cold foam. Why settle for black tar when I can have the good stuff?"

He crooked his finger, and I automatically leaned in closer as if my chin were attached to his hand with a string.

"We're both aware of the size of my cock, buttercup. It can take extra cold foam."

I blinked again, heat creeping up my neck as I yanked my head away, fumbling with a cup. "You're ridiculous," I scoffed, my voice coming out far too breathy considering my girds were supposed to be loined—or whatever the correct way to say that was. His gaze caressed my skin as I somehow managed to combine the rest of the ingredients. Hopefully I was doing this right. It was a little difficult to concentrate when he was watching me like he wanted to eat me alive.

He'd smelled good. *Why did he have to smell so good?* My chest tightened with a cruel ache. Callum had been a cold shadow who had choked me the entire time I'd been with him. But Jace . . . Jace felt like a wildfire, burning too bright, too close, and I couldn't help but feel the heat.

"Ridiculous is part of my charm, cupcake," he said, sipping the air like he was already tasting his drink, his voice dropping flirty and low. "And while you're at it, yes, I would love for you to be my date to the tailgate tonight. One shot, Riley St. James—me, you, whatever your choice of beverage is, and a whole lotta me looking cute for you. Thanks for asking me out, I accept."

Callum's voice filled my head.

"You're not smart enough, not talented enough. For fuck's sake, you're not even pretty enough." Callum let out a slow exhale, like he was disappointed in me. *"Pathetic little thing, always trying so hard. But for what? You think anyone actually sees you?"*

I slid the macchiato across the counter with a trembling hand as my dream from last night played through my head like a horror film. The cold foam was piled high with a pink sugar dusting that looked absurdly dainty for him, and I kept my eyes on it as I tried not to fall apart. "My answer hasn't changed, Thatcher. You should take a hint. What we're doing is just sex. That's all." My legs shook underneath me as a wave of exhaustion swept over my skin. I'd been pushing myself too hard lately, and it was constantly in the back of my mind that any day now . . . my body was going to revolt.

He took the cup, smirking like I'd handed him a golden ticket instead of a no. "I know we came to an understanding last night, Riley-girl—it's not just sex. We both know that. I'm not willing to accept the *no* when your eyes are screaming *yes* so loudly. As well as all the other parts of you that have been . . . screaming so loudly lately."

I blushed at his reminder of just how loud I'd been *screaming* last night.

"C'mon—one tailgate." He took a sip of his drink, cold foam catching on his full lip, and somehow I caught my tongue licking along my own lip, like it was practicing to trace his. Jace's gaze grew hungry as he watched me, and I was annoyed about how achingly hot he was.

"Worthless. Weak. No one could love you but me."

Callum's words stomped through my head, reminding me . . . you couldn't risk your heart on a man who shone like the sun . . . when you were just *ash*.

Jace didn't move away from the counter. He just continued to sip his frilly drink, watching me like he'd already mapped every crack in my armor.

"Do you need something else?" I said, fiddling with my apron while trying to look everywhere but at him.

"You're making this very difficult, Riley St. James, aka Riley Thatcher, aka buttercup." He set the cup down with an exaggerated sigh that made my lips twitch despite myself. "And you've left me with no choice."

Before I could react, he hoisted himself onto the counter—a full sprawl, his legs dangling, his arms behind his head like he was lounging on a picnic blanket. My jaw dropped as his legs draped around the cookie containers, all while he grinned at me like some kind of lovesick fool. To make it even more outrageous . . . his abs were flashing—six ridges of tanned, sculpted muscle that seemed to gleam under the fluorescent lights like this was a commercial and he'd just been oiled up. I stared.

Because how could I not?

Lust coiled in my belly, hot and unbidden. One thing I hadn't done . . . taste those abs. I was suddenly desperate to trace all that skin with my tongue.

Why did he have to look like he'd been carved from every fantasy I'd ever had?

Jace took his sweet time lowering his arms, letting the shirt drape slowly back down, smirking like he knew exactly what he'd done to me by that little flash of skin. Customers seated at the tables froze, the guy that had been standing behind him actually had to lean over Jace's body to order a flat white, glaring at me like this was my mess.

"What are you doing?" I hissed, my voice cracking as my eyes lingered on where his abs had been, my heart a frantic jumble. Jen, my boss, peeked out from the back . . . and then shrugged, like it was no big deal.

Someone needed to have a discussion with the student body at this school and let them know that football players weren't actually gods.

I peeked back at the sliver of skin showing as Jace stretched out some more.

Okay . . . maybe *he* was a god. But this was unsanitary at the very least.

"I'm staging a lie-in, baby doll," he said, shifting like he was trying to get comfy, his voice all flirty velvet. "A la sixties vibes, Riley-style. I'm not moving until you say yes. Call it a protest against your stubborn streak, or a show for my favorite barista. Take your pick."

"You're insane," I said for what must have been the millionth time since I'd met him, but my voice faltered, a laugh slipping free as my chest ached with want. My cheeks were burning from the fact that everyone in the store was staring at me. A woman reached over his legs for sugar, and I rubbed my temples, unsure what to do.

I'd just ignore him. He couldn't stay here forever.

Right?

I began wiping the counters . . . around his body, refilling sugars, grabbing milk . . . leaning over him for lids—all while he stayed here, watching me with that grin.

Fifteen minutes stretched like a lifetime, and unfortunately, my resolve started splintering at the seams.

"Move, asshole," a guy demanded. Jace just winked.

A woman muttered, reaching over his legs for creamer; another glared as she ordered a chai tea, forcing me to stretch across his stupid abs again.

I finally snapped and threw my rag down.

"Fine—one party . . . or tailgate . . . or whatever it's called. I'll show up alone. No picking me up. No . . . nothing crazy . . . or I leave," I told him, trying to ignore the butterflies going off in my stomach as we locked eyes.

A slow, sexy, *victorious* smile slid across his lips before he moved off the counter, his abs flexing again as his shirt came up, like somehow he was doing it on purpose. He leaned toward me, his eyes blazing like I'd handed him my soul. "Deal, Mrs. Thatcher," he said, brushing off his jeans with a flourish. "You won't regret this, Riley-girl. It's going to be the best night of your life."

"Doubtful," I muttered, but my voice softened, and he caught it—his grin turning sweeter, melting me further. He tossed a twenty on the counter. "For the drink and the eye candy." He sauntered out, leaving me staring after him, my chest a tangle of irritation and . . . yearning.

Fuck.

It kind of felt like I was falling.

CHAPTER 12

RILEY

The glow of the bonfire danced against the night sky, painting long shadows across the field as the air buzzed with life. Laughter floated over the crackle of burning logs, mixing with twangy music from a truck's speakers and the sharp scent of smoke and beer. People were everywhere—crowded around the flames, stretched out on the grass, leaning against tailgates with red cups in hand, their voices loud and bright.

Too many people.

I lingered at the crowd's edge, my fingers twisting the sleeves of my hoodie, the soft fabric bunching under my grip. It was so loud, voices overlapping, cups glinting in the firelight, bodies weaving in a blur that made my chest tighten. The energy hummed, wild and overwhelming, and I wasn't sure I could step into it. Maybe this was a mistake. Maybe I should just turn back, slip away to my dorm before anyone noticed I'd even—

My feet left the ground, the world tilting fast. I gasped, a quick little breath, as strong arms scooped me up, lifting me like I was as light as air. A startled squeak slipped out, high and silly, before I felt a warm, solid chest press against mine, spinning me through the air until my head spun and my heart raced. Jace. It had to be Jace.

He grinned down at me, his golden hair catching the fire's light, his lips flashing like he'd just found a prize. "There's my girl," he said, his voice warm and steady, wrapping around me like a blanket I hadn't asked for but couldn't push away.

My sneakers skimmed the ground again, soft dirt under my feet, but he didn't let go; his hands stayed on my waist, firm and warm through my hoodie, sending a flutter through me I couldn't shake. I blinked, breathless, my hands hovering like I didn't know where to put them. "Y-you can put me down," I stammered, my voice small, tripping over itself.

"Just celebrating the fact that the night's actually perfect now that you're here," he said, his grin widening, all smug and pleased. His eyes sparkled, mischief glowing in the brown, the fire's reflection flickering like something wild and alive.

I stared, my thoughts scattering, my heart doing a nervous little dance in my chest. He leaned closer, too close, his breath brushing my cheek, his nose almost touching mine. "I followed you from your dorm," he said, casual as anything, like it was no big deal. "I had to make sure you showed up."

My breath caught, eyes widening as I tried to process it. "You followed me?" I asked, my voice barely above a whisper as my stomach flipped around—part shock, part something soft and warm I didn't want to name.

Jace's smirk deepened as he dipped lower, his voice a low, teasing murmur. "Yeah, babycakes," he said. "Couldn't let my favorite girl slip away before I caught her."

A rush of heat climbed my cheeks, and I ducked my head, tugging my sleeves over my hands. He always did that . . . said things like they were sweet, not completely unhinged, and for some reason I was never as weirded out—or scared—as I probably should be.

Jace slid me down the length of his body, slow and deliberate, like he wanted me to feel every hard inch of him, his chest, his stomach, and then . . . okay . . . the firm, undeniable press of his erect length against my hip as I moved past it. My breath hitched, a quick, shaky pull, and he groaned softly.

"I would tell you to ignore *him*, but I don't really want you to," he said with a wink.

I scoffed, unable to help the grin that slipped past my lips.

I didn't really want to ignore *him*, either.

His hands stayed on my waist, thumbs brushing my ribs through my hoodie, soft and teasing, while he looked at me—really looked—like he was soaking me up, memorizing every nervous blink. I fidgeted, my fingers twisting my sleeves, unsure where to hide from the sudden warmth tingling through me.

Then he smiled, soft, devastating, and entirely too sincere. He winked, quick and playful, and my heart stumbled, caught in my throat. "Riley-girl," he said, his voice dropping low, husky, the glow of the flames painting gold across his sharp jaw and his messy hair. "You're fucking gorgeous. Prettiest girl I've ever seen."

Callum had never called me beautiful after that first night. He'd replaced any compliments with critiques and criticism, and I'd believed every harsh word that had come out of his lips.

Jace said these things like they were a revelation, and I had no idea how to respond. Heat rushed up my neck, my breath stalling, a lump I couldn't swallow. "Jace—" I started, voice wobbly, but my brain blanked, words slipping away like sand.

"Welcome to our first official date," he said, grinning like he hadn't just flipped my world upside down, like this wasn't a total ambush that left me dizzy. His arm went around my shoulders, tugging me into his side, warm, solid, smelling like pine and smoke as he steered me toward the bonfire. "Come on. I gotta introduce you to my bestilicious bros."

I blinked up at him, my head spinning. "Your what?" I asked, my voice small, tripping over his words as I stumbled to keep up with his long strides.

"You know," he mused, guiding me through the crowd like it was nothing, his hand steady on me while bodies parted around us, laughing, shouting, cups sloshing. "My boys. My ride-or-dies. My No Drama Llama brothers from other mothers . . ." He smirked, obviously thinking he was funny, even though I had no idea what he was talking about. "They've all been *dying* to meet you."

Panic squeezed my ribs, sharp and sudden, my sneakers faltering on the uneven grass. "Jace, I don't—" I swallowed, my voice quivering. "I think it's too soon. Don't you?"

He stopped dead, turning to face me, one eyebrow arching high, all fake innocence and teasing light in his eyes. "Too soon?" he echoed, like I'd said something hilarious. "Huh. That's weird." He tilted his head, gold hair falling over his forehead. "Did I feel like a stranger in my Jeep yesterday?"

My stomach flipped, a quick, hot twist, and I glared, cheeks burning. "That's different," I said, my voice a little colder, though it trembled at the edges as I remembered—his hands on me, the Jeep's leather seat cool against my back, the way he'd touched me like he belonged there.

He grinned, wide and wicked. "Is it?"

"Yes," I huffed, crossing my arms tight, trying to ignore the memory.

"Interesting," he said, dragging the word out before he sighed big and dramatic, like I'd wounded him. "You and Matty both need wake-up calls. I'm always right."

I scoffed, a tiny laugh slipping out despite my nerves. "Those words are never going to come out of my mouth," I said, shaking my head, my ponytail swaying as I peeked up at him.

Jace's grin was never-ending as he steered me forward again, his arm a warm weight I couldn't shake. "We'll see, sweetheart," he said, his voice dipping low, teasing and sure. "We'll see."

A thrill shot through me, curling low in my stomach.

I shouldn't have liked this—him pushing, teasing, refusing to back down no matter how much distance I tried to put between us. But I did. More than I should. More than I wanted to admit.

I tucked my lip between my teeth, trying to suppress the smile threatening to break free, but the warmth was already spreading through me, traitorous and undeniable. He made me feel wanted. Chased. Like he had no intention of letting me slip through his fingers.

And maybe—just maybe—I didn't want to slip through.

Not when it was him.

As we wove through the chaos of the bonfire party, the night pulsed around us, wild and loud, like it had a heartbeat of its own. People shouted Jace's name from every direction—teammates in sweat-stained jerseys, girls in tight sorority crop tops giggling too loud, random guys waving for fist bumps, their voices slurring over the crackle of the fire. Every few steps, someone lunged into our path, trying to snag him for a laugh or a story, their red cups sloshing beer onto the grass. The air smelled like smoke, spilled liquor, and the faint sweetness of burning wood. It pressed in, heavy and warm, making my head spin a little.

Jace barely slowed, his long strides cutting through the crowd like it was nothing. His arm stayed locked around my shoulders, firm and steady, his fingers brushing my collarbone through my hoodie every time he shifted. It was like he was binding me to him, keeping me from floating away in the mess of bodies and noise. I clung to that feeling with all my might, my sneakers scuffing the uneven ground.

"This is Riley," he said, over and over, his voice smooth and sure, introducing me to every single person we passed—some linebacker with a goofy grin, a girl with glitter on her cheeks, a guy balancing four cups like a circus act. No hesitation. No secrecy. Just Jace, tossing my name out like it belonged there, loud and proud, his smile flashing in the firelight.

"Hey, Jace, man, come take a shot with us!" some guy hollered from behind a makeshift bar where kegs and coolers were stacked in the dirt, a folding table wobbling under bottles. His voice was thick, half drunk, cutting through the music blaring from a truck nearby.

Jace didn't even turn his head as we kept moving, his grip on me tightening a fraction. "Can't. I'm with my girl," he called back, casual as anything, like it was the easiest thing in the world to say.

My girl.

The words hit me like a jolt, and I stumbled, my sneaker catching on a clump of grass. My heart did a quick, clumsy flip as it thudded hard against my ribs. I glanced up at him, wide-eyed, searching his face. He wasn't looking at me; he just kept steering us forward, cool and composed, his golden hair in some kind of half-up, half-down hot messy bun that I was pretty sure no other man could make so incredibly sexy, his jaw sharp and unbothered. Like he hadn't just dropped a bomb in my chest and walked away whistling.

It kind of seemed like Jace Thatcher—one of the gods of UT football, the star wide receiver, the guy everyone wanted a piece of—was introducing me—*me*—as his girlfriend. Proudly. Casually. Like it was obvious. Like it was no big deal. With him, I wasn't some dirty secret he'd tuck away when the spotlight got too bright.

A pang twisted in my chest, tight and sudden, stealing my breath.

With Callum, I'd been hidden away, kept quiet, made to feel like I wasn't *worthy* of being acknowledged. I'd been something to control, to keep in the dark, shoved in the shadows until he wanted me. Someone who was *his*, but only behind closed doors.

Like that one night . . .

The house was alive with the murmur of conversation, the clinking of glasses, and the low hum of classical music piped through the sound system. My mother's voice rang out in a practiced laugh as she charmed some politician's wife, and my father stood near the bar, swirling a glass of whiskey, looking entirely disinterested in his own event.

I'd been told to dress appropriately. Which, in my mother's language, meant something elegant but demure. Something that wouldn't draw attention in the wrong way but would still present me as the perfect daughter in the St. James family.

I'd spent the evening like a ghost, floating from room to room, sipping a watered-down drink, pretending to be fascinated by whatever conversation was happening around me. But my stomach had been in knots since the second I saw him.

Callum. With her.

Age-appropriate her. The kind of woman Callum should be with. She was perfect. Polished. Laughing in all the right places, touching his arm with an ease that made my stomach churn.

And Callum?

He seemed to be eating it up. Smiling at her, leaning in, whispering something that made her blush.

I told myself I didn't care. I told myself it didn't matter. That he didn't love her, not like he loved me. But the sharp edge of jealousy was a knife in my ribs every time I saw his hand skim the small of her back. Every time she smiled up at him like he was hers.

I was supposed to be used to this. To watching him parade around with her, a woman who fit the mold perfectly. To seeing him be the man he was expected to be while I stood in the shadows.

It didn't matter that I was the one he really wanted. It didn't matter that it was my bed he'd crawled into countless nights before.

None of it mattered.

Because Callum belonged to this world, and I belonged to him. And he never let me forget it. He never let me be free.

I spent the night avoiding him. I tried to pretend I was fine, that the sight of his hand ghosting over her hip didn't make my skin crawl. I avoided his eyes, avoided being in the same room with him when I could.

But I should've known better. Callum never let me avoid him for long. He liked to taunt me with her. He liked to put me in my place. Because he knew there was nothing I could do about it.

The party was winding down, and she had gone home when I felt it—that prickle on the back of my neck. I turned, and he was there. His tie was loosened. His eyes were dark.

"You've been avoiding me," he murmured, stepping closer.

My heart pounded against my ribs. I forced a brittle smile. "You seemed occupied."

His lips twitched. "Jealous?"

I scoffed, but the sound barely left my throat before his fingers were curling around my wrist, his grip firm.

"You know better than that, Riley."

I hated how easily I let him pull me with him.

The hall was empty, the distant hum of the party fading as he tugged me into the closet under the stairs. The second the door shut, his hands were on me.

His fingers slid into my hair, tugging, forcing me to look at him.

His lips grazed my jaw. "You've been a little brat tonight."

I swallowed hard.

Callum sighed, his patience razor-thin as he flicked his gaze over me. "You know why I have to be seen with her, Riley. No one would take me seriously if they knew the truth. I have to keep you tucked away because you're not old enough, you're not polished enough to stand beside me where it matters."

He stepped closer, his voice dropping, cool and cutting. "So stop pouting. You know the deal. I do what I need to do, and you stay exactly where I put you. And right now? You can make it up to me for the attitude you've been throwing all night."

His thumb traced my bottom lip. My breath hitched.

I knew what he wanted.

I knew what he expected.

And I knew I was going to hate myself even more . . .

But I sank to my knees anyway.

I blinked hard, the bonfire snapping me back, the heat of it licking at my face as Jace's arm tugged me closer. He was the complete opposite of Callum. There didn't seem to be any shame, any hesitation. It was just him, holding me tight, making sure every drunk idiot here knew I was his. He seemed so proud of that. Flaunting me, like I was everything.

His thumb brushed my shoulder again, a soft, absent touch that sent a shiver down my spine, and I swallowed, my throat thick with something I couldn't name.

I didn't say anything. My voice was stuck somewhere between my racing heart and the lump in my chest. Because deep down, in a quiet little corner I didn't want to peek into, I liked it. I liked the way he said *my girl* like it was a fact, I liked how his arm felt like a shield, I liked how he didn't care who saw us. It was new, dizzying, and a little . . . terrifying.

Because what if this wasn't real?

What if he found out who I really was . . . the girl Callum had seen . . . and changed his mind? My body was a trip wire that could go off at any minute. What if it did—and he decided he didn't want to handle it?

We continued weaving through the crowd, his arm a steady weight around my shoulders, until we reached a giant black truck parked at the edge of the field. Its tailgate was down, flipped open like a makeshift stage, and a small group lounged around it—laughing, cups in hand, their voices loud over the music thumping from a speaker propped in the bed. I slowed as I took them in, trying to school my face so I didn't look too freaked out, but Jace didn't pause.

"No Drama Llamas," he called, his voice cutting through their chatter, easy and confident as he pulled me in front of him, his hands sliding to my hips like he was presenting me. "This is my angel cakes, babylicious, most fantastical girl on the planet—my girlfriend, Riley."

My breath caught, a little hitch in my chest, and I froze, heat creeping up my neck. Girlfriend. He said it like it was carved in stone, and my eyes darted up to his face, feeling some kind of weird relief at how confident he looked when he said it. The group turned, heads swiveling, and I shrank a little under their stares, my fingers twisting the hem of my hoodie.

"I was beginning to think you'd made her up, Jace-face," one guy said, stepping forward with a laugh.

Jace nudged me toward him, grinning wider. "Riley, this is Parker—our quarterback, resident big brain, and bestilicious number one."

Parker was tall, matching Jace inch for inch, with broad shoulders that filled out his shirt like some kind of model and dark hair that fell in his face. His grin was all perfect teeth—and his blue eyes glinted as he reached out a hand toward me. "Hey, Riley. Heard a ton about you," he said in a booming voice, smooth and deep, like he was born to command a room—or a field. Before I could even move, Jace swatted Parker's hand away midair, a quick smack that made Parker laugh, low and easy.

"No touching," Jace said, voice sharp but smirking, stepping closer to me, his hand sliding to my hip, gripping tight, possessive as hell. I froze, caught off guard, my smile wobbling as Parker raised his hands in mock surrender, still grinning like some kind of otherworldly, gorgeous creature.

Jace leaned in, his lips brushing my ear, breath warm as he whispered in a low growl, "Parker sometimes has magical powers with women, so we best not risk it."

The gorgeous girl next to Parker snorted, rolling her eyes, and I watched as Parker pressed a soft kiss on the top of her head, looking at her with the same wide-eyed awe that I'd seen before . . . whenever Jace looked at me.

"I only use my magical powers on *one* woman," Parker commented, sounding a bit growly as he pulled the girl closer to him.

My stomach did its weird twisty thing again.

"Nice to meet you," I murmured, barely audible over the noise, my cheeks heating up as Jace's fingers squeezed my hip, steady and sure, staking his claim.

Jace gestured to the girl next to Parker. She was beautiful, with long dark hair, sharp cheekbones, and big, bright eyes that sized me up quick—not mean, just curious.

"This is Casey," Jace said, his voice softening a little. "Smartest one here, keeps us in line, and the love of Parkie-Poo's life."

Parker beamed at that intro, and Casey blushed and looked down at the ground, like she wasn't sure how such a thing could be true, either.

"Hey, Riley," she said, her voice calm, a little husky, and she smiled—just a small curve of her lips, but it felt real.

"Good to meet you." I nodded back, my hands fidgeting, feeling a little less lost with her steady gaze.

"And *this* is Matty," Jace said as a guy with a mop of wavy black hair leapt off the tailgate, landing with a *thud* that rippled the ground, all lean muscle and swagger in one hot package. Matty had bright blue eyes that were piercing, the kind that'd stop traffic. He was gorgeous—wide and solid, his arms sculpted under a faded UT shirt that clung to every muscle.

There was a pause as he stared at Jace like he was waiting for something.

"Why are you acting weird?" Jace asked. "You're going to make her think I hang out with weirdos."

"I'm just waiting for the rest of my introduction," Matty snapped. "You had a whole bunch of nice things to say about Parker, so where are *my* nice things?"

"Oh, you're feeling insecure about the 'bestilicious number one' thing," Jace said with a nod. "That's only because I met him first. It's not a ranking thing, *per se*."

"*Per se* . . . That was a good one," said Parker.

Jace beamed at him. "Thank you. I knew you would like that one."

I couldn't keep the grin off my face.

"I'm still waiting," said Matty, sounding very disgruntled as he crossed his arms over his chest. "And I don't think we ever agreed on the No Drama Llamas thing. I think there are better options. Like not having a name at all."

"He's just mad that he didn't think of the group name first," Jace whispered—loudly—in my ear.

Matty grunted again, and Jace sighed like he was being very put out. "Riley-girl, this is Matthew. Star tight end, known for his *tight end* and his missing *quarter* inch. Bestilicious number two."

Matty's face got a little red, and we were all laughing as he stared at Jace like he was going to kill him.

"What's the quarter inch thing?" I asked.

Matty got even redder.

"Nothing. Absolutely nothing," he said in a weird, high-pitched voice as he waved his hand at me and jumped back on the tailgate.

Last was another girl, leaning against the truck, her blonde hair catching the firelight like it was made of gold. "This is Natalie," Jace said, grinning again. "Casey's BFF, our resident fireball. She has a mean right hook, we've learned, but so far she hasn't used it on any of us."

Natalie rolled her eyes, but looked very proud of her introduction. She was tall and curvy, her smile wide and bright, like she was ready to charm the whole world. Her blue eyes sparkled as she waved at me enthusiastically, her nails painted orange to match her UT shirt. "Riley! Oh my gosh, you're adorable," she said, her voice bubbly and fast, like she couldn't wait to spill a hundred stories. "You and Jace are the cutest. Do you like Nerds Gummies and football? It's okay if you don't like football. We can work on that."

I blinked at all the hurried sentences falling out of her mouth as Casey laughed, high and sweet.

"You're going to scare her off, Nat. And then she won't want to be friends with us."

"Of course she's going to want to be friends with us," Natalie retorted, like Casey had said something ridiculous. "We're awesome."

Natalie glanced over at me. "You want to be friends with us, right?"

I blinked at her, blushing furiously again as I squeaked out, "Of course."

Natalie looked at Casey triumphantly. "See?!"

Jace chuckled behind me, his breath warm against my ear. "Told you they'd love you," he murmured, low enough that only I could hear, and my heart skipped, caught between nerves and something softer. "It's impossible not to."

I swallowed hard, my pulse betraying me with the way it stuttered in my throat.

Jace's voice was smooth, easy—like this was just another one of his crazy, offhand remarks. Like it was nothing.

But it *wasn't* nothing.

Not to me.

Not when his breath skimmed my skin, low and intimate, like a secret just for me. Not when his words *lingered*—sank deep and settled into the place I never let anyone reach.

It's impossible not to.

My stomach flipped, my body reacting before my brain could catch up.

Because it almost sounded like he . . .

Like he *loved* me.

Which was ridiculous.

Right?

And yet, as I felt the heat of his body pressed against my back, as his fingers brushed lightly over my wrist like he couldn't *not* touch me—

I wasn't exactly sure.

———

I was next to Jace, our legs dangling over the edge of Parker's truck as the bonfire's roar sliced through the night. Its flames stabbed fifteen feet high, flinging embers that twirled like frantic moths above the Knoxville crowd, a pulsing swarm of coeds, alumni, and stragglers mashed together under a star-slashed sky. Their shouts and slurred laughter hammered my ears over the relentless *thud* of bass from warped speakers.

And somehow—*somehow*—this was the most fun I'd ever had.

The group had been good to me, welcoming in a way I wasn't used to, like I belonged there just as much as any of them. I'd laughed more tonight than I could ever remember laughing in my life, loud, real, unrestrained laughter that had my stomach aching from the sheer force of it. Parker and Matty had drunkenly declared me an honorary Llama member, and Casey and Nat had all but glued themselves to my side, already making plans for us that I couldn't help but hope were real.

And then there was Jace.

He'd been *everywhere*—his body always close, his hand brushing my thigh, his knuckles grazing my wrist. He never left my side except to grab me food, and even then, he'd thrown a wink over his shoulder like he *dared* me to miss him. And maybe I did. Maybe I'd spent every second hyperaware of the way his eyes always found mine first, the way he'd light up just a little whenever I smiled at him.

I was warm from it all. The alcohol, the heat of the fire, the way my chest *felt* different—light and heavy all at once.

My head buzzed, foggy from the four or five beers I'd downed. I clutched my latest bottle, already half empty, the condensation slicking my fingers.

And for the first time in a long, long time . . .

I felt *happy*.

The opening chords of "The Only Exception" floated through the night air, soft and lilting, cutting through the thumping bass that had owned the bonfire all evening. The gentle strum of the guitar rippled out, a whisper against the chaos, softening the wild shouts and laughter into something quieter, something sweeter. The crowd shifted, a subtle hush falling over the field as the song's melody wove through the smoke and firelight. It felt like the world exhaled, just for a moment, and I sat there on the tailgate of that giant black truck, taking it all in.

Jace was in front of me then, his strong hands sliding around my waist, his fingers warm where they moved against my skin.

"Come here, sweetheart," he murmured, his voice thick and low, wrapping around me like the song itself, pulling me in before I could think to pull away—not that I wanted to, not really.

His hands tightened, and then he lifted me off the tailgate with that ridiculous ease of his, like I weighed nothing. The world tilted as he set me down on the grass, and I swayed for a second—the buzz of the beer making my head light, my movements slow and clumsy. But Jace was there, his hands guiding me, steady and firm, pulling me into him until my chest brushed his, the solid warmth of him grounding me as the music swirled around us.

The firelight danced over his golden hair, turning the messy strands into something glowing, something almost mythical, like he'd stepped out of a story I'd dreamed up. His grip was firm, protective, his arms wrapping me close as he swayed us side to side, slow and deliberate, the crowd fading into a blur beyond us. I pressed my palm against his chest, feeling the steady thud of his heartbeat beneath his shirt, strong and alive, matching the rhythm of the song. His warmth seeped into me, melting the tension in my shoulders, softening me against him.

I exhaled, a shaky little breath, and let myself melt into it, into him, lost in our own tiny world, the bonfire's crackle and the distant chatter falling away.

This wasn't just a dance.

This was something *more*.

Jace's fingers splayed wide against my back, tracing gentle, lazy circles over my hoodie, like he was mapping me out, memorizing every inch he could touch. It wasn't just holding—he was *keeping* me, his hands possessive but so tender it made my chest ache.

I rested my cheek against his shoulder, inhaling the scent of his skin—clean, warm, so *him*—and let my eyes flutter shut.

"I think I was always gonna end up here," Jace murmured, his voice barely a whisper against my ear. "With you."

My breath caught, a quick, sharp hitch that lodged in my throat, and my fingers tightened on his shirt, clinging to the fabric like it could steady me.

It wasn't a declaration. Not quite.

But it *felt* like one, heavy with quiet truth, sinking into me like rain into dry earth.

I pressed closer, my forehead brushing his collarbone, the heat of his skin radiating through his shirt, and he shifted, one hand sliding up to cup the back of my neck, his thumb brushing my hairline, soft and slow. The firelight flickered behind my closed eyes, painting little bursts of gold and orange, but all I could feel was him—his heartbeat under my palm, his breath against my temple, the way he held me like I was something precious, something he'd never let slip away.

"Riley," he said, so quiet it was almost lost in the music, and I peeked up at him, my lashes lifting slow and hesitant. His face was close—too close— his eyes locked on mine, warm and unguarded, the fire reflecting in them like tiny sparks. His lips curved, just a little, soft and real, and my stomach flipped, a slow, sweet twist that left me breathless.

The song dipped, the lyrics curling around us, wrapping us in its quiet promise, its aching *hope*.

And I knew.

Knew what it meant to truly fall for someone.

It wasn't grand gestures or flashy moments. It was this. The quiet, the certainty, the way someone could hold you like they'd never let you go. The thought that maybe . . . he'd be able to handle me . . . That he wouldn't think I was a burden.

I gripped the back of his shirt and *clung* to him, because I wasn't sure I wanted to let go, either.

Not yet.

Maybe not ever.

"You're perfect," he whispered, his voice rough at the edges, like it slipped out before he could stop it, and I ducked my head fast, my cheeks burning, a tiny laugh bubbling up despite myself. He chuckled, too, soft and low, his chest rumbling against mine, and he pressed his lips to my forehead—a quick, gentle kiss that sent a shiver racing down my spine.

The song faded, its last notes drifting into the night, but Jace didn't let go, he didn't step back. He just held me there, still swaying, like the music hadn't ended, like it never would. And I stayed, my arms around him, my cheek against his shoulder, the firelight glowing soft and golden around us, feeling—for the first time in a long time—like I was exactly where I was supposed to be.

The night stretched on, the bonfire's glow dimming as people trickled away, their laughter fading into the dark. Jace stayed close, his arm around me as we said goodbyes—Parker's laugh, Matty's sloppy wave, Casey's quiet nod, Natalie's bubbly hug filling my insides up with a heady, sparkling warmth. And then he led me to his Jeep.

"Are you alright to drive?" I murmured as he helped me into my seat.

"I didn't drink anything, Riley-girl," he said, reaching over to snap my seat belt into place.

"You didn't?" I asked with a frown, before realizing I'd only seen him sipping water the whole evening.

"I didn't want anything about this night to be blurry," he answered with a wink as he closed my door.

My head was still light, the beer's buzz lingering, but his hand in mine felt like an anchor as he drove. There was a part of me that thought I should be asking him to take me back to my dorm—but I couldn't get my mouth to actually say the words.

I didn't want this night to end.

The hum of the engine and the soft country tune on the radio filled the space between us. I leaned my head against the window, watching the blur of trees and streetlights, my heart still fluttering from the dance, from him.

We pulled up to the house he'd told me he shared with Matty, a small place off campus with a porch light flickering. Jace turned off the engine and looked at me with a soft smile. "C'mon," he said in a gentle voice, and I followed him inside, my steps echoing across the floor as he flicked on a lamp, casting a warm glow over the living room.

My eyes widened when I saw the room. I'd been expecting some grimy jock crash pad, maybe a futon and a pile of beer cans. But it was way nicer than I'd pictured. The living room stretched out, sleek hardwood and plush vibes—a big leather couch, a glass coffee table gleaming under a soft lamp, and a shelf lined with shiny football trophies that caught the light just right. A huge flat-screen hung on the wall, and the air smelled faintly of cedar, warm and inviting, like it was actually lived-in, not just a pit stop.

Jace tossed his keys onto a polished side table with a *clink*, then turned to me, his hands shoved in his pockets, looking almost . . . shy? Like he wasn't sure how to play this now that we were here. "How are you feeling?" he asked, stepping closer, his brown eyes locking on mine, searching, like he was looking for some sign from me. "It's late. I can drive you back if—"

"No," I said, too quick, my voice soft but firm, surprising even me. I swallowed, my hands fidgeting at my sides. "I want to stay. With you."

His brows lifted, a flicker of surprise crossing his face, then that grin crept back, slow and warm. "Yeah?" he said, stepping closer still, until

I could feel the heat of him again, that pine-and-Jace scent wrapping around me.

We stumbled down the hall, a tangle of limbs and quiet laughs, my hoodie slipping to the floor as we made it inside a bedroom. I didn't even bother to look around—didn't care about the walls, the furniture, the shadows cast by the dim light spilling in from the hall. My focus was all on him, on Jace, his golden hair mussed from my fingers, his brown eyes catching mine with that warm, steady glow that made my heart skip. He sat down on a king-sized bed, the mattress dipping under his weight, and he tugged me onto his lap, his hands finding me like they always did—curling around my hips, sliding up my back, and threading through my hair.

I felt alive, electric, the buzz of the beer I'd sipped at the bonfire sharpening into something bright and clear, like the night had peeled back every layer until it was just us, raw and real.

His touch was everywhere, in his warm palms pressing into my spine, his fingers brushing the bare skin where my shirt had ridden up, tangling gently in my ponytail.

I couldn't get enough, I couldn't stop the way my breath hitched, the way my hands pressed against his chest, feeling the hard muscle beneath his shirt. I pulled back, breathless, my fingers tracing the line of his jaw, the faint stubble prickling my skin, and I looked at him, really looked, seeing the flush on his cheeks, the way his lips parted, soft and waiting. My chest fluttered, a wild, nervous beat, and I slid off his lap, slow and deliberate, kneeling between his legs, my hands resting on his thighs, the denim rough under my palms.

"Riley—" he started, his hands reaching for me, hovering like he wasn't sure if he should pull me back or let me go. His eyes widened, a flicker of worry cutting through the heat, but I shook my head, my decision settling firm and warm in my chest, a quiet certainty I hadn't felt in so long.

"I want to," I said, looking up at him, my voice steady despite the flutter in my stomach. His jeans were tight, the outline of him hard and obvious against the fabric, and I reached for his belt, my fingers trembling but sure, the metal cool against my touch.

This wasn't just impulse—it was more, something I'd been turning over in my head all night, maybe longer. I wanted to show him, really show him, how much he meant, how much I liked him—how much I liked the way he made me feel seen, safe, *wanted*.

With Callum, this had been a chore, a demand I'd hated, something I'd dreaded every time his voice turned harsh, his hands too heavy. I'd always felt small after, hollowed out, like I'd given up a piece of myself I couldn't get back.

But with Jace? I wanted to give him this—not because he asked, not because I had to, but because I *chose* it, because it felt right, like a gift I could wrap around him, something tender and mine to offer.

"You're drunk," Jace murmured, catching my wrists, his voice uneven as his thumbs brushed my pulse points, gentle but firm. His eyes searched mine, wide and worried, his breath shallow like he was fighting himself. "Babycakes, you don't have to—"

"I'm not," I cut in, shaking my head, my voice soft but fierce. "I feel more alive, more *alert*, than I ever have." I met his gaze, unwavering, my heart pounding with something bold, something new. "I want this. With you."

He stared at me, his grip loosening, and then he exhaled, a shaky, awed sound, his hands falling to his sides. "Okay," he whispered, his voice raw, and I smiled—a small, real smile—before unbuckling his belt, sliding it free, my fingers brushing the heat of his skin as I unzipped his jeans.

"Get on your knees." Callum's voice echoed in my head, but I blinked him away, the warmth of Jace's bedroom flooding back, his brown eyes locked on mine—soft, worshipful, nothing like Callum's.

This was different. This was *me* choosing, *me* taking, and it felt like light breaking through a crack I'd forgotten was there.

He lifted his hips, and I tugged his jeans down, his briefs next, and he sprang free—thick, hard . . . huge. The sight of him sent a shiver through me. It wasn't fear, though, it was *want*. I leaned in, my hands moving up his thighs, feeling the muscles tense under my touch as I pressed a soft kiss to the tip, tasting the drop of salt and heat already beading from his slit.

Jace groaned, low and deep, his head tipping back as his hands fisted the comforter. "Riley—" he breathed, my name a prayer on his lips, and I smiled against his skin, my heart swelling with something powerful . . . something mine.

I took some of him into my mouth, slow and deliberate, my tongue tracing his length, learning him, savoring the way he shuddered, the way his breath hitched with every move I made. It wasn't rushed, it wasn't forced. It was tender, intentional . . . a gift I wanted to give.

His hands hovered, like he didn't know where to put them, and then they settled in my hair. He didn't push, he just rested them there, his fingers threading gently through the strands.

"Fucking hell, baby," he rasped in a breaking voice. I glanced up, meeting his eyes—wide, awestruck, glowing with something that made my chest ache. I moved faster, my lips sliding over him, my hand wrapping around the base, stroking in time with my mouth, and he moaned, a raw, beautiful sound that sent a thrill racing through me.

I felt strong, alive, every shudder of his body a testament to my choice, my power. This wasn't Callum's cold demand—this was Jace, open and vulnerable, giving himself to me as much as I was giving to him. I swirled my tongue, teasing the sensitive spot beneath the tip, and his hips jerked, a choked "Riley" spilling out, his voice thick with wonder. I hummed softly, the vibration making him gasp, his fingers tightening in my hair just enough to feel real, to feel connected.

Time blurred, the room fading to just us. The soft creak of the bed, the ragged rhythm of his breathing, the warmth of him against my lips.

I took him deeper, my throat relaxing, my hands steady, and he trembled, his control fraying, his moans growing louder, more desperate. "Riley— I'm—" he warned in a strained voice, but I didn't pull back, didn't stop, wanting him to feel it, to know this was mine to give.

He came with a groan, loud and shattering, his body arching, his hands clutching my hair as he pulsed against my tongue, hot and overwhelming. I stayed with him, swallowing every drop of his cum, my heart feeling like it was glowing inside me until he stilled, his chest heaving as his fingers caressed my jaw. I pulled back slowly, wiping my lips with the back of my hand as I looked up at him.

My breath was uneven, my cheeks were warm.

Jace stared down at me, his eyes wide and glassy, his mouth parted like he couldn't find words. "Riley," he finally said hoarsely, his voice soaked with wonder as he reached for me, pulling me up into his lap, his arms wrapping tight around me. "Holy shit, babycakes," he breathed, pressing his forehead to mine, his hands trembling as they cupped my face. "You're . . . you're incredible."

I smiled, small and shy, my heart overflowing, and I nestled into him, my cheek against his chest, feeling the steady drum of his heartbeat—fast, wild, *alive*. This wasn't just a moment; it was *everything*. A collision of fate and fire, a quiet storm of something undeniable, something that made me feel seen, *whole*.

Later that night, as I listened to his quiet breaths, our limbs tangled in his bed, I had so many thoughts.

Sex with Callum had been transactional. A carefully orchestrated game where I was always two steps behind, where I never quite knew the rules until it was too late. His touch had been firm but distant, rehearsed in a way that made it clear he was more interested in controlling me than in making me feel anything.

With Callum, I had been something to be handled. A possession, a trophy, a thing to be claimed rather than cherished. He had never once looked at me like I mattered, never once let me lead, never once given me space to breathe.

I never felt safe.

Even when I thought I wanted him, there had always been a hesitation. A wrongness pressing against my ribs, something dark curling in my gut. He made me feel small. Trapped. Powerless.

And I hated that, for so long, I had convinced myself that was just how it was supposed to be.

Because Jace?

He was everything Callum wasn't.

Jace touched me like I was something holy. Like I was made of delicate, breakable things but strong enough to take whatever he gave me. His hands were rough but attentive, his mouth soft but insistent. He listened. He worshiped. He made me feel wanted, not owned.

And the biggest difference?

With Jace, I never felt afraid.

Not once. Not even when his grip tightened in my hair, not even when he pressed me into the mattress, not even when he kissed me so deeply I forgot my own name.

Because Jace didn't just take—he gave.

Every touch was a question. A promise. A demand wrapped in devotion.

And for the first time, I understood.

It was never supposed to hurt.

It was never supposed to feel like a cage.

It was supposed to feel like . . . this.

CHAPTER 13

JACE

The ball cut through the crisp night air, spiraling perfectly as it came down toward me.

I tracked it effortlessly, the lights burning overhead, the roar of the empty field like a promise of what was coming. My fingers closed around the leather, the impact reverberating up my arms as I pulled it in and took off, juking past an imaginary defender before turning back and tossing the ball to Matty.

"Damn, you're locked in today," Matty called, shaking his head as he caught my pass.

I grinned, jogging back to the line of scrimmage. "Gotta be ready for Saturday, *Matthew*."

"Yeah, but usually by the end of practice you're coasting," Parker muttered, stepping up beside me. He pushed his helmet back, eyeing me like I was a puzzle he hadn't quite solved. "What's wrong with you?"

Matty scoffed. "Riley's probably avoiding him again."

I wrinkled my nose, thinking it was probably too unhinged that I didn't like him even saying her name.

Parker raised an eyebrow. "Oh yeah, that's probably it."

Matty shot me a smirk, one that quickly faded when I nodded to the silver car in the parking lot where *his stalker* was watching practice. Like usual.

I dropped into my stance as Coach barked out another play, and I didn't deign to answer them until I'd caught another pass.

"She's not ignoring me," I said. "She just . . . doesn't want to spend the night tonight."

Both of them nodded, like that was the same thing.

"She slept over last night, though," Matty said slowly.

Parker scoffed, shaking his head. Because he understood. Matty hadn't been infected yet. He hadn't gotten that hit of feeling what it was like to hold the person you were obsessed with in your arms.

He wasn't understanding that I might not be able to sleep until I was snuggling with my Riley-girl again.

Which would be a problem. Because I needed my beauty sleep.

I might have been killing it tonight, but that was only because of my raw talent. My head was filled with her.

The way her breath hitched when I touched her. The way she looked at me like she wanted to run—but couldn't bring herself to do it. The way she fit against me, like she belonged there.

I ran the next route at full speed, snatching the ball from the air before my feet even hit the turf. My blood was already buzzing, my pulse thrumming in time with the need crawling up my spine.

I had to be with her tonight.

Practice finally wrapped, and I didn't even wait for the huddle to break before I was yanking off my helmet and turning to Matty.

"I need you to help me with something."

Matty groaned. "Fucking hell, not again."

I ignored him, slinging my helmet under my arm and wiping the sweat off my forehead. "She's probably at the library right now."

Parker rolled his eyes. "And how would you know that?"

I grinned, thinking of the tracking app on her phone. "Not telling."

Matty barked out a sound that was a cross between a dying cow and a moose. "You're a psycho, Thatcher."

I shrugged. "So? Are you helping me or not?"

"Why can't *I* help?" Parker said, practically pouting.

I gave him a thumbs-up because that was the energy I was looking for. "Because I need someone single for my plan," I told him, nodding at Matty.

Matty sighed dramatically, like this was such a hardship for him, fulfilling his best friendship duties. "Fine. I haven't recovered from the last time I helped you. But what's the plan?"

I was already walking off the field, eager to get back to my locker so I could find out where Riley was right now. "We're gonna make sure I see Riley tonight. Whether she likes it or not."

Matty snorted. "Yeah, because that doesn't sound like stalking."

I just smirked.

It wasn't stalking if she *wanted* me there.

Even if she didn't know it yet.

Sneaking into Riley's room required two things: precision and a sucker.

Fortunately, I had Matty, and a very precise, three-step plan. One that definitely showcased my big brain.

Step one: Get Matty to entertain her creepy-ass roommate.

Step two: Slip into Riley's room unnoticed.

Step three: Sleep under her bed like a psycho, as nature intended.

We got into the locker room, and I gave a little fist pump when I checked my phone and saw that I'd been right, Riley *was* in the library.

"Alright, here's the deal. Riley's roommate only leaves her room for class. So, I need you to *distract* her."

Matty's lips curled up in suspicion. Probably thinking of the Darla Pinswallow situation. This was going to be a piece of cake compared to that.

Probably.

Maybe.

"Distract her how, exactly?" he asked.

I slung an arm over his shoulders, noting my superiority, because out of the three of us, I was the only one who didn't stink right now. "I don't know, Matty. How do you usually get girls?" I asked sarcastically. "Talk to her, charm her, maybe ask about her hobbies . . ." I rolled my eyes, because seriously, this shouldn't be too hard for him.

"What if her hobby is murder?" Parker asked. I paused at that thought before waving him off.

"Then this is a great opportunity for personal growth," I finally answered.

Matty snarled and shook off my arm. "You are the worst."

I smirked as I headed toward the shower, eager to get out of here and into Riley's room.

I was waiting down the hall from Riley's room, and Matty was not here. Instead, he was freaking out somewhere, frantically texting me and wasting precious time.

> Matty: Wait . . . wait, wait, wait. A thought just came to me. And it seems crazy. But I need to check . . . because it's you.

THE WRONG PLAY   165

> Matty: Are you trying to sneak into Riley's room?? Without her knowing . . . !?

> Me: I don't like how you make it sound illegal.

> Matty: BECAUSE IT IS!

> Me: You sound like a cop.

> Matty: You sound like a future inmate.

> Me: If I go down, I'm taking you with me.

> Matty: What the hell does that mean??

I checked my app again, making sure Riley was still in the library. She was still there, but she'd been acting very tired when I dropped her off this morning. So, she probably would be heading to her room anytime now. He needed to get his ass moving.

> Me: You're up, buddy. Go get her.

> Matty: WHAT??

> Me: Just keep her occupied for like, a while. You got this, champ.

Matty was a lot of things—nosy, annoyingly good at video games . . . a worrywart of the highest order—but one thing I'd never truly appreciated was his ability to charm a woman. The man actually had game.

From my position down the hall, hidden in the shadows like the world's hottest criminal, I watched as he strolled up to Riley's room, knocked twice, and leaned into the doorframe, displaying a confidence that made me a little hot, as a matter of fact.

The door swung open, revealing her.

Emma.

The roommate. A little creepier than I'd anticipated, but we couldn't control what happened to us. Only how we reacted to it.

Or at least that's what I would be advising Matty on later.

I braced myself, fully expecting Matty to choke, to panic, to possibly scream. But no. The man did something *incredible*.

He smiled. Tilted his head just so. Dropped his voice to the kind of murmur that probably had the freshman girls sighing into their overpriced lattes.

I actually felt proud. *Look at him go.* Matty, in the wild, putting on a clinic in *wingmanning*.

Emma blinked up at him, her expression blank.

Then, after he said something I couldn't hear, and a long pause in which I held my breath the entire time . . . she stepped out of the room.

Matty walked her down the hall, and I decided he'd just moved up in the friendship rankings. *Per se*, of course.

Mission. Freaking. Accomplished.

As they got closer to where I was hiding out, I noticed Emma was a little . . . off.

Not in the usual freshman girl trying too hard kind of way. Not even in the sorority girl who thinks she's better than you kind of way. No, Emma moved like she was floating just slightly above the ground, like her feet barely touched it, like she wasn't quite tethered to this plane of existence.

But it was her *face* that made the back of my neck itch.

Her eyes were *wrong*. Wide. *Too* wide—pupils dilated like she'd just crawled out of a sensory deprivation tank and hadn't yet readjusted to reality. She didn't blink. Not once. She just . . . *stared*. Right at Matty's ear. Not his face. Not his body. His *ear*.

Matty, to his credit, looked like he was holding back the kind of fullbody shudder you get when a bug skitters across your skin.

I could see it all over him. The way his face had gone pale. The way his movements were stiff, almost robotic, like he had just survived some kind of horror movie encounter and wasn't fully *processing* it yet.

A man above men, right there.

He pulled out his phone, and a second later, I got a text.

> **Matty:** I don't think she blinked once the whole time we talked.

Alright, well, not ideal. But if he could manage Darla, he could manage this chick . . . hopefully.

> **Me:** You're doing your country proud.

> Matty: She said something about how the stars tell her secrets.

I grinned, watching as they passed before I slipped around the corner toward Riley's door.

> Me: Maybe that means you're soulmates.

I thought the middle finger emoji he sent back was a little *dramatic*, but we couldn't all be patient kings.

Sliding the key from my pocket—the one I'd "borrowed" long enough to make a copy of—I opened Riley's door.

Slipping into her room was the easy part. The harder part was not laughing at Matty's suffering in real time. I eased the door shut behind me and took in her room. It was easy to know which side was hers; she didn't have a creepy poster on the wall of my worst enemy—a certain red-haired clown. I shivered, resisting the urge to tear it off the wall.

Moving closer, I took in the small things that made it Riley's—the faint scent of vanilla in the air, the books stacked neatly on her desk, the sweater draped over the chair that I had seen her wearing just days ago.

On her desk, a hair tie sat next to her books. I picked it up, running my fingers over the soft fabric before slipping it onto my wrist. It was still warm from the now-set sun streaming through the window, but I imagined it was warm from *her*.

Her dresser was next. I opened the top drawer and nearly groaned. Lace, silk, delicate fabrics in muted colors—things that clung to her body, things I had imagined peeling off her. I reached in and pulled out a pair of panties, pressing it to my nose and inhaling deep. The scent of her made my head spin, and before I could second-guess myself, I slipped them into my pocket.

Then I moved back to her desk, pulling open the drawers one by one. Pens, notebooks, folded letters I didn't dare open. And then—a photograph.

A man I didn't recognize. His face half shadowed, his expression unreadable. But it wasn't the picture itself that caught my breath—it was the thick, red letters scrawled over it. *Remember.*

I frowned, staring at it a second longer before slipping it into my pocket. Later, I would find out who he was. Later, I would know why she had it.

My phone buzzed again.

Matty: Jace.

Matty: I hate you.

Matty: She just looked at me like she could see my soul.

Matty: SHE STILL HASN'T BLINKED!

I sighed, because really, I didn't have time for this. I was still investigating.

Me: Maybe she's impressed by your aura.

Matty: Or she's deciding how to season my corpse.

Me: Either way, you're doing great.

I turned to the wall above Riley's desk. If I was going to be in her space, I might as well take advantage of the opportunity. I reached into my jacket, pulling out the tiny camera I had brought. It was barely the size of a quarter, discreet enough that she would never notice. I affixed it in the corner of the wall, angled perfectly toward her bed.

Once it was in place, I stepped back, satisfied.

Checking my phone again, I saw that she was almost back to the dorm. *Shit.* I used her bathroom, knowing I wouldn't be able to go for the rest of the night.

I was about to take a sip from her water she'd left on the desk when my phone buzzed again.

Matty: This is a hostage situation.

Matty: She just asked if I believe in the astral plane.

Me: Go with it. Say you visit often.

Matty: . . .

I grinned, crawling underneath Riley's bed, settling in like I belonged there.

Another text.

> **Matty: Jace. JACE, she's smiling.**

> **Matty: I've never known fear like this.**

I typed out a quick *You're a hero*—just to bolster his self-esteem.

> **Matty: I swear to fuck, if I make it out of this, I'm setting your bed on fire.**

That was dramatic. I happened to like my bed. Especially after Riley had slept in it last night.

I tucked my hands behind my head, feeling pretty damn accomplished. Mission success. Riley had no idea I was here, Matty was out there making a new "spiritual connection," and all was right with the world.

Now, all I had to do was wait.

I had never been so fucking comfortable in my life.

Sure, I was lying flat on my back, crammed under Riley's tiny bed like some deranged stalker, my shoulder wedged against a rogue notebook she must've kicked under here at some point. My legs barely fit, and if I shifted too much, I'd probably take out the bed frame altogether.

But I didn't care.

Because I was going to be close to her.

I listened as the door finally creaked open, as her soft footsteps padded across the room. The rustling of her bag dropping to the floor. The sigh she let out—deep, tired. The sound of her kicking off her shoes, one hitting the wall near the desk, the other landing suspiciously close to my head.

I smirked.

Fucking perfect.

The bed dipped slightly as she sat on the edge, and I had to close my eyes, forcing myself to stay still. My entire body went tense at the realization that all I had to do was roll out from under this bed, and I could be touching her. My fingers curled into a fist against my chest.

You can do this, Jace. You're a legend. Absolute iron discipline inside you.

Her soft hum filled the room as she moved around, getting ready for bed. The sound of a drawer opening. The rustling of clothes. A pause. A tiny sniffle.

My smirk dropped. What the fuck? I turned my head slightly, trying to gauge her movements.

She sniffled again, and the sound hit me straight in the fucking ribs. Was she . . . crying?

I clenched my jaw. I'd burn the world down before I let anything make her cry.

Then, the sound of a yawn.

I exhaled slowly, relaxing against the cold floor. Not crying. Just exhausted.

That, at least, I could fix.

She'd been putting on a brave face, but I needed to pay more attention to how much sleep she was getting. Everything I read had said she needed a lot of rest with her condition, and I'd been messing it all up.

Riley shuffled again, and I listened intently as she climbed onto the bed, the mattress shifting above me. I could picture it so fucking clearly—the way she'd be curled up, her dark blonde hair spilling over the pillow, the soft rise and fall of her breath as she started to drift off.

So close.

If I lifted my hand, I could press my palm to the underside of the mattress, directly beneath where she was lying.

I wanted to.

To touch her, even if she wouldn't know.

Instead, I just listened. Memorized every tiny sound.

There was a long beat of silence, and then her breathing slowed . . . deepened. She let out a cute little sigh as she got comfortable.

She was asleep.

My chest fucking ached at how much I loved it, at how much I wanted this every single night.

At how much I'd do to make sure I got it.

I smirked to myself, adjusting slightly so I wasn't crushing my arm under my body. Tomorrow.

And then—

A barely there moan, softer this time.

Okay . . . so she wasn't actually asleep. I'd read that wrong.

I swallowed hard, my fingers curling against the floor beneath me. The sound was small, almost nothing. But I knew better. I *knew* her.

The mattress shifted again, and then there it was—the hushed intake of breath, the softest whimper.

My head tilted. My pulse roared in my ears.

Fuck.

She was touching herself.

Heat slammed through my chest, my throat, my gut. I bit down on my tongue, hard, trying to keep my own breath steady, but my control was slipping, fraying at the edges as I listened.

Another little sound. A breathy inhale that had my fists clenching, my cock going painfully hard beneath my jeans.

Did she know?

The thought sent a dark thrill through me. Was she thinking of me? Had she sensed me somehow? Had she noticed the missing things—

Or was she just *that* desperate for it tonight?

She shifted again, and I imagined it. Her hand slipping lower, fingers dragging over the softest part of herself, teasing, pressing—

My eyes squeezed shut, my control hanging by a fucking thread.

My cock ached, pulsing with every breath she took, every tiny sound that slipped past her lips.

I couldn't stop myself. My hand was already working at my jeans, dragging the zipper down as silently as I could manage. My dick was thick and desperate, the tip already slick as I wrapped my fingers around it, drawing in a tight breath as I gave it a slow stroke.

Was she thinking about what *my* fingers could do? How they pushed inside her. How I always found that perfect spot that drove her crazy every time?

The air in the room changed. Grew heavier. Charged.

Her breath hitched again, sharper this time, and I imagined her fingers slipping lower, circling, pressing inside. My grip tightened as I matched her pace, my breath growing uneven. I bit down on my lip, hard, barely holding back a groan.

The bed creaked as she moved, a soft exhale spilling from her lips. The sound sent a violent shudder through me. I pumped faster, my entire body strung so fucking tight I thought I might snap.

Another moan—higher now, breathier, her movements growing urgent. Her breath hitched, and then, barely above a whisper, she moaned my name.

"Jace . . ."

Fuck. Fuck. Fuck.

I kind of wanted to scream I was here, but that would probably ruin the vibes. We'd have to talk about this moment later on. We'd probably both agree how hot this was.

I wasn't going to last. It was a good thing I'd already proven how good my stamina was in previous encounters.

I clenched my teeth, my body going taut, burning with need as I worked myself harder, faster, my other hand trying to grip the floor like it might keep me from unraveling. But nothing could stop it now. Nothing could stop the way my body locked up, the white-hot pleasure that tore through me, so intense I saw spots behind my eyes.

I came harder than I ever had in my life, my body shaking as I spilled over my hand. My breath was ragged, my mind clouded with heat and hunger and something darker, something possessive.

Above me, the bed creaked one last time as she let out a soft, sated sigh.

I dragged in a shuddering breath, my cock still throbbing in my grip.

Fuck, that was hot.

————

A door slammed, and I jerked awake, disoriented, my heart thumping against my ribs.

For a second, I forgot where the hell I was.

Then I moved—*bang*—smacking my head against the damn frame of Riley's bed. *Right.*

I'd fallen asleep. *Under her fucking bed.*

Like a fucking lunatic. My hand covered in dried cum.

In my defense, it had been an *incredible* night—an orgasm straight from the gods, Riley's body above mine, her quiet, sleepy breaths in my ear as she drifted off. I'd planned on sneaking out before sunrise, but evidently my body had decided to sleep deeper than it ever had before.

I listened for movement, my ears straining for the sound of her breathing. But there was nothing.

Fuck. I'd been sleeping so deeply, I hadn't even heard her getting ready for the day.

I let out a slow breath, waiting a few extra beats just in case my ears weren't working. But the dorm stayed quiet, empty.

Carefully, I inched over, peering out from under the frame.

The coast was clear.

I slid out with practiced ease, rising to my feet and stretching out the stiffness in my muscles.

Her scent was still everywhere—wrapped in the sheets she'd just abandoned, clinging to the air. I inhaled deeply, letting it settle into my lungs, feeling it curl around my ribs like something that was attaching itself to my insides.

I stared at her bed, my fingers twitching with the need to take something from it.

Just a little *piece* of her.

Reaching down, I brushed my hand over her pillow, feeling the warmth still lingering from her skin. And before I could stop myself, I stripped the pillowcase off, bringing it to my nose and taking a deep inhale.

Vanilla. A little bit of citrus. A hint of something deeper, something uniquely *her*.

Yeah. This would do.

I bunched it into my pocket, smoothing out the bed like nothing had happened.

Tonight, when I went to bed, I'd have her scent wrapped around me. A reminder of last night. A promise of what was to come.

The first of many things she'd bring to my house.

Even if she didn't know it yet.

CHAPTER 14

JACE

Rolling my neck around because it turned out that sleeping on a cold, hard floor was actually not that comfortable, I headed across the green to the athletic building for weights. Pulling out my phone, I scrolled through it, blocking girls who had messaged me. I was going to have to change my number or hire an assistant to block numbers full-time because the amount of texts I received just through the night was ridiculous.

Now that I'd found the drama to my llama—my baby love to my . . . wow, I maybe should have spent more time sleeping and less time listening to the sound of Riley breathing. I would probably be making a lot more sense right now.

Ah, I'd missed some texts from Matty. He probably wanted to thank me for his fun night.

Oh . . . I'd missed *a lot* of text messages.

> Matty: Mayday. Mayday. HELP!

> Parker: Sorry, Matty-kins. It's date night.

> Matty: It doesn't matter if you are about to walk down the fucking aisle, I've got a major problem here.

> Matty: JACE!

Parker: Are you going to tell us what happened? Or are you just going to yell about it?

Matty: She's sitting across from me, and she did that thing.

Parker: I didn't know you had a date tonight?

Matty: Don't act like an idiot, Davis. We both know that Jace Fucking Thatcher asked me for a favor and then left me for dead while he does who the hell knows what.

Matty: Fuck. Fuck. Fuck. I'm scared to move. This is how horror movies start. With her.

Parker: Who's her? What's going on?

Matty: She's doing that thing.

Matty: Where you flip your eyelid inside out. She's doing it. Fuck. She just picked up a knife.

Parker: Casey and I are coming.

Matty: NO. DON'T BRING CASEY! IT'S TOO DANGEROUS!

The texts ended there. Huh, I was just getting into it.

The weight room smelled like sweat and rubber, the clank of metal on metal filling the space as I glanced around for Parker and Matty.

Slackers. If you weren't early, you were late. Or at least that's what someone had said to me once. I'd definitely have been late if it hadn't been for Riley so lovingly waking me up this morning, slamming her door as she left for class completely unaware that I was still in her room.

That reminded me. I pulled out my phone, checking to make sure she'd made it to her class okay.

> Me: I missed you last night.

I stared at the text I'd just sent her, hoping that it came across as more *I'm hopelessly devoted to you* than *I spent the night under your bed.*

Parker sidled in. My man looking very well fucked. "I hope you have a really good explanation for last night."

"The turntables have turned, QB," I told him as I laid down on the bench. He was going to love where I'd been last night. Possibly. *Probably.*

"What does that even mean?" he asked.

Before I could respond, the door burst open. Matty stumbled in like he'd been in a bar fight with a tornado, his hair a mess. He plopped down on the bench, a weird, haunted look on his face. He hadn't even looked this terrified when we had to help Parker dig up that old woman for his Sphinx trial.

"What happened to you?" Parker hissed. "I was all prepared to save your life, and then you never texted me back."

"Why didn't you just track him?" I asked, confused.

They both shot me a look, Matty's a little less friendly than necessary.

"I don't know, Jace. Maybe because I don't have a tracker on him."

"Only on Casey?" I said, wiggling my eyebrows at him.

He grinned and winked.

"Can we focus?" Matty hissed, poking me in the chest. I moved around my pectorals, and he scoffed.

"Just giving you something to aim for," I said, coughing and pretending to add more weights to the bench press bar as one of the coaches came in.

Parker casually grabbed some weights and started doing lunges.

"I just want you to know that you're going to owe me for the rest of my life," Matty spat, and he started spotting me.

"Dropping this bar on me is not going to make you feel better, my dude," I told him as I pushed the bar up.

"I'm not sure about that," he growled, and I shivered. Matty was definitely being spooky sexy right now. "She was a fucking lunatic." He glanced around like she was hiding in a corner and was going to overhear our conversation.

"Why are we whispering?" I whispered.

"Someone like that, you have to whisper about." He shivered.

I blew out a breath as I did another set.

"First of all, who is *she?*" Parker asked, sounding miffed because he didn't know what was going on.

"The love of my life's roommate," I answered matter-of-factly, causing both of them to give me the side-eye.

Which was ridiculous, honestly—at least on Parker's part. While Matty was still in the "multiple vaginas, one dick club," Parker was a bona fide rabid little love muffin, so wrapped up in Casey that I was pretty sure he wasn't aware that other women even existed.

Just like me.

"The love of your life's *psycho* roommate," Matty corrected me.

"Potato, Puh-tat-oh," I told him.

He ran a hand through his hair, his fingers shaking a bit. "I was supposed to keep her occupied, right? So I figured, easy, just take her somewhere to eat, make small talk, distract her for a while, and then I'd bounce."

"Good plan," I said with a nod.

His eyes widened, a strange, crazy glint in them as he stared up at me.

I stood my ground, because I wasn't an idiot. When a wild bear was staring at you, you had to stand your ground, or else it would eat you.

"It would have been a great plan, Thatcher, if you had answered your fucking phone and told me that you were going to be there *all night*. I wasn't going to let her in there with you while you were asleep. Who the hell knows what would have happened to you!"

"Huh, I don't remember getting that text," I mused, wondering if it had come during Riley's and my little orgasm sesh.

Parker did another lunge. "Can we get to the point?"

"Sorry my spiraling is too much for you," Matty growled.

I held in my snort as I racked the weights and pulled a protein bar out of my hoodie that I'd forgotten I'd put there.

"How can you have an appetite at a time like this?" Matty gasped like one of those olden-day maidens right before they fainted.

"Pretty sure Jace pulls out cookies during sex." Parker grunted, his face scrunched up as he sank down into another rep.

"That was one time," I drawled. "And I'll have you know, that an orgasm is much better with the taste of chocolate chip cookies in your mouth."

"You got crumbs on her boobs," Parker snarked.

"And then I got to lick them off," I said with a grin, before I remembered I hated all other boobs and all other girls, and no one else existed anymore except for Riley.

I was a born-again virgin starting from the moment I'd spotted Riley across that bar.

Matty made a strange choking sound, and we both looked over at him, concerned. His eyes were now bugging out a little bit, and there was a red color on his face that made him look a little like that Kool-Aid pitcher guy who Jagger used to be terrified of as a kid.

"She didn't blink," he choked out, even though I thought we had moved on and were talking about cookies now.

"That's not possible," Parker inserted helpfully as he started doing box jumps.

"I thought maybe I was imagining it, so I timed her. We were sitting in the common area, and she just *stared* at me. For a full two minutes. Straight face. No reaction. Nothing."

Parker grimaced. "Okay, that's a little creepy."

Matty snorted. "*A little*, he says. How about this? At one point, she started talking about dreams. Specifically, how she likes watching people sleep and then tries to guess what they're dreaming about. Like it's a hobby of hers."

We blinked at him.

"And *then* she asked if I ever wondered what people dreamed about right before they died. And THEN she *laughed*. Not a normal laugh, either. Like a movie villain laugh. Like she had a body in her closet just waiting for the right moment."

I wrinkled my nose at that. It wouldn't matter soon enough because I planned on moving Riley in with me as soon as possible, but thinking of her roommate watching my girl was unacceptable. Only I was allowed to watch Riley sleep, obviously.

Matty had my full attention now.

"Go on," I told him.

He scoffed, like I wasn't being super magnanimous.

I gave myself another pat on the back because my continued use of that word was excellent. Real *big brain* material. And they called Parker the smart one.

Scoff.

Matty ran a hand down his face. "So, at this point, I'm thinking I need to get somewhere *public*, fast. I suggest we go grab some food because, you know, normal people do that."

He sucked in a breath, eyes still wild. "Joke's on me."

Parker and I exchanged glances. "What happened?" Parker asked, like he already regretted it.

Matty threw his hands up. "She orders a glass of milk—with ice—stares at it for a full five minutes without drinking it."

"Where did you take her?" I asked.

Matty stared at me, aghast. "Does it matter?"

"I'm just saying . . . I wouldn't exactly call you a foodie," I noted.

"This coming from the man who thinks corn dogs and milk are a complete meal."

"Says the person who's never tried it. Trust me, if you've tried it, you would be talking differently. Iceless milk, of course, though."

"I took her to Ashwood Café. Are you appeased?"

"*Appeased*. I like that word, Matty-kins. Good job."

"Me too," Parker said with a grin. A supportive king right there. "But also, someone drinking ice with their milk is a sign of a monster."

"True serial killer behavior," I added so I could be supportive, too.

Matty side-eyed me like he didn't believe me.

"Continue."

"I tried to keep it light. Make conversation. I asked her what her major was. She answers, 'I study the way people fall apart.'"

Parker made a choking sound.

"She said this as the waiter showed up. He looked at both of us like we were nuts."

"Probably prevented him from spitting in your food," I offered.

Matty rolled his eyes.

"I ordered chicken—"

"As one does when there are no corn dogs around," I interrupted again.

"As one does when they are supposed to be *following* the team nutritionist's plan," Parker commented snarkily.

Okay, so he wasn't always a supportive king.

"I ORDERED CHICKEN . . ." Matty repeated loudly. Tank, one of our offensive linemen, looked over at the mention of food, and I waved him off.

As you were, gentlemen.

Parker and I both leaned in, sure the story was about to get good.

"So, she stares at my plate and then begins talking about how different bones taste. You know, *hypothetically*. She then says that she thinks femurs would be the best cut, if properly prepared."

"What the fuck?" Parker gasped, freezing on top of the box he'd just jumped on—right, we were supposed to be working out.

"Yeah. And then she just . . . *tilts her head* and goes, 'It's fascinating how marrow keeps us alive, isn't it?' Like she's personally tested the theory. As she drinks her iced fucking milk!"

Alright . . . I was feeling genuinely disturbed now. That girl slept by my angel cake every night.

"It got worse," Matty said, flopping back on the bench and staring at the ceiling. He possibly was going to need therapy after this. Unfortunate, but necessary, I guess.

The sacrifices we made for love.

"What could be worse than what you've already said?" Parker asked, looking flabbergasted.

"She asked me if I ever thought about what human flesh tasted like."

We both blinked at him.

"Sorry, what?" I asked, losing my appetite for what may have been the first time in my entire life. I slowly pulled the wrapper back over my protein bar and shoved it in my pocket.

"You heard me." Matty looked *traumatized.* "She said—*and I quote*— 'There's a reason people always compare it to pork. At least that's what the studies say.'"

"What did you do?" Parker asked, glancing around like he was now expecting her to pop out of the corner, too.

"You left, right?" I asked.

"Of course I left," Matty practically screeched. "I faked a phone call and told her my 'cousin' was in the ER. And you know what she did next . . ."

"What?"

"She just smiled—fucking *smiled*—and said, 'That's a shame. I was hoping to give you some . . . brain.'"

"Nope," I said, pulling out my phone and double-checking that Riley was still in class and not anywhere near this psychopath.

Parker gulped. "What kind of brain do you think she meant?"

"DOES IT MATTER?" Matty's voice was high-pitched again, and I rubbed my ears because that was . . . unpleasant.

The story *and* the voice.

"Moral of the story is . . . you owe me for the rest of your life."

"Do I, though?" I asked as I picked up my weights and started my lunges. "Because it sounds like you put me at risk for spending the night with a serial killer—the exact opposite of what I asked you to do, obviously."

His eyes were doing that bugging out thing that looked a little unhealthy. "Well, what were you doing? What did she do when she discovered you in her room?"

I waggled my eyebrows at him. "You're acting like she discovered me."

He hesitated. "This sounds worse than iced milk . . ."

I snorted and opened my mouth to tell him, of course, it wasn't worse than iced milk, it was true love—when Coach's booming voice echoed through the weight room. "Why the hell are all of you sitting around gossiping like sorority girls instead of lifting? You think the SEC is gonna roll over for you just 'cause you're funny?"

Matty let out a strangled noise, probably over the fact that Coach didn't seem to think his night with a demon was more important than working out.

Coach narrowed his eyes at the sound, because somehow he had ears like a bat—literally and figuratively. "You know what you need, Adler? Shuttle runs. Fifty of them. Now."

Matty let out another weird noise and a "motherfucker" and headed toward the door, only looking back to do that thing where you point at your eyes with two fingers and then point at the other person—me.

I huffed and turned back to my workout because, honestly, I wasn't the one who had failed in my duties.

And then I promptly turned my attention to what I was going to do to get Riley out of her dorm and safe at my place.

"What's that look?" Parker grunted as he started squats.

I just grinned at him. Because out of the three of us, he knew best what that look meant.

It meant I was going to win.

CHAPTER 15

RILEY

I stood in front of my closet; the door creaked open wider than my resolve, my hands hovering over hangers like I could *will* the perfect outfit to jump out at me. Jace's game was in an hour, and Casey and Natalie were meeting me there, which felt lifesaving, because the thought of sitting alone in that massive stadium made my stomach twist into a nervous little knot.

But what was I supposed to wear? Jace seemed to think I was hot no matter what I was wearing—case in point, my hoodie at the bonfire. But I kind of wanted to dress cute for once. The only UT apparel I had was from freshman orientation, and it was three sizes too big and fit like a tent. I chewed my lip, shaking my head as I reached out to grab it anyway.

Then I saw it . . . tucked between my cardigan and a pair of leggings, hanging there bold and smug like it owned the place. Jace's jersey. Orange and white, oversized, his number 77 stitched in block letters, his last name—*Thatcher*—sprawled across the back in a way that felt like a claim I hadn't agreed to yet.

I blinked, my hand freezing mid-reach, and I let out a soft, exasperated huff, rolling my eyes so hard I almost saw stars.

How did he even get it in here?

I hadn't seen him since yesterday when he'd dropped me off after class with that stupid, perfect grin, and I *definitely* hadn't invited him to sneak into my dorm and play wardrobe fairy.

But there it was, staring me down, and I couldn't help the tiny smile tugging at my lips, the way my heart did a quick, fluttery skip despite myself.

Jace Thatcher had a way of worming into my life, and I was starting to just . . . accept it.

I pulled the jersey off the hanger and held it up, my nose wrinkling as I debated. It smelled faintly of him—pine, sexy musk, that warm Jace-ness that made my cheeks heat—and I sighed, tossing it onto my bed. Fine. I'd wear it. Not because he'd planted it here. Okay, maybe a little because of that . . . but because it was easy, and maybe it would be alright to . . . give in for once.

I tugged it on over a white tank top, paired it with my favorite jeans, and yanked my fingers through the waves in my hair as I glanced in the mirror. The jersey swallowed me, the sleeves dangling past my elbows, his name huge across my shoulders, but . . . it looked cute. Maybe a cap would look good too.

I rolled my eyes again, muttering, "You win this one, Thatcher," under my breath.

A sudden knock rattled my door, and I jumped.

"Riley! Open up, woman!"

Natalie's voice burst through, loud and bright, followed by a softer, "C'mon, we're on a mission." That had to be Casey. I lifted an eyebrow. I was supposed to meet them at the stadium. Had I mixed up the plan? Hurrying over, I flipped the lock, and the door swung open to reveal Natalie bouncing on her toes, her blonde hair a wild halo, orange streaks painted on her cheeks like war stripes. Casey leaned against the frame dressed in a Parker Davis jersey, hands in her pockets, her silver-looking eyes calm but tinged with that quiet solemnness I'd noticed at the tailgate party.

"Hi? I thought we were meeting at the game?" I asked.

"Change of plans!" Natalie chirped, shoving past me into the room, her energy filling the tiny space like a glitter bomb. She spun around, hands on her hips, and grinned at Jace's jersey. "Oh my gosh, yes! Look at you, rocking the Thatcher vibe! He's gonna lose his mind when he sees this."

Casey stepped in more slowly, a small smile tugging at her lips. "Jace told us to come get you," she said.

Natalie made quotation signs with her hands. "He said to make sure his 'love muffin' showed up at all costs. His words, not mine, obviously. I would have used *sexy beast* or something much better than *love muffin*."

Casey snorted, grinning at Nat.

I blinked, a flush creeping up my neck. "He—what?" I squeaked, my hands fidgeting with the jersey's hem. "I was already going!"

"Psh, he wasn't taking chances," Natalie cut in, flopping onto my bed like she owned it, her legs kicking in the air. "He's, like, obsessed with you, Ri. He told us yesterday after practice—" Her voice dropped into a low growl that sounded nothing like Jace. "'Get her there. I don't care how, just do it.' So, here we are!" She grinned, wild and unapologetic, and I couldn't help the tiny laugh that slipped out, even as my stomach did a wild flip.

Casey leaned against my desk, examining the poster that Emma had hung over her wall, her dark hair spilling over one shoulder. "These No Drama Llamas tend to be pushy," she said with a grin. "But they mean well. *Mostly.*" Her eyes flicked to mine, and I got the distinct impression she was thinking of a specific situation I knew nothing about.

"I think we should change the group name to that Inner Sanctum one. It sounds much cooler," Natalie mused as she went through my closet like she was trying to see if I had anything she wanted to borrow—spoiler alert, I didn't.

"Group name?" I asked as I grabbed my school ID and some lip gloss off my dresser.

Natalie's eye roll was so epic I decided I needed to learn it. "Jace seems to think we need a group name. No one else agrees, but it's Jace, so we go along with it. What do *you* think our group name should be?"

"Oh, I—don't know. I mean, that's up to you guys," I said shyly.

Casey slid her arm through mine suddenly. "You *are* in the group, Riley," she said gently. "Welcome to the No Drama Llamas."

Natalie whooped and linked her arm through my other one. "We think you got a lot of potential, Riley St. James; don't let anybody tell you any different."

I grinned. "*Pretty Woman.*"

"See! Inner Sanctum material right there for knowing my favorite movie."

The girls dragged me out the door, and the walk to the stadium was a blur of girl talk, the late afternoon air crisp and sharp with fall. Natalie led the charge, her voice bouncing off the trees lining the path. "So, Ri, spill— how's it going with Jace? Like, are we talking full-on boyfriend vibes yet, or is he still in the 'I'm gonna charm her 'til she caves' phase?" She wiggled her brows, her orange nail polish glinting as she waved her hands.

I laughed, soft and shy, my cheeks heating. "I don't know," I admitted, tugging my cap lower. "He's calling me his girlfriend. But he's . . . a lot. It's nice, though. *He's* nice." My voice dipped, almost a whisper.

"And hot," Natalie responded helpfully.

I had an image of how he'd woken me up when I'd spent the night this week, his head in between my thighs.

Yes, very hot.

Natalie smirked as if she could read my mind.

"It's overwhelming, isn't it?" Casey murmured. "All that attention. Parker's the same way with me." Her eyes met mine, steady and kind.

"All that *attention*." Natalie rolled her eyes again, bumping Casey's shoulder. "You mean absolutely unhinged. Because Parker and Jace definitely have that going on." Natalie's grin was infectious. "Seriously, though, he's, like, a *smitten kitten*, Ri. I love this for you." She sighed. "I need to talk to my fairy godmother about the fact that the only football player I found was a cheating cockface." She muttered something that sounded a little bit like *That's all I deserve*, and I tilted my head, noting an edge of sadness in her gaze, a faint cloud I couldn't quite read.

"At least you had a chance to show off what a badass you are. You're practically famous now," offered Casey.

Natalie's face regained its smug, confident grin. "We believe in retribution in the No Drama Llamas. Hunter's just lucky I punched him in the face and not the dick."

I had no idea what they were talking about, but I was still smiling as I listened to them, loving this feeling of . . . belonging.

Jace's group was really good at that.

Jace was really good at that.

By the time we made it to the stadium, the energy in the air was a living thing, buzzing and crackling with excitement. The towering stands were already packed with fans decked out in orange and white, their voices a dull roar beneath the fight song blaring through the speakers.

Casey led the way, weaving effortlessly through the crowd as Nat clutched my wrist, dragging me behind her like an eager golden retriever. We maneuvered past the student section, heading lower, closer—so much closer—to the field than I expected.

A prickle of familiarity crawled up my spine.

My feet slowed as we reached the seats, my stomach twisting when I realized where we were. *The same seats Tasha had taken me to the last game.* Right up front.

"Wait." I glanced between them, suspicion creeping in. "How did you guys get these seats?"

Casey shrugged like it was no big deal. "Parker usually hooks us up. But these ones?" She grinned. "Jace."

Nat nudged me with a smirk, her eyes gleaming. "Jace wanted to make sure you had the 'best' view of him. Again, his words, not mine. He's nothing if not considerate."

I blinked, my brain struggling to catch up.

Jace.

Jace, who had once again gone out of his way to orchestrate another crazy spectacle.

The realization hit like a slow, warm flood in my chest. That sneaky, manipulative, insufferable—

I shook my head in mock exasperation, but I couldn't fight the way my lips twitched up, the way my stomach flipped in that dangerous, weightless way that only he could cause.

I was swooning.

Like, full-on, stomach-floating, heart-squeezing, brain-melting *swooning*. God help me.

"I'm just happy to be along for the ride when y'all's men get you such prime football real estate," Natalie declared, flopping into her seat, kicking her legs over the railing like she owned it. She undid the lid to her water bottle, taking a dramatic sip, then grinned. "Told you—he's got it bad."

Casey sat beside me, stretching her legs out, her hands clasped in her lap. "Natalie considers herself Tennessee's biggest fan," she said, a faint smirk playing on her lips.

"I don't consider it, I know I am," Natalie retorted. I giggled softly, but my attention was on the field. Watching a certain football player whose golden hair was peeking from under his helmet.

My heart skipped, my hands tightening on the seat's armrests, and I leaned forward, watching . . . my boyfriend showing off on the field.

A warmth bloomed in my chest despite the nervous flutter. The crowd roared louder, the drums kicked up, and I couldn't look away, caught in the glow of him, wondering what he'd do next.

The game began, and I could barely keep up with what was happening on the field. But every time Jace exploded across the turf, my stomach clenched, my breath catching in my throat. The way he moved, powerful and controlled, sent a thrill through me that had nothing to do with the game itself.

A burst of excited squeals erupted around me as the kiss cam flashed onto the giant screen above the field. The camera panned across the stadium, zeroing in on unsuspecting couples, each reaction more entertaining than the last. Casey and Nat immediately perked up, elbowing each other and giggling as they watched the awkward, sweet, and sometimes downright hilarious kisses play out. Some played along, kissing sweetly while the crowd cheered. Others got caught in awkward situations—one girl straight-up rejected the guy next to her, causing an entire section of the stadium to howl with laughter.

"Fuck, yes," Natalie wheezed. "That guy just went in for a kiss and got denied. That's what I like to see." She crossed her arms in front of her chest, nodding wisely. "You have to make them work for it."

I laughed, shaking my head as another couple popped up on the screen— an older man and woman who, despite looking a little shy, kissed to the roaring approval of the fans.

Casey nudged me. "See, football is fun."

Natalie scoffed, looking offended. "This is not football," she said primly. "This is human suffering in action."

Casey shook her head in amusement.

Another round of couples flashed on the screen, the camera lingering on a guy who had been sitting next to a woman clearly uninterested in him. The second she turned her head and started talking to someone else, the entire stadium booed him.

I was mid-laugh when the camera panned again—

And landed on me.

I froze.

Natalie sucked in a sharp breath, her hand flying to her mouth.

"Oh, shit," Casey whispered.

I barely had time to process the collective cheers that erupted around us before the camera zoomed in like it knew exactly what it was doing.

My mouth opened, shaking my head furiously. No. *No, no, no.* This was not happening.

Casey and Natalie were dying.

The camera wasn't moving.

"Seriously," I hissed, turning toward them. "Do something!"

"Like what?" Casey giggled. "Kiss you?"

I shot her a glare, my face blazing as I turned back toward the screen. Still there. I shook my head again, trying to silently convey for the camera to move on, please move on. But that only seemed to encourage the crowd, because the noise escalated, the whole stadium feeding off my embarrassment.

I was seconds away from sinking into the concrete when the screams suddenly intensified.

Like the entire stadium had collectively lost its mind.

I frowned. What was going on?

And then I saw him.

Charging straight off the field. Helmet off. Mouth guard gone. Number 77. Jace Thatcher.

My stomach dropped.

"What is he doing?" I choked out, hands flying to my face.

Jace leapt up on the railing in front of us. His golden hair was damp with sweat, his eyes locked right onto mine with deadly intent.

A whole stadium full of people screamed, chanted his name, and lost their damn minds.

I just sat there, completely paralyzed.

This was *not* happening.

And then it was.

Jace grabbed me by the back of my neck and kissed me senseless.

The world shattered. My brain short-circuited.

His lips crashed against mine with a ferocity that left me gasping, his fingers threading into my hair like he was trying to own me completely. I barely had time to react before he tilted my chin, deepening the kiss, his tongue sliding with mine in a way that sent fire straight through my veins.

A thunderous roar exploded around us.

People were screaming. Chanting. Whistling.

None of it mattered.

Because Jace. *Jace, Jace, Jace.*

The heat of his body, the grip of his hands, the absolute certainty behind every movement—I was drowning in him. His mouth moved against mine like he was starving for this. For me. Like he had wanted this for years. Like he needed me more than air.

I melted into him, clutching his jersey, letting him consume me.

I felt everything in that kiss.

Possession. Obsession. A promise.

By the time he finally pulled back, I was dizzy, my lips swollen, my entire body wrecked. Jace stared up at me, breathless. His eyes burned, his fingers tightening around my jaw like he couldn't believe I was real.

The stadium was still screaming, but I could barely process any of it.

Because Jace. Jace was looking at me like I was his entire world. "I've got one for you." He grinned, leaning forward so his lips brushed against mine once again.

"What is it?" I asked, an answering smile already forming on my face, noting that his eyes were a little dazed-looking, like he was just as affected by this as I was.

"What has two butts and kills people?"

"Um . . ."

"An *ass*assin."

I snorted, pressing my mouth against his for one more quick kiss because he made me so happy.

And then, because he was Jace, he did the most ridiculous thing imaginable. Somehow balancing on the railing, he raised his fists in the air like he had just won the Super Bowl, and then he jumped off the railing, back on the field and he . . . danced.

A whole-ass victory dance. Complete with hip thrusting that was definitely targeted at me.

The crowd went absolutely feral.

I gawked at him, still trying to get oxygen back into my lungs.

Before I could finish, Jace turned straight toward the camera, grinning like he had zero regrets about what had just happened.

And then—he shouted it. Into a microphone. On live television.

"I'M OBSESSED WITH RILEY ST. JAMES."

The stadium erupted again.

I thought the place had been loud before. But I was wrong.

Because now? Now, it was chaos.

Cameras zoomed in on my mortified expression, broadcasting my humiliation to a national audience.

And Jace? Jace looked so proud of himself. Like he had planned this entire thing.

Which—knowing him? Was not out of the question.

A furious roar from the sidelines broke through the moment. I glanced over and saw a guy—I assumed was one of the team's coaches—wearing a headset, his face nearly purple, veins bulging in his neck as he pointed an accusatory finger at Jace and barked something unintelligible.

Jace winced.

Nat snorted. "He's in so much fucking trouble."

Casey grinned. "Worth it."

Jace winked at me before—finally—trotting back to the sidelines, completely unapologetic.

"Chill, Coach. I was just"—he jerked his head toward me—"making the right play."

I groaned.

I was so, so screwed.

CHAPTER 16

RILEY

I pulled my phone from my bag, fingers absentmindedly swiping through my notifications as I waited for Jace to finish up in the locker room. The stadium crowd was thinning, the lingering hum of victory still buzzing in the crisp night air. My cheeks ached from smiling so much, my throat raw from cheering.

For once, I'd let myself enjoy the moment.

But then my phone dinged. I looked down, and my smile dropped. It was an email. From *him*.

My stomach plummeted, a sharp, ice-cold feeling cutting through the warmth that had been filling my chest just moments before.

The subject line was empty. Just my name.

And the message?

I can't wait to see you soon.

I stopped breathing.

A ringing noise filled my ears, drowning out the distant cheers and conversations around me. My body went cold, my fingers tightening around my phone so hard I thought the screen might crack.

No.

No, no, no.

I blinked fast, trying to swallow the panic, to shove it down into the deepest part of me where it couldn't suffocate me, but it was too late.

Because my mind had already cracked open.

And the memories spilled out like poison.

I was crying.

Soft, silent tears streaking down my cheeks as I sat on the edge of his bed, my hands clutching the sheets, gripping the fabric like it could somehow ground me.

"Don't be like this, Riley." Callum sighed, his voice laced with exasperation, like I was the one in the wrong. Like I was overreacting.

I wasn't. I knew that. But he was so good at making me doubt myself.

"You're hurting my feelings," he continued, his footsteps slow and deliberate as he crossed the room toward me.

My shoulders hunched automatically. Bracing. For what? I didn't know. Maybe for the words that would come next. Maybe for the hands that always followed.

I hated when he was disappointed in me. I hated when I made him upset. I hated that I cared so much.

"You didn't even try," he murmured, stopping in front of me. His fingers brushed against my cheek, his nails scraping lightly down my jaw. "You just lay there."

I flinched.

"I told you I wasn't in the mood," I whispered, but my voice was pathetic, breaking on the last word.

"You're never in the mood."

His fingers slid lower, wrapping around my throat, not squeezing, just holding. A quiet reminder.

A warning.

"But I always make it good for you, don't I?" he asked softly, lips tilting in a knowing smirk.

I nodded because it was easier. Because it was safer. Because I knew if I fought him on this, it would only get worse.

And I didn't want worse.

I shuddered, snapping back to reality so fast it made my head spin.

The stadium lights suddenly seemed too bright. The air too thick, pressing down on me like a weight I couldn't shake. I squeezed my eyes shut.

I was safe now. I was away from him.

He was still there, though, wasn't he? In my inbox. In my mind. In the way my body still reacted like he was standing right behind me. I glanced around, almost expecting him to be in the crowd, watching.

But of course, he wasn't.

I sucked in a deep breath, forcing my expression into something neutral. Something that wouldn't make Jace look too closely and see the cracks.

Just in time.

Because there he was.

His presence crashed into me before I could even prepare for it—arms wrapping around my waist, feet leaving the ground as he spun me in the air like I weighed nothing.

"Helloooo, Riley-girl," he murmured, grinning up at me as he held me close, my feet still dangling above the pavement. His eyes were so bright, so full of victory and joy and *me*.

I faked a smile, forcing lightness into my voice as I let my hands tangle in his damp hair. He deserved this—deserved my happiness, my excitement, my unwavering support. Jace had worked for this, bled for this, and the last thing I wanted was for my mess to taint it. So I lifted my chin, let my lips curve just enough, and pretended that the weight in my chest wasn't pressing down so hard it hurt.

"You were amazing, Thatcher."

And as he kissed my cheek, murmuring something cocky and sweet against my skin, I clung to the feeling.

To him.

The room was dark except for the faint sliver of moonlight filtering through the curtains, casting soft shadows over the sheets tangled around us. My body still hummed from him, my skin warm where his hands had been. But the afterglow wasn't enough to chase away the anxiety clawing its way through my chest.

"Riley," Jace murmured, his voice thick, aching with something deeper than just satisfaction. Love. I could hear it in the way he said my name. Felt it in the way his fingers traced my bare shoulder, slow and reverent.

I blinked, and before I could stop it, a tear slipped down my cheek, hot and unbidden.

Jace noticed immediately. His brows pulled together, concern flickering in his gorgeous brown eyes. He reached up, catching the tear with the pad of his thumb. "Hey," he whispered. "What's wrong? Did I—"

"Don't." I cut him off, my voice barely above a breath. I shook my head, swallowing past the lump forming in my throat. "You can't say my name like that."

He went still, watching me. "Like what?"

"Like you love me."

Silence stretched between us, thick, heavy. His hand lingered on my cheek, thumb brushing over my skin like he could smooth away the cracks forming inside me. But nothing could smooth them. Nothing could make them go away.

"Riley," he said again, softer this time, like a prayer, like he was trying to hold on to something slipping between his fingers. "I—"

"No," I interrupted, my voice breaking. I pulled back, needing space, needing air. "You don't get to love me, Jace. You don't understand. Love—real love—it doesn't save you. It ruins you. It takes everything you have and leaves you bleeding. And I can't—" My breath hitched, my fingers curling into the sheets. "I can't watch you bleed for me."

His expression didn't change. He didn't flinch or look away. He just watched me like he was trying to map every fracture, every hidden wound I refused to show.

"Who hurt you?" he asked, his voice quiet but firm.

I closed my eyes. Shook my head. "It doesn't matter."

His jaw tensed. "It matters to me."

I exhaled shakily, pressing my palm against my chest as if I could hold in everything threatening to spill out. But I couldn't. Not yet. Maybe not ever.

"Just don't say my name like that again," I whispered. "Please."

Jace swallowed hard, his fingers twitching like he wanted to reach for me again. Instead, he nodded, though the anguish in his eyes made my chest feel even tighter.

A war raged inside me, screaming at me to take it back. To let myself believe, even for a second, that maybe love wasn't what I thought it was. That maybe Jace wasn't like *him*. But the scars on my soul whispered the truth.

I turned away from him, curling onto my side, staring at the wall as another tear slipped free. I wanted to believe love could be something other than pain. But I knew better.

And Jace deserved better than me.

Minutes passed in silence, the only sounds the soft, steady rhythm of our breathing. My body was exhausted, my mind frayed, and eventually, my eyes drifted shut. But just as I teetered on the edge of sleep, I felt it—his fingers ghosting over my arm, the weight of his presence still wrapped around me like something unshakable.

Then, in the quietest voice, barely more than a breath, he whispered, "Someday, I'm going to say it. And someday, you're going to believe it."

I didn't move, didn't let him know I was still awake.

But the words slipped into the cracks of my heart, settling deep.

CHAPTER 17

JACE

There were exactly three things I didn't want to wake up to, especially after such a nice night of cooking a steak, having sex, and then watching my favorite movie before Riley had made me take her back to her dorm: One: A crying voicemail from my mom about her fear of dying before I give her any grandbabies.

Two: Darla Pinswallow's boobs.

Three: A fucking blindfold strapped over my face while I was clearly not in my own bed.

Guess which one I woke up to?

The answer: *all three*, if you counted the fact that Darla drunk texted both me and Matty in a group chat a photo of her guzzling a bottle of wine with her tits out. And then when I tried to delete it, I opened a voicemail instead and had to listen to my mom's existential crisis, sobbing about the fact that she'd probably die before I ever gave her grandbabies—which was actually Jagger's responsibility as the oldest, obviously.

Although now that I'd found my babycakes . . . I could probably be persuaded to fulfill that wish sooner rather than later.

But that was after I had ripped a blindfold off my face. After I clumsily reached for my phone to check the time and got bombarded instead. After I'd shoved it back in my pocket and realized I was not in my own bed.

I was instead . . . outside. High up. And judging by the way the air sliced across my bare chest like a fucking blade, I was nowhere safe.

I sat up fast, my body already on high alert, gravel crunching under my palms.

A slight tilt to the ground made my stomach lurch. And then—the wind, howling and ripping around me. And the distant wail of traffic below.

Looks like my second Sphinx trial had begun.

I blinked at the blinding city lights below me—*below* being the important word there. Because . . . I was on a rooftop. A high one. One that was still under construction if the unfinished concrete and steel beams sticking out like ribs were anything to go by.

I blew out a breath, dragging a hand over my face, wincing at the bits of roof gravel stuck to my palm. How the fuck had I been passed out hard enough not to notice being dragged out of my fucking bed? Had they drugged me somehow? I glanced around, trying to see if there were cameras watching me or something.

"Motherfuckers could've at least given me coffee first," I muttered, thinking longingly of that macchiato Riley had made me the other day.

That's when I noticed the envelope.

A red envelope, the Sphinx symbol stamped into the wax seal, sitting right next to me like a taunt. I sighed, snatching it up and tearing it open.

congratulations, jace. trial #2 begins now.

retrieve the item at the edge of the rooftop.

blindfolded.

no safety harness.

one way down.

find it yourself.

I stared at the note, then turned my head slightly to look at the very distant edge of the rooftop.

Then back at the note.

Then at the skyline, stretching out in front of me.

Then back at the note.

I dragged a hand down my face. "You've gotta be fucking kidding me."

"Alright, Thatcher," I muttered under my breath, rolling my shoulders. "You've survived worse."

Which—objectively—was debatable, considering I had never *actually* had to *blindfold myself and walk a fucking rooftop ledge* before.

But hey. First time for everything.

You know what would have been much better than this trial? Literally anything else.

What about a cook-off? Who could heat up a corn dog the fastest? Or a milk-drinking contest—no ice, obviously. Ooh, what about an obstacle course?

All of these things would be much more appropriate for a fucking *college* student.

Something else I would leave in my feedback along with my comment about welcoming snacks before trials. A cookie would have been great right about now.

This was the moment, though. The moment where any sane person—hell, even an *insane* person—would weigh their options.

Option A: I could just walk away. Call their bluff. Refuse to be their trained monkey. This wasn't exactly a legally binding contract. What were they gonna do, give me a bad Yelp review?

Option B: I could do the dumbass thing. Walk blindfolded across the ledge like I had some kind of death wish, risking a quick splat on the pavement below for the sake of a game I wasn't even sure I *wanted* to play.

It wasn't a hard choice. I *should* walk away. I should turn around, find the exit, and tell them to shove this little hazing ritual up their cryptic, Sphinx-worshiping asses.

But then . . .

Jagger's face appeared in my head.

My mystery of an older brother. My *Sphinx-member* brother.

If he had done this and survived, there was no way in hell I was backing out now.

Because I knew him. I knew he'd be sitting on his throne of smugness, just *waiting* to give me shit for failing the second trial. Even if I died, he would figure out a way to rub it in my face.

And there was no fucking way I was giving him that satisfaction.

I exhaled slowly, rolling my neck.

"Alright," I muttered. "Jagger lived. I'll live. Surely they wouldn't let me die, right?"

Right?

I pulled out my phone and fired off a text to Jagger.

> Me: Thanks a lot, asshole, for making me probably about to die due to our stupid sibling rivalry that shouldn't even be a rivalry because I'm obviously superior.

He didn't answer me.

I grabbed the black cloth that I'd tossed off earlier, feeling the rough, scratchy fabric between my fingers. *Cheap bastards.* "Blindfolded, huh?"

I mused, already tying it around my head. "Could've at least gone for silk. Maybe some lace, make it sexy."

I adjusted the knot, tugged it tight, then exhaled through my nose. And stepped forward.

The first thing I noticed?

The sound.

Wind howled past me, whistling through the unfinished beams like a fucking ghost orchestra. Every step forward made the gravel crunch, every shift in weight had the ledge feeling one gust away from taking me out.

This was so much worse than a football field.

On the field, I could see the chaos coming. I could anticipate the hits. I could feel the pressure but control it.

Here?

Nothing.

Just the wind, the height, and the fucked-up knowledge that one wrong step meant a headline that would probably read something like "College Football Star Mistakes Himself for a Bird."

I inched forward, feeling with my feet. My bare feet—since I'd been brought to this trial dressed in only my jeans. Considering I went to bed naked, that meant someone had handled me while I was unconscious.

"I hope you enjoyed the show, assholes!" I yelled into the night. "Must be tough knowing you'll spend the rest of your lives feeling inferior in the face of my dick size. Hope it was worth it."

These weren't even my favorite pair of jeans. They could have at least managed to put me in those.

I shivered because it got disturbing if I thought about it for too long.

One step.

Another.

Each one slow.

Each one deliberate.

Each one made me fully aware of the thousand feet of nothingness below me.

The fucked-up part? The one that probably made me a certifiable badass and something I would definitely be rubbing in Parker's and Matty's faces . . .

I liked it.

The rush. The pure, unfiltered adrenaline tearing through my veins.

My heart pounded, my body thrumming with that same high I got on the field—only bigger.

Darker.

Something about it felt good. The risk. The recklessness.

The certainty that one bad move could cost me everything.

I was made for this.

Just as I reached the edge, the whisper of a sound cut through the wind— a faint scuff of movement, barely there, but enough to send every nerve in my body firing at once.

My muscles tensed, instincts kicking in before my brain could catch up. The hairs on my arms rose, my breath stilled in my chest, and some deep, primal part of me screamed that I was no longer alone.

Before I could turn—before I could react—something slammed into my back.

A shove.

Hard. Brutal. Right between my fucking shoulder blades.

Air rushed past my ears as my body tilted forward, weight tipping over the ledge, gravity yanking me toward the abyss below. For half a second, I pictured it in my head—the vast stretch of city lights beneath me, a glowing sprawl of streets and steel, the dark ribbon of pavement that would have been my grave. Concrete death, waiting.

Then—

A yank.

A sharp, brutal snap at my waist, the sudden force jerking me mid-fall, snapping my body back so violently my teeth rattled.

I wasn't falling anymore. I was swinging.

A fucked-up human pendulum, arms flailing, legs scrambling for purchase as I dangled hundreds of feet above the city, my body twisting through the open air.

My brain barely managed to catch up before the sheer panic hit. My pulse roared, my breath coming too fast, too unsteady. I should be dead.

But I wasn't.

Something held me.

I fought to get my bearings, sucking in air, my stomach flipping as I twisted midair like a rag doll. My belt. There was something attached to my belt. I ripped off my blindfold.

A rope.

A near-invisible, black climbing harness had been clipped to me at some point—thin, sleek, strong enough to stop my fall but impossible to notice in the dark.

I clenched my jaw, dragging in one long, shuddering breath as realization over what had happened sank in. They'd fucking pushed me!

They'd fucking wanted me to believe I was going to die!

This wasn't just about seeing if I had the balls to walk blindfolded across the ledge. This was about trust. About seeing if I would hesitate. If I would question the game. Or if I would throw myself into the void, blindly believing the Sphinx had no intention of letting me die.

I forced my hands to unclench, flexing my fingers, feeling the tremor still running through my limbs. Slowly, I exhaled.

And I grinned.

"Alright, motherfuckers," I muttered under my breath, voice raw from the adrenaline still ripping through me. "I see how it is."

The line above me tightened.

I felt myself being reeled back up, slow and deliberate, my body dragged toward solid ground as if some unseen force had decided I'd had enough fun for one night.

Within moments, I'd flopped over the edge of the building, my heart still hammering like a war drum as I pulled myself all the way onto the roof.

And there, standing just a few feet away, was a single masked figure. Watching. Silent. His expression unreadable beneath the black mask.

In the thick, charged air between us, he clapped. Once. A slow, deliberate sound, slicing through the night like a knife.

Then, without a word, he turned and walked away, disappearing into the shadows.

I stood there, breathing hard, hands braced on my knees, my entire body humming from the experience.

Then I let out a low, breathless laugh, shaking my head.

"They really need to start providing cookies."

———————

I woke up to pain.

Not the dull, lingering ache of sore muscles or the bruises forming from my latest attempt at impressing a group of masked psychopaths. No, this was from a sharp, bone-rattling impact after I hit the floor face-first, limbs flailing, blankets twisting around me like some kind of fabric straitjacket.

The mattress above creaked. A slow, menacing breath filled the silence. And then—

"Jace."

I peeled my face off the floor just in time to see Matty's furious, sleep-creased face peeking down at me from the edge of the bed, his eyes bloodshot, his hair sticking up in seventeen different directions.

"What," he said, his voice flat, dangerously calm, "are you doing?"

I blinked at him. Took a second to assess.

Right. I had been in his bed. Not mine. That made sense. After barely surviving the trial from hell, I must've crawled in here at some point.

"I was snuggling," I admitted, pushing myself up onto my elbows. "Duh."

Matty's nostrils flared. "With WHO?"

I squinted. "With you, obviously. You were just asleep for it."

A vein in his forehead visibly pulsed. "So you got into my bed—without my consent—and snuggled with me?"

I scratched the back of my head, offended that he looked so angry. "I mean . . . yeah. No one was around to distract Riley's roommate, so I had to snuggle someone after my NEAR-DEATH EXPERIENCE!"

Matty launched a pillow at my face.

The door creaked open just as I caught the pillow, and Parker walked in because, even though he lived next door with Casey, apparently he had to start the day with his bestilicious bros.

He stopped short, eyes flicking from me on the floor to Matty looking homicidal, piecing together the fact that there clearly had been two people crammed into one bed before my abrupt eviction.

A long pause.

A very long pause.

Then, slowly, Parker nodded to himself, pivoted on his heel, and walked back out without a word.

Matty threw up his hands. "See?! Even Parker knows this is fucked!"

"Yeah, but he also just accepted it immediately," I pointed out. "Which, honestly, says more about us than him."

Matty groaned and flopped onto his back, muttering something about needing a new roommate and possibly an exorcism.

He kept mentioning that—an exorcism. Maybe I should just contact a church on his behalf. Or the Ghostbusters. It would be a nice little surprise for him.

I tossed the pillow back onto the bed and grinned, stretching like a cat.

"Anyway," I said, standing up and cracking my back. "We cuddling again tonight, or what?"

Hopefully by tomorrow, when my plan went into effect, Riley would be the one cuddling me, but in a pinch, Matty would have to do.

CHAPTER 18

RILEY

I stepped into the hallway of my dorm, my stomach full but my nerves frayed from the long day. All I wanted was to crawl into bed, pull the covers over my head, and pretend the world didn't exist for a few hours.

But as I got closer to my door, the heavy bass thudding against the walls sent a spike of dread down my spine.

What the hell?

A burst of laughter rang out from inside my room, followed by the unmistakable sound of a beer can being cracked open. I quickened my pace, sure that Emma must be watching a movie or something, because there was no way—

I shoved the door open . . . and about passed out. The room was packed wall-to-wall with bodies. I hadn't even known it was possible to fit this many people into that small of a room. Strangers lounged on my bed, red Solo cups in their hands. Smoke curled toward the ceiling, the thick pungent scent of weed mixing with stale beer. A group of guys were by the window, shouting over the music, a bottle of something dark being passed among them. Someone had draped a string of blinking lights over my desk, turning the entire space into a makeshift frat house.

What the *fuck*?

"Hello?" I shouted over the noise.

No one even looked at me.

I pushed through the crowd, my pulse pounding in my ears. A girl in a crop top stumbled past me, giggling as she sloshed her drink onto my room-mate's rug.

Speaking of my roommate.

Emma was sitting on her bed, pressed against the wall, her eyes bugging out as she stared at everyone. This was probably prime people-watching for her. I appreciated her sitting there while a group of strangers invaded our space.

Or were these her friends?

Glancing over at the mess of bodies, it didn't seem likely, but why else would she have let them in?

I grimaced when a girl fell back, her drink spilling all over my comforter. Seeing how sweaty the partygoers were . . . it was probably going to be cleaner for me to sleep out on the front lawn at this point.

"Get out," I snapped at the nearest person.

A guy with a backward hat and a glazed-over expression turned toward me, blinking slowly like he was trying to process my words. Then he laughed. *Laughed.* "Chill, sweetheart. It's just a party."

I clenched my jaw, my hands curling into fists at my sides. "I can see that. Now get out."

Someone cranked the music up higher, drowning out my words. More laughter. More people shoving into the room until I felt so claustrophobic I was close to passing out. I couldn't even move, there were so many people in here.

Before I could even *attempt* to get control of the situation, a loud knock boomed against the doorframe. Two figures stood there, silhouetted by the dim hallway lights. The taller one had a square jaw and a buzz cut, his uniform crisp, his expression unreadable. The other was shorter, stockier, with a tired look that said he had broken up one too many of these parties before. Their presence was enough to suck the air out of the party. The entire room seemed to freeze for a second before the music was cut off abruptly.

Campus security had arrived.

The two officers pushed their way inside, their eyes sweeping over the disaster that used to be my room. The smell of weed was undeniable despite the fact that someone had thrown open the window, and I could see things flying out as people tried to get rid of their contraband. One of the officers kicked an empty beer can aside before scanning the room, unimpressed.

"Alright," the taller officer barked. "Who's responsible for this?"

There was a beat of silence. Then, as if rehearsed, multiple hands lifted and pointed right at me. "It's her room," one of the girls—who I'd never seen before in my life, by the way—slurred to the officers confidently. "She invited everyone to the party."

"That's not true!" I screeched, panic rising at the look of disbelief on the officers' faces. I glanced around for Emma, who was suddenly conveniently missing. How had I missed her leaving? "I just got here. I don't even know these people!"

The shorter officer sighed, apathetic to my situation. "Well, that's not what the whole room is saying. We've got illegal substances, alcohol violations, and noise complaints. You've violated at least ten campus policies. Effective immediately, you're being removed from the dorms. You'll get a hearing later to decide if the campus will have further disciplinary measures."

My stomach plummeted. "But you have to listen to me. This isn't my party!"

"Pack your things. You've got until tomorrow morning to vacate."

The room erupted into murmurs as my world crumbled around me. The crowd, eager to escape consequences, started slipping out the door, leaving me standing in the wreckage.

A minute later, the room had emptied out, and the officers began their write-up.

"Where am I supposed to go?" I whispered as the shorter officer held up a device for me to sign, acknowledging I was receiving a ticket. I noticed there was nothing in the text forcing me to agree I'd committed the so-called crime.

"There's plenty of off-campus housing," he said, not sounding the least bit sympathetic to my plight. "Just be glad it's not any worse. It's going to take Campus Services days to fix this room up."

I glanced behind me, noting that most of the damage to the "room" happened to be *my* stuff and not the actual room itself. You could just throw it all away, and the room would be almost back to normal.

I decided to give it one more try. This couldn't be how the system actually worked—that you could be kicked out like this.

"Please. I didn't do this. I—I didn't even drink anything! You can do a Breathalyzer test on me! I literally just got here."

My voice cracked, and suddenly, I couldn't hold it in anymore. The overwhelming exhaustion, the stress, the sheer unfairness of it all hit me like a tidal wave. Tears welled in my eyes before spilling over, and once I started crying, I couldn't stop.

"I swear, I had *nothing* to do with this. I was at dinner, I came back, and my entire room was full of strangers! I told them to leave, but no one listened. Please, I *can't* get kicked out—I have nowhere else to go!" My shoulders shook as I swiped at my face, completely humiliated but unable to stop myself.

The shorter officer shifted uncomfortably. "Uh—"

The taller one sighed, rubbing a hand down his face. "Damn it."

The RA, who had arrived just in time to witness my breakdown, crossed her arms, eyeing me with something almost like sympathy. "She's right. I've never had trouble with Riley before. She's not the kind to throw a party."

The taller officer let out another sigh, looking more tired than annoyed now. "Fine. But if anything like this happens again, you're out. No warnings next time."

I nodded rapidly, still sniffling. "It *won't* happen again. I promise."

"Alright," he muttered, shaking his head and mumbling something and left. The RA followed them out of the room.

I slumped onto my bed, rubbing my temples. Falling back, I winced when I felt something wet, and I remembered that someone had spilled beer all over my sheets.

I exhaled sharply, staring up at the ceiling, my mind spinning.

At least beer-stained sheets could be fixed.

Too bad I couldn't say the same for the rest of my life.

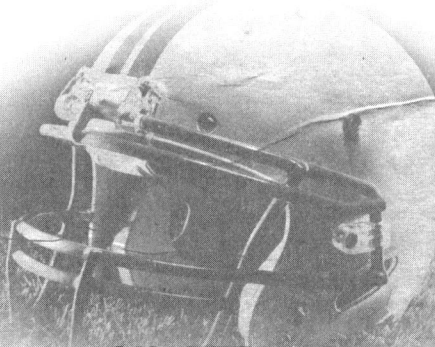

CHAPTER 19

JACE

Something was off. I felt it the second I dropped into my seat, the sense of something missing settling over me like a weight I couldn't shake.

Not because of anything obvious—not because my gut was twisting in warning or because my instincts were screaming at me to pay attention. No, it was something much simpler.

She wasn't here.

Riley was always here.

Parked near the window with her laptop open, pretending to be focused on something important while totally people-watching instead. I'd watch the way her eyes would flicker over the room, cataloging everything, catching every whispered conversation, every unspoken tension.

And the second I slid into the seat next to her?

She'd roll her eyes, let out that little exasperated sigh when I handed her the coffee that she loved, like my presence was an inconvenience, like she wasn't hyperaware of me, like she wasn't stealing glances when she thought I wasn't looking.

But today?

Her seat sat empty.

I pulled out my phone, flipping through my texts, searching for something—anything—but there was nothing. No memes. No sassy insults. No response to the lovesick text I'd sent her this morning just to get a reaction.

A weird, unwelcome feeling crawled up my spine, slow and suffocating.

Had I done something? Had I pushed too hard? Said something to scare her off?

I frowned. She hadn't been feeling well the last couple days. I'd caught the way she yawned between classes, the way she rubbed at her temples when she thought no one was paying attention. Riley never admitted when she felt like shit, never let on when she was running on empty, but I noticed.

I always noticed.

A sharp pulse of unease settled deep in my chest.

I needed to see her.

Now.

I pulled up the app, tapping into the camera feed I'd installed in her dorm. The screen flickered for half a second before settling into focus, and my chest tightened the second I saw her.

Riley.

In her bed, lying so still it almost didn't look real. Her body was curled toward the wall, one arm tucked beneath her pillow, the other resting limply on top of the blanket like she hadn't moved in hours.

I stared, my grip tightening on the phone, waiting for something—anything—to change. To show that maybe she was just sleeping in.

But she was too still, too silent, like the weight of something heavy had pressed her into the mattress and refused to let go.

A prickle crawled up my spine, my skin going tight, my instincts screaming at me that something was wrong. The longer I watched, the harder my stomach twisted, like a fist had lodged itself beneath my ribs and squeezed. I knew Riley. I knew how she moved, how she curled and stretched and burrowed under the covers when she slept. But this? This wasn't rest.

This was something else entirely.

What if it was her condition? What if she was having an episode? Fuck.

I shoved my chair back so hard the legs screeched against the floor, the loud sound cutting through the murmur of the classroom. The noise barely registered. My body was already in motion, muscles tensed, instincts screaming at me to move. My brain hadn't even caught up yet, but it didn't have to.

Because I knew.

The professor barely got a word out before I was halfway to the door, moving with a singular focus . . . my blood thrumming with urgency.

"Mr. Thatcher, where do you think you're—"

I didn't answer, and I definitely didn't slow down.

I didn't give a single fuck about whatever consequence was waiting for me for ditching class. Because nothing in that classroom mattered. Not the lecture. Not the grade. Not the fact that football depended on me keeping passing grades. None of it.

Not when something was wrong with *her*.

I sprinted across campus like a lunatic, shoving past people, ignoring the weird looks and the muttered complaints as I bulldozed through the crowd. The pavement blurred beneath my feet, dread growing with every step.

By the time I reached her dorm, my breath was coming fast, my entire body thrumming with urgency.

I didn't bother knocking. My fingers curled around the cool metal in my pocket, gripping it tight, and I slid the key I'd made into the lock, turning the handle and pushing the door open in one smooth motion.

The room was completely silent.

Riley was still curled up on her bed, in the exact same position as she'd been when I'd first looked.

Pale. Unmoving.

Fuck.

I moved toward her on autopilot, dropping onto the bed beside her. My fingers grazed her cheek. "Hey, Riley-girl," I murmured, my voice rougher than I meant it to be. "You decide that Ethics wasn't worth it anymore?"

Her honey-colored eyes flickered open and stared at me with complete . . . hopelessness.

Something in my chest twisted, deep and unrelenting.

Fuck this.

———

Riley

I knew the moment I drifted toward consciousness that getting out of bed today wasn't going to happen.

Not because I didn't want to—because fuck, I *wanted* to.

Because I *couldn't*.

My eyelids felt heavy, weighted down like they had been glued shut. Each time I tried to lift them, they fluttered back closed, my body refusing to cooperate, betraying me in the way it always did when I needed it most. It felt as if a lead blanket had been draped over me, pressing me into the mattress, siphoning away whatever energy I might have had left.

Every inch of me ached. A dull, relentless throb radiated through my limbs . . . through my bones. My head pounded in time with my heartbeat, and my muscles burned like I had been running in my sleep. But I hadn't been. I hadn't done *anything*, and yet my body still felt like it was punishing me.

I let out a quiet groan and forced my eyes open, only for my vision to swim.

The weak morning light barely slipped through the gap in my curtains, but even that was too much, the brightness stabbing through my skull like a blade. The sharp, searing pain in my temples made me wince, my entire body curling inward instinctively.

No.

Not today.

I couldn't afford this today.

I sucked in a shaky breath, pressing the heels of my palms into my eyes as if I could somehow will the exhaustion away, but it didn't work. It never worked.

I had already missed too many classes.

I was already so far behind.

I *had* to get up.

Swallowing hard, I blinked at the ceiling, trying to ignore the way my throat felt tight, like something was lodged there.

I could do this.

I *had* to do this.

Slowly, I forced myself to roll onto my side, bracing my hands against the mattress before pushing myself upright.

Pain shot through my back and down my spine, and the moment my feet hit the floor, nausea slammed into me like a freight train.

I sucked in a breath and bit down hard on my lip, trying to steady myself, but the room tilted.

I swayed, my knees buckling, and barely managed to catch myself against the nightstand.

My fingers dug into the wood as I squeezed my eyes shut, waiting for the dizziness to pass.

Just get ready. Just push through it.

I let go of the nightstand and shuffled toward the bathroom, every step feeling like I was dragging myself through wet cement. By the time I reached the sink, my hands were trembling, my breath coming too fast, too shallow.

Still, I turned on the faucet and splashed cold water onto my face, hoping it would help, hoping it would *do* something.

It didn't. Everything still felt *wrong*. Like my body had simply given up on me.

With shaking fingers, I grabbed my toothbrush, but the second I tried to lift it to my mouth, my arm barely made it halfway before it gave out.

The toothbrush slipped from my grasp, clattering into the sink.

I stared at it, my throat tightening, a lump forming that I couldn't swallow past. Tears burned the backs of my eyes.

This wasn't *fair*. I *hated* this.

I hated that no matter how hard I fought, no matter how much I pushed myself, my body still failed me.

I *wanted* to go to class. I *wanted* to be normal.

Grinding my teeth, I forced my body to move, snatching the toothbrush with a grip so tight my knuckles turned white. I wasn't going to let this stop me.

I *couldn't*.

But when I tried again, forcing my muscles to work, my legs buckled. I barely felt myself sink to the floor, gasping, my forehead dropping against the cabinet.

A strangled sob tore from my throat, and I covered my face with my hands, trying to keep it in, trying to breathe, trying to tell myself that this was just another bad day.

That it would pass. That it *had* to pass.

But sitting there on the cold bathroom tile, my body too weak to even hold itself up, it didn't feel like it would. It felt like this was going to be the rest of my life.

And Jace—he couldn't know. He couldn't see me like this. I didn't want him looking at me the way Callum used to, with thinly veiled disappointment, with impatience masked as concern. *"You're too fragile, Riley. Too much work. Too much trouble."*

Jace had fought for me, chased me down like I was something worth keeping. If he knew . . . if he saw me like this, broken and pathetic, would he still want me? Would he still look at me like I was his?

I squeezed my eyes shut, forcing down the nausea, the frustration, the fear. No. I wasn't letting him see this part of me. I wouldn't give him a reason to walk away.

I didn't know if I could handle that.

I had no idea how long I sat there, curled up against the cabinet, shaking, crying—hating every second of it.

Eventually, my body forced itself into autopilot. I crawled back to bed, my limbs screaming in protest. The second I hit the mattress, I pulled the blankets over my head and squeezed my eyes shut, ignoring the wetness staining my cheeks.

I'd set an alarm. I'd try again in an hour.

But deep down, I already knew.

I wasn't getting up today.

CHAPTER 20

RILEY

The weight of exhaustion pressed down on me. I wasn't just physically tired. I wasn't just tired from the ache of a sleepless night or the constant push and pull inside my own head—I was tired in my soul.

I stared at the ceiling, each second I lay there dragged, stretching out into eternity.

Would it always be like this?

Would I always feel like I was carrying something too heavy to put down?

I exhaled shakily, my fingers curling into the sheets. It hurt to exist. It hurt to wake up every day, to pretend like I wasn't suffocating. Jace made it easier, but even he couldn't fix what was broken inside me. And one day, he'd see that. He'd realize I was nothing more than a burden, a weight dragging him under.

What was the point in fighting the battle if the war had already been lost?

The thought crept in slowly, insidiously. Maybe it would be easier if I just stopped. If I let it all go. If I let the darkness take me.

No more struggling. No more fighting. No more pretending to be okay when I wasn't.

I rolled onto my side, staring at the sliver of sunlight filtering through the curtains. My heart thumped dully in my chest, a slow, steady beat that felt too loud in the quiet.

I just wanted it to stop.

Tears slipped silently down my cheeks, and I didn't bother wiping them away. What was the point? What was the point of any of it?

The exhaustion was crushing now, pressing against my ribs, wrapping around my throat. And for the first time since I'd left home . . . since I'd left Callum . . . I wasn't sure I had the strength to fight it anymore.

I squeezed my eyes shut, whispering a plea to no one.

I just wanted to rest.

I just wanted it to be over.

A key sounded in the lock, and I couldn't even muster the energy to look at the door.

The door clicked open.

I felt him before I saw him.

That ridiculous, overwhelming presence. That force of nature that bulldozed his way into my life and refused to leave.

The bed dipped, and warm fingers smoothed over my cheek, tracing along my skin like he was memorizing every inch of me.

"Hey, Riley-girl," he murmured, his voice low, teasing, but laced with something deeper. Something *worried*. "You decide that Ethics wasn't worth it anymore?"

I forced my eyes open.

He was staring down at me, his brows drawn tight, his jaw clenched. His hair was a mess—like he'd dragged his hands through it on the way over—and his hoodie was pulled on haphazardly, the strings uneven.

He looked . . . tense. Restless. *Wrecked.*

Over *me.*

My throat tightened.

"Jace . . . why are you here?"

My voice barely made it past my lips.

His hand curled into a fist on the blanket, his whole body tensing. "Better question—why the hell haven't you told me you weren't feeling good?"

I swallowed, my head pounding, my body so drained that even shifting on the bed sent a wave of exhaustion crashing through me. I tried to sit up, to prove I wasn't as weak as I felt, but the second I moved, sharp pain lanced through my body, and I collapsed back onto the pillow, gasping.

Jace cursed, his hands hovering over me like he wanted to *do* something, like he wanted to *fix* me. But there was nothing to fix.

This was just . . . *me.*

"Jace, you don't have to be here," I whispered, my voice weak.

His jaw clenched, his entire body going still.

The silence stretched, heavy and thick, and then—

"Don't *ever* say something like that again."

The words were quiet, but they were packed with so much frustration, so much *anger*, that I couldn't breathe.

I turned my face away, ashamed. I hated this. Hated feeling like this. Hated that he was seeing me like this.

"I'm just . . . tired," I whispered.

A muscle ticked in his jaw. His eyes darkened, a storm raging behind them.

"Yeah, I know," he said, voice low. "That's why you're stuck with me until you feel better."

"Jace—"

"Nope. No arguments." He shifted, stretching out on the bed beside me, bracing his head on his hand, his other arm draping across my stomach like he was *staking a claim*. Like he was *never leaving*. "You're mine, Riley. That means I take care of you. End of discussion."

———————

The room was quiet.

Jace hadn't moved.

I should've told him to leave. I should've shoved him off my bed, told him to go home, told him that I could handle this on my own.

Because that was how it always was.

How it always had to be.

I had spent my entire life being "too much" for people. Too much to deal with. Too much work.

They'd accused me of faking it, of being lazy, of exaggerating what was happening to my body so I could get attention.

I had learned a long time ago that the safest way to protect myself was to just . . . not let people in.

Because no one really cared.

No one *ever* chose me, prioritized me, tried to understand what I was going through.

Jace would be no different.

Except—

He was still here. He hadn't flinched. Hadn't pulled away. Hadn't *run*.

Tears burned in my throat.

I sucked in a breath, willing myself to push them back, but Jace—of course, *Jace fucking noticed*.

His fingers brushed against my jaw, turning my face toward him.

"Baby," he murmured, his voice softer now, like he was handling something fragile. "What's going on in that pretty little head of yours?"

I swallowed. "You're not supposed to be here."

"And yet, here I am."

I shut my eyes. "You don't . . . you don't understand. I don't get better. I get *through* it, and then it happens again. And again. And eventually, people get tired of dealing with it. Of dealing with *me*."

He was quiet for a long moment.

And then—

"You think I scare that easy?"

My eyes snapped open. Jace was looking at me like I had just personally *offended* him.

Like I had *wounded* him.

His fingers traced my cheek, his gaze burning into me. "I don't get scared, Riley."

I didn't blink. "I know I'm a burden," I whispered.

His eyes flashed. "Not to me."

Jace's voice was quiet but steady, filled with a kind of certainty that made my breath hitch. His thumb trailed over my knuckles, his grip warm, solid—like he was grounding me in place.

"You keep acting like letting me take care of you is some kind of burden, like it's asking too much," he murmured, his gaze locking onto mine. "Like I'm supposed to be scared of this . . . of you. But, Riley, that's not how this works. That's not how *we* work."

His fingers curled around mine, holding on like he had no intention of letting go. "Loving you isn't some fucking chore. It's not a weight around my neck, not something I have to suffer through. You *think* you're hard to love, but you don't get it. You don't understand that loving you is the easiest thing I've ever done."

I swallowed, my throat thick because he'd said it.

He'd said the L-word.

But he didn't stop.

"You think taking care of you is some kind of sacrifice, but it's a privilege, Riley. You hear me? *A privilege.* Every time you're struggling, every time you think you have to fight alone, I want you to remember that. I want you to remember that there's nothing in this world I'd rather do than stand beside you, carry you when you need it, and hold you up when you feel like you're falling."

His jaw clenched like he was trying to keep himself in check, but there was something raw in his expression, something that made my chest ache. "I love you, Riley. I love you when you're strong . . . I love you when you're barely holding on. I love you when you push me away, when you fight me, when you try to tell yourself you don't need me. And I will love you through every single bad day you have . . . through every single moment where you think you're too much."

He lifted my hand, pressing a kiss against my palm. "You're never going to be too much for me, sweetheart. You *are* my fucking world. And I'll spend every single day proving that to you if I have to."

I sucked in a shaky breath, terror gripping me in a way I didn't understand.

Because he said it like it was fact.

Like he had already decided.

Like I had no say in the matter.

Like I wasn't something that *burdened*—but instead, I was something that should be *protected*.

Jace leaned closer, so close our noses brushed. "Let me make something clear, Riley-girl."

My breath caught.

His fingers curled against my jaw. "You are mine. And I always take care of what's mine."

I exhaled sharply, my body too weak to do anything but *let* him hold me.

Jace pulled me against him, pressing my head to his chest, his heartbeat steady beneath my ear. "So stop fighting me on this, yeah?"

I wanted to.

God, I wanted to.

But I had spent my whole life fighting for myself. How was I supposed to just . . . stop?

Jace pressed a kiss to my forehead. "Close your eyes, Riley. Just this once, let someone else fight for you."

I squeezed my eyes shut.

And for the first time in forever—

I let myself believe that maybe, just maybe—

I wasn't alone anymore.

Maybe I should have fought harder when Jace picked me up.

I should have insisted that I could take care of myself, that I didn't need him to play hero, that I wasn't some fragile thing he needed to rescue.

But the second he lifted me into his arms, I was done for.

Because for the first time in my life, being taken care of didn't feel like weakness.

It felt like *safety*.

After driving us to his place, Jace carried me effortlessly through the front door, his arms wrapped securely around me, as if letting me go wasn't even an option he'd considered. His grip was firm but careful, his body warm and solid against mine, like he could steady me even as I drifted further into exhaustion. His familiar scent, pine and masculine . . . it was everywhere, pulling me deeper into the haze pressing down on me.

His hold on me never faltered as he moved through the house, his footsteps steady, purposeful, as if he had already made up his mind that this was exactly where I was supposed to be. When we reached his room, he didn't hesitate. He walked straight to the bed and gently laid me down, his movements careful, as if I were something precious, something fragile. The warmth of his arms disappeared as he straightened, and I instantly missed it, missed *him*, though I would never admit it out loud.

"You stay put," he said, pointing a finger at me like I was some kind of unruly child who might bolt the second he turned his back.

I sighed, my body already sinking into the comfort of his bed. "Not like I'm going anywhere."

He gave me a look like he didn't quite believe me, but after a second, he turned and walked out of the room without another word.

I let out a slow breath, staring up at the ceiling, waiting for the usual panic to settle in. Waiting for Callum's voice to fill my head.

But his ghost was unusually silent.

I found myself curling into the soft, warm blankets and letting my body sink deeper into his bed, letting the exhaustion take over before I could come up with a good enough excuse to push Jace away. By the time he returned, I was somewhere between sleep and consciousness, my body unwilling to fully let go, but the scent of peppermint and something warm pulled me back from the edge.

"Up," he ordered, his voice softer than usual but still carrying the same stubborn determination.

I cracked an eye open to find him standing beside the bed, holding a mug in his hand, one brow raised expectantly.

I groaned. "Jace . . ."

Ignoring me completely, he sat on the edge of the bed, slipping one arm beneath my neck to help me sit up, his touch careful but unyielding, like he had already decided there was no room for argument.

"I made you tea," he said simply, as if that explained everything.

I blinked at him. "You *made* me tea?"

His mouth twitched slightly, as if he were fighting a smirk. "I do have culinary skills greater than just heating up corn dogs, Riley-girl."

I eyed him suspiciously before hesitantly taking the mug from his hands, feeling the warmth seep into my fingers. "What kind?"

"Something for pain and nausea," he said casually, like he hadn't just admitted to looking up remedies for my symptoms. "I did my research."

Of course he did.

I took a small sip, the warmth spreading through my chest, the taste surprisingly pleasant. "It's not bad."

His smirk widened. "That's the highest praise I've ever received. I might frame a cross-stitch of that."

I rolled my eyes but kept drinking, ignoring the way he watched me like I might disappear if he looked away.

Then, without warning, he reached for my legs.

I stiffened immediately. "What are you doing?"

His hands curled around my calves, his thumbs pressing gently into the sore muscles.

"You get leg cramps sometimes, right?"

I sucked in a sharp breath.

Because, yeah. I did.

A side effect of the exhaustion. Something I just accepted, something I had never expected *anyone* to notice.

But Jace had.

His fingers moved slowly, carefully kneading the tension out of my muscles, his touch strong but soothing, and despite myself, I felt my body relax against the pressure.

I wanted to tell him to stop.

I wanted to tell him I was fine, that I could handle it, that I didn't need him taking care of me like this.

But the words wouldn't come.

Instead, a traitorous sound of relief slipped past my lips, and I immediately smacked a hand over my face, mortified.

Jace chuckled, the deep vibration sending warmth down my spine.

"See?" he said, his voice full of smug amusement. "I *do* know what I'm doing."

I glared at him from between my fingers. "You're—"

"Amazing? A gift? The best thing to ever happen to you?"

I groaned. "Something like that."

His grin was downright *obnoxious*.

But I let him keep massaging my legs.

And when he was done, he pushed the mug back up to my lips, watching with that same infuriating intensity as I drank.

"You don't have to do all this," I mumbled.

His jaw ticked. "I know I don't."

I swallowed, setting the mug aside. "Jace—"

"Riley."

He reached out, brushing a knuckle down my cheek, his touch impossibly gentle.

"You think I'm doing this because I *have* to?" His voice was quiet now, low and firm, like he was willing me to believe him.

I didn't answer.

Because I didn't know how.

Jace exhaled, his forehead dipping to rest against mine, his breath warm against my skin.

"Listen to me," he murmured. "You could be tied to this bed for weeks, and I'd still want you. I'd still be here."

Tears burned my eyes.

Because he *couldn't* mean that.

"You say that now," I whispered. "But I'm a burden."

His grip tightened on my jaw, not enough to hurt, just enough to make me focus.

"That's the last time you *ever* say that to me."

I swallowed. "But—"

"No. I don't do pity, Riley. You think I love you because you're perfect? You think I give a shit if you need extra care?"

I couldn't breathe. Because . . . I wanted to believe him. So badly.

He leaned in, voice dropping to a whisper. "I'll ruin anyone who makes you feel like you're too much. *Even yourself.*"

A tear slipped down my cheek.

Jace caught it with his lips, kissing it away like he could take the pain with it.

I didn't know what to say.

So, I didn't say anything.

Instead, I finally exhaled.

I finally let go.

And when Jace pulled me into his arms, I let myself be held.

Because maybe, just maybe, he meant every word.

For three days, he had been there—skipping drills and dodging his coach's wrath, sleeping next to me when I drifted off, waking me with water, his voice a low hum through the fog.

Jace . . . He held me like I was worth it, like my broken pieces fit his jagged ones. By the fourth day, the fog lifted, my body lightened, and he grinned, all teeth and triumph. "There she is—my girl's back."

I'd laughed, weak but real, and knew then—he'd carved a space in me no one else could touch.

That night, the air in the bedroom shifted—soft and heavy, a quiet hum from the radiator weaving through the stillness, blending with the sound of our breaths as we sat on the bed. The comforter was a tangle around our legs; it kind of felt like a shield against the world outside. Jace was sprawled beside me, his golden hair a beautiful mess from my fingers running through it earlier, his shirt clinging to the broad lines of his frame, hinting at the strength beneath. I caught his gaze—those brown eyes, warm and glinting with something softer than his usual cocky smirk—and my chest tightened, a pull I couldn't resist . . . a pull I didn't *want* to resist.

Not anymore.

"Jace," I whispered, my voice a fragile thread as I reached for him. My fingers brushed his jaw, rough with a day's stubble, and he caught my hand, pressing it to his lips. His breath was warm against my skin, a tender kiss that sent a shiver racing through me, and the world shrank—just him, just me, this delicate, perfect moment suspended in the dim glow of the bedside lamp.

"You want some more peppermint tea, don't you?" he said proudly, moving to get off the bed.

I huffed softly, because he was a professional at making peppermint tea at this point. But what I wanted . . . was something more.

"Jace," I murmured, brushing my hand down his chest. His eyes widened, and he gulped dramatically.

"Riley-girl, I—"

"Give me what I want, Jace Thatcher."

"Are you sure?" His voice was raw, quiet, a plea edged with restraint. "I don't want to rush you, sweetheart. Not if you're not ready."

The sweetness in his words made my chest tighten, stealing the air from my lungs.

I swallowed hard, my fingers curling around his, brushing over the rough calluses on his palm—the marks of a man who had clawed his way to the top with sheer will. And now . . . now he was here, looking at me like I was something he was willing to fight for, too.

"Jace," I murmured. "I want this. I want you. More than anything." I blew out a breath. "I *need* you."

His breath hitched at that, the sound making warmth unfurl in my stomach, slow and aching. He gripped my waist, his fingers spreading across my skin through the thin fabric of my tank top, like he was memorizing every inch.

"Fuck, Riley," he whispered, his voice breaking with awe. "I've missed this."

He lifted the hem of my shirt, peeling it up with care, baring my skin to the soft light, and I shivered—not from the chill. But from him . . . from the way his eyes traced me, like I was a treasure he'd uncovered, a star he'd pulled from the night sky.

I raised my arms, letting him slip the tank top over my head, the air cool against my flushed skin as it fell away. My breath caught as his fingers grazed my ribs, mapping me with a tenderness that felt like a promise, like he was seeing every part of me, the scars, the freckles, the shaky rise and fall of my chest . . . and loving it all.

My hands were trembling as they moved to his shirt, tugging it up and off. I needed to feel him, his warmth, his skin against mine. He helped me, pulling it over his head, and I traced the planes of his chest with my fingertips, worshiping all the taut muscle . . . the abs that made me wet just thinking about them.

"Please," I breathed, my voice laced with need as I pulled him down, our mouths meeting in a kiss. It was gentle at first, then deepened, our tongues tangling together as he licked into me. He groaned, a low, reverent sound that vibrated through my chest.

Pulling back, his eyes met mine . . . searching. "You're sure?" he pressed again, his voice thick with concern. "You *really* feel up to this?"

"I'm sure," I whispered as I leaned in, kissing him again, slow and deep, pouring every ounce of trust into it. He exhaled against my lips, a shaky, relieved sound.

"You're so fucking beautiful," he rasped, his voice gravel and silk as his lips trailed fire down my throat, nipping my pulse hard enough to make me gasp. My head tipped back as he kissed lower, hungry and relentless. He palmed my breasts, his thumbs flicking my nipples until they were hard points, and a spark of pleasure shot straight to my core.

I moaned, loud and unashamed, and his smirk was dark and wicked as his mouth descended, sucking one peak harder, his tongue swirling, teasing . . . driving me wild.

"Jace—" I whimpered, my hands fisting his hair, tugging as he devoured me, his teeth grazing just enough to sting, then soothing with a slow, wet lick that had me writhing beneath him. His fingers dug into my hips, sliding down to rip my leggings off with my panties in one rough tug so I was completely bare.

I was dripping, my legs falling open as I panted for him. My nerve endings ignited until it felt like I was *glowing*. I clawed at his shoulders, pulling him back up, my lips crashing into his, tasting him as I ground against his hard body, desperate for more, for all he could give me.

He yanked off his sweats, and my breath snagged, a sharp, needy gasp as my eyes locked on his cock, heat surging through me.

It was always a treat when he didn't wear briefs.

He was hard and thick, a gorgeous, pulsing promise in the half-light, and I bit my lip, my thighs clenching as a desperate ache flared deep in my core. My hands trembled, itching to touch, and I reached for his cock, my fingers grazing his hips, pulling him closer as my voice broke free, low and ragged.

"Come here," I begged, a hungry edge to the whisper, and he obeyed, hovering over me, his body a scorching shield, his skin blazing against mine as he pinned me to the bed.

Jace's mouth found mine in a fierce kiss. It was a clash of lips and tongues, and he devoured me, his groan vibrating through my chest. I arched up, pressing myself into him, my nails raking down his back, feeling the flex of muscle as he growled against my lips, the sound igniting me further. His hands gripped my waist, rough and urgent, and I shivered, bare and burning under his gaze, his brown eyes dark with lust, drinking me in like I was his last breath.

"My gorgeous girl." His voice was a broken plea as his hands roamed over my skin, gripping my thighs, spreading me wider as he slid his dick against my thigh, hot and insistent. Every inch of him was a tease that made me ache.

I reached down, my fingers wrapping around his length—hard, velvet steel under my touch—and he hissed, a feral sound that sent a thrill racing through my insides. I guided him to me, rubbing his tip against my wet folds, teasing us both until I couldn't stand it, until my hips bucked up, demanding him.

"Now," I pleaded, my voice cracking with want, and he groaned, low and guttural, his hands clamping onto my hips as he thrust in, deep, hard . . . filling me in one fierce stroke that stole my breath. My head slammed back against the pillow with a cry.

"Fuck, Riley," he growled, his voice rough and exultant, his hips snapping against mine in a rhythm that was wild and relentless. Every thrust was a claim, a fire searing through me. I wrapped my legs around him, my heels digging into his ass as I pulled him deeper.

I met him, thrust for thrust, our bodies slamming together in a desperate, perfect dance. Jace's mouth found my neck, and he sucked hard, marking me, his teeth grazing my skin as I moaned, loud and free. The sound was raw and untamed as it echoed off the walls . . . a song I never wanted to end.

"Yes, yes, yes," I chanted, my hands clutching his shoulders, my body arching as he drove into me. His cock was hitting that spot deep inside that made my vision blur . . . that made sparks ignite behind my eyes. His rough fingers found my clit, rubbing fast and firm, slick with my arousal.

I shattered, a scream tearing from my throat as pleasure crashed through me—hot, blinding. My walls clenched around him, pulsing hard as I came, shaking and lost in the wildfire of us.

"Riley—fuck, that's it," he groaned in a broken voice. He kissed me, swallowing my cries as he thrust through my orgasm, dragging it out in a faltering rhythm, his hips jerking as he chased his own release. I clung to him, urging him on, and he growled, a primal, desperate sound as his hands gripped my thighs hard enough to bruise.

He slammed into me one last time, his cock pulsing inside me as he came . . . a shudder ripping through him, his groan loud and ragged against my ear.

We collapsed in a sweaty, trembling tangle as his weight pinned me to the bed. His chest was heaving against mine as we gasped for air, our breaths harsh and mingled in the quiet. Pressing his forehead to mine, he kissed me . . . slow and messy and perfect.

Jace's hands cupped my face, holding me like I was fragile, precious, even after all that heat. "Riley," he rasped in a hoarse . . . awed voice. "You're— Fuck, you're everything."

I shivered, every part of me still tingling as my hands traced his back, feeling the marks I'd left. I was shaky and sated as I smiled, my lips brushing against his.

"I love you," I whispered. The words spilled out of me, soft . . . and true.

His groan was almost pained this time as he rolled us so that I was sprawled across his chest. His arms wrapped tight around me as his heartbeat thundered beneath my cheek.

"I love you, too," he murmured, his voice a low rumble, and I looked up at his face, only to grow wide-eyed as I watched a tear slide down his cheek. "Always."

The word wasn't just spoken—it was etched into the space between us, into the warmth of his body pressed against mine, into the quiet reverence in his eyes as he looked at me like I was his world. His voice, thick with emotion, wrapped around me like a vow, binding us tighter than anything physical ever could.

Another tear slid down his cheek, catching in the faint light, and something inside me clenched—something deep, something fragile, something I hadn't dared to name before him. I reached up, brushing it away with my thumb, lingering, memorizing the way his skin felt beneath my touch, the way he didn't flinch, didn't pull away.

Jace Thatcher, reckless and untouchable to the world, was letting himself break for me.

I had never seen anything more beautiful.

My heart ached in the best way as I whispered, "Say it again."

His lips curled in the faintest, most heartbreakingly tender smile I'd ever seen. And he leaned in, his forehead pressing against mine, our breaths mingling . . . our souls stitched together in the silence.

"Always."

A promise. A truth. A love so deep it felt inevitable, like gravity itself had brought us here.

And as I held him, as his arms tightened around me like he never intended to let go, I knew—he wasn't just saying it.

He meant it.

I dozed off against his chest, feeling our hearts beating, basking in the glow he brought me.

But there was a shadow that crept in. The one that always hovered over me. And now that I'd given myself fully to Jace, that shadow rooted to me with real fear.

Because he loved me.

But he didn't know my secret.

And he never could.

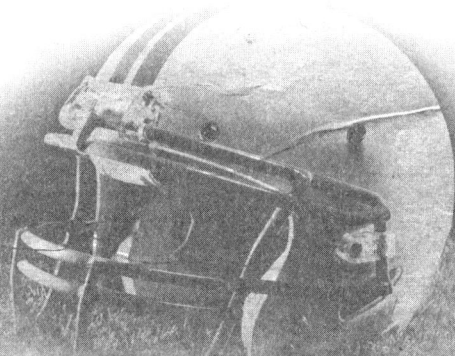

CHAPTER 21

JACE

I leaned back in my chair, staring at my laptop screen, frustration burning a hole in my patience. The party had *somehow* failed to get Riley kicked out of her dorm. I blamed her hotness. And her sweetness. *And* her overall perfection. Campus security would have had no choice but to let my baby angel face off the hook.

I should have thought of that.

Planted a body in there or something. I bet they would have had to kick her out, then. Except I was trying to get her kicked out of the dorms . . . not the school . . . so maybe murder was a bit too extreme.

And then I'd thought after I'd taken care of her that she would just *want* to move in at that point, unable to part with the love of her life.

But nope. Riley was nothing if not stubborn.

So, I was on to my next plan.

"I thought the World Wide Web was supposed to be helpful," I muttered, scrolling through an article titled "How to Get Someone Evicted From Student Housing Without Actually Committing a Crime." It was shockingly *unhelpful*. And possibly fake because these ideas were really bad.

"Why do you always call it the 'World Wide Web'? Why don't you just call it the internet?" Matty mused.

He was across the room, lying on our couch, eyes glued to his phone, idly scrolling through whatever nonsense occupied his tiny attention span.

"Because that's not its name. What do you think 'WWW' even stands for, Matthew?" I drawled, clicking out of yet another worthless article. He let out a half-hearted grunt, which evidently was about as much effort as he was willing to put into this conversation.

I sighed, rubbing my temples because it turns out thinking was hard.

I was too pretty for this.

"What's your worst nightmare as far as sleeping arrangements go?" I mused, willing my big brain to wake up.

Mine was clowns. Waking up with one of the freaky devils leering over me with those red balloons. Not sure they all came with balloons, but they probably did. That would be sure to get Riley out of her room.

And possibly into a mental institution.

An image of Emma's wall poster came to mind then. Riley had to look at that every day. Apparently, clowns *weren't* actually an issue for her.

I shivered thinking of the poster . . . and Emma.

I would still only go there as a very last resort. Just in case. There were some things you just couldn't come back from.

Matty didn't even look up. "A cult moves in next door and tries to recruit me."

I rolled my eyes. "Be serious."

"I *am* being serious."

"Okay, give me a different one."

"Darla's mouth." He shivered and then finally glanced at me. "Why?"

I shrugged, feigning casual interest. "Just curious."

Matty squinted at me. "Why are you saying it like that? It's definitely for a reason." He sighed. "Am I going to have to track you again? Because I really don't think I can do it." His gaze took on a wide, haunted look. "I can't go through that again."

I snorted. I still wasn't convinced of his whole cowboy hat story.

That shouldn't make you haunted. That should make you . . . learn technology better.

"You'll only need to track me if it's a worst-case scenario, Matty," I told him reassuringly. He shivered like he was imagining it right now.

The front door opened, and Mr. QB himself, Parkie-Poo von Davis, walked through the door. *Alone.* Which was surprising. He and Casey were usually attached at the hip outside of football hours.

"Just the man I was looking for, since Matty over here has the imagination of a geriatric squirrel."

Parker raised an eyebrow, a smirk on his face as he glanced between the two of us. Matty was muttering to himself, but that wasn't anything new, so I ignored him as I continued my quest.

"What's your worst nightmare as far as sleeping arrangements go, Davis?" I drawled, clicking on another link that was titled "Kidnapping and Why It's Effective."

He stretched, cracking his neck as he thought about it. "I dunno. Rats? No, wait—roaches. No, wait—*bedbugs*." He shuddered. "Yeah. Definitely bedbugs. Once you got 'em, you gotta burn your whole damn life down and start over. Walker once had bedbugs in a hotel during an away game, and he had to get rid of everything he had with him." He shivered again.

Something clicked in my brain.

I straightened in my chair and typed *buy bedbugs* into the search bar. The second the results loaded, I grinned and let out a victorious whoop.

Parker cocked his head. "Why do I feel like I just helped you with something crazy?"

I winked at him. "It's only crazy if it doesn't work. Everyone knows that."

Matty shook his head. "Literally no one says that. How have I become the reasonable person in this group? Do you know what that says about us?"

"Good things, Matty, my man. Only good things. You'll definitely need that level head once you fall for that stalker of yours," I said, clicking on a link to a sketchy-looking pest control supplier.

Matty scoffed, but I ignored him again because my plan was finally back on track.

I looked up at Parker. "Davis, I could kiss you. This is definitely going to work."

Matty sat up, alarm creeping into his expression. "Oh no."

I turned the screen toward him. "Oh yes, you mean. You can buy dead bedbugs in bulk. *Bulk*, Matty. This is my destiny."

Matty recoiled like I'd just suggested we start eating raw sewer rats. "What the *fuck* is wrong with you?"

"Where do I even start?" I clicked the add to cart button. "We sprinkle some of these in her bed, tip off the RA, and—boom—housing crisis. She'll have to leave."

"Okay, first of all, this is deranged. Second, do you *hear* yourself? You are willingly ordering *dead bugs* off the internet."

"Sounds like true love, if you ask me," Parker said, sounding completely serious. A man above men right there, obviously.

"Your cock hasn't experienced true love, Matthew. It's still tainted by Darla. One day you will understand."

Matty groaned and flopped back onto the couch. "For the hundredth time, Darla's mouth did not touch my cock. And also, you better pray I never do fall in love. Because if I become like you—something that will never happen, mind you—we'll be lost and probably all end up in prison."

I ignored him, clicking through the checkout process. "Standard shipping or overnight?"

Matty covered his face with both hands. "Oh my God."

"Overnight it is."

I hit confirm, then sat back, feeling deeply, profoundly satisfied.

Matty peeked at me from between his fingers. "You do realize that when Riley finds out, she's going to actually murder you, right?"

Parker leaned on the table next to me, grinning as he looked at the screen. "You mean *if* she finds out."

I also grinned. "*If* is my new favorite word."

Matty let out a long sigh, staring at the ceiling. "I'm totally going to have to use the tracker again."

Riley

I dragged myself into the room, every muscle in my body aching. I was still recovering from my episode, and even though I was a lot better—thanks to Jace—I wasn't back to normal. Or at least *my* normal . . . which was still much more exhausted than most people.

Now that I'd opened up to Jace . . . now that I told him that I *loved* him . . . a strange terror had taken over my insides. Like how at any moment he might find out about Callum and change his mind. I'd been tempted to tell him about it while we lay on his bed yesterday, tempted to test how far that "always" extended . . . but I couldn't bring myself to do it.

Jace . . . was becoming a necessity, a tether to what felt like my own personal miracle when the rest of my world felt like it was slipping through my fingers. He was the sun cutting through my storm clouds, a god I wanted to worship even as I feared what it meant to need him.

I just need sleep, I decided. I needed to let the darkness pull me under for a few hours, and when I woke up . . . my head would be on straight, and I wouldn't be so weirdly terrified.

Emma was staring at a textbook and not me at the moment, so I might as well take advantage of it.

I yanked my covers down, desperate to disappear beneath them—until I saw it.

Something small and dark. And *scuttling*.

I shrieked, scrambling backward so fast I nearly fell off the bed. My pulse was pounding in my ears as I watched the tiny shape disappearing into the folds of my sheets.

"No, no, no," I muttered, pressing a hand to my chest, forcing myself to breathe. "Woman up, Riley. It's probably just lint. Lint with legs. Lint that moves."

I glanced over to see Emma . . . watching me.

Because, of course she was. Now I'd gotten her freaking attention.

"I thought I saw something in my bed," I offered lamely, even though I didn't owe her an explanation. Not since she'd solidified herself as the world's worst roommate a hundred times over after that party.

When she didn't say anything, I turned back to the bed, tempted to just sleep on the floor rather than deal with this.

I leaned forward and peeled the covers back again. My stomach twisted.

Definitely not lint. It was small, oval-shaped, and a sickening reddish-brown. Okay, but it wasn't moving.

Any relief went away when I pulled the cover back more and saw a whole bunch of the same spindly-legged creatures.

I was going to be sick.

"Ah!" I screamed.

Across the room, Emma was moving off her bed. "What—" she murmured, before stiffening. Her eyes flew open. "What is that?!" she shrieked, flinging herself upright, her hands slapping wildly at her arms and legs like she was being electrocuted.

"Oh my gosh. They're on your bed, too?" I gasped, standing on my tiptoes like that would protect me from the infestation currently happening.

"THEY'RE ON ME! THEY'RE ON ME!" she wailed, still swatting at herself.

And then in a truly spectacular display of blind panic . . . she turned too fast, lost her balance, and smacked straight into the wall with a *thud*.

Silence.

"Emma?" I whispered.

She slid down the wall, eyes fluttering shut as she crumpled into a heap on the floor.

Okay, sometimes it felt like I actually lived in an alternate reality since coming to this school . . . and this was one of those moments.

I gawked at her unconscious body, my heart still racing.

Shoving my hair out of my face, I forced myself to move, peeling back my sheets farther. My stomach churned as more of the tiny brown shapes scattered.

Nope. Nope, nope, nope.

My whole body recoiled as the realization sank in. *Bedbugs.*

As if summoned by my misery, the RA burst into the room, breathless. "What's going on? I heard screaming—" Her gaze dropped to Emma, still unconscious, then to my bed, then back to me.

"Emma?" she yelled, dropping to her knees next to Emma's body.

"There's bugs," I squeaked, pointing to my bed.

On cue, Emma groaned from her place on the floor. Her eyelids fluttered, and for a second, she just lay there, blinking sluggishly at the ceiling. Then, realization dawned in her expression. Her head snapped up, her gaze darting wildly around the room until it landed on me, then the bed.

"Are they gone?" she asked, her voice small and hoarse.

I hesitated. "Uh—"

She let out a bloodcurdling scream. "THEY'RE STILL HERE! FUCK! THEY'RE IN MY HAIR!"

Emma shot upright, flailing like a possessed marionette, slapping at her arms and shaking out her hair so violently that I instinctively took a step back.

"Emma, breathe—"

"I CAN FEEL THEM CRAWLING! THEY'RE EVERYWHERE!" she screeched even louder, spinning in panicked circles before she ran straight into the dresser. The impact sent her sprawling back onto the floor with a groan.

The RA exhaled sharply, rubbing her temples. "Fucking hell. I don't get paid enough for this."

Emma groaned from her place on the floor. "Where are we supposed to go?"

The RA pinched the bridge of her nose, looking genuinely stumped. "That . . . is a great question. You can't sleep here, but I don't exactly have a backup plan for a full-on bedbug infestation. Um . . . ." She glanced around like someone was going to pop out from the closet or something and give her an answer.

My phone buzzed in my pocket. I pulled it out with shaky fingers, my brain still trying to process the nightmare unfolding around me.

Jace: Miss you.

I stared at the screen, my heart stuttering. My chest felt tight, like the weight of the entire evening had suddenly doubled. Before I could overthink it, I typed back.

> **Me: There are bedbugs in my room. Emma knocked herself out. I'm being evicted.**

The three little dots appeared almost instantly.

> **Jace: Be right there.**

I blinked at the screen, still dazed. I wasn't sure what response I expected, but it definitely wasn't that.

Barely ten minutes later, the sound of heavy footsteps pounded down the hall. The door flew open, and there he was—Jace, dressed in sweatpants and a Tigers hoodie, his eyes immediately scanning the room before locking onto my sheets. He took one step closer, leaned over the bed, and squinted.

Then he gagged. Loudly.

"Nope. Absolutely not," he announced before marching straight toward me. Before I could protest, he scooped me up effortlessly and slung me over his shoulder like I weighed nothing.

"Jace! Put me down!" I yelped, pounding at his back.

He ignored me completely, adjusting his grip like I was a damn duffel bag. "Buckle up, buttercup. You're staying with me."

CHAPTER 22

RILEY

T he second Jace carried me over the threshold like some old-fashioned groom, I knew I was in trouble.

Not the kind of trouble where you get caught sneaking back into your dorm after curfew. But the kind of trouble where the ground beneath you shifts, where you look around and realize you've walked straight into the lion's den. And the lion? He was grinning like he'd already won.

Jace kicked the door shut behind him, his grip on me firm like he thought I'd try to bolt. To be fair, I probably should have. Instead, I was too busy processing the absolute absurdity of my life. I had bedbugs. My dorm was unlivable. My weird-ass roommate had screamed herself into a concussion. And now, I was being princess-carried into the home of the man who was way too happy for a college junior about to have a live-in girlfriend.

Matty was slumped on the couch, a bag of chips open on his lap. He took one look at me, one at Jace, and exhaled like he had seen this coming from a mile away.

"Dude." Matty's tone was pure resignation. "You actually did it. You kidnapped her."

Jace smirked, finally setting me down, but not before his fingers flexed like he was reluctant to let go. "She came willingly."

Matty gave me a look that said *Did you, though?*

I ignored it because if I thought too hard about how fast all of this had happened, I might actually scream.

Jace didn't give me time to process anything. He took my hand and pulled me toward the hallway. "Come on, Riley-girl. Let's get you settled."

"Do you have a guest room?" I asked, because as bad as it was to be moving into his house . . . it was definitely too much for me to be in his space every day, sharing his room.

"Nope." He led me into his room and did a little *ta-da* move.

Jace didn't hesitate. The second we stepped inside, he strode over to the dresser and got to work. I hovered near the doorway, watching as he grabbed my bag, unzipped it, and started pulling out my clothes, neatly stacking them in one of the open drawers.

"Wow," I muttered, crossing my arms. "No fear at all, huh?"

He barely glanced at me, his smirk pure arrogance. "Fear of what?"

I gestured vaguely. "I don't know . . . The possibility that my stuff is now riddled with microscopic parasites?"

Jace scoffed, completely unconcerned. "Nah."

I narrowed my eyes. "Nah?"

He shot me a look over his shoulder, like I'd just said the most ridiculous thing in the world. "Not worried about it."

I frowned. "You're not worried about bedbugs?"

"Not even a little."

That was . . . odd. Most people would be at least mildly concerned. Hell, I was concerned. I'd spent the entire drive over mentally cataloging everything I owned, trying to determine what could be salvaged if the infestation had made it into my things. But Jace? Zero hesitation. Like he knew something I didn't.

A strange feeling slithered down my spine, but before I could dwell on it, he kept unpacking, pulling out my socks, my shirts, my sleep shorts—each one folded and placed away like he'd done this a million times.

That was when I saw it.

Not the drawer he was filling. The one he wasn't.

It was already full.

My steps slowed as I took it in.

I stopped cold. "Jace."

He turned, looking at me with that lazy, infuriating confidence, like he knew exactly what had me gaping. "Yeah?"

I lifted my hand, pointing toward the dresser. "Is that—"

"Your drawer?" he finished for me, strolling over to pull it farther open. Inside were things that *should not be there*. My favorite brand of socks. A sleep shirt that looked suspiciously like it was my size. Even the same type of hairbrush I used.

I moved to the closet next, opening the door, my stomach tightening when I saw hangers. Empty space. Room for me.

His bathroom? My shampoo. My conditioner. My brand of body wash.

I turned slowly, my pulse a steady drumbeat in my ears. "Jace."

He leaned against the doorway, arms crossed, expression unreadable. "Riley."

I swallowed. "What the hell is all this?"

He pushed off the frame, walking toward me, every step deliberate. When he stopped in front of me, he tilted his head as if he were amused I'd even asked.

"I like to be prepared." His voice was smooth, just the right mix of teasing and something darker. "And this? Was always going to happen."

A shiver ran across my skin, and I wasn't sure if it was from his voice, his presence, or the sheer weight of what he had just said.

I opened my mouth. Closed it. Then finally managed, "I can't decide if this is the creepiest thing anyone has ever done for me or—"

Jace cut me off before I could finish. "Charming."

I narrowed my eyes. "That's not what I was going to say."

"Sure it was." His lips twitched. "Riley-girl, you wouldn't be standing here if you didn't like it."

I made a sound that was dangerously close to a scoff, even as I was very aware that he was right. "That's a bold assumption. This is only until I can find another place."

His grin sharpened. "I don't assume."

There it was. The thing that set Jace apart from every other guy I had ever met. It wasn't just confidence—it was certainty. He pursued me with the same single-minded focus he probably used in a game. No hesitation. No doubt.

I stepped back because I needed space. He let me, but there was something in his gaze that said *only for now.*

I swallowed, then turned abruptly, heading back toward the living room because I needed to be anywhere else before I did something stupid.

Matty was still on the couch, halfway through his bag of chips, completely oblivious to the emotional warfare I had just endured.

He glanced up, raising an eyebrow. "You good?"

I sat down hard, grabbing a handful of his chips and stuffing them into my mouth before answering. "No."

Jace strolled in like he owned the place—because, well, he did—and dropped onto the couch next to me, throwing an arm over the back like it was the most natural thing in the world.

Matty chewed thoughtfully. "You look like someone who just realized they're in over their head."

I pointed at him. "Exactly."

Jace made a dismissive noise, reaching over to pluck one of Matty's chips out of the bag. "She's fine."

I turned to glare at him. "I haven't decided if I'm fine yet."

He flashed that lazy, arrogant smirk that made me want to throw things. "You will."

I groaned and flopped back against the couch, my mind spinning with everything that had happened tonight.

This was insane—*we* were insane.

Jace winked, though, all cocky confidence and unshakable certainty, and I couldn't stop my answering grin. The warmth that spread through me wasn't fear or doubt—it was something terrifyingly close to *right*. Like no matter how twisted or obsessed we were, this was exactly where I was meant to be.

Jace

She was finally here for good. In my bed. Wrapped in my sheets. Breathing in my space.

I lay beside her, watching the slow, steady rise and fall of her chest. Her lips were slightly parted, her hair a mess against my pillow, the strands catching the moonlight filtering through the blinds. Too pretty. Too perfect. And completely mine.

She slept with one hand curled beneath her cheek, her body relaxed in a way I'd never seen before. That should have been a good thing, but all it did was remind me how much I needed to keep her here.

My cameras—strategically placed—gave me every angle of the room so I could watch her when I couldn't be here. There was one trained on the bed and another covering the entrance. A final one was in the corner near my dresser, positioned to capture the room's entire layout.

I should have been satisfied, I should have closed my eyes and gone to sleep, but I wasn't done.

My fingers curled around the tiny device Jagger had sent me. Small. Subtle. Undetectable. Just like he promised.

I moved carefully, pressing it against her skin and firing the tracker beneath the soft curve of her shoulder. She stirred slightly, a quiet moan escaping her lips. My breath caught, watching her lashes flutter, but the sleeping pill I'd slipped into her drink at dinner had done its job. She didn't wake.

A slow grin curled my lips. Perfect.

I tucked the device away and shifted closer, pulling her against me, inhaling her scent. Soft. Sweet. Addictive.

She was finally right where she belonged.

———————

By the time the sun filtered through the curtains, I was already up, moving silently in the kitchen. Matty sat at the kitchen island, freshly back from a jog, drenched in sweat and looking like he wanted to murder someone. He was stirring his protein shake aggressively, eyes narrowing at me as I cracked eggs into a pan.

"What are you doing?" Matty grumbled, eyeing the ingredients I had set out.

"Making breakfast."

"For yourself?"

I smirked. "For Riley."

He groaned, taking a long gulp from his drink. "You're acting suspicious."

I flipped the eggs with practiced ease. "I'm always suspicious."

"No, this is worse." He leveled a glare at me. "You look . . . smug."

"I have a lot to be smug about."

Matty groaned. "Jace. There's obsessed, and then there's Parker. Think about who you want to be when you grow up."

I grinned, sliding the eggs onto a plate. "Maybe Parker wants to be *me* when he grows up."

Matty shook his head, muttering something about how I was insane. I ignored him and piled Riley's plate with exactly what I knew she liked— fluffy scrambled eggs, crispy bacon, and a stack of pancakes with just the right amount of syrup. I grabbed a fresh cup of coffee, made exactly how she drank it, and balanced it all on a tray before heading back to the bedroom.

When I pushed open the door, Riley was stirring, her hair a tangled mess, her skin flushed with sleep. She stretched, blinking up at me as I set the tray down beside her.

"You made me breakfast?" she mumbled in a husky voice.

I smirked, leaning in and brushing a kiss against her lips before moving the tray over her lap. "You've finally given me what I want, and surprise— there are major rewards."

She scoffed and grabbed her fork, stabbing a big bite of eggs. "I slept so good last night," she said as she slipped the food into her mouth . . . looking appropriately impressed with my kitchen skills.

I fought back another smirk, knowing exactly *why* she'd slept "so good." I made a mental note—next time, no sleeping pill. I had better ways to make sure she slept soundly, ones that involved more orgasms, which were always better than drugs.

She took a sip of her coffee and shook her head in disbelief. "A girl could get used to this, Thatcher."

"That's the goal," I murmured, watching with satisfaction as her jaw dropped and a slow blush crept up her cheeks.

Good. Let her start getting used to the idea. Because she wasn't going anywhere.

CHAPTER 23

JACE

Practice wasn't supposed to be easy. It was supposed to push us until our lungs burned, our legs screamed, and our heads pounded like we'd been each smacked with a brick.

And for the most part, it did.

But that didn't mean we weren't gonna talk shit the whole way through it.

"Being a dick won't make yours bigger, Matty," I told him as I lined up wide, rolling my shoulders as Parker barked out a new play. Matty was next to me, cracking his knuckles like we were about to throw hands instead of running drills. He scowled at the reminder of his missing quarter inch.

"Alright, listen," I called as Parker took his stance. "If you're gonna risk your life for a secret society, you should at least get something out of it. I don't feel like I'm getting the proper respect from these people."

I caught the ball from the JUGS machine and turned upfield, shaking my head. "And why do I feel like my life isn't worth as much as Parkie-Poo's? Do they not even realize how awesome I am?"

"I mean they haven't given me much." Parker grinned. "A mysterious envelope with pictures I happened to need to secure my future wasn't much of a gift, considering they made me dig up a fucking body."

Parker rifled a pass straight at Matty's chest—hard enough that he staggered back a step when he caught it.

"I would like to point out that I helped dig up that body, too," Matty said, his eyes doing that bugging-out thing again. "And what have I received? Nothing."

"Did you help, though, *Matthew*? All I can picture from that night is you all pale and shaky, while Parker and I dug up a corpse."

"Do you hear yourself right now? You just dropped the word *corpse* like it's the same thing as walking a dog," Matty griped.

"'Corpse' is just another word for *dead broad*—which means *woman* for all you non-big-brained people out there." I caught another ball from the JUGS machine, making it look easy as usual. "And I happen to be very good with women."

"This is a really weird conversation," Manning, one of our freshman wide receivers, commented from a few feet away.

"That's why it's rude to eavesdrop," Matty said, all of a sudden getting all growly and scary-looking. I could see it when he did that, how it was possible for him to get the ladies.

Not to mention having a dedicated stalker.

All I'd had stalk me so far was the three-nippled girl.

The eighth wonder of the world when you thought about it. Must be those baby blues Matty had going on. They must be stalker-worthy to some people . . . who obviously hadn't seen me yet.

"I'm just saying," I said, jogging past him. "Two near-death experiences and a fun new fear of blindfolds."

"And absolutely no snacks," I muttered as an afterthought.

Matty snorted. "Maybe your third trial will be easy."

"Wouldn't that be nice." I reached for my helmet, flipping up the visor. "What's the ROI on getting shoved off a building, though? Parker, you got anything in that big brain on that subject?"

Parker flicked the ball at me, shaking his head. "It seems like they help out when you least expect it."

"The problem is that they gave us all those expectations when they put the bags over our heads and shoved us into the basement. Remember all the 'You will be rich and powerful' things," Matty said in a weird, deep voice. "That was a mistake on their part. They set the expectations too high. My trials haven't even started yet."

"I agree with that," I said, holding up my hand for a high five in solidarity . . . which he ignored.

"Why do you sound so shocked about agreeing with me?" he growled, his eyes straying over to the silver car sitting in the parking lot . . . the one that happened to always be in the parking lot at practice.

I slung an arm around Matty's shoulder and nodded toward it. "So, Matty . . . are we ever gonna acknowledge her, or are we going to keep pretending she doesn't exist? Because I'm thinking she's your soul-mate."

Matty groaned. "Or she's related to Darla . . . and I can't live through that again."

Parker raised a brow. "It sounds like you've put some thought into it, though—the whole soulmate thing."

Matty muttered something under his breath. "I have not put *any* thought into it."

I hummed the first lines of "Love Story," and he acted like he didn't even know what I was humming, even though everyone knew I had excellent pipes.

He could ask Riley—she'd seen my performance firsthand.

I grinned. "Matty's in loooove."

"Or Matty's about to lose his teeth. She could have one of those walls in her house that she's decorated with memorabilia," mused Parker.

"We should talk to Riley and Casey about upping their game in that regard," I said, once again thinking it was irrational that Matty had such dedication.

"Agreed," Parker said, giving me the high five of solidarity that Matty wouldn't, and showing why he deserved his place as number one bestili-cious bro today.

"Can we just focus on football?" Matty groaned, running a hand down his face. "Fuck. You guys act like I'm about to get kidnapped."

I squinted at the car again, at the girl hidden behind a big pair of sun-glasses . . . and hat. Because evidently, she didn't think that was obvious. "I mean . . . we don't *not* think that."

Matty threw up his hands. "I hate both of you."

Coach's whistle blew again, and we lined up for another rep. I flexed my hands, ready to run the route, when Parker called out, grinning, "Alright, run it back, and it would be great if both of you could try not to get murdered before the season's over."

Matty groaned.

Parker snapped the ball.

And I took off, grinning the whole fucking way.

———

I was in such a good mood after practice, I couldn't help but fuck with Jagger.

Me: How's the mafia?

Jagger: I don't know how many times I have to tell you . . . I'm not in the mafia.

Me: I'm positive that's exactly what someone in the mafia would say.

Jagger: . . .

Me: I'm going through my checklist here.

Jagger: Your checklist?

Me: Yes, my mafia checklist. And it's quite clear . . . you're definitely in the mafia.

Jagger: Okay . . . this list. Tell me five things on it that make me mafia.

Me: You wear suits all the time.

Jagger: So do a lot of people who work.

Me: You do sketchy things at night that you tell me you can't talk about.

Jagger: I don't think I've ever said I can't talk about them.

Me: Ok, so talk about them.

Jagger: Maybe I don't feel like talking about it right now. And besides, we're supposed to be going through your list, so it wouldn't be relevant.

Me: Right. I'm going to go ahead and check that one off.

Jagger: Thank you.

Jagger: Wait, by check it off, you mean check it off, right. As in, it's not applicable.

Me: Applicable. I like that word. Seems like a mafia sort of word.

Jagger: . . .

Me: As I was saying . . . you have lots of money. Despite me not knowing what exactly you do.

Jagger: Just because you don't understand what I do, doesn't mean that I've been weird about it.

Me: Okay . . . tell me what you do.

Jagger: As I've told you, I'm in the procurement industry.

Me: As in guns.

Jagger: Don't say guns!

Me: Why? Because the FBI is monitoring your texts.

Me: Because you're in the mafia.

Jagger: . . .

Jagger: Don't say mafia.

Riley chose that moment to walk through the door, and I swooned a bit at the thought of her using the key I'd given her. And her living with me every day.

And her having lots of sex with me. Starting right now, obviously.

Me: Gotta go, Mafia Man.

I ignored the middle finger he texted back because one, it was rude . . . and two . . . I had better things to do.

Or better said . . . I had a Riley-girl *to do*.

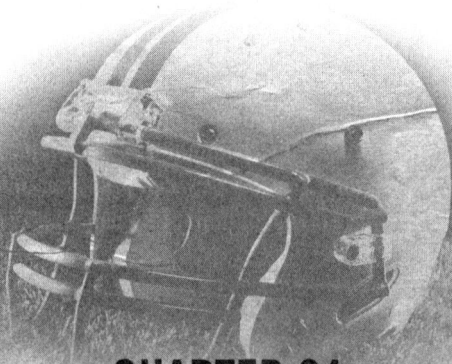

CHAPTER 24

RILEY

I couldn't stop the smile stretched across my face. It seemed like it had been a permanent piece of me for the last week, ever since I'd moved in with Jace and discovered . . . life could actually be fun.

I was sitting in class, waiting for our professor to appear, when a text came in.

> Jace: What's up, buttercup?

> Jace: You're dreaming about me, aren't you?

> Jace: I bet you are.

> Jace: Probably thinking about my hands on you, and that little tongue trick I did this morning.

I rolled my eyes, but a smile tugged at my lips despite myself. I was going to ignore that comment . . . I didn't need to be getting horny when class was about to start.

> Jace: No response?

> Jace: I'll take that as a yes.

Me: I'm in class. You're being stalkerish again.

Jace: So, tell me to stop.

My fingers hovered over the keyboard. But, of course . . . I didn't tell him to stop.

I was past the point of wanting him to.

Jace: Learning anything important?

I shook my head, trying to ignore the warmth curling low in my stomach. I needed to focus.

The professor still wasn't here yet, but the lecture hall was already buzzing. Students filled the seats around me, pulling out laptops, flipping through notebooks, and leaning across tables to whisper. Some of them weren't even trying to be discreet.

I caught the sideways glances. The murmurs just low enough to be obvious.

Jace.

His name threaded through the air like static electricity, sparking in snippets I tried to ignore but couldn't quite escape.

I was getting used to the stares. The rumors. The fact that half these people probably had an opinion about me, one way or another.

That was the price I paid for dating someone who was a campus celebrity, though.

Good thing he was worth it.

I glanced at my phone to see what else Jace had sent, and then it happened.

A voice sliced through the chatter, deep, smooth, and rich with authority.

"Good afternoon, everyone."

My entire body locked up. Every muscle in me turned rigid, my fingers turning ice cold where they gripped my pen.

No.

No, no, no, no.

That voice.

The voice that had once whispered in my ear, wrapping around me like silk, like chains. The voice that had slithered through my nightmares long after I thought I had escaped.

A sound I would know anywhere, no matter how much time had passed.

I turned my head toward the front of the room slowly, dread thickening like tar in my veins.

My stomach dropped into a bottomless black pit of nothingness.

Callum.

Standing at the front of the lecture hall like he belonged there. Like he hadn't just stolen the air from my lungs.

The world around me tilted, my vision blurring at the edges. This wasn't happening. This wasn't real.

But the room hadn't changed. The lecture hall was still packed with students—laughing and murmuring, completely oblivious to the chaos ripping through me.

"Wait, who is that?" someone whispered from a few seats over.

"Why do we have a new professor halfway through the term?"

"Does anyone know anything about him?"

"Well, damn," a girl behind me murmured. "If all historians looked like that, I might actually pay attention."

A few quiet chuckles followed.

They didn't know.

None of them had any idea.

They just saw a polished, well-dressed professor standing with effortless confidence, sharp in his suit and refined in his posture. They saw someone intelligent. Someone impressive. Someone who had stepped into this room like he owned it.

But me?

I saw a monster in a tailored suit.

Callum adjusted his cuffs, smoothed his tie, exuding effortless confidence. His blue eyes swept over the room, casual, indifferent—until they landed on mine.

And he smiled.

A private little smirk.

Like a secret only we knew.

Like he hadn't just destroyed me all over again.

I barely registered the students around me, I didn't hear their murmurs or the scrape of chairs as people settled in. All I could hear was the blood roaring in my ears, the thunderous pound of my pulse. Every instinct in my body was screaming at me to get up and leave before he spoke another word. Before his voice wrapped around my throat like a noose.

But I couldn't move.

I was paralyzed, locked in place as Callum took his time scanning the room. "Good afternoon, everyone. My name is Professor Callum Westwood," he said, his voice settling over the lecture hall like death incarnate. "I apologize for the sudden change in your syllabus, but *I* will be filling in as your professor for the remainder of the semester. It is my hope that we'll have an intellectually stimulating experience together."

A few murmurs rippled through the students, but he continued, unbothered.

"I'm sure some of you have questions, but rather than waste time on introductions, let's jump right in."

Bile rose in my throat.

"History," he began, his voice calm, deliberate, "is not simply a collection of dates and wars. It is a record of power—who seizes it, who wields it, and who is left in its wake."

"You see," he mused, locking eyes with me for just a fraction of a second before moving on, "throughout history, there have been individuals who do not wait for permission to take what they desire. They do not waste time on trivial concerns like morality or rules set by those weaker than them."

I curled my fingers into my palms, my nails biting into my skin.

"Consider Alexander the Great," Callum continued, pacing in front of the room. "A man who carved an empire with his *bare hands*. A man who didn't stop because someone told him no. Who didn't hesitate because an obstacle was in his way. He saw what he wanted. And he took it."

A chill ran down my spine.

I knew what this was.

He wasn't talking about history.

He was talking about *us*.

He was talking about *me*.

"In the end, history does not remember those who hesitate. Those who cower, who run. No, history remembers the ones who act. The ones who do whatever it takes to ensure that what belongs to them . . ." He paused, his eyes coming back to mine. "Stays with them."

The air around me turned suffocating. I wanted to run.

I *needed* to run.

But I couldn't.

I was stuck, trapped beneath the weight of his words, of his eyes, of the knowledge that he was standing here, right in front of me, and there was nowhere to hide.

He had found me.

He was *never* going to let me go.

The class murmured in interest, some nodding in agreement, completely oblivious to the deeper meanings of his words.

"Some people . . ." he went on, tone casual, almost conversational, "think they can escape their past. They think they can rewrite their own story. But history . . . well. History has a way of catching up to you. Doesn't it?"

A few students shifted, glancing around like they sensed the tension but couldn't place it.

He turned, slowly pacing, his voice dipping lower. "And in the end, the only thing that matters is this—who is willing to do whatever it takes to win?"

He stopped and looked at me.

"Because those are the ones who always do."

A memory flashed through my head.

His fingers tightened around my throat.

I gasped, my nails clawing at his wrist, but his grip only tightened—cutting off the little air I had left.

"Shh," Callum murmured, smiling down at me. Like this was normal. Like this was just another lesson in how to please him.

Like it didn't feel like he was killing me.

My vision blurred at the edges. Tears spilled down my cheeks. I tried to shake my head, to get some air, but he just tilted his head, watching me like I was fascinating.

His other hand cupped my jaw, thumb stroking my cheek as he pressed me into the mattress. "Look at you," he mused, voice dripping with amusement. "So desperate."

I choked. My body convulsed, instinct screaming at me to fight.

But I didn't.

Because I had learned by then.

Fighting only made him squeeze harder.

I forced my body to go still, forced myself to surrender.

And just like that, he loosened his grip.

Air rushed into my lungs so fast it burned.

My chest heaved, a violent sob tearing out of my throat, but Callum only sighed, brushing a hand over my damp cheek.

"There you go," he murmured. "That's better."

I jerked back to reality, breath coming fast and shallow as I tried to remind myself I wasn't there. I wasn't his anymore.

But it didn't matter.

Because he was here. Standing at the lectern. Watching me.

The rest of the lecture blurred together, my brain barely processing anything but him. Every word he spoke was laced with meaning only I could decipher. Every glance my way felt like a warning.

By the time the hour was up, my pulse was a wreck.

The second he dismissed us, I shoved my notebook into my bag, keeping my head down as I practically ran for the exit.

I was so close.

Just a few more steps and—

"Riley."

My stomach dropped, and I froze.

I turned slowly, my legs numb. The last few students passed by, oblivious to the way my entire body had gone rigid, like prey caught in a trap.

The door clicked shut, and I was alone with him.

He leaned against the desk, casual, like this wasn't some twisted nightmare I couldn't wake up from. His suit was crisp, dark navy, the sleeves perfectly fitted to his frame. The gold of his cuff links glinted beneath the harsh fluorescent lights, his wedding band gone, like he never even had one. Like his wife's existence had never mattered.

Like I was the only thing that had ever mattered.

"It's been a long time, *darling*."

The sound of that word—the way it slithered off his tongue, snaking around me, tightening with every syllable—sent a hollow weight sinking deep in my veins.

I swallowed, my nails digging into my palm. "Don't call me that."

His lips twitched, amusement flickering in his blue eyes. "You always hated when I called you that. And yet . . ." He tilted his head, eyes raking over me, soaking me in like he was remembering every inch of me.

"Look at you," he murmured. "It's been just a few months, and yet you look like you've changed . . . like you've grown up."

He looked a little disappointed by that, and bile was in my throat again.

His gaze flicked to my bag, my fingers curled so tightly around the strap that my knuckles had gone white. "Running off already?" He pushed off the desk, closing the distance between us with lazy, confident strides. "That's disappointing. I really thought you were going to want to catch up."

I stepped back, and he smiled.

A slow, knowing smirk. Like he could see inside of me. Like he could still reach into my chest and twist his fingers around my heart, my throat, my everything.

Callum's voice curled through the air, low and smooth and terrible. "Stay," he said softly, like it was a request, but I knew better. It was a command.

The word slid down my spine like ice, every muscle in my body locking up. His tone was too familiar, too calculated—the same one that had whispered in my ear in dark rooms, had slithered into my bones until I didn't know where I ended and he began.

But I wasn't that girl anymore.

I forced myself to breathe, to push past the way my skin prickled under his gaze. "I don't want to stay." My voice wasn't as strong as I wanted it to be, but it was steady. It was mine.

Callum tilted his head, his smirk lazy, indulgent—like he was already two moves ahead of me in a game I didn't even want to play. "Yet here you are," he mused.

I hated him.

I hated how easily he made me doubt myself.

I hated that even now, after everything, after running, after starting over, some part of me still tensed like I was waiting for his approval.

He reached for me, a slow, deliberate movement, and I flinched before I could stop myself, jerking back like his fingers were fire and I'd been burned one too many times.

A flicker of something crossed his face—dark amusement laced with something sharper, something colder. And then he laughed, soft and condescending, his eyes drinking in every inch of my reaction.

"Still so jumpy," he murmured, lowering his hand, but not before I saw the cruel edge in his gaze. "I'd almost think you were afraid of me."

The breath in my lungs turned stale, every fiber of my being screaming at me to get out, to put as much distance between us as possible.

"Why are you here?" My voice wavered, my pulse hammering against my ribs.

He leaned in just enough that his scent hit me—cedarwood and leather. The same cologne, the same intoxicating mix of power and poison that used to cling to my sheets, my clothes, my skin.

The past came rushing back so fast it stole my breath.

"You think you can leave me, darling?" His voice echoed in my skull, a ghost of another time, another place. *"You think you can run?"*

I blinked hard, yanking myself out of the memory, forcing air into my lungs as he hummed, watching me with that same calculating stare. "I suppose you could say . . . I missed you." He exhaled, feigning wistfulness. "I was so distraught after you left, I could hardly function."

A shudder raked through me, bile rising higher in my throat.

"That's not true," I whispered.

"No?" His smirk deepened. "I did tell you that you'd never get away from me."

His voice was almost gentle now, like he was soothing a skittish animal. "Tell me, Riley. Did you really think I wouldn't find you?" His eyes softened just enough to make it worse. "Did you really think some state school in a different city would make you disappear?"

My stomach twisted into knots, the air between us turning suffocating.

He took another slow step forward, his voice dipping into something quieter, something laced with dark amusement. "Imagine my surprise when I turned on ESPN . . ." He sighed, like he was recounting a fond memory. "And there you were. Headlining." His eyes darkened, glinting with something possessive. "All over the screen. All over *him*."

The shift was subtle, but I felt it. The barely there clench of his jaw. The faint edge creeping into his voice as he said, "That *boy*."

Jace.

My stomach dropped.

Callum didn't say Jace's name. He didn't have to. The disdain, the warning—it was all there.

"Riley," he murmured, lifting his hand as if to touch me again, trailing his fingers just beneath my chin before I yanked my head away.

His expression didn't change, but his eyes flashed. A glint of something wicked.

He was enjoying this. Enjoying my fear. "I'm divorcing her."

My eyes widened in surprise, feeling the pure threat. Because if he did that, he would have even more freedom to come after me. To try and trap me.

Without living his double life with his *wife*.

I swallowed hard, my voice shaking. "You don't belong here."

He smiled then—the kind of smile that could kill. "I'm not so sure about that."

I forced myself to stand still, to breathe, even as my chest ached with the effort.

He took a step back, like he'd had his fun, like he'd already won. "Stay away from me," I managed to grit out.

His smile widened, condescending, patient. "Oh, Riley . . ." He shook his head, sighing like he was disappointed in me, like I was being difficult.

And then, just as I turned to leave, his voice caught me like a hook sinking into my ribs.

"I'll be seeing you."

I nearly stumbled.

But I didn't look back.

I forced one foot in front of the other, made my way to the door, my breath uneven, my hands shaking.

I didn't run.

Even though everything in me was screaming to.

By the time my shift at the coffee shop ended, my entire body ached, but not from exhaustion. Not from the hours spent on my feet or the countless cups of burnt espresso I'd poured.

No, the ache was deeper. Heavier.

Callum had found me.

And I had to pretend like everything was fine.

I walked into Jace's house and tried to breathe. The air smelled warm and familiar—faint traces of his cologne in the air.

Safe.

I wanted to sink into it, let it wrap around me, pretend the day hadn't happened.

Jace was in the kitchen, as usual, because I'd learned that he couldn't exist for more than a few minutes without food, and I took a deep breath before walking into the room.

He didn't say anything for a second. Just stood there, eyes flicking over me, assessing. Then, without a single ounce of warning—

"That's it. I can't take it anymore."

Before I could even process what was happening, he lunged across the kitchen, grabbing me by the waist and hauling me up into his arms like some kind of dramatic movie hero. A very dramatic, very unhinged movie hero.

I squeaked, instinctively wrapping my arms around his neck as he spun us in a circle, my hair whipping into my face. "Jace!"

"I missed you," he groaned, squeezing me tighter, like he was physically incapable of functioning without having me in his orbit. "It was so tragic. So painful. I think I might have withered away from sheer heartbreak. Did you even think about me today? Did you even mourn my absence?"

I huffed out a laugh, trying to wriggle free, but his grip was ironclad. "I was in class and then at work, you lunatic."

He gasps. "Even worse! You left me to fend for myself. What if I had perished from neglect?"

I rolled my eyes, but my cheeks ached from smiling. "You were at practice, Thatcher."

He ignored me, setting me down just long enough to grab my face between both of his hands, his thumbs brushing my cheeks like I was some delicate, tragic thing. "I've come to a decision." His voice dropped, solemn and serious. "You should carry me around in your pocket. Just—fold me up, shove me in there, and keep me close at all times. That way, we'll never have to be apart again."

I stared at him, deadpan. "You're six four, Jace."

He waved that off. "And yet, I believe in you. I believe in *us*."

I laughed, shaking my head, but he just wrapped his arms around me again, pulling me into his chest, his chin resting on the top of my head like he had no plans of letting go.

"Missed you, Riley-girl," he murmured, his voice softer now, still playful but edged with something *real*.

I swallowed hard, trying not to cry as I pressed my cheek against his chest, letting myself sink into him for just a second. "Missed you, too."

And for just a moment, I let myself pretend it was that simple.

"I've got a new one today," he said, still holding me close as he grabbed a cookie from the counter and started munching it. I snorted as a crumb fell on my nose.

"What is it?" I asked, trying to force a grin across my mouth.

"What do you call a man with a two-inch penis?"

I blinked, trying to think of what the answer could possibly be. "I have absolutely no idea," I told him, shaking my head as *another* cookie crumb fell on my face.

"Just-in," Jace said proudly.

It took me a second, and then a strange cackle came from my mouth.

"See, you have a much better sense of humor than Parker and Matty. I need to have a talk with them about how much they've slipped in the *per se* rankings lately."

I forced a smile as he pulled me back so we could look at each other. "Yeah, you better get on that," I told him softly, trying to keep that smile on my lips.

His brows drew together as he studied my face. "Riley." His voice was careful, his eyes running over me like he was cataloging every inch, every flicker of something off.

"Yes, Jace."

"What's wrong?"

I opened my mouth, hesitating while I tried to think of what to say.

"It was just a long day at work. I swear the entire freshman class of UT came in for caramel macchiatos all at once." I exhaled a laugh like it was funny, like it was normal. Like I hadn't spent the last three hours gripping the counter so hard my nails had nearly splintered, Callum's words replaying in my head over and over like a curse.

Jace didn't look convinced. His gaze lingered, his jaw ticking slightly.

"Yeah?" He leaned against the counter, crossing his arms. "You sure that's all?"

I nodded too fast. "Yep. Just tired."

He didn't say anything. Just watched me.

And I felt it.

Felt his gaze on me all evening.

Through dinner, when I barely ate. Through the movie we half watched, when I curled into his side, pretending that the warmth of his body was enough to keep the cold fear at bay. Through every tiny moment when I felt my mind drifting, my fingers gripping the fabric of his hoodie, needing something solid to hold on to.

Because if Jace knew—

If he knew that Callum was here, that he was watching, waiting, already sinking his claws in—if he knew that Callum had been as old as my father . . . and married . . .

Would he still look at me the same way?

Or would he see me as something broken?

As something ruined?

I pressed closer to him, breathing in his scent, feeling the solid warmth of him under my fingertips.

Jace Thatcher was a lot of things—reckless, cocky, infuriatingly overconfident.

But he was also safe.

And if I could pretend—just for tonight—maybe I could let myself believe that safety was real. That I could have this, even if only for a little while.

So, I smiled when he kissed my temple. Laughed at something Matty said from the other room. Forced my body to relax even as the fear coiled deep inside me, whispering what I already knew.

Jace wouldn't just let this go.

And when he found out the truth—

I wasn't sure if he'd still want me at all.

CHAPTER 25

JACE

I popped another handful of popcorn into my mouth, leaning back on the couch as I watched the screen. The coffee shop's security footage played in perfect HD, and there she was—Mrs. Buttercupalicious herself, completely unaware as she wiped down the counter with a look of concentration on her face.

She was adorable. And perfect. And mine.

The sound of the front door opening barely registered until Parker and Matty walked in, still laughing about something. They headed straight for the fridge before Parker turned, finally noticing the screen.

He froze, and Matty frowned next to him. "Uh . . . what are we looking at there, Jace-face?"

"Surveillance," I said smoothly, popping another kernel in my mouth.

Matty blinked. "Is that—"

"Riley?" Parker finished, grinning. "Hell yeah, it is." He came over to give me a high five because he understood true love.

Matty's horror was instant. "Are you serious right now? You hacked the coffee shop's cameras?!"

"Obviously." I gestured at the screen. "How else am I supposed to keep an eye on her? She came home from work last night, and she was acting different, and I want to know why."

Matty ran a hand down his face like he was personally suffering. "Did you ever think of just asking her?"

I snorted, because that was hilarious. That would have gone as well as me "asking" her to move in with me.

Meaning, it wouldn't have worked at all.

Parker, meanwhile, had pulled up a chair. "How many angles do you have?"

"Three," I said smugly. "One at the register, one at the counter, and one covering the back room."

Matty groaned. "You two are *both* insane."

Parker pointed at the screen, watching as Riley leaned over the counter, oblivious to us watching her. "Damn. Look at my future sister-in-law, just killing it at customer service."

I preened at the recognition that I was his brother from another mother. "It's temporary."

Matty gaped. "What do you mean it's temporary? Are you planning on getting her fired now?"

I tilted my head. "'Fired' is such a strong word, *Matthew*. I prefer 'reallocated.'"

Matty threw his hands in the air. "Reallocated?! This is a bad idea."

Parker grinned, nudging Matty with his elbow. "This could be you. If you just gave in to your stalker."

"Or Darla," I supplied helpfully, ignoring the way Matty was cracking his knuckles again like he was thinking about introducing them to my face.

"How are you planning on doing it?" Parker asked, ever the supportive king, and still ahead of Matty in the rankings.

I tapped my chin thoughtfully. "Accidental plumbing issues? Health code violation? Maybe a break-in. Something *minor*, of course. Just enough to shut the place down for a bit."

Matty groaned again, rubbing his temples like he was developing a stress headache. "I'm not going to be able to break you out of jail. It's not in my skill set."

I waved him off. "Relax. It's not going to come to that. Hopefully. But something has to be done. Something is making her upset."

I studied the footage. "Coffee shops are dangerous. Slippery floors. High risk of burns. Annoying customers. It could be any of those things."

"Or she was just having a bad day," Matty deadpanned.

I shrugged. "Possibly."

Parker snickered. "Matty, he can't leave things to chance. Come on."

Matty let out a long, suffering sigh. "Okay, so what exactly is wrong with her working there *right now*?"

Like the universe itself wanted to assist in proving my point, the answer strutted right through the door.

A guy.

I narrowed my eyes, watching as some dude in a leather jacket sauntered up to the counter, all confidence and cocky grin—all things that were firmly in *my* realm. Riley didn't seem to notice at first; she was too busy being an excellent employee and wiping down the espresso machine. But when she finally looked up, he leaned against the counter, saying something that made her lips possibly twitch a little.

I didn't like that.

I didn't like that at all.

I set my popcorn down, sitting up straighter. "She's *definitely* done with that job."

Matty threw his hands up. "He's a customer. She's just being nice."

"Well, of course, she's being nice, Matty. *He's* the one not being nice."

"I don't think this has anything to do with her bad mood yesterday, Jace."

"*Think* is the operative word in that sentence, sir. You need to leave the big-brain thinking to QB and me if that's the energy you're bringing to this conversation."

Matty sniffed in outrage.

Parker smirked. "What's the plan, big guy? You've got that twinkle."

I grinned. "Oh, I've got a few ideas . . ."

Matty groaned. "Of course you do."

Parker leaned closer to the screen, watching Leather Jacket make another move, and then he snapped his fingers. "We could kidnap him, take him out to one of those lakes where they've been finding gators, and make him fight one. See if he's still feeling brave then."

I turned my head slowly to stare at him. Matty did the same.

I blinked. "I was thinking more along the lines of breaking his nose, but sure, Parker. Let's start with reptilian combatives."

Matty shook his head slowly, still staring. "You always go straight to kidnapping. It's honestly concerning."

Parker just shrugged, completely unbothered. "You guys never wanna have any fun."

Matty crossed his arms. "I have a crazy idea—you just let Riley exist in the world without orchestrating a hostile takeover of her entire life."

I turned to him, unimpressed. "That was your *crazy* idea?"

Parker shook his head in disgust. "What's your *non*-crazy idea?"

Matty groaned into his hands. "You guys are insane."

I turned my attention back to the screen, watching as Riley shook her head at whatever the guy said. She wasn't interested—that much was clear—but it didn't matter.

Because now, I had a new mission.

I clapped my hands together. "Alright, gentlemen. Time to find Riley some new hobbies."

Parker grinned. "Ooh, can we make her a football fan?"

"We'll see," I mused, already mentally drafting a list. "Step one: Get rid of the coffee shop job. Step two: Get her *occupied* so she doesn't notice step one."

Matty groaned louder. "I hate that this is an actual conversation happening right now."

Parker nudged him. "Oh, shut up. You're just mad because Jace is making moves, and you're still scared of your stalker/future soulmate."

Matty scowled. "We don't even know what my *stalker* really looks like. Besides *blonde*. It's possible it's Darla." He shivered in horror.

I didn't blame him. Darla had come outside in a muumuu yesterday, the same one from that infamous boob pic, and I'd been traumatized all morning.

But back to my problem . . .

I wasn't totally sure if it was Riley's job that was making her upset, but it was best to cut out all variables when it came to her happiness.

Because when it came to my babylicious, there wasn't a single thing I wouldn't burn to the ground to keep a smile on her face.

"Hey," Jagger answered, sounding suspiciously out of breath.

"What's wrong with you? Did you answer in the middle of sex again? Because I told you that was rude."

Surprisingly, the girl he'd been with hadn't been upset at all. Probably because of our superior genes. It was a known fact that Thatcher genes drove women crazy. Her moans had only increased during the call—which maybe would have been hot if it wasn't my brother who was balls deep inside her.

Jagger scoffed like I'd said something outrageous. "No, I'm not in the middle of sex. That girl was a one time thing. Obviously, since she was bad enough in bed that I answered the phone."

"I just thought that you were answering because I'm your brother and I could have been in mortal danger."

"Oh, is that a thing football players in college experience often . . . mortal danger?"

"It is when your family is a member of the mafia," I snapped, a little miffed because it sounded like he'd only answered because he was bored.

Also, considering the Sphinx had left me for dead at the top of that building the other night, football players, aka *me*, were actually in mortal danger quite often around here.

Jagger made a weird growly sound. Huh, he and Matty were both good at that one.

"Alright, so are you working out? Did you just get done riding a bull?"

"Did you just ask me if I just got done riding a bull?" he asked . . . or more like gasped since it sounded like he was now running.

Several bangs sounded through the phone, and I almost dropped it. That sounded like . . . gunshots.

"Motherfucker," Jagger growled, sounding even more out of breath now.

"Oh . . . let me guess. You're at your job. Doing boring office work . . . procurement work. Absolutely nothing exciting happening on your end at all," I drawled sarcastically.

Here was the thing about Jagger: I knew he did something nefarious at his job. And he knew I knew he did something nefarious at his job. But apparently, he wasn't ready to talk about it. He was only ready to get me questionable items—like when Parker needed those pharmaceuticals—or to provide me with mysteriously large sums of cash to invest.

"And that definitely wasn't fucking GUNSHOTS that I just heard, either," I added calmly.

"Is there a reason that you called?" he snapped. "I . . . have to take this package to the mail room."

My eye roll was probably a thing to behold. I should've taken a picture of it and sent it to him because even he would've been impressed.

"Well, I'm calling about two things," I said. "First, I just tripled the money you sent me last week, and I'm definitely taking that ten percent you offered me on account of the fact that I'm the smartest, best-looking, absolutely *amazingest* person that you know."

Another bang.

"You can have five percent," Jasper hissed, cursing under his breath about whatever had just happened. "Because it's so fucking easy for you, and you shouldn't prey on me when I was just having a weak moment that day."

"A weak moment because of the dead body you had in the garage? Right . . . but also, you shouldn't get a discount on account of my big brain. I bet you don't give discounts because of your big—"

"I think we've discussed I'm not a hooker, Jace. But you can keep trying."

"This is where you tell me thank you and then go do whatever . . ."

"The mail room. I'm taking something to the mail room," he corrected me.

"Someday, I'm going to figure this out," I warned him.

He huffed, like he thought I was being funny.

"And your second reason for calling?" Jagger drawled.

"I need a favor."

There was a short pause, then an amused chuckle. "Well, that's going to cost you the five percent."

I scoffed. "Well, since it was actually ten percent, I still get five percent, so we should be all good."

My fingers drummed against my thigh. "I need the coffee shop Riley works at closed for a while. Something . . . inconvenient, but not too serious."

Jagger hummed, considering. "Pipes bursting?"

I smirked. "Sounds perfect."

"You know, normal people just ask their girls to quit. Offer to take care of them for a while."

"Normal people are boring," I muttered. "Besides, she's stubborn. This way, she thinks it's out of her hands."

Jagger laughed. "I'll make some calls. Expect a water disaster by morning."

I grinned. "That's why you're my favorite brother."

"I'm your *only* brother, dumbass."

I ended the call and went back to watching her on the screen, a satisfied smirk settling on my face. Problem solved. Now, I just had to figure out how to get that bookstore downsized, too.

The next day, Riley came home, her brows furrowed in worry as she dropped her bag onto the counter.

"You won't believe this," she said, running a hand through her hair. "The coffee shop flooded overnight. Something about busted pipes. It's going to be closed for a while."

I schooled my expression into one of soft concern. "That sucks, Riley-girl. Are they still paying you while it's closed?"

She shook her head, sighing. "No. I mean, I still have the bookstore job, but it's going to be tight for a while. Even with you not letting me pay any rent for this place."

There was a cute little growl at the end of that sentence that made me want to bury my face between her legs . . . but I controlled myself. Instead, I made a sympathetic noise, stepping closer and brushing my knuckles along her jaw. "Maybe this isn't such a bad thing."

She arched a brow. "How do you figure?"

I leaned against the counter, my gaze locked onto hers. "You're always running around, working, studying . . . stressing yourself out. Maybe this is the universe telling you to slow down a little."

She huffed. "Or maybe it's just the universe being a jerk."

I chuckled, tilting my head. "Look at it this way—you get more time to yourself now. More time to relax, sleep in, maybe even let me take care of you a little."

She rolled her eyes. "I don't need to be taken care of."

"I know," I said smoothly, my fingers tucking a loose strand of hair behind her ear. "But that doesn't mean you don't *deserve* to be. And think of the orgasms. You can have so many more orgasms with that free time."

She hesitated, her lips parting like she wanted to argue but couldn't quite find the words. I could see the flicker of uncertainty in her eyes, the way she fought against the idea of letting herself *be* taken care of. It only made me more determined.

"Come on, Riley-girl. Think about it," I murmured, running my hands up and down her arms. "No more dealing with customers who don't tip. No more aching feet after standing all day. Just . . . free time. And me. And orgasms. Sounds pretty great, don't you think?"

She exhaled slowly. "I guess when you put it like that . . ."

I grinned. "Exactly. You deserve a life of leisure. One where you can focus on what really matters."

She smirked. "And what exactly do you think *really* matters?"

I leaned in, my voice dropping. "Me, obviously."

Her face heated, and she quickly turned away, grabbing a glass of water. "You're insufferable."

"I believe the word you were looking for . . . is cute." Riley scoffed, of course.

I watched her closely, my smirk widening. If she thought this was the end of it, she was wrong. Because next, I had my sights set on that damn bookstore job.

She might not realize it yet, but soon enough, she'd have all the time in the world.

And she'd spend it exactly where she belonged—*with me.*

———————

As I drew her in my arms that night after an hour spent giving her the promised orgasms, there was one thing still bothering my mind.

She still had that haunted look in her eye.

And I still didn't know what was causing it.

CHAPTER 26

RILEY

The email hit my inbox at exactly 8:04 a.m.

> *Subject: Academic Standing*
> *Dear Ms. St. James,*
> *Please report to the Administration Office at your earliest convenience regarding an urgent academic matter.*
> *Best,*
> *Dr. Elaine Morrison*
> *Dean of Academic Affairs*

I stared at the screen, my stomach twisting.

Nothing good ever came from being summoned by Academic Affairs.

I wasn't failing—at least, not at the moment. Sure, I had missed those classes at the beginning of the semester, but I was finally getting caught up. Or, I thought I was.

Something felt off.

I swallowed the lump in my throat and forced myself to move, shutting my laptop and shoving it into my bag. It wasn't like I had a choice. Ignoring it wouldn't make it go away.

By the time I reached the Administration Office, my hands were ice-cold and my pulse was a drum in my ears.

I stepped inside, the scent of printer ink and too-strong coffee filling the space. The front desk attendant barely looked up before pointing to the office at the end of the hall.

"Dr. Morrison is expecting you," she said.

I walked in on legs that didn't feel like my own.

Dr. Morrison was already seated, her thin-framed glasses perched on the end of her nose as she sifted through a file. Her office was too neat, too sterile, the kind of space that gave bad news with a polite smile.

"Ms. St. James," she greeted, gesturing toward the chair across from her desk. "Thank you for coming."

I sat, gripping the armrests like they were my lifeline. "Is something wrong?"

She folded her hands over the file and sighed.

"There have been concerns raised about your academic performance this semester," she said. "Particularly, your attendance early on."

My stomach bottomed out.

"I know I missed a few classes at the start of the semester, but I've been keeping up—"

Dr. Morrison lifted a perfectly manicured hand, silencing me. "Professor Westwood brought his concerns to our attention."

Ice. Cold, unrelenting ice slid through my veins. I could barely hear her over the sound of blood roaring in my ears.

Callum.

He did this.

I forced myself to breathe, to school my face into something neutral even as panic gripped me. "Concerns?" I asked, keeping my voice as steady as possible.

She sighed again, flipping open my file. "Professor Westwood informed us that you've been struggling in his class, and that given your early semester absences, you're at risk of falling behind."

Every muscle in my body locked up.

Struggling? I wasn't struggling in that class—at least not before Callum had taken it over.

But that wasn't the point, was it?

The point was control.

The point was Callum making sure I couldn't escape him.

I opened my mouth to protest, to explain that I was doing just fine, that *Professor Westwood* wouldn't know how I was doing because I'd literally had one class with him, but she was already continuing on, flipping a page in the file like my fate was a formality.

"We take our students' academic success very seriously, Ms. St. James," she said. "Which is why we're implementing an academic intervention plan for you."

My pulse thundered in my skull.

"What does that mean?" I asked, though I already knew.

Dr. Morrison adjusted her glasses. "It means we've arranged for Professor Westwood to tutor you privately, effective immediately."

My breath stalled.

My skin felt too tight, too hot, too suffocating.

"No," I said immediately. "I don't—I don't need a tutor."

Dr. Morrison gave me a look—the kind that told me she'd already made up her mind and my opinion on the matter didn't count. "Given your academic record, this is nonnegotiable. Professor Westwood has generously volunteered his time, and we expect you to comply."

Nonnegotiable.

I gripped the armrests so hard my nails ripped into the fabric.

This wasn't happening.

This couldn't be happening.

I shook my head. "I— There are other tutors, right? The campus tutoring center, peer tutors, someone else—"

Dr. Morrison's eyes sharpened. "Professor Westwood is highly qualified, and as your professor, he is the most suited to help you succeed in this course."

I couldn't breathe.

I was trapped.

Caught in his web, exactly where he wanted me.

"You will attend your scheduled tutoring sessions," she continued. "Failure to do so could result in an academic hold being placed on your account."

Academic hold.

A polite way of saying they could block me from registering for future classes.

He had me.

I could see it now, clear as day.

Callum had backed me into a corner. He'd gone to the administration, played the concerned professor, and now he had complete control over me.

I wanted to scream.

Instead, I forced my face into something resembling compliance because I knew how this game worked.

I had learned the hard way.

Dr. Morrison must have seen my acceptance because she nodded, closing my file with a crisp snap. "Good. You'll receive your tutoring schedule by the end of the day."

I stood, my legs barely holding me up.

"Thank you for your time, Ms. St. James," she said, dismissing me like she hadn't just handed me over to a monster.

I nodded stiffly, turned on autopilot, and walked out of the office.

I barely registered where I was going.

One second, I was pushing through the doors of the admin building. The next, I was standing outside, my breath coming in short, shallow gasps.

I needed air. I needed out.

I stumbled toward the nearest bench and sat, my entire body shaking.

I knew Callum was ruthless, but this?

This was a new level.

He'd done what he always did—made sure there was no way out. Made sure I had no choice but to sit across from him, week after week, knowing exactly what he was capable of.

My hands curled into fists.

I needed a plan. I needed to figure out a way to get out of this.

But how?

If I refused, my future was on the line.

If I complied, I was handing myself over to him.

I couldn't win.

The realization crashed over me like a wave of nausea.

I wrapped my arms around myself, hating the way my body still shook.

Somewhere in the distance, the bell tower rang, signaling the start of the next class. Students milled past, laughing, talking, completely oblivious to the war raging inside me.

Callum had me exactly where he wanted me.

And I had no way out.

The door creaked open, and I felt it before I even saw him—the shift in the air, the quiet intensity that followed him like a shadow.

I kept my eyes on the ceiling, my pulse a slow, steady thrum beneath my skin, even as my body hummed with the awareness of him. The weight of his stare pressed against me, heavy and unrelenting.

Then his voice—low, hushed, threaded with concern.

"Tell me what's wrong," Jace murmured.

I swallowed, forcing my expression into something neutral before turning my head toward him. He was standing in the doorway, his long hair damp from a postpractice shower, his broad shoulders stretching the fabric of his Henley. His brown eyes flickered in the dim light of the bedside lamp, scanning me like he could read the wreckage inside me if he looked hard enough.

I should have known he'd notice. Jace wasn't the kind of man you could hide things from.

I exhaled softly, shifting against the pillow. "I got called into the Academic Affairs office today."

His brows furrowed, and in one fluid motion, he leaned against the doorframe, arms crossing over his chest. "For what?"

I hesitated, a weight pressing against my ribs. "Academic concerns."

His expression twisted into confusion. "What? But your grades are fine."

That made me pause.

I lifted a brow. "And how exactly do you know that?"

Something flickered across his face, too fast to catch, too fleeting to decode.

Then he schooled his expression, casual, easy, but there was something off—something tense beneath the surface.

"You've mentioned it," he said after a beat, but his voice had shifted, like he was testing the excuse as he said it.

I didn't argue. Because, right now, it honestly didn't matter.

All that mattered was the way he was looking at me—the way he always looked at me. Like I was something fragile but untouchable, something wild but his to protect.

Jace pushed off the doorframe and stalked toward the bed with slow, measured steps. He sank down beside me, the mattress dipping beneath his weight, and he didn't speak.

He just waited.

For me to tell him the truth. For me to trust him with it.

But I still couldn't bring myself to do it.

So instead, I did something reckless. Something desperate.

I reached for him.

My fingers curled into the fabric of his shirt, and before he could react, before I could think better of it, I kissed him, panicked and frantic, like I needed him to tether me before I drifted into the abyss.

Jace made a noise of surprise against my lips, but he didn't hesitate.

His hands came up, rough and warm and grounding, framing my face as he kissed me back, consuming me, like he was trying to pull every unspoken word from my tongue.

I climbed into his lap without thinking, my knees pressing into the mattress on either side of his hips, my hands threading through his damp hair as his fingers dug into my waist.

I didn't want to think.

I didn't want to feel the way Callum's presence was crawling under my skin like poison.

I wanted this. Wanted Jace.

His touch, his warmth, the way he always made me feel like I was something worth protecting.

His grip tightened, his lips parting like he was about to say something, but I beat him to it, the words tumbling out before I could stop them.

"Do you mean it?" I whispered against his mouth, breathless, desperate.

His fingers flexed against my skin at my question, his lips hovered over mine, just an inch away.

"When you say *always*. Do you mean it?"

Jace pulled back just enough to look at me, really look at me.

His warm brown eyes—wild and molten in the soft glow of the lamp—searched mine, trying to piece together what was unraveling inside me. Then he exhaled, the sound rough, raw, like it physically hurt him that I even had to ask. He reached up, brushing his knuckles along my jaw, a touch so tender it nearly broke me.

"Riley."

His voice was deep and steady, but there was an edge to it, something fierce, something unshakable. "*Always* isn't something I just say."

My throat tightened.

"But—"

He cut me off.

"No." His grip on my waist tightened, like he could physically hold me together, keep me from slipping away into whatever storm was raging inside my head. "You don't get to doubt that. Not with me."

His other hand found the back of my neck, his thumb brushing soothing circles against my skin, his hold firm but gentle, like he was tethering me to this moment.

I closed my eyes, swallowing down the lump in my throat, willing my body to believe him.

But Callum's voice still echoed in my mind.

"You think you can leave me, darling?"

A shudder raked through me, and Jace felt it.

Of course he did.

Because Jace Thatcher didn't just see me.

He *felt* me.

His forehead pressed against mine, his breath fanning across my lips.

"You're mine, Riley," he murmured, soft, but so damn sure. "Not because I own you, not because I control you, but because you are the best fucking thing that has ever happened to me. And I'm never letting you forget that."

My chest constricted so painfully I thought I might break apart right there in his arms.

"Jace—"

"No." His hand slid to my cheek, tilting my face up until our eyes locked again. "No running, Riley. No second-guessing me. If I say *always*, I fucking mean it."

Something cracked open inside me—something deep, something terrifying and warm and devastating all at once.

A breath hitched in my throat, and without thinking, I kissed him again— slower this time, softer, like I was memorizing the shape of his lips, like I was imprinting the feel of him onto my skin.

Jace groaned low in his throat as his arms wrapped around me. His hands splayed across my back . . . his hold became an unspoken vow.

Mine. Always.

Jace kissed me again, slower, deeper, like he was trying to erase every doubt, every fear still lingering beneath my skin. His hands were warm, steady, moving down my back, over my hips, before gripping my thighs and guiding me back onto the bed.

I let him.

Because I needed this.

I needed him.

The weight of him pressed against me, solid and familiar, as his lips traced a slow, burning path down my throat. I arched into him, my breath hitching when his teeth grazed my collarbone, when his hands roamed like he was memorizing me all over again.

"Jace . . ."

He hummed, the sound low and knowing, vibrating against my skin as he pushed my shirt up until I was bare beneath him. His hands skated down my stomach, his mouth following, leaving kisses that weren't just kisses but promises—soft, reverent, possessive.

His fingers hooked into the waistband of my leggings, dragging them down slowly, teasingly, until I was left in nothing but lace. His hands settled on my thighs, spreading me open, his breath hot against the sensitive skin.

"You know why I love doing this?" he murmured, his voice like warm whiskey and sin, pressing a kiss to the inside of my thigh.

I swallowed hard, my fingers tangling in the sheets as my body automatically arched for him . . . reached for him.

"Why?" I breathed.

He kissed higher. Too slow. Too soft. His tongue flicked out, teasing, making me whimper.

"Because you fall apart for me." His brown eyes burned as he glanced up. "Because I can feel you. Every shiver. Every sigh. Every time you gasp my name like you can't help it."

And then he kissed me there.

A slow, soft press of lips, before his tongue parted me, licking through my slick folds with a lazy, devastating stroke. My breath hitched, a sharp, startled sound, and Jace made a sound of satisfaction, his hands gripping my thighs, holding me open like he wasn't planning on letting me go anytime soon.

I was already trembling.

Already lost.

His tongue flicked over my clit, gentle, teasing, before sucking it into his mouth, and I nearly came off the bed.

"You're a god at this." I gasped, immediately embarrassed that those words had come out of my mouth.

Jace laughed against me, the vibration sending another wave of pleasure spiraling through me. "I prefer *Jace*, but I'll take it."

I barely had time to glare at him before he buried his face deeper, licking and sucking with slow, torturous precision, his hands gripping my hips to keep me from squirming.

"Jace—" My voice broke on his name, my thighs trembling against his shoulders.

He growled, deep and low, like my voice alone could unravel him.

"Yeah, Riley-girl. Just like that."

He slid one finger inside me, slow and deep, curling just right, and I gasped, my hips jerking, desperate for more, more, more.

"Jace, please—"

"I got you, babycakes," he promised, adding another finger, his tongue working my clit in tight, perfect circles, pushing me higher . . .

Until I shattered.

My body arched, my hands flying to his hair, my mouth falling open on a strangled cry.

Jace groaned against me, licking me through it, dragging it out until I was trembling, spent, barely able to breathe.

Only then did he pull back, his lips slick, his eyes burning as he crawled up my body.

He kissed me slowly, letting me taste myself on his tongue, like he wanted me to know exactly how much he loved wrecking me.

I clutched his face, pulling him closer, needing to feel all of him, needing him to take me completely.

"I need you," I whispered, my voice raw with desperation, my nails sinking into his shoulders as his thick length throbbed against my stomach through his sweats.

Jace groaned, the sound dark and wrecked, his forehead pressing against mine as he shoved his pants down, his cock springing free, hot and heavy as he dragged the tip along my slick heat and lined himself up with agonizing precision.

"You sure, baby?"

I nodded.

He exhaled, a shaky, reverent sound.

And then—

He pushed inside me, sinking into me inch by inch, until there was nothing left between us.

I gasped as I drowned in the feeling of him.

"Fuck, Riley," he groaned against my mouth. "I'll never get enough."

He stilled, his body taut with restraint as he gave me a second to adjust to the enormous shaft that had just taken over my insides.

I kissed him, slow and deep, rolling my hips up, a silent plea for more— needing him, needing this. My fingers curled against his back, pressing him closer, desperate for the friction, the heat, the overwhelming sensation of him.

"Move, Jace," I whispered against his lips, my voice breathless, needy.

And he did.

His thrusts were deep and controlled, like he was savoring every second. His forehead pressed against mine, his hands roaming, gripping, caressing, like he couldn't decide which part of me to hold on to the tightest.

"Mine," he murmured against my lips. "Every fucking inch of you."

I moaned, arching into him, matching his rhythm, meeting every thrust, every movement, feeling him everywhere.

It was slow. It was intense. It was everything.

He kissed me through every moan, every gasp, every quiet cry of his name.

And then—he shifted, angling his hips just right, and I shattered again, my body tensing, then releasing all at once.

Jace let out a low, guttural groan, his thrusts growing rougher, more desperate as he chased his release. His breath came in hot, unsteady bursts against my skin, his grip on my hips tightening like he couldn't stand even an inch of distance between us.

And then, as if the need to claim me wasn't enough, as if he had to remind me that I was his in every way, he softened—his movements slowing, his lips seeking me.

His lips skimmed over my temple and my cheek before finally capturing my mouth in a slow, lingering kiss—like he needed to taste me, to keep me close. His arms tightened around me, holding me like I was something rare, something he'd never let go of.

Like I was the most precious thing in the world.

I shivered as he tucked me against his chest, his heartbeat a wild, erratic drum against my skin.

Neither of us spoke.

There was no need.

Because this?

This was *everything*.

CHAPTER 27

JACE

I was in my happy place, lying next to a very naked Riley, her warm body tucked against mine, her slow, even breaths ghosting against my collarbone. She was actually sleeping soundly, and I was not about to mess with that.

Which, obviously, meant something was about to ruin it.

Buzz. Buzz.

I cracked one eye open, barely lifting my head from the pillow as I reached over and grabbed my phone off the nightstand.

Unknown Number.

I swiped it open.

Unknown: Walk outside.

I stared, then contemplated throwing my phone at the wall and pretending I never saw it.

This would also be noted in my comment card to the Sphinx because they should have better timing than this. Naked soulmates were a line that should not be crossed.

Rubbing a hand down my face, I blew out a breath. I didn't need a second text to know that ignoring them would only lead to something worse. Like them dragging me out of bed themselves. Or worse, waking up Riley. Which would probably lead to jail time on my part, and I was way too pretty for prison.

I glanced at the babycakes in question. She hadn't stirred, blissfully unaware that I had been summoned by the secret society from hell. Her face was soft and peaceful, her hair fanned out on my pillow like a fucking wet dream. A dream I really didn't want to leave.

Sighing, I pressed a kiss to her forehead before grudgingly slipping out of bed and grabbing the sweats I'd thrown on a chair earlier today, along with a pair of shoes. At least I had the opportunity to be dressed for *this* fun adventure. That was an improvement to waking up practically naked on a rooftop.

Maybe I'd note that in my comment card as well.

I walked through the house, grabbing a bag of cookies as a to-go snack as I silently cursed the Sphinx and their obsession with making my life as inconvenient as possible.

When I stepped outside, the cold night air hit me like a slap as I glanced around for some masked weirdo.

And then I saw it.

A black sedan idling in front of the house, its headlights off, its trunk . . . open.

I paused and tilted my head, questioning the eternities. Then I slowly turned my gaze toward the masked driver sitting behind the wheel.

"Seriously?" I called, shoving my hands into my pockets.

No response.

Just silence and the gaping, open trunk.

I let out a deep, soul-weary sigh.

"Alright, let's break this down, buddy. You text me from a random number in the middle of the fucking night, drag my ass out here in the cold, and now you expect me to willingly climb into the trunk?"

Still nothing.

Just the faintest twitch of the driver's head.

I groaned, rolling my shoulders.

"Do you know how inconvenient this is for me? *Do* you? Because I just got her to sleep. I was having a perfectly nice moment in there. And now, instead of getting laid or sleeping like a normal human being, I'm out here contemplating whether or not I want to end up *murdered*."

Silence.

I exhaled through my nose, tilting my head up toward the sky.

"Fine," I muttered, already knowing I was going to do it. "Fuck, I hate this club."

I trudged toward the car, dragging my feet just to be petty. When I got to the trunk, I glanced inside.

Dark. Empty. Literally the perfect murder setup.

"Just so we're clear," I said, looking back toward the driver. "If this is some kind of murder plot, I hope you know I'll haunt the hell out of you. I'll be terrifying, knocking over glasses and whispering creepy shit in your ear forever."

Still fucking nothing.

"I love this for me," I muttered as I climbed in.

A moment later, the trunk slammed shut.

And just like that, I was off to my latest terrible decision. But at least there wasn't a blindfold involved this time.

I woke up groggy as hell. Which, given the circumstances, was probably not a good thing.

My head was foggy, my limbs felt like lead, and there was a distinct lack of oxygen in my life.

For a second, I had no fucking clue where I was. Then reality came back in bits and pieces.

The Sphinx. The masked driver. The fucking trunk.

And then—oh, yeah. I had inhaled a decent amount of gas fumes before I passed out.

Fantastic. There goes my big brain.

Through my semiconscious state, I realized that the car had stopped. The faint hum of an engine was gone, and somewhere in the distance, I heard . . . wind? Rustling leaves? Definitely not civilization.

The trunk had been popped open.

Which meant either they were letting me out, or they had finally decided to finish the murder they'd been subtly working up to.

I blinked, trying to clear the probable brain damage I'd just acquired before pressing my palms against the trunk's interior and shoving it all the way open. Cold air rushed in, hitting me right in the face.

I squinted, blinking blearily against the sudden darkness that stretched in every direction. Woods. I was in the middle of the fucking woods.

A sigh left my lips, part exhaustion, part deep-seated annoyance at the constant and utter disregard for my comfort.

I groaned, sitting up and swinging my legs out of the trunk, taking a second to assess the bullshit.

Tall trees towered around me, their jagged limbs clawing at the sky. The area was completely devoid of streetlights, roads, or anything remotely resembling an exit. Nothing but a dirt path behind the car and the ominous feeling that I was very much alone.

Well, aside from whoever the hell had driven me here.

Speaking of . . .

I turned toward the driver's seat, ready to ask what fresh hell they had in store for me now. Except—the car was empty.

I squinted. Then checked again. Still empty.

My ride had fucked off into the night without a single explanation.

Because, of course.

I rubbed my temples, trying to ward off the incoming headache that was already forming.

Alright.

Waking up in a gas-induced coma inside a car trunk in the middle of nowhere? Not ideal.

The fact that I was now completely alone with zero clue what I was supposed to be doing?

Definitely worse.

"Cool," I muttered to myself, standing up and stretching out my very kidnapped limbs. "I'll also be noting this in my feedback."

I pulled my cookies from my pocket and started to eat them as I took a slow, assessing look around, my shoes crunching against the dirt as I turned in a slow circle.

No lights.

No signs.

No cryptic Sphinx assholes waiting with a neatly typed-out here's-what's-about-to-ruin-your-life instruction sheet.

Just . . . the forest.

And the fact that the only thing I had going for me was my sheer stubborn refusal to die like a freaking squirrel.

A rustle behind me sent a sharp shock through my spine.

I whirled around, fists clenched.

I told myself it was just the wind. Just an animal. A raccoon, maybe. A deer, if I was lucky. Something nonmurdery.

Except . . . it didn't feel like something.

It felt like someone.

Watching.

"Don't let us get you, Thatcher," a voice suddenly cut through the silence, distorted and mechanical, warped by a voice changer. "Run."

I waited. Breathless. Tensed for whatever came next.

A beat of silence.

Then—laughter.

Low. Amused. Hungry.

The kind of sound a predator makes before it pounces.

My stomach clenched. My pulse thrummed. And then I did exactly what the voice ordered . . . because I wasn't a fucking idiot.

I ran.

The uneven forest floor snagged at my shoes, roots jutting from the dirt like trip wires. I leapt over a fallen log, my foot slipping on wet leaves before I caught myself and shoved forward again.

Branches clawed at my skin, leaving thin, stinging cuts on my arms.

Then—a metallic crack split the night air.

My body jerked on instinct, muscles screaming for cover.

What the fuck was that?

And why couldn't I hear crickets? Where the fuck were the crickets? Or the squirrels? Give me a deer or something!

How had they managed to find the creepiest forest in all of Tennessee?

Or at least, I assumed I was in Tennessee.

Laughter echoed through the trees again.

I jumped.

And not just any kind of laughter.

Clown laughter. The distinct, nightmarish kind. The kind inspired by Emma's poster.

And then it wasn't distant anymore.

It was closer.

I was being hunted. By clowns. Of fucking course.

A whizzing sound zipped past my ear. I flinched, twisting mid-stride— just in time to see pink paint explode against a tree trunk beside me.

I blinked. Paint?

They were hunting me with paintball guns?

I snorted.

Because now all I could picture was a group of Sphinx members in ski masks, sprinting through the woods, giggling like gremlins as they tried to snipe me with Dollar General warfare.

If Matty, Parker, and I actually made it into this society, we were revamping their trial system immediately.

A second shot whizzed past me, closer this time, nearly grazing my shoulder.

Okay. Less funny.

I ducked, rolling under a low-hanging branch, my muscles burning. This extra workout wasn't ideal, if I was being honest.

The trees were thinning ahead—maybe, probably, hopefully. Then a faint sound reached me, low but steady—an engine.

A car.

I veered toward it, ignoring the sharp sting of a branch slashing across my cheek as I pushed forward. The forest spat me out onto asphalt, my boots skidding slightly against the rough pavement.

A weak streetlamp flickered in the distance, casting a dim, stuttering glow over the road. And just beyond the curve ahead, I saw it—a gas station, glowing faintly, a beacon of questionable salvation.

Then—headlights.

A car barreled toward me, cutting through the dark. My stomach clenched, but I stumbled forward anyway, throwing up an arm, hoping like hell they saw me in time because being hit by a car wasn't on my approved list of ways in which I would die.

The tires screeched, rubber burning against pavement as the driver slammed the brakes, stopping just inches away.

A beat of silence.

Then the window rolled down, and a middle-aged man, clutching a Styrofoam cup, blinked at me like he'd never seen something more shocking in his life.

"Hell's bells, kid. You trying to get yourself killed?"

I held up a finger. Because, one, I was slightly out of breath. And two . . . this guy could be my ticket out of whatever *Blair Witch* fever dream I'd been dropped into.

"Lost—got separated—no phone." My words came out uneven. "Can you—take me?"

Wow. Fuck. How far had they chased me? A hundred miles?

The man's gaze flicked behind me into the woods. His lips pressed into a thin line, like he was weighing his options.

I didn't blame him.

Judging by what I could see, I was several inches taller than him and outweighed him by all muscle. Not to mention I looked like I'd just crawled out of a horror movie.

Dirt-streaked. Sweat-drenched. Probably one bad decision away from completely feral.

Then there was a new sound . . . of boots. Pounding against the asphalt. Steady. Purposeful. Way too close.

My stomach twisted as I turned, and there—emerging from the trees, stepping onto the road—was a masked figure. Just standing there on the road. Still. Watching. Waiting.

More shadows lurked behind me, barely visible in the darkness, shifting like specters at the tree line. The air thickened, pressing against my chest, heavy with something unspoken, something dangerous.

The man in the car followed my gaze, his face draining of color as he muttered, "Nope." His grip tightened around his Styrofoam cup like it was a lifeline.

Before I could react, he slammed the gas and the tires screeched, the car fishtailing slightly, and then . . . he was gone.

Rude.

The red taillights of my only shot at escape disappeared around the bend, leaving me standing in the weak glow of the flickering gas station sign. The distant hum of the car's engine faded, replaced by the rustling of leaves and the whisper of shoes on pavement . . . way too many shoes.

The masked figure in the road still hadn't moved. But the others, they were shifting, creeping forward at the edges of my vision, coming out of the trees like the zombies in that show Matty liked to watch.

I blew out a slow breath, rolling my shoulders. *Think, Thatcher. Use that big brain.*

My body was still humming from the sprint, my lungs still burning, and my hands were braced on my knees as I tried to decide whether I was screwed or just *mildly* screwed.

The lead guy finally took a slow step forward, and I straightened, trying to look less like a guy who was two seconds from dropping dead of exhaustion and more like a guy absolutely ready to throw hands.

News flash . . . I was absolutely *not* ready to throw hands.

"Alright, gentlemen," I said, voice steady despite the fact that I could literally hear my own heartbeat in my ears. "I think I've passed this one, we should call it good."

They said nothing.

I sighed dramatically. "Great. That's exactly the answer I was hoping for."

My gaze flicked to the gas pumps. Then to the rusty old truck parked beside them, its driver inside the store.

And then—to the set of keys hanging right from the ignition.

Bingo. I bolted for the truck, and shouts rang out . . . footsteps pounding after me.

I threw myself at the driver's side door, yanking it open so fast it nearly took me with it. My foot hit the step, my hands gripping the wheel, my other hand slapping the lock down.

Just as one of them grabbed the handle.

Too late, *sucker.*

I twisted the keys—and the engine roared to life.

The guy outside yanked on the door hard, and I shifted into drive, slamming my foot down so that the truck lurched forward, jerking him off-balance.

I wasn't usually one for *Grand Theft Auto* . . . but also, don't leave your keys in your vehicle at a shady gas station at two in the morning. That's just common sense.

The bell above the gas station door jingled, and I barely had time to process it before a voice bellowed from behind me. "HEY! WHAT THE HELL—THAT'S MY TRUCK!"

Shit.

I could hear the guy storming out of the store and the unmistakable sound of a six-pack *thunking* to the ground as he realized his ride was peeling out of the parking lot without him.

"SON OF A BITCH!" he roared, and yeah—he was not happy.

Which was fair. But in my defense, I was dealing with some larger issues at the moment.

I floored it, speeding out of the lot as the masked freaks lurked by the pumps, watching as I made my escape.

Unfortunately, I wasn't that lucky.

I took the first turn out of the gas station, gripping the wheel as I barreled down a back road, my heart still hammering. The truck rumbled like an earthquake, the shocks barely hanging on, and the check engine light flicked on in a way that made me genuinely concerned that this thing might just die mid-escape.

But I didn't have time to dwell on it, because, sure enough—headlights appeared behind me.

They were following. Of course they were.

"Satan's left tit," I muttered, adjusting my grip, scanning the road ahead. I didn't have a long-term plan yet, but I had a short-term one.

Step one: Get the hell off the main roads . . . and figure out how to get to campus.

Step two: Get this truck close enough to campus that I could ditch it without immediately being tackled by campus security.

A sharp turn loomed ahead, and I took it too fast, the back tires skidding. Gravel sprayed up as the truck bounced onto an unpaved path, jostling me like I was on a fucking mechanical bull.

I gritted my teeth, barely keeping the thing straight. The road was narrow, winding, more of a suggestion than an actual road, but it was exactly what I needed—thick trees, fewer eyes, and plenty of room to lose my new fan club.

I sped up, rattling over dirt and rocks, glancing in the mirror. The headlights were still there, but they were farther back now. Hesitating.

Probably deciding whether their shady masked society rules allowed for off-roading pursuits.

Spoiler alert: I didn't care.

Up ahead, I spotted a clearing. A break in the trees, just wide enough to see the lights of campus in the distance.

Perfect.

I veered toward it, the truck bucking over roots and potholes like it was personally offended at my driving decisions, and then—finally—I hit the main road.

I was just outside campus.

I slowed down just enough to make sure I wasn't about to plow through a pedestrian and then yanked the wheel, cutting toward a deserted lot near the athletics building.

The truck screeched to a stop, and I threw it into park and jumped out.

And booked it.

I slipped into the shadows of the nearest building as the sound of the truck's engine ticked in the silence, and I'd barely made it twenty feet before the black cars came screeching onto the road behind me.

I ducked behind a dumpster, chest heaving, watching as they rolled to a stop near the abandoned truck.

Doors opened.

Figures stepped out.

I stayed crouched behind the dumpster, my breath still coming fast. There might have even been a little blood in my mouth from the fact that my lungs were still recovering from having been chased through a fucking forest.

The blacked-out SUVs idled near the truck, their engines humming low in the quiet night. For a second, I thought they might get out and come searching. That I'd pushed my luck too far, veered too far off script.

But then one of the masked figures stepped out.

He turned toward me, and I froze, every muscle coiled, my pulse hammering against my ribs like it was trying to escape my body.

But he didn't move toward me. He just stood there, watching. Creepily.

He nodded, a slow, deliberate gesture of acknowledgment.

Like I'd done exactly what they wanted.

Like I'd pass the third trial, as a matter of fact.

I exhaled, tension unwinding in slow, measured increments. My hands, still curled into fists at my sides, finally relaxed.

The masked guy lingered for another moment before turning, slipping back into the car without another word. The doors shut in near-perfect unison, and then, with a smooth purr of the engines, the SUVs peeled away, leaving me alone in the parking lot, standing next to a stolen—borrowed—truck and way too many questions.

I didn't move right away. I just watched the taillights disappear down the road before finally letting out the breath I'd been holding.

Then I glanced at the truck.

I should probably . . . Yeah.

I yanked the driver's side door open, reached inside, and killed the headlights. Left the keys on the seat. Figured the poor bastard who'd owned it deserved some kindness after I jacked his ride and sent him into cardiac arrest.

With one last glance at the empty road, I shoved my hands in my pockets and started walking.

Back toward campus.

Back toward my life.

Back to where Riley was still hopefully laying naked in our bed.

I was elbow-deep in chili when Matty shuffled into the kitchen, squinting like he had just been reborn into the world and wasn't happy about it. His hair was a wreck, his sweats were half falling off his hips, and he looked like he had just been punched awake by the clown on Emma's poster.

He stopped in the doorway, rubbing his face, and blinked at me.

I ignored him and kept stirring—this recipe was finicky.

Matty cleared his throat. "Uh . . . what are you doing?"

I gestured at the pot like it was obvious. "I don't know, *Matthew*, after my latest near-death experience with the 'Elite League of Lunatics,' maybe I worked up an appetite."

He stared at the simmering pot, then at me, then back at the pot.

"For *chili*? At eight a.m.?"

I turned off the burner and lifted the wooden spoon like I was about to give a TED Talk on the philosophical importance of comfort food. "Chili is an elite post-trauma meal," I said, dead serious. "Hearty. Protein-packed. Warms the soul. If I were on death row, this would be my last meal."

Matty pulled out a chair, dropped into it, and rubbed a hand over his face. "Why does chili sound good to me right now?"

"Because you have good taste, obviously."

He groaned, shaking his head, but he still reached for a spoon, which meant I won.

I set a steaming bowl in front of him, and he eyed it like it might fight back.

"Do you even know how to make chili?"

I froze mid-stir, spoon hovering in the air. Slowly, I turned to glare at him. "Do I—Do I know how to make chili?"

He lifted a skeptical brow. "Yeah. 'Cause I'm pretty sure I once saw you google 'how do I turn on an oven.'"

I crossed my arms. "That was for science."

Matty sniffed the air dramatically, as if he were a bloodhound on a case. "Right. And what's your scientific conclusion? That this is edible, or that my intestines are about to file for legal emancipation?"

I jabbed the spoon in his direction. "Eat it or starve, *Matthew*. Those are your options."

With a long-suffering sigh, he dipped his spoon into my creation. "Fine, but if I die, I expect you to lie at my funeral and say I was your favorite."

I grinned as I scooped up my own first bite. "Oh, I will. And I'll say you died doing what you loved."

Matty scowled but begrudgingly took a bite, chewing like he was preparing for an exorcism.

I was ready to defend my honor, but then my bedroom door creaked open, and Riley stepped out looking . . . *Fuck.*

Hair messy, tank top loose against her shoulders, bare legs peeking out from beneath my boxers.

Adorable. Sexy. Sleep-rumpled perfection.

She stretched, and my brain went static.

Matty exhaled dramatically. "Fucking hell. Can you keep it in your pants for, like, five minutes?"

I shoved a piece of cornbread in my mouth so I wouldn't say something deeply inappropriate.

Riley blinked blearily at us, then at the table, then at the chili. Her brows furrowed. "Are you two seriously eating chili at"—she glanced at the clock on the stove—"eight in the morning?"

I swallowed the cornbread and pointed my spoon at her. "You don't get to judge. You're wearing my underwear."

She grinned, completely unbothered. "You don't wear your underwear, so someone has to. And besides, your underwear is comfy."

"Chili is *comfy*."

Matty groaned. "It's too early for this."

Riley shook her head and padded toward the cabinets, muttering, "I will be opting for cereal."

I smirked. "Your loss, sweetheart."

Matty snorted, and I narrowed my eyes at both of them.

Betrayal.

Absolute betrayal in my own kitchen.

But fine. More chili for me.

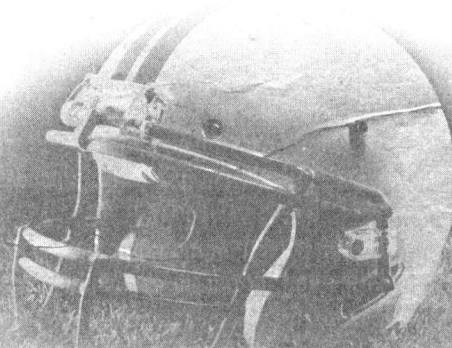

CHAPTER 28

RILEY

The campus library was nearly empty on a Saturday morning, but that was exactly why I'd chosen it. Tucked away in the farthest corner, I curled into my chair, trying to drown in the pages of my textbook. My coffee had gone cold an hour ago, my notes sat untouched, and the clock on my laptop inched farther and farther away from ten—the time I was supposed to be at my first tutoring session with Callum.

I hadn't gone. I wasn't going to go.

He could manipulate the university all he wanted, twist reality in whatever way suited him best, but I wasn't going to sit in a room with him and play his games. He wanted control? Let him fume over the fact that I refused to show up.

I'd also decided I was going to tell Jace. He'd had to spend last night at a hotel with the team in preparation for the game tonight, but I was going to tell him tomorrow.

And accept whatever came after that.

I exhaled slowly, unclenching my fingers from where they'd been digging into my palm. Maybe this would be it. Callum would realize he wasn't going to win, and we could both move on . . .

Maybe . . .

A cluster of students walked past my table, their voices breaking my focus. At first, it was just background noise, muffled murmurs about the upcoming game, last night's party, a test they were all dreading. I tuned it out, forcing my attention back to the open book in front of me.

And then I heard it.

"She was obsessed with him."

The words slammed into me like a physical blow. My breath caught, fingers tightening around my pen as my ears zeroed in on the hushed conversation happening just a few feet away.

"Like, full-on stalker mode," a redhead from one of my classes, who always had a designer handbag and an omnipresent smirk, whispered. "He told me she wouldn't leave him alone. It was bad."

My stomach flipped.

"Wait, Riley St. James? The one who's dating Jace Thatcher?" a guy scoffed, his voice laced with disbelief. "She doesn't seem like the type."

The girl let out a huff, like she was annoyed he wasn't buying it outright. "That's how people like her get you. She seems normal, but he said she used to show up at his house, uninvited. Sent letters, emails—threatened to hurt herself when he wouldn't give her what she wanted. He had to let her down gently because she was so unstable."

The air around me turned razor-sharp, slicing into my skin. My hands went numb, my pulse roaring in my ears as my mind fought to keep up.

No. No, no, no.

Callum.

Of course it was Callum.

I forced in a slow breath, gripping the edge of my table so hard my knuckles turned white. He was doing it again. Warping the past, twisting reality, painting himself as the victim while making me into something pathetic, something broken, something dangerous.

And people were believing him.

I stared down at my textbook, the words blurring together as nausea churned inside me. How was it all so effortless for him, that he could have just arrived and already be wielding so much power?

The girl sighed, her voice softening—but it wasn't pity. It was satisfaction. "Honestly, I feel bad for him. Can you imagine how scary that must've been? He's such a nice guy. He probably felt responsible for her."

I swallowed back the bile rising in my throat.

I had to get out of here.

My chair scraped against the floor as I pushed back abruptly, the sound cutting through the low hum of voices around me. Heads turned. A few people blinked in curiosity, eyes flicking to me before shifting away, but I felt the weight of their attention like a crushing force.

I shoved my notebook into my bag, my hands jerky, clumsy. I still had more studying to do, but I couldn't stay—not here, not when my lungs felt like they were collapsing in on themselves.

The girl didn't even pause in her conversation.

"I mean, I wouldn't be surprised if she still kept tabs on him. Someone needs to warn Jace."

The words followed me as I walked away.

The moment I stepped out of the library, I felt it—that creeping sensation slithering down my spine, the weight of unseen eyes pressing against my back. I told myself I was being paranoid. I turned the corner, heading toward the courtyard when a hand clamped around my wrist, yanking me into the alcove between buildings. My breath shot out of me in a sharp gasp as my back hit the cold brick, my body locking up at the sudden touch.

"Riley." His voice was silk over steel, smooth and coaxing, but with that ever-present undercurrent of cruelty. The kind of voice that promised destruction hidden beneath a charming veneer.

I tried to yank free, but his grip tightened, fingers pressing into my skin like shackles. "Let go."

Callum clicked his tongue, shaking his head like I was some troublesome child. "Now, now, is that any way to greet your mentor? I was worried about you, Riley. You missed our session." His smirk was infuriating, full of condescension. "And we both know that wasn't optional."

My stomach twisted. "I thought you would let it slide, considering the false pretenses," I hissed.

He arched a brow, amused. "You wound me, Riley. False pretenses?" He scoffed. "I think you need someone looking out for you. Because, *darling*, you've got quite the reputation these days, haven't you?" He leaned in, voice dropping to a whisper. "People are talking, Riley. And not in a way that benefits you."

I stiffened. "You did this." My voice shook with fury, but he just tilted his head, eyes bright with feigned innocence.

"Me? You're cutting me, truly." He let out a low chuckle, his thumb stroking over the pulse point in my wrist. "But let's be honest. You never really needed my help ruining yourself, did you?"

I swallowed hard, pulse hammering in my throat. "Why are you doing this to me?" I hated the vulnerability in my voice, but Callum thrived on it, feeding on weakness like a parasite.

His smirk widened, his grip loosening just enough to trail his fingers up my arm, slow and deliberate. I flinched, a violent shudder rolling through me, but he only hummed in amusement. "Because, my dear Riley, I find it *entertaining*. Watching you scramble, watching you fight so hard to stay afloat when we both know you're drowning."

I gritted my teeth. "You don't own me, Callum. And you don't know me, either. Not anymore."

His gaze darkened, the glint of something vicious flashing across his face. "Don't I?"

I felt it then, the true weight of his power. Callum had always known how to make me feel small. And right now, with his hand pinning me against the wall, his voice dripping with amusement, I felt utterly powerless.

"You know what I could do to that boy you're living with, don't you? One little whisper to the right people, and his name disappears from every draft board. His dream of the NFL? Gone. Just like that." His voice was a blade slicing through the air.

"Leave him out of this."

Callum sighed dramatically, as if my request genuinely inconvenienced him. "Oh, but that's the thing, Riley. You make it impossible. Moving in with him? Makes me wonder . . . does he even know what you are?"

My pulse pounded in my ears, but I forced myself to stand tall. "If you do anything to him—"

He held up a hand, feigning offense. "Now, now, don't be so dramatic. I don't *have* to do anything. I just have to . . . suggest a few things, let the right people come to their own conclusions." His smile sharpened. "You think I ruined *your* reputation? Imagine what I could do to *his*."

Pain bloomed in my chest, panic threatening to consume me. Jace had already done so much—protected me, loved me. And now, Callum was holding him over my head like a guillotine.

"I don't want to hurt him, Riley." His voice was soft now, mockingly gentle. "But if you really love him, you'll leave him before he gets caught in the cross fire. You'll come back where you belong. Because if you don't, I'll make sure the whole world sees him as nothing more than the fool who let an obsessed little liar ruin his life."

Tears burned behind my eyes, but I refused to let them fall.

I hated him. I hated how he always knew exactly where to strike, how he could sink his claws into my weakest points and rip me apart like it was nothing.

"You don't get to control me," I whispered.

Callum's smirk returned, lazy and triumphant. "I already do."

Then he was gone, disappearing into the crowd like he hadn't just torn my world apart. I stood frozen, my breath ragged, my heart screaming in protest.

The stadium pulsed with life, packed with fans draped in orange and white, their cheers rising and crashing in an unrelenting rhythm. The air vibrated with anticipation, thick with the scent of stadium food and the syrupy sweetness of spilled soda—the kind of atmosphere that usually felt intoxicating, impossible to resist.

But tonight, it was different.

The noise didn't vibrate through me the same way. The energy didn't lift me; it pressed down instead, heavy and suffocating. Every cheer, every chant, every roaring reaction to the game blurred into a meaningless hum, drowned out by the low, insidious echo of Callum's voice in my head. I tried to focus, to latch on to the distractions around me—the laughter of students, the familiar rhythm of the fight song, the distant sound of whistles cutting through the chaos—but none of it could shake the cold weight lodged in my chest.

Jace was out there, moving like he was untouchable, like nothing could shake him. But I knew better. Callum had set his sights on him, on us, and suddenly, game day didn't feel like an escape. It felt like a countdown to something I couldn't stop.

I sat wedged between Natalie and Casey, both of them fully invested in the action unfolding on the field. Casey was on the edge of her seat, elbows on her knees, eyes locked on Parker like he was the only player out there. Natalie, on the other hand, had spent most of the game alternating between screaming at the refs and using her phone camera like a sniper scope to zoom in on Tennessee's offensive line.

I was . . . pretending.

Pretending I was just another girl in the stands, wearing her boyfriend's number, cheering like everyone else. Pretending I wasn't holding myself together with frayed stitches.

Callum was here.

I hadn't seen him yet, but I felt him. That insidious, crawling sensation of being watched, of being studied, like a hand pressing between my shoulder blades, a whisper at the back of my head.

I forced my gaze to stay locked on the field, to focus on Jace, lined up at the thirty-yard line, his stance loose but lethal, fingers twitching at his sides as he waited for the snap. It should've calmed me. The familiarity of him, the certainty. But even Jace—the safest thing in my world—couldn't keep the dread from knotting in my stomach.

"Riley?" Casey nudged me, dragging me back to the present.

I blinked, realizing I'd been gripping my knee so hard my knuckles had gone white.

"What?"

"You okay?" She frowned, tipping her head.

Natalie waved down the guy selling bottled water without waiting for my answer. "She's fine, she's just stress-watching because they're playing like this," she announced, handing me a bottle. "Hydrate. Hydration fixes everything. Except for heartbreak and bad grades, but you're not failing, and you're definitely not heartbroken, so drink up." She eyed me until I took a sip before patting my hand. "Jace will probably do something ridiculous soon, and we need you conscious for it."

I tried to laugh, but it felt hollow.

If only that was the case . . .

Callum had won.

I could admit that now.

He'd walked into my world like I'd never left his.

And he'd won.

I sucked in a breath and let my eyes drift toward the stands. And there he was.

Standing a few sections over, too still in the chaos of the crowd. He wasn't cheering. He wasn't watching the game. He wasn't even pretending to blend in.

He was watching me.

A slow, knowing smirk curled at his lips, his head tilting slightly—like he was amused, like he'd caught me in some invisible trap, like I'd played right into his hands just by existing.

The crowd swarmed around him, oblivious, cheering and laughing, lost in the game while he lifted a hand, barely a movement, just enough for me to see. Just enough to remind me he was there.

My stomach twisted violently.

I couldn't do this. I couldn't sit here, pretending everything was fine while his stare stripped me down to nothing. I felt exposed, flayed open under his gaze, every breath too shallow, every nerve on fire.

I shot to my feet so fast my knee slammed into the metal in front of our seats. Casey startled beside me, blinking up in confusion. "Riley?"

"I'll be right back," I muttered, barely hearing myself over the blood pounding in my ears.

Natalie frowned. "Where are you—"

But I was already moving.

I shoved past the people crammed in the row, barely hearing their complaints as I reached the stairs. My hands trembled, my legs carrying me on pure instinct.

Not toward him.

Away.

I had to get away from that stare. Away from the sick feeling twisting in my gut, from the phantom touch of his fingers on my skin, from the past slamming into me with every beat of my heart.

I took the stairs two at a time, blind panic nipping at my heels.

I didn't stop.

I couldn't stop.

CHAPTER 29

JACE

Right before the play, I happened to glance up at Riley, my good luck extraordinaire . . . and my stomach fucking dropped.

She was running.

Not just moving through the crowd—running. Full speed up the stairs, her blonde hair flying, her shoulders tense, her head snapping over her shoulder like something—someone—was chasing her.

Fear. I could see it, carved into the stiff line of her spine, the way she gripped the railing like she needed something to steady her.

The ball snapped.

I didn't fucking move.

Didn't even hear the play happening around me, didn't register the footsteps pounding against the turf, my teammates shouting, the crowd roaring.

All I saw was her.

And then—she disappeared.

Gone. Vanished into the tunnel at the top of the stairs.

My chest tightened like someone had laced my ribs with barbed wire. My cleats felt glued to the field, my fingers twitching with the need to rip my helmet off and sprint after her.

Someone slammed into me, and I barely registered the hit. A blur of orange shot past me, Parker's pass landing clean in Chris Jordan's hands. The crowd erupted as he tore down the field.

None of it mattered.

The second the whistle blew, I was gone.

I ripped off my helmet, tossed it without thinking, and sprinted for the sideline.

"Thatcher!" Coach Everett's voice boomed from the sideline, pissed as hell. "Where the fuck do you think you're going?"

I didn't answer. I didn't even look at him.

The assistant coach stepped forward like he thought he could block me, and I shoved past him without a second thought.

"Thatcher, you step off this field, you're benched for the rest of the season!" Everett bellowed, his voice cutting through the roaring crowd.

But I didn't hesitate, not for a second. Because Riley was out there somewhere. Terrified.

Nothing else fucking mattered.

The crowd was a blur. A blur of team colors and screaming fans and pounding music. Of bodies pressing in too close as I shoved my way through them, barely seeing anything beyond the frantic need to find her.

I didn't have my phone, so I couldn't track her.

All I had was the memory of her face. That terror, sharp and raw in her wide eyes as she'd looked back over her shoulder.

I cut through the concourse, scanning every doorway, every exit, searching for any sign of her. My pulse was a steady drum in my ears, drowning out the mayhem of the stadium.

The girls' bathroom.

I didn't even hesitate.

A few girls squealed when I pushed inside, their eyes going wide at the sight of me storming through the doorway. Someone muttered something about me being lost. Another gasped, clutching her friend's arm. I ignored them all.

"Riley!" My voice echoed off the tiled walls.

No answer.

I strode deeper, feeling desperate. If she wasn't in here, I didn't know what I'd do.

Then a stall door creaked open.

And there she was.

Her eyes were red, her cheeks damp, her lips trembling as she stared at me like she couldn't believe I was standing there.

"Jace," she whispered, shaking her head. "What— Why are you here?"

I exhaled sharply, relief flooding through me now that I could see her, touch her. "I saw you running," I said, my voice softer now, but still laced with the adrenaline thrumming through my veins. "I saw you look back like something was after you. You really think I wouldn't come for you?"

She swallowed hard, her throat bobbing, but she wouldn't meet my eyes.

"You need to go back," she whispered. "You're— Jace, you're in the middle of a game. You can't just—"

I sighed, scrubbing a hand over my face before stepping closer, cupping her jaw, tilting her face up to mine.

"I don't give a shit about the game right now, Riley." My voice was firm, steady. "You're crying in a fucking bathroom, and I need to know why."

She shook her head again, faster this time, stepping back, arms wrapping around herself.

"I'm fine." The words were a lie, shaky and weak.

I scoffed. "Yeah. You look real fine."

Her breath hitched. She sucked her bottom lip between her teeth, like she was trying to keep herself from breaking apart.

Fuck that.

I reached for her, pulling her against me, arms locking around her, holding her tight against my chest.

She didn't fight me.

Didn't push me away.

She just . . . collapsed.

A soft, shattered sound escaped her throat as she buried her face in my chest, her hands clutching at my jersey, fingers twisting into the fabric like she needed something solid to hold on to.

I felt her shaking. Felt the way her body trembled against mine, the way her breath stuttered, uneven and ragged.

I wanted to demand answers.

Wanted to tilt her face up, make her look at me, make her tell me who the fuck had done this to her.

But I didn't.

Not yet.

Instead, I just held her.

Held her like she was the most important thing in the world. Because she was.

And when she cried into my chest, silent and broken, I tightened my arms, pressed a kiss to the top of her head, and made a silent promise.

Whoever had done this?

Whoever had put that fear in her eyes?

They weren't going to get away with it.

Riley

I buried my face in Jace's chest, my fingers fisting in the fabric of his jersey like I could somehow hold on to this moment—hold on to him—forever. His arms were wrapped around me, strong and unyielding, like nothing in the world could touch me as long as he was here. I could feel his heartbeat steady and sure against my cheek, feel the warmth of his breath in my hair as he pressed a kiss there.

But then . . . the roar hit.

It rumbled through the stadium like an earthquake, before surging into a deafening eruption of sound. The kind that sent energy crackling through the air, the kind that made the ground tremble beneath our feet. The kind that told me something big had just happened out there on the field.

I stiffened.

Jace felt it immediately, his grip on me tightening, like he knew exactly where my mind had just gone. But I wasn't thinking about myself anymore. I wasn't thinking about Callum or the weight of his threats pressing down on my chest like a vice.

I was thinking about Jace.

About the fact that he wasn't where he was supposed to be.

I pushed back, my hands flattening against his chest, forcing space between us as I lifted my gaze to his. "Jace." My voice came out hoarse, but I forced strength into it. "You need to get back out there. Right now."

He hesitated. Conflict flickering in those sharp brown eyes, his jaw clenching.

"Go. You can't be here. I'm—I'm fine," I insisted, the lie tasting like ash on my tongue.

His expression hardened, his hands still firm on my waist. "I swear to everything, Riley," he muttered, his voice low and edged with warning. "If you need me . . ."

"I'm fine," I promised, even as my stomach twisted. "I'll explain everything later."

He didn't look convinced.

But there was no time to argue.

"Fine," he muttered. "I'll go back out there."

Relief flickered in my chest . . . until he smirked.

"But first," he said, grabbing my hand, "I have a plan."

Before I could argue, before I could ask what the hell that meant, he was already moving, dragging me through the concourse, past the sea of fans swarming the hallways, past the flashing screens and the beer carts and the murmur of conversations that barely registered in my buzzing brain.

I wiped my face, trying to erase any evidence of my tears as he led me to the suite level, past a security guard who didn't even blink at our entrance.

"Jace," I hissed, tugging at his grip. "Where are we—"

He stopped in front of a door, knocked once, then pushed it open.

And suddenly, I was staring at two people I'd never seen before in my life.

A man stood near the floor-to-ceiling windows, hands tucked in the pockets of his jacket, his frame broad and sturdy, like Jace's but older. His hair was dark brown, peppered with gray at the temples, his jaw strong, his nose slightly crooked like it had been broken once, maybe twice. His eyes were those same striking brown eyes I'd fallen for, and they locked onto me with curiosity, the corners crinkling as he smiled.

Sitting beside him, a woman in a wheelchair turned slightly, her blonde hair falling over one shoulder in thick waves, one of her legs in a bulky, blue cast. She had warm green eyes, and her hands, delicate and graceful, rested in her lap, her fingers adorned with simple silver rings.

They both looked at me.

Then at Jace.

Then back at me.

The woman arched a brow. "Jace . . . honey, what exactly is going on? Why aren't you out on the field right now?"

Jace grinned, totally unfazed. "Pops, Mom—meet Riley. She's the love of my life. My heart. My everything."

My breath caught. Oh my gosh. What a freaking day to meet his parents. I whipped my head toward him, eyes wide, heart slamming against my ribs. "Jace—"

He ignored me, turning his attention back to his parents.

"I gotta get back out there, but I need you to take care of her while I do. Make sure she's okay, make sure she's safe, make sure she doesn't freak out and try to bolt." His eyes flicked back to mine, lips quirking. "Because she will. She's kind of like a jumpy little bunny."

His mom blinked, clearly trying to catch up. "Honey?"

"I'm serious," he said, all traces of humor gone. "She means everything to me. Just . . . please. Make sure she's okay."

His dad stepped forward, still looking very concerned as he clapped a hand on Jace's shoulder. "Of course, son."

His mom softened, her eyes moving to me, studying me closer now that she knew I was something to her son. "It's nice to meet you, Riley."

I opened my mouth, then shut it again, frantically wiping at my face, trying to make myself look at least halfway presentable.

Jace smirked. "She's really cute when she's flustered."

"Jace," I hissed.

He just laughed, kissed my forehead, then turned and jogged out of the suite, leaving me standing there, still half wrecked, staring at his worried-looking parents while my brain tried to reboot.

They both stared after their son for a moment before his mom finally forced a smile, her fingers anxiously adjusting the blanket in her lap. "Would you like to sit down, sweetheart? I would come and hug you, but as you can see, trying to paint my bedroom did not go well for me," she said, pointing to her cast.

I nodded, swallowing thickly, my pulse still erratic.

His dad moved to a mini fridge, cracking open a bottle of water and handing it to me.

"You good, Riley?" he asked, voice calm, steady.

"Yep," I whispered, feeling incredibly awkward.

Now I was the one forcing a smile, smoothing my palms down Jace's oversized jersey. "Sorry about that," I said lightly, like I didn't have red-rimmed eyes and trembling hands. Like I wasn't *actively* spiraling. "Jace should *not* have done that."

His mom reached out, placing a gentle hand over mine. "That boy's had a stubborn streak a mile wide since he could crawl," she said, her voice warming up as she talked about her son.

His dad didn't seem to be buying what I was selling, though. His brown eyes stayed on mine, quiet, assessing, like he could see straight through the cracks I was trying to plaster over. "You in some kinda trouble?"

"I—I promise I'm okay," I lied, pasting on another brittle smile. "I just need to sit for a while. Really." I looked between them, guilt gnawing at me like acid on my skin. "Jace has enough to focus on right now—he doesn't need to be worrying about me."

His mom's lips pressed together, her sharp gaze flicking over me again, like she could sense the storm raging inside my head. "You sure about that, honey?" she asked quietly, leaning forward and patting my knee, like she really did care what my answer was.

I had an urge to cry again, at the kindness the two of them were showing me when my own parents could show me none.

I nodded, too quickly. "Positive."

She hesitated. Finally, she nodded, too, but I could still feel their eyes on me. Watching. Worrying. Seeing too much.

I sat down next to her. Halftime had just begun, and I could only imagine what Jace was going to get from his coach.

I was already *ruining* him.

Even without Callum making a move, just knowing I existed in Jace's world was enough to put a target on his back. Jace had just risked his entire season—his entire future—to chase after me, to make sure I was okay. And his parents? They deserved to watch their son shine. They deserved to see him reach everything he'd worked for, not to have it all come crashing down because of me.

The realization settled like a stone in my gut.

I had to go.

I had to leave before I completely wrecked his life.

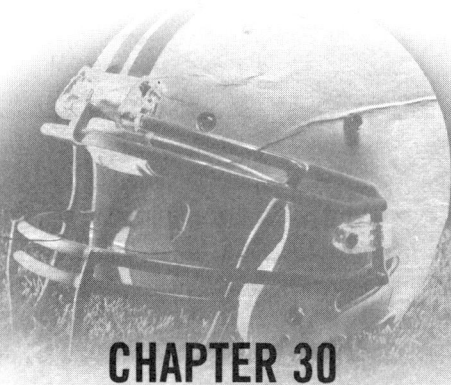

CHAPTER 30

JACE

The second I stepped foot into the locker room, I knew I was about to get obliterated.

Coach Everett was already waiting for me, his face redder than a damn stop sign, veins popping out of his neck like he'd swallowed a beehive whole. His clipboard—his favorite weapon of choice—was clenched in his hand so tightly I half expected it to snap in half.

"Thatcher," he barked, and the whole room went dead silent. "What the hell was that?"

I barely had time to drop my helmet that I'd retrieved from the sidelines before he was in my face, close enough that I could smell the spearmint gum he was furiously chewing like it was the only thing keeping him from ripping me apart.

"You don't get to walk off my field in the middle of a fucking game, Thatcher!" His voice boomed through the locker room, rattling through my skull. "You don't get to abandon your team—your brothers—because you suddenly have something better to do!"

I clenched my jaw, swallowing hard. "Coach, I—"

"I don't give a rat's ass what your excuse is!" he snapped. "I don't care if your house is on fire or if the fucking commissioner himself called you personally to tell you he needed a wide receiver! You don't do what you just did, and you sure as hell don't expect to get away with it!"

I exhaled, staring straight ahead. I took the hit. I didn't fight it. He had every right to be pissed. Hell, I'd be pissed, too.

"Congratulations, Thatcher," Coach said, his voice dripping with anger. "You're benched. For the rest of the damn season."

A low murmur rippled through the locker room.

Matty and Parker both jerked their heads toward me, wide-eyed, looking like someone had just kicked each of them in the gut. The rest of the team shifted uneasily, some muttering under their breath, others frozen in place, afraid to move.

"Coach . . ." Parker started, stepping forward. "Come on—"

Coach shot him a glare, cutting him off immediately. "I don't want to hear it. I don't care if we're winning or losing, if it's the fourth quarter or overtime, Thatcher is done."

Silence.

The kind that stretched heavy and suffocating, the weight of his words slamming into my chest harder than any tackle ever could.

Without another word, he stormed out, slamming the door so hard behind him the walls trembled.

I stayed frozen in place, fists clenched at my sides. My pulse pounded in my ears, my entire body thrumming with adrenaline and frustration.

Benched. For the rest of the season. Just like that.

Parker ran a hand through his hair, pacing. "What the hell was that?"

Matty looked like he might throw up. "Dude. Where did you go?"

I exhaled sharply, shaking my head. "I had to make sure Riley was okay."

Matty groaned, dragging a hand down his face. "Bro, I love you, but how the fuck are we going to fix this?"

Parker stopped pacing, leveling me with a hard stare. "You realize what this means, right?"

I knew. Oh, I knew.

The NFL. The scouts watching. Any possibility of a future in football. All of it—gone.

Because of one choice.

And I didn't regret it.

Not one bit.

The door slammed open again, and everyone went stiff. Coach stormed back in, but this time, something was different. The color in his face had cooled, and his jaw was no longer clenched like he was about to spontaneously combust.

He exhaled heavily, rolling his shoulders like he was shaking something off, and then he pointed at me. "You're back in."

Silence.

Dead silence.

I blinked. "What?"

"Don't make me say it twice, Thatcher. I've decided to give you one more chance."

Matty and Parker shared a look of absolute confusion. The rest of the team was equally stunned, staring at Coach like he'd just announced practice was canceled for the rest of the year.

I opened my mouth, then shut it again. Something was off. Coach never changed his mind. Not like this. Not after making a declaration that strong.

But I wasn't about to question it.

I grabbed my helmet. "Yes, sir."

Coach pointed at me. "Don't screw this up." His voice dropped, rough and unyielding. "You pull another stunt like that, and I don't care how good you are—I'll bench you so fast your head will spin. You so much as breathe out of line, and you'll be watching the rest of this season from the fucking stands. You hear me, Thatcher?"

I nodded and jogged back out with the team, the adrenaline roaring back through my veins like fire. We took the field, and the energy in the stadium shifted the second I stepped back on the turf.

The second half was ours.

We dominated.

The final score? 35–17.

We didn't just win. We shut them down.

By the time we got back to the locker room, the celebration had already started. Water bottles were sprayed, guys were yelling, everyone was going nuts.

And then I saw it.

An envelope.

Sitting on my locker.

Red-colored, thick paper. My name scrawled across the front in dark ink.

I grabbed it, my pulse kicking up as I flipped it over and pulled out the card inside.

Two words.

you're welcome.

Below it, in smaller print, another line:

courtesy of the sphinx.

My stomach dropped, and my hand automatically went to my chest where a brand-spanking-new Sphinx tattoo was inked into my skin. A shady guy had shown up to the house the day after I'd passed the third trial, armed with a tattoo kit, and I hadn't been a fan of the resulting new ink.

But I was rethinking my stance right about now.

Parker stepped up beside me, brow furrowing. "Is that what I think it is?"

I swallowed hard, showing him the note in my bag before anyone else could see it.

Matty squinted at me, catching my expression, an impressed smile sliding across his face.

I shook my head, feeling a bit dizzy from all that had happened over the last three hours. "Apparently, that ROI on my three near-death experiences has just improved quite a bit."

Parker snorted. "I'm thinking so."

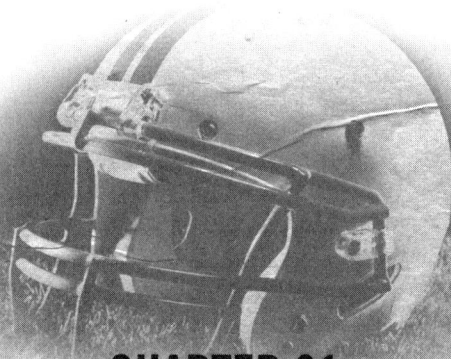

CHAPTER 31

RILEY

I practically ran back to Jace's house after the game, every step fueled by the suffocating weight of Callum's threats. My hands shook as I burst through the door, my breath coming in shallow gasps. I didn't have much time. If I could get out before Jace got back from the game, I could disappear before he even realized what was happening.

I grabbed my bag and started shoving clothes inside, not bothering to fold them. My toiletries, my books—anything that I could fit—I packed in a frenzy, my heart pounding so hard it hurt. Jace had made room for me here, carved out space in his life like I was a permanent part of it. But I wasn't. I never had been.

By the time I zipped my bag shut, my eyes were burning from the urge to cry, and it felt like something was wrong with my chest, like something had reached in and grabbed my heart. The ache got stronger with every move I made to leave him.

I ignored the pain and threw my bag over my shoulder before grabbing my car keys and running out the door, my mind screaming at me to go faster.

Sliding into the driver's seat, I shoved the key into the ignition. My fingers trembled as I turned it.

Click.

Nothing.

"No," I whispered, trying again. *Click. Click.* Nothing.

I slammed my palm against the steering wheel, panic clawing up my throat as I stared out the windshield at the rain that had just started to fall. My car had never had issues before. This wasn't happening.

I tried again. And again. Each failed attempt sent me spiraling further into despair.

I couldn't stay here. I *had* to go.

Abandoning the car, I grabbed my bag and ran through the rain. The bus stop wasn't far—just a few blocks away. My only chance. My legs burned as I sprinted down the sidewalk, dodging pedestrians, my breath ragged. Every time I slowed, Callum's voice echoed in my head. *"But if you really love him, you'll leave him before he gets caught in the cross fire."*

Tears blurred my vision, mixing with the rain pelting my face as I reached the bus stop. I fumbled to check the schedule, my fingers shaking so badly I could barely read it.

I had to get out. Before it was too late. Before Jace found me. Before Callum destroyed everything.

Clutching my bag tighter, I swallowed back the sob threatening to break free.

I didn't have a damn clue where I was headed—just away. The bus stop squatted under a flickering streetlight, a rusted bench and a graffiti-smeared pole marking the edge of nowhere. My sneakers scraped the cracked pavement as I dropped onto the seat, the cold seeping through my jeans like a punishment.

The wind sliced through my jacket, whipping my wet hair into my face, but I didn't bother fixing it. I just needed to go—somewhere, anywhere, away from the shitstorm I couldn't seem to escape no matter how hard I tried.

Callum's voice clawed at my skull, digging in deep, ripping at every weak spot he'd ever found. I'd shut my phone off, killing the lifeline to Jace, because one buzz from him and I'd break. I'd run right back, and he'd be screwed. Callum would see to that.

The street was a ghost town, just the low growl of traffic in the distance and the occasional skitter of trash across the asphalt. I pulled my knees up, hugging them tight, my breath hitching as a sob finally escaped my chest.

I'd left him. Jace. The only person who'd ever seen me—really seen me—and I'd had to leave him. My chest burned, the ache spreading so violently I wasn't sure I could survive it.

But I had to do it. He deserved more than my chaos, more than Callum's venom poisoning his life.

Headlights slashed through the dark, and I stiffened, squinting as a Jeep screeched to a halt across the street. My heart slammed into my ribs. *No.*

Fuck, no. The driver's door banged open, and Jace stepped out, his frame taut with rage. Even from here, I could feel the anger rolling off him, those brown eyes gone black with something feral. He slammed the door, the crack cutting through the sound of the rain hitting the pavement, and stormed toward me, every step the stalk of a predator.

"Riley," he snarled, voice rough and low, slicing through the wind. "What the hell are you doing?"

I scrambled up, my bag tipping over, pulse pounding in my throat. "Jace, go back home. Please."

He didn't slow, closing the gap until he loomed over me, a wall of fury and muscle blocking out the light. Up close, he was all heat. His jaw locked tight, a muscle ticking under the strain. "Where do you think you're going?" he demanded, his eyes drilling into mine, sharp and unyielding.

I stumbled back, my sneakers catching in a crack as I sat back on the bench. "Away. I—I can't stay."

"Why would you run? Why would you *leave* me?" His voice was agonized, disbelieving that I could hurt him like this.

I stared at him through my tears, my throat burning, my chest caving in. He stood there, soaking wet. His hands were clenched at his sides like he was trying to hold himself back from shaking me, from gripping my face and making me look at him the way he always did—like I was something he refused to let slip through his fingers.

But he didn't know.

He didn't know what I'd done.

And once he did, once I said the words out loud, I knew he'd look at me differently. He'd see what Callum saw—what Callum made me believe.

I sucked in a breath, forcing the words through my tight throat. "Jace . . . I—" My voice cracked, and I shook my head, squeezing my eyes shut for a moment before forcing myself to look at him. "I didn't leave because I wanted to. I'm leaving because I have to."

His brows furrowed, frustration flickering across his face. "The hell you do! Why would you have to leave?"

I let out a shaky breath, tears spilling faster. "You don't understand. I'm trying to protect you."

"From what?" His voice softened just slightly, but the intensity in his eyes didn't waver. He dropped to his knees in front of me, gripping the bench on either side of my legs, locking me in place. "Riley, what the hell is going on?"

I choked out a broken laugh, tilting my face to the sky, my vision blurring with rain and tears and exhaustion.

Sucking in a deep breath, I forced myself to *look* at him, to let myself feel the weight of what I was about to say. I wiped at my face with trembling fingers, my voice barely above a whisper. "Before I came here . . . before I met you . . . there was someone else."

His head tilted just slightly, his brows pulling together.

I swallowed hard, my fingers twisting into the fabric of my soaking wet sweatshirt. "It started right after I graduated high school," I continued, my voice cracking on the words. "He's my dad's best friend. He . . . he was married."

Jace went utterly still.

"The first time he looked at me, really *looked* at me, I felt . . . wanted. Like I wasn't just another girl. Like I was special." I let out a broken laugh, shaking my head. "I was so stupid."

Jace's jaw ticked, but he still didn't say anything.

I exhaled shakily, wringing my hands together as I talked. "He made me believe that what we had was something real—something I needed." I shuddered. "And I fell for it. I fell for *him*. I let him pull me into his world, let him mold me into what he wanted. And by the time I realized what he really was, what he was doing to me, it was too late."

Jace's fingers twitched. "Did he hurt you?" His voice was quiet, but there was something lethal beneath it. It hit me then, how ironic it was that Callum had once asked me that same thing . . . yet he ended up hurting me far worse than anyone else ever had.

I hesitated. Not because I didn't know the answer, but because I didn't know how to say it.

Finally, I whispered, "Yes."

His entire body tensed, his breath coming slower, heavier. "Riley . . ."

I swallowed, forcing the words up like poison in my throat. "He destroyed me."

Silence. Thick, weighted, suffocating silence.

Jace's hands clenched at the bench, his knuckles stark white, but I couldn't look at him. I couldn't bear to see the rage, the fury, the devastation.

So I kept talking.

"He never asked. He would just . . . take," I murmured, my voice hollow. "Whenever he wanted. No matter how I felt. No matter if I was sick, if I was exhausted, if I said I wasn't up for it. It didn't matter. Because he owned me. That's what he always said."

Jace sucked in a breath, sharp and lethal, but I kept going, because I had to. Because this was my truth, and I was done keeping it locked inside.

"He had a way of making me feel like I was the problem," I whispered. "Like I was ungrateful. Like I was lucky to have him. He'd tell me how much he risked for me, how much he sacrificed. That I owed him."

I shuddered, rubbing at my arms, trying to erase the ghost of his touch. "He'd say things—cutting, cruel things that made me feel like I was nothing. That I was a burden. That I was lucky anyone even wanted me."

Jace's chest rose and fell in ragged, uneven bursts. His jaw was clenched so tightly I thought he might break his teeth. A noise erupted out of him— low, guttural, dangerous. "That fucking piece of—" He cut himself off, his entire body vibrating with emotion.

"I shut down," I admitted. "I stopped saying no. I stopped fighting. It was easier that way. And I—I wanted to be easy. I wanted to be good. I wanted . . . to be enough. I wanted to be more than the dirty secret he told me I was." I sucked in a breath, my chest tightening at the memories. "And then there was my condition."

Jace's head snapped up, his gaze burning into mine. "What about it?"

I let out a trembling breath. "He hated it. Hated when I was too tired to go to him. Hated when I had to cancel plans because I was in too much pain. He'd sigh, like I was some inconvenience. And then he'd tell me I was weak. That I was lazy. That if I just tried harder, I wouldn't be such a burden." My throat thickened. "And the worst part? I believed him."

I shook my head, trying to steady myself, because I'd just admitted so much . . . and there was still so much more to go.

"When I was finally done, when I knew I had to get away . . . he told me I'd never escape him," I continued. "So, I cut ties completely. Changed my number. Changed everything. I took off without even telling my parents where I was going because they refused to help me. I thought—I *thought* I got away from him." My throat burned. "And then . . . he found me."

Jace's frown deepened. "What do you mean, he *found* you?"

I wiped at my face, sucking in a shaky breath, hating myself for the way my voice shook when I spoke. "He's here. He's been here for weeks, watching me. He—he's a visiting professor, Jace." I laughed bitterly, my hands curling into fists. "I was waiting for class to start one day, and then I heard his voice, and there he was . . . standing at the lectern. Just standing there, like he owned me. Like he always has."

"Riley . . ."

"He's been threatening me," I whispered as I wiped at my cheeks. "Watching me, waiting, enjoying the fact that I know I can't do anything about it. When I met you, I thought maybe—maybe—I could have something real. Something different than what I had with him. But now . . ." My breath shuddered. "Now, he's making sure I know he still owns me. That I can't have a life without him in it."

Jace's fingers flexed against the metal, and it made a cracking sound this time. "What has he been saying to you?" His voice was lethal. Low and dark and steady.

I let out a humorless laugh. "It's not just me anymore. It's you." I met his gaze, my stomach twisting at the rage burning there. "He told me that if I didn't walk away from you, he'd ruin your life." My voice dropped to a whisper. "And I couldn't let that happen."

Jace's breath came hard and fast, his entire body coiled tight, like a storm seconds away from unleashing its fury.

I pressed my hands to my face, my voice barely above a whisper. "I thought if I left, if I walked away, you'd be safe. I thought—" My voice cracked, and I dropped my hands, looking into his eyes. "I thought if you knew the truth, if you knew what I'd done, you wouldn't want me anymore."

That did it.

Jace moved.

One second he was gripping the bench, and the next, his hands were on my face, tilting my chin up, his fingers sliding into my hair, his forehead pressing against mine as he exhaled hard. "Say it again," he whispered.

I blinked, my breath stuttering. "Jace—"

"Say it *again*," he growled in a raw, shaking voice. "Tell me you really believe I'd walk away from you because of *him*."

I swallowed, tears slipping down my cheeks. "I—"

"Riley." His grip tightened, his thumb stroking my cheek with devastating tenderness. "You never belonged to him. You hear me?" His voice was rough, desperate. "*Never*."

I let out a shaky breath, holding my palms to his chest. His heart was slamming against my hands, just as wild as my own.

His forehead pressed harder against mine. "You belong with me."

A sob clawed its way up my throat. "I was scared," I whispered. "I didn't know what else to do."

Jace let out a shuddering breath. "You don't run from me, Riley. Ever." His hands slid down, gripping my shoulders, his voice shaking with restraint. "If you think for one second that I'd *ever* let you go because of what he did to you, then you don't know me at all. I'm not worried about that sick bastard."

Tears spilled faster as I clutched at his hoodie.

"I would burn the world down before I let him take you from me," he whispered, his eyes burning as he stared at me. *"Burn it all down."*

My breath hitched. "I can't—I can't let him touch you. I love you too much."

He swore and pulled me into his chest, and I sobbed against him, a strange relief flooding my veins because he knew. He knew . . . and he was still here.

The second my breath steadied, the second my sobs had quieted, he pulled back just enough to look me in the eyes. His grip was firm, his touch warm, grounding. His brown eyes gleamed with something fierce, something unshakable.

"We're going home," he said in a voice so resolute, there was no chance of me arguing.

I barely had a second to process before his arms were under my legs, lifting me effortlessly off the cold metal bench. I let out a startled breath, my arms instinctively looping around his neck as he cradled me against his chest.

"Jace," I mumbled, feeling my face heat.

"Don't even start, Riley-girl." His voice was firm but gentle, the sound of it smoothing over the raw edges inside me. "You're done running."

The world blurred as he carried me toward the Jeep, my head tucked against his shoulder. The smell of rain lingered on his hoodie, mixing with the warmth of his skin, and for the first time in hours—maybe days—I let myself relax.

He pulled open the door and set me down on the passenger seat like I weighed nothing, his hands lingering on my waist for a second before he pulled the seat belt over me. His fingers brushed my collarbone as he clicked it into place.

"Stay put."

Like I was going to try and escape again.

Jace shut the door and jogged around the front of the Jeep. As he slid behind the wheel, the bus pulled up in the distance, headlights flashing against the dark, tires hissing against wet pavement. I swallowed hard, watching as the doors opened, waiting for passengers that now wouldn't include me.

I squeezed my eyes shut, inhaling deeply. *I hope I made the right decision.*

Jace's hand slid over mine, and he threaded our fingers together. He didn't say anything—he didn't have to. He just held on, his thumb brushing against my knuckles, a silent promise in the way he refused to let go.

The Jeep rumbled to life, and he pulled away from the curb, driving us back toward campus. The streetlights flickered by in golden streaks, the hum of the engine a steady pulse in the silence.

It was only a few minutes before I turned to him, my voice quieter than usual. "How did you find me?"

Jace didn't even blink. "I was tracking you."

I scoffed, half expecting a smirk, some cocky little grin to tell me he was joking. But he didn't look at me. His eyes stayed on the road, his thumb still moving in slow, absentminded circles over my skin.

I blinked. "Wait . . . *What?*"

Now he smirked, just a little. "Relax, babycakes. I'm not crazy."

I narrowed my eyes. "That's exactly what someone who *is* crazy would say."

He shrugged. "It's just a precaution." His tone was casual, like we were talking about checking the weather. "You disappear a lot, Riley. I figured I should make sure I could find you when you get it in your head to run."

A strange tension coiled in my stomach, but not in the way it should have. I should have been freaked out. I should have pulled my hand away.

But instead, warmth spread through my chest.

Because even if he wasn't joking—even if he'd really found a way to keep tabs on me—I didn't mind.

Because it was Jace.

Because he had always found me, even when I was breaking, even when I was slipping through the cracks.

And I'd been an idiot for ever thinking I could leave him.

Callum's control had been about power—about diminishing me, keeping me small and hidden—while Jace's possessiveness was about protection, about pulling me into his world and making sure I never had to face anything alone again.

I squeezed his hand back, staring at him in the dim glow of the dashboard. At his sharp jawline, the focused set of his mouth . . . the warmth in his brown eyes, even when he was looking at the road instead of me.

This is home.

I exhaled softly, turning back to the window, watching the world blur by as he drove me back to where I belonged.

Jace didn't let go of my hand, not for a second. His grip was firm but careful, his touch steady against my skin as he pulled me inside the house. The door clicked shut behind us, the quiet hum of the house wrapping around us like a cocoon. My pulse hammered, not from fear—but from the weight of everything pressing down on us, on me.

He guided me through the living room, past the soft glow of the lamp by the couch, past the framed photos on the wall and the jacket he'd left draped over a chair. The warmth of the house, of him, settled into my skin, loosening something tight in my chest.

And then, we were in his room.

Our room.

The one he'd made mine without ever asking, the one I'd never once resisted making ours. My things were woven into his space like I had always belonged there—clothes tossed across his desk chair, a book left open on the nightstand, hair ties scattered around the room. A quiet invasion I hadn't realized was happening until it was already done.

Jace let the door swing shut behind us, but it wasn't violent. It didn't slam. It just settled, like the shift in the air. Thick with something unspoken, something heavy.

I turned to face him, my breath catching at the storm in his eyes.

Dark. Feral.

Like holding back was costing him.

"You don't leave me." His voice was rough, low, and filled with something dangerous . . . something desperate. He stepped closer, slow but deliberate, each movement pressing into my space until I had nowhere to go. "Ever."

The word crackled between us, raw and possessive, burning through my skin. My heart slammed against my ribs, my hands curling into fists at my sides as I fought the urge to reach for him.

Jace's jaw clenched as his fingers flexed. "Do you have any idea what it did to me?" His voice was quieter now, but no less intense. "First, watching you run away terrified at the game? Then finding out afterward that you'd left me?"

I swallowed hard, my throat dry. "Jace—"

His hands found my hips, dragging me the rest of the way into him, his body a furnace against mine. His grip was firm but careful, like he was fighting himself, like the line between anger and something deeper was thinning with every second.

"You don't *get* to do that to me, Riley," he murmured, his forehead dropping to mine. His breath fanned across my lips, hot and uneven. "I'm always going to come after you."

That was another difference. Callum had chased control, keeping me caged in shadows, but Jace—Jace chased *me*, refusing to let me disappear, refusing to let me believe I was anything less than his entire world.

I trembled in his hold, every part of me caught between wanting to fight and wanting to fall.

"Tell me you get it," he said, his breath thick. His fingers curled tighter at my waist, his body practically vibrating against mine. "Tell me you understand."

I met his eyes, searching the fire in them, the wreckage, the need. My heart pounded, my skin burned, but I nodded.

"I understand," I whispered.

His lips parted, a shaky breath slipping free.

And then he kissed me.

Hard.

Jace didn't give me space to hesitate, he didn't give me time to second-guess. His mouth captured mine with fierce possession, hot and consuming, his teeth grazing my bottom lip before he soothed the sting with a slow, deliberate stroke of his tongue. His body pressed into mine, solid and unyielding, pinning me back against the wall with a heat that sent shivers cascading down my spine.

"You're mine," he rasped, his voice thick with something dark, something desperate, vibrating against my lips. His hands gripped my hips, pulling me flush against him, and I felt him—*all* of him—hard, insistent, undeniable. A fire ignited low in my belly, a need so sharp it left me breathless.

"Jace," I gasped, but he didn't let me speak. Didn't let me run.

"Say it," he demanded, his fingers slipping beneath my shirt, the rough calluses on his palms dragging over my bare skin, setting me ablaze. "Say you're mine."

I sucked in a ragged breath, my head tilting back as his mouth trailed down my jaw, his teeth scraping the sensitive spot beneath my ear. He didn't *need* me to say it—he already knew—but still, he wanted to hear it.

I didn't answer. Not yet. Maybe because some small, reckless part of me wanted to make him prove it.

His grip tightened, his hands firm but not rough, not cruel—just claiming. "You don't run from me," he murmured, his voice softer now, but no less resolute. He traced patterns against my stomach, dipping lower, teasing, testing my resolve. "You don't leave. You don't ever leave."

I shuddered as his hands moved lower, skimming the waistband of my jeans. A warning. A promise.

Just as I opened my mouth to reply, Jace lifted me, carried me away from the wall, and tossed me onto the bed. My breath hitched, my body sinking into the mattress as he loomed over me, eyes dark and unreadable, his chest rising and falling with deep, controlled breaths.

My heart pounded as he dragged his soaking wet hoodie and shirt over his head, the muscles in his arms flexing, his tattoos shifting with every movement. The rest of his clothes followed. "You think I'd ever let you go?" he murmured, shaking his head as if the thought itself were absurd. "You think I could?"

I didn't answer because we both knew the truth.

I whimpered, heat pooling low as his tongue traced my throat, his grip tight and alive. He released my wrists and then tore at my jeans and under-wear, yanking them down with a roughness that stole my breath. I kicked them off, exposed under his stare, and he groaned, low . . . primal, his eyes raking over me like I was his to devour.

His body was a wall of muscle and intent as he climbed over me, and his mouth crashed into mine again, fierce and unrelenting, while his hands roamed—grabbing my thighs, spreading me wide. "You don't get to leave," he snarled again as his fingers slid between my legs, and he found me wet and aching. I arched, a cry ripping out as he teased me, brushing softly against my clit as I gasped for more. "This is mine. You're mine."

"Jace—" I cried, but he didn't ease up as he plunged two fingers inside me, curling them hard. My hips bucked, pleasure spiking fast and brutal, and he smirked victoriously.

"That's it," he muttered, pumping deeper, his thumb circling my clit with merciless precision. "Feel me."

I broke, my orgasm crashing through me in a flood of heat and light, my body clenching around him. He didn't stop; he kept going, dragging it out until I was shaking, raw, clawing at his shoulders. "Jace, please . . ."

"Please, what?" he soothed, pulling his hand free only to drop his mouth there, his tongue diving into my core, licking me open. I screamed and fisted the sheets while he consumed me relentlessly, pushing me toward another edge.

"I, I can't . . ." My voice splintered, but he didn't care. He sucked on my clit harder, sending me spiraling again. The second orgasm hit like a storm, leaving me trembling, breathless, tears leaking from my eyes.

Jace climbed up my body until his face was only inches from mine, his cock pressing against me, thick and demanding. "You don't decide," he said in a low, lethal voice as he pushed in—slow at first, then deep, filling me until I couldn't breathe. "*I* decide. And *I'm* keeping you."

That was another difference between Jace and Callum. Unlike with Callum, with Jace . . . I wanted to be kept.

I moaned as my legs wrapped around him, and he thrust harder, each stroke a claim, a punishment, a vow. "Fuck, you feel so good," he growled as he gripped my hips, tilting me to take him deeper.

The pace built, savage and perfect. His mouth was on my neck, my chest, leaving biting marks all over my skin like he was carving his name. I came again, a shuddering wreck, my nails raking his back as he fucked me through it unyieldingly, chasing his own end. "Say it," he demanded hoarsely as his hips slammed into mine. "Say you won't leave."

"Jace . . ." I whimpered. I was lost in him. Another orgasm was building too fast; it was too much.

But he didn't stop, he drove me higher, his grip bruising as his eyes locked on mine.

"Say it, Riley," he snarled, his thrusts erratic as I teetered on the edge. "You're mine. Fucking say it."

"Yes," I finally sobbed as I shattered again, pleasure tearing me apart as he groaned and spilled his hot cum inside me. It filled me up until it was leaking down my thighs, soaking the bed underneath us. "I'm yours . . . I won't leave."

Jace collapsed over me, breathing hard, his weight pinning me as aftershocks rippled through us. But he wasn't done. He pulled out, flipped me onto my stomach, and slid in again, slower now, deliberate . . . drawing it out. "Good girl," he murmured in a dark, thick voice as his hands roamed my back, my ass. "But we're going to keep going to make sure you truly understand. You. Are. Mine!"

I lost track of the orgasms, each one stripping me bare, leaving me raw and limp. He fucked me until I couldn't speak, couldn't think . . . until I was just a quivering mess, his name a broken plea on my lips. "Never," he whispered, final and fierce, as I came one last time, the world fading to black as I passed out, spent and his.

One more thing hit me, though, as I drifted into unconsciousness. There was another difference between Jace and Callum.

I'd never loved Callum.

The only man I'd ever truly loved was . . . Jace.

———————

Jace

The first rays of morning light crept through the blinds, casting soft, golden streaks over Riley's sleeping form. She was sprawled out on our bed, her cheek pressed into the pillow, her long blonde lashes fanning against her skin. The sheets were tangled around her legs, one arm stretched above her head, the other . . . well. The other was cuffed to the headboard.

With a furry, pink handcuff.

I crossed my arms, leaning against the dresser, watching her chest rise and fall in a slow, steady rhythm. Even in sleep, she looked smug, like she already knew she had me wrapped around her little finger. Which, yeah. She did.

But that didn't mean she could just leave me.

My jaw ticked, the memory of yesterday slamming into me like a full-body hit. That sinking feeling in my gut when I checked her location. That cold, sharp panic when I saw the blinking dot on my phone screen—far away from here, seemingly waiting at a bus stop at the edge of town.

She'd been running.

And if I hadn't gotten there in time, she would have left me.

Imagine if I hadn't disabled her car before I'd left for the team hotel the night before. Who knows how far she would have gotten?

The thought still made my ribs ache.

I'd done what any reasonable man would do. Hauled her ass back here, made sure she knew she wasn't going anywhere, and then spent the entire night proving it. Again. And again. And again.

I knew she was exhausted, fucked into oblivion, mind too hazy to even think about leaving now. But just in case . . . I'd taken precautions.

The pink handcuff was a nice touch. Her favorite color. It seemed only fair.

Riley stirred, murmuring something unintelligible as she shifted beneath the sheets. My lips curled as her wrist gave a little tug, the chain rattling against the headboard. Her brows furrowed, her nose scrunching up like something wasn't quite right. And then, slowly, her eyes blinked open.

It took a second. A long, slow second where I could practically see her sleepy brain processing why one of her arms wasn't moving freely. And then her gaze snapped to her wrist, her entire body going rigid.

"What the hell?" she croaked, her voice rough with sleep. She yanked at the cuff once. Then again. The pink fur made a delightful little contrast against her skin. "Jace?"

"Morning, Riley-girl." I smirked, pushing off the dresser.

She lifted her head, looking at me, then back at her hand, and then back at me. "Jace," she repeated slowly, like she was trying to determine whether I'd actually lost my mind. "Are you serious?"

I nodded. "Deadly."

Her mouth parted, her breathing still thick with sleep. "You . . . handcuffed me to the bed?"

"Sure did."

"With furry, pink handcuffs?"

"Best I could find on short notice."

She closed her eyes for a moment, inhaling through her nose, exhaling through her mouth. "Jace."

"Yes, baby?"

"I swear to God, if you don't uncuff me—"

I raised a brow. "You swear to God? Really? That's a strong accusation coming from someone who was at a fucking bus stop yesterday."

She flinched, guilt flashing across her face. She opened her mouth, then closed it, her lips pressing into a tight line.

I stared down at her, my arms crossed again. "You did leave, Riley." My voice wasn't teasing anymore. "You ran."

Her throat bobbed as she swallowed.

I exhaled sharply, shaking my head. "Do you have any idea what that did to me?" I murmured, my voice lower now, rougher.

Her expression softened.

"I love you," I said fiercely. "I don't know how else to say it. I don't know how to make you believe it enough to stay."

Her eyes welled up, but she blinked fast, like she was trying to hold it together. "Jace . . ."

I climbed onto the bed, bracing myself over her, one arm on either side of her head. "No more running," I murmured, pressing my forehead to hers. "No more leaving."

She didn't answer right away. Instead, her free hand came up, sliding into my hair, gripping the back of my neck as she pulled me down, her lips brushing against mine. "I won't leave you," she whispered.

I sighed, the knot in my chest loosening slightly.

She pulled back, a small, amused smile tugging at the corner of her mouth as she lifted her cuffed wrist. "But this is a little excessive."

"Disagree."

Riley rolled her eyes, but there was no real heat behind it. "Jace."

She was giving me the look. That half glare, that half-exasperated are-you-actually-serious-right-now expression that I'd come to know intimately since she'd entered my life.

I, however, was unbothered. Entirely unbothered.

She stretched her fingers, testing the chain again, as if in the last thirty seconds some magical shift had occurred and she'd suddenly be free. When, in reality, all she was doing was proving that I'd done a damn good job making sure she stayed right where I left her.

I smirked. "You're gonna make yourself sore if you keep yanking on that."

Her eyes narrowed. "Take this off."

I clicked my tongue. "Hmm. No can do, babycakes."

She sucked in a breath, clearly wrestling with every ounce of patience in her soul. "Jace."

"Riley." I grinned, settling onto the bed beside her.

She flopped back against the pillow, exhaling through her nose in a loud burst. "You cannot actually be serious."

I propped myself up on my elbow, trailing a finger down her bare arm, ignoring the way her skin shivered at my touch. She definitely needed some rest after our . . . activities last night. "Deadly serious."

"Jace." Her voice dipped into that dangerously sweet tone. "I swear, if you don't—"

"It's just until I get back from my meeting with Coach," I cut in smoothly, pressing a quick kiss to her jaw. I'd explained what had happened after the game in between one of our fucking sessions last night.

She stilled. "Wait. What?"

I leaned over her, my lips brushing against her ear. "Just a little insurance, babycakes," I murmured. "To make sure you don't get any ideas while I'm gone."

Riley made a sound of pure disbelief. "I already said I wasn't leaving!"

I pulled back, looking down at her, gaze lazy and amused. "Yeah. And you also said you weren't gonna run in the first place."

Her mouth opened—then snapped shut.

Checkmate.

She groaned, flopping back against the pillows again, and I bit back a chuckle.

"You cannot keep me like this," she muttered.

I shrugged. "Sure, I can."

"This is kidnapping."

I pressed a finger to her lips. "It's temporary containment."

She licked my finger.

I jerked my hand back, scowling as she grinned, smug and unrepentant. Little menace.

I sat up, shaking my head. "You're impossible."

"And you're insane."

I smirked. "Welcome to the No Drama Llamas, Riley-girl."

Her glare could've melted steel.

Still, I didn't miss the way her lips twitched.

"Now," I said, standing up and grabbing the remote from the nightstand. "Since you're gonna be here a while, I took the liberty of setting up your favorite show." I turned on the wall-mounted TV, and theme music filled the room. "And"—I grabbed the bag I'd set on the dresser, tossing it beside her—"snacks."

Her eyes darted from me to the TV to the bag of food. "You're bribing me?"

"Sure am." I winked. "You like peanut M&M's and BBQ chips more than you like being mad at me. I give it twenty minutes before you forget you're even cuffed."

She clenched her jaw, stubborn as hell, but she didn't not glance at the bag like it was calling her name.

Yeah. That's what I thought.

"Be good while I'm gone," I murmured, leaning down to brush a kiss against her forehead.

She huffed.

I grinned.

And then I walked out, leaving my girl cuffed to our bed with her favorite snacks and show, knowing that a few minutes from now, she'd be fully immersed, only remembering she was technically being held captive when I came back to let her go.

Or not.

That part was still to be determined.

CHAPTER 32

JACE

I sat at my desk, fingers drumming against the wood, my eyes burning from staring at the screen for so long. The house was quiet. Too quiet. Riley was in class, and I had my app up, checking her location constantly to make sure she hadn't gone anywhere.

It was probably going to take a minute for me to not feel the need to handcuff her for the rest of my life . . . but that couldn't be helped. I'd be tracking her even in the bathroom from now on. Although I didn't think that would be a problem for her.

Just like I'd predicted, when I got back, she was completely engrossed in her show, curled up in our bed like she hadn't been handcuffed there against her will for the past couple of hours. The second she actually noticed me, though, she put on her best scowl—one that had all the bite of a pissed-off kitten who still wanted cuddles.

"You're back," she said flatly.

I leaned against the doorframe, arms crossed, smirking. "What, no dramatic escape attempt? No using sheer willpower to chew through the headboard?"

She scoffed, huffing as she turned back to the TV. "I was formulating a plan."

"Uh-huh." I walked over and perched on the edge of the bed, glancing at the screen. "Looks like your plan involved getting emotionally invested in a fictional couple instead."

Riley narrowed her eyes at me. "Shut up. You left me with nothing but this show and snacks. What was I supposed to do? Sit here and stew in betrayal?"

I tilted my head like I was considering. "That *was* an option."

Her glare intensified, but again, kitten. More adorable than intimidating.

So, naturally, I climbed onto the bed and took full advantage of my adorable, pretend-angry girlfriend. And by *took full advantage*, I meant I spent the next hour between her thighs, making damn sure she didn't actually hate the cuffs as much as she claimed.

Which, for the record, she absolutely *did not*.

When she finally regained the ability to speak, her breathless little, "Okay, maybe keep them," was all the confirmation I needed.

I grinned down at her, pressing a kiss to the inside of her thigh. "That's my girl."

I forced myself to stop reminiscing and concentrate on the fact that my computer was a mess of notes, tabs, and bullshit I had pulled together on Callum Fucking Dipshit—or whatever his real last name was. I was elbow-deep in the university's faculty directory, sifting through an absurd amount of academic drivel, when my bedroom door creaked open.

Matty strolled in, uninvited, might I add, balancing a paper plate stacked with corn dogs in one hand and a bottle of mustard in the other. His usual shit-eating grin was in place as he kicked the door shut behind him.

I glanced up, immediately setting my laptop aside with newfound respect.

"Matty," I said, solemn as a funeral priest. "You are a man above men."

He smirked, setting the plate down next to my laptop. "I know." Then his eyes narrowed as he took in my face. "You good?"

I grabbed a corn dog and bit into it like it had personally wronged me. "I will be," I muttered around the mouthful. "After Professor Westwood is disposed of."

Matty sighed and rubbed a hand down his face. "So, we're committing murder now?"

I side-eyed him, chewing thoughtfully. "I had something else in mind, but I appreciate the commitment." I pointed my corn dog at him. "You've just moved up in the best-friendship rankings."

Right then, Parker wandered into the room, also uninvited. "What rankings?" he asked suspiciously.

"These are still the *per se* rankings," I told him absently, reaching for the mustard bottle. "But I'm fine with you guys competing for ways to stay on top."

Parker frowned. "I thought you said there wasn't a ranking."

"Yeah," Matty added, nodding. "Pretty sure last time I asked, you said something about 'friendship being a sacred, ranking-less bond' and 'don't ask stupid questions, *Matthew*.'"

I waved them off. "That was last week. Things change."

Parker crossed his arms. "Corn dogs were an unfair move. I'd like to file a complaint."

I nodded sagely. "You could probably get me some milk to go with them—iceless, of course."

Matty snorted and took an obnoxious bite of one of my corn dogs before pointing it at Parker. "Step it up, QB."

Parker rolled his eyes but didn't argue . . . and he didn't leave the room for my milk.

Disappointing.

Instead, his gaze flicked toward my laptop screen. "So, what's the plan?"

I leaned back in my chair, licking mustard off my thumb. "I'm currently trying to strategize," I told them, nodding at all the open files on my screen. "There's got to be something here. If he was doing all that shit to Riley . . . he must've been doing that shit to someone else, too."

Parker dropped onto the armchair in the corner and stretched out like he was settling in for a show. I shot him a finger gun and picked up my phone. "Let's see what Jagger has to say about this."

Matty looked confused. "I don't think a parking meter guy is going to be able to help you with this."

Parker snorted, like he thought that Matty was being funny. He wasn't. That's just what I'd told Matty one day when I was annoyed with him.

I ignored both of them, scrolling to Jagger's number. This was all based on speculation, of course. But if there was anyone who thrived on making people's lives miserable in creative and legally questionable ways . . . if there was anyone who I knew most likely to be involved in shady shit . . . it was him.

I fired off a text:

> Me: I need ideas for ruining a man's life. Open to suggestions.

Jagger's response was almost instant.

> Jagger: . . .

> Jagger: Nice to hear from you, too, little brother. Can you narrow it down? Psychological or physical?

I tapped my chin, considering.

Me: Ideally, both.

Jagger: Okay . . . who's the target?

I scoffed. That was such a mafia thing to say.

Me: Professor. Mid-forties. Wears suits he thinks make him look important. Generally looks like the type of guy who collects leather-bound books and has never made a woman come in his life.

Jagger: What'd he do?

Me: Hurt Riley.

Jagger: Say no more. Do you want humiliation or complete annihilation?

Me: Obviously, why choose?

Jagger: That's what I like about you. Okay, let's start with what we can dig up. Most guys like this have skeletons in their closet, and if they don't, we make some.

Me: Excellent thinking, brother from the same mother.

Me: P.S. You're definitely in the mafia.

Jagger: P.P.S. Don't say mafia.

I sent Jagger the miniscule amount of docs I'd already found—some faculty emails, a suspiciously empty financial record, and a few complaints that had been conveniently buried. It wasn't much, but it was enough to start setting the stage. When I was finished, I looked up and realized Parker and

Matty were still in the room . . . watching me. A little bit worshipfully look-ing if I cocked my head a certain way.

"It's surprisingly easy to ruin someone's life," I mused.

Matty had been chewing another bite of my corn dog, and he swallowed theatrically. "Why are you saying that so threateningly?"

Parker didn't look frightened at all, though, probably because he wasn't eating my corn dog at the moment and had thus moved back into the number one position. I would tell him about his rise in rankings.

Later.

It was good to keep them on their toes.

Glancing down at my phone, I watched as the little typing bubbles popped up on Jagger's end.

> Jagger: This is going to be easy. Do you want it messy or a slow burn?

I grinned.

> Me: Both.

I smirked, shaking my head as I turned to my laptop and got back to work. I had a feeling that Callum had built his life on control—controlling his students, his reputation . . . Riley. He had spent years making sure people feared him more than they questioned him.

But fear only worked when you weren't up against someone crazier.

Lucky for me, I had no moral compass when it came to protecting Riley.

———————

I cracked my knuckles, rolling my shoulders as I leaned closer to the laptop screen, my fingers flying over the keyboard with sharp precision. The dim glow of the monitor was the only light in the room, casting jagged shadows against the walls as I worked.

I'd waited until Riley was asleep to get back to it, not wanting her to know what I was doing until it was done. Every so often, I glanced over at the bed and got the pick-me-up I needed to pull another all-nighter. Time was of the essence here, though. He'd sent her another email today, remind-ing her of their next "tutoring" appointment. He'd be coming after me any day now.

People were lazy as hell when it came to cybersecurity. Callum West-wood . . . sorry, *Professor* Callum Westwood . . . was no different.

Tonight, it had taken me only ten minutes to crack into the university's database. Five minutes after that, I was scrolling through his login credentials. And at the fifteen-minute mark?

I was deep inside his inbox.

The guy didn't even try to make his passwords complicated, probably some variation of a pet's name, an old birthday, maybe even a pretentious Latin phrase. Hell, the first one I tried was *FortunaFavetFortibus1* and boom—I was in.

Pathetic.

I clicked through the usual academic drivel—emails from faculty members about meetings, half-finished drafts of research proposals . . . an obnoxious amount of correspondence with the dean, kissing ass over some upcoming funding.

Bingo.

A folder titled *Research Proposals.*

I frowned, clicking it open. It seemed harmless enough—Callum was a professor, after all, and reviewing proposals was part of the gig. But as I scrolled through the contents, a familiar, sick feeling started curling in my gut.

Half of these files? They weren't research at all.

I spotted an email chain buried in the folder, the subject line *Re: Follow-Up on Discussion.*

I clicked.

The first few messages were clean, basic faculty-to-student conversations about research methodology and scheduling meetings. But then, as I kept scrolling?

The tone shifted.

Callum started getting too comfortable.

There were compliments—subtle at first. *Your insight is always so refreshing. I wish more students were as mature as you. You have such a natural intelligence—so rare to find these days.*

Then, the timing of the emails got . . . odd. Messages sent past midnight. Responses riddled with overly familiar phrasing, unnecessary punctuation.

I narrowed my eyes, scrolling faster.

There it was.

A thread between Callum and one of his grad student assistants.

I sat up straighter, the air in my lungs coming out in a loud gasp.

The first few emails seemed normal enough—she had asked for clarification on a project she was assisting him with. He had responded.

But then . . .

Callum had offered her a better research position.

In exchange for . . . private meetings.

My hands clenched into fists.

The girl had refused, flat out, without any hesitation. Her reply was clear and professional. She stated she wasn't comfortable meeting off campus. She didn't think it was appropriate. She thanked him for the opportunity, but she was not interested.

And Callum? He had responded by tanking her entire recommendation letter.

I exhaled slowly, dragging a hand through my hair.

This was it. This was the kind of shit that could end him.

I copied everything. Screenshots, attachments, the whole fucking thread. But I wasn't done. Not yet.

Because if I was going to take Callum out, I wasn't going to do it halfway. Destroying the good professor's career and reputation wasn't just about exposing what he'd already done.

It was about making sure no one would ever doubt it.

I cracked my knuckles again and leaned forward, my focus razor-sharp as I pieced together something that looked airtight.

First, I adjusted the time stamps. Made it seem like the emails weren't from years ago but were much more recent . . . like he had *just* tried to pull the same disgusting move with another student last week.

Next, I planted a fake complaint. A carefully crafted, anonymous email from a "former student," detailing inappropriate conduct, coercion, and academic tampering. I kept the language vague enough that it didn't seem forced but specific enough that it would be undeniable.

Then came the paper trail.

With a few keystrokes, I linked his name to a dummy email account I'd created, one that "accidentally" housed multiple attachments of inappropriate messages sent to "various students" over the years. It wasn't just about one case anymore—it was a pattern of misconduct.

People didn't react to singular scandals. They reacted to multiple scandals.

Callum was about to become a textbook example of a predator with a pattern.

I sat back, staring at the mess I'd created, my heart thudding hard in my chest.

Now, I just needed to drop the bomb.

I leaned back in my chair, rolling my shoulders as the email draft glowed on the screen in front of me. My fingers hovered over the keyboard, tension coiling in my chest. This wasn't just about sending a message—it was about completely erasing Callum Westwood from the face of academia.

If the university thought they could bury this, if he thought he could get away with what he did to Riley—what he'd probably done to God knows how many others—they had another thing coming.

I cracked my knuckles and reread the email one more time.

Subject: URGENT: Misconduct Allegations Against Professor Callum Westwood

To Whom It May Concern,

This is a formal complaint regarding Professor Callum Westwood's ongoing misconduct involving multiple students.

Attached, you will find documented evidence of inappropriate behavior, coercion, and academic tampering. Multiple individuals have been impacted, some of whom have remained silent out of fear of retaliation.

If the university does not take immediate action to investigate and remove him from his position, this information will be forwarded to major media outlets, alumni donors, and the state education board.

This is your opportunity to do the right thing—before the public forces your hand.

Sincerely,

A Concerned Party

I stared at the screen, my pulse thudding against my ribs.

The university would try to protect him, I knew that much. Institutions like these? They cared about reputation first, not justice. But the moment this thing reached public ears, they'd have no choice but to distance themselves.

That was the goal.

I hesitated for only a second.

Then, I clicked send.

But I wasn't stopping there.

While that email was worming its way into the inboxes of every tight-lipped administrator on campus, I grabbed my phone to text Jagger.

Me: Wake up.

Three dots appeared instantly.

Jagger: This better be an emergency.

I snorted.

Me: This one bad in bed, too?

Jagger: . . .

Jagger: Yes.

Me: Good, then you'll have no problem helping me. I need you to get something in front of a journalist ASAP.

Jagger: You found something?

Me: Yep, I've got the receipts. I just need the megaphone.

Jagger: My favorite kind.

I attached and sent the files.
A few beats of silence. Then—

Jagger: Holy. Fucking. Shit.

Me: Yeah.

Jagger: He's done.

Me: Make sure of it.

A few minutes later, another text popped up.

Jagger: Sent it to a reporter at *The Tennessean*. He's running it by his editor now. If they hesitate, I'll nudge it to someone who won't.

Me: Good. Keep me posted.

I set my phone down on the nightstand, the screen still glowing with Jagger's last text. The wheels were in motion now. Callum's career, his reputation—everything he'd built—was already starting to crumble. And by the time Riley woke up, it would be in free fall.

I let out a slow breath, dragging my gaze to her.

She was curled up in the middle of the bed, completely wrapped in the blankets like some kind of sleep-drunk burrito, one arm stretched over my pillow. Her hair was a mess against the sheets, her lips slightly parted, breath soft and steady. Peaceful.

She actually looked like she felt safe, and I couldn't wait for that to be her reality.

I rubbed a hand over my face, exhaling before I climbed into bed beside her. The second my weight dipped the mattress, she stirred, her body instinctively gravitating toward mine like she knew I was supposed to be there.

My chest clenched.

"Everything okay?" she mumbled, her voice thick with sleep as she pressed closer, her fingers grazing my stomach.

I wrapped an arm around her, tugging her against me, my chin resting at the top of her head. "Everything's great," I murmured, kissing her hair, my lips brushing against the soft strands.

I couldn't wait for her to find out just *how* great.

I stood outside the admin building, hands in my pockets, watching as the doors swung open. The late afternoon sun hit just right, casting long shadows across the steps as two uniformed officers flanked Professor Callum Westwood, gripping his arms as they led him out in handcuffs.

Beautiful. Absolutely fucking beautiful.

Callum's face was tight, lips pressed into a thin line, his carefully curated, upstanding-professor mask cracking under the weight of reality. His suit was rumpled, his usually slicked-back hair a little out of place, and there was something wild in his eyes—the look of a man who'd finally realized he wasn't untouchable.

And then those eyes found me.

I smirked, tilting my head slightly as I slipped one hand from my pocket and lifted it in a lazy, two-fingered salute.

His jaw clenched, his whole body going rigid.

Fuck, this was satisfying.

I cocked a brow, letting the moment stretch between us, letting him sit with the fact that he wasn't the one in control anymore. That he never had been. That his whole world was crumbling while I stood here, solid, smug, and victorious.

The officers muttered something to him, nudging him forward, but he didn't move for a second—just stared, a muscle jumping in his jaw, a storm brewing in his glare.

Poor guy. He really should've known better. I took out my phone and took a picture of him, for Jagger . . . and posterity's sake.

His face only got angrier.

Finally, he was yanked forward, forced to stumble down the steps, the sound of his dress shoes scuffing against the pavement so much louder now that he was no longer the one calling the shots. Fury radiated off him in waves, but there wasn't a damn thing he could do about it.

I smiled wider, watching as they loaded him into the police cruiser.

Then I turned, slipping my hands back into my pockets, my work here done.

And Riley's nightmare? Officially *over*.

CHAPTER 33

RILEY

I wasn't sure when I'd started shaking.

Maybe it was when I first saw the headlines on my phone. Maybe it was when the whispers started floating through campus. Maybe it was when I walked into class and every single person was either talking about it or reading about it.

"Professor Callum Westwood Under Investigation"

"University Suspends Professor Amid Scandal"

"Police Confirm Criminal Charges Against University Professor"

I reread the words again and again, my vision blurring, a strange lightness threading through my veins.

It was real. He was actually gone.

I had spent so long suffocating under the weight of him, trapped in a current I could never escape. Whether in person or lurking in the shadows of my mind, he was always there—haunting me, hunting me. His voice had weaved through every quiet moment, his threats slithering into my thoughts, a constant reminder that no matter how far I ran, I'd never be beyond his reach.

He didn't need to stand beside me to corner me, he had mastered the art of making me feel caged with nothing but a whisper, a glance, the unshakable knowledge that he was watching. Always watching. Always waiting.

But now?

Now, *he* was the one losing everything.

I covered my mouth with my hands, a sob breaking loose from my throat.

I should have felt relieved.

I should have felt safe.

Instead, I felt overwhelmed.

The pressure, the fear, the suffocating weight I had carried for so long suddenly cracked apart all at once, and the pieces collapsed over me in waves.

I stumbled back, bracing my hands against the table, struggling to catch my breath.

And then . . .

Warm hands grabbed my waist.

A familiar grip. A solid, immovable force.

Jace.

I barely registered how I got outside, how I was suddenly in his arms, his strong hands cupping my face, tilting my chin up so I had no choice but to look at him.

He was searching my eyes like he could fix me just by holding me.

"Breathe, babycakes." His voice was low, soothing, but edged with something rougher. "You're okay."

I shook my head, another sob escaping. "I— He's— Jace, he's—"

"I know."

His thumb traced the tear sliding down my cheek, and I felt it like a brand.

I let out a broken laugh. "It's over."

His jaw clenched tight, but his eyes softened, filled with something deep and aching. "Yeah, Riley-girl. It's over."

I grabbed fistfuls of his hoodie, pulling him closer, burying my face against his chest. He was so warm, so solid, his arms wrapping around me, holding me together even as I was falling apart.

I felt his lips press against the top of my head, lingering, like a silent promise.

"You never have to be afraid of him again."

A fresh wave of tears burned in my throat. "Jace—"

His grip tightened. "Shh. You don't have to say anything. I got you."

I pulled back just enough to look at him, really look at him—the strong lines of his face, the way his hair was slightly damp from practice, the shadows under his eyes that told me he had barely slept.

Like he had been watching over me this whole time.

The realization hit me like a punch to the chest.

"Jace." My voice trembled. "Did you—"

His smirk was slow, smug, and infuriatingly beautiful.

"Did I what, baby?"

I sniffled, narrowing my eyes. "You know what I'm asking."

He tangled his fingers in my hair, tilting my head back so I was trapped in his gaze.

And then . . . he smiled.

That dark, knowing, I-would-burn-the-world-down-for-you smile.

"I told you, didn't I?" His voice was soft, almost teasing. "You're mine. No one gets to touch what's mine."

A shiver ran down my spine.

"Jace."

He leaned in, brushing his lips over mine, a whisper of contact that stole every bit of air from my lungs.

I couldn't breathe, the heat of him, the sheer intensity of him swallowing me whole.

"Jace," I whispered, my voice barely more than air, curling into him, drawn to him like gravity itself. "I don't know how to do this without you."

His chuckle was low and rough, his grip tightening on my hips as he pulled me flush against him. "Good thing you don't have to."

I stared up at him, that strange lightness spreading. "You always—" My throat tightened, emotion clawing its way up. "You always take care of me."

"Damn right, I do," he murmured, his breath warm against my lips, his eyes dark with something fierce and unshakable.

A half laugh, half sob tumbled from my lips. "You can't just . . . just erase everything bad in my life."

His smirk deepened, wicked and sure. "Watch me."

And then his lips crashed into mine.

No warning. No hesitation. Just heat—raw, all-consuming, mind-destroying, world-ending heat.

I gasped into his mouth, and he swallowed the sound, his fingers digging into my waist, pressing me back against the wall like he wanted to sink into my bones, like he wanted to mark me from the inside out.

It wasn't gentle.

It wasn't soft.

It was desperate, possessive . . . full of every promise he had ever made.

And as my knees went weak, as my body melted against his, I didn't fight it.

I let him catch me.

———

The room was still bathed in the afterglow of what we'd just done, our breaths still uneven, the heat of Jace's body pressing against mine as we lay tangled in the sheets. My head rested on his chest, the steady rhythm of his heartbeat soothing, anchoring me in the quiet darkness. His fingers lazily traced circles on my bare back, his touch soft, unhurried.

I could have stayed like that forever.

But then I shifted, stretching slightly, and my hand brushed against his ribs.

He flinched.

I froze, my fingers barely skimming his skin. Jace Thatcher was not a man who flinched.

Frowning, and before he could stop me, I lifted myself onto my elbow, peering down at him through the dimness in the room to see if he had some bruise from football that I hadn't noticed.

His smirk was lazy, satisfied, but his eyes flashed with something almost . . . *nervous.*

That should have been my first warning.

"What was that?" I asked, my voice still husky from multiple orgasms and *him.*

"Nothing." His grip on my hip tightened slightly, like he was trying to distract me. "Come back here, Riley-girl. I wasn't done with you yet."

I narrowed my eyes. He was hiding something.

And when Jace hid something, it usually meant chaos.

I pushed myself up farther, shifting the sheets down his body, and that's when I saw it.

Ink.

Of my name.

Etched onto his ribs like it had belonged there all along.

I sucked in a breath, my heart hammering. "Jace . . . what the hell is that?"

His lips twitched, but his hand reached for me again, like he knew I was about to freak the hell out.

"Riley, before you—"

"You tattooed my name on your ribs?" I hissed, my palm flattening against the inked skin like I needed to confirm it was real.

And it was.

His skin was still warm from the healing process, slightly raised, the ink fresh. My full name stretched across his ribs in an elegant, bold script, right beneath the edge of his heart.

I gaped at him.

He grinned up at me like a man who knew exactly what he was doing. "I was going to wait until the right moment to show you, but . . ." He exhaled, cocky and completely unrepentant. "You're evidently a nosy Nelly, babycakes."

"Nosy? I'm nosy?" My voice pitched. "Jace, you tattooed my freaking name on your body!"

"Yeah," he said, completely unbothered, dragging a hand through his messy golden hair. "And?"

I blinked at him. *And?*

"Jace," I whispered, my fingers still pressed against the ink. My head was spinning. My heart was pounding. "Why . . . why your ribs?"

His expression changed, softening just slightly, the teasing smirk giving way to something deeper. His fingers brushed over mine, pressing my palm against his skin like he wanted me to feel the weight of it.

"Because," he murmured, voice quieter now, rougher, "your name belongs right here." He tapped his ribs, just over the ink, just over his heart. "Every breath I take, I want you to be part of it. Every time I move, I want to feel you with me. I don't want you on my arm where it'll fade in the sun. I don't want you on my back where I'll never see it. I want you here, Riley. Where you can't be ignored. Where you can't be erased."

My chest clenched.

Emotion swelled in my throat, choking me.

I stared down at him, at this ridiculous, reckless, beautiful man who had just branded himself with *me*.

"You're insane," I whispered, because what else could I even say?

Jace smirked. "I think at this point that's old news."

I wanted to run my fingers over the letters. I wanted to trace every line, every curve, to press my lips against the proof that he had made me a part of him—permanent, unshakable, like I was something that could never be erased. I wanted to scream, to laugh, to cry, because Jace had gone and inked me onto his body like it was the most natural thing in the world. Like I had always belonged there. Like I always would.

Like he never had a single doubt about it.

I swallowed hard. "I think this means you're serious about me, Jace Thatcher."

His smirk softened, and those eyes—warm brown with flecks of amber catching the light—held me captive. Steady. Unyielding. Certain. Like he already knew how this story ended.

"I told you," he said simply, "you're mine."

I drew in a breath, the kind that felt like it reached the deepest parts of me, stirring places I'd long thought abandoned.

Jace Thatcher.

Fierce and reckless. Unyielding and mine. A storm I should've feared, but instead, I had run straight into it, finding shelter in the very thing that could destroy me.

I exhaled, my fingers brushing over his skin, mapping the warmth of him, the solidity, the unwavering presence that had become my foundation.

And in that moment, something within me, something fragile and aching, mended, not with stitches, but with fire, sealing every crack with the only thing strong enough to make me whole.

Him.

CHAPTER 34

JACE

Parker and I were lounging on the couch, watching football, when the front door slammed open so hard I thought it might fly off the hinges. Matty stormed in like a man on a mission, eyes locked onto me like I was his mortal enemy.

"You are *still* tracking me?" he bellowed, hands on his hips like a pissed-off suburban mom.

I popped another cheese puff into my mouth, completely unfazed. "You hadn't answered any of my texts," I pointed out, licking cheese dust off my fingers.

Matty threw his hands in the air. "I was on a date, Jace. A *date*."

I nodded sagely, reaching for another cheese puff. "Yeah, and that date could've been a cleverly orchestrated kidnapping attempt. You never can be too careful these days."

Parker snorted, but I kept my face neutral, like I was genuinely concerned about the state of Matty's safety.

He scowled. "Kidnapped? By *Courtney*?"

I shrugged, stuffing another handful of snacks in my mouth. "Listen, I don't know Courtney personally. Maybe she seemed sweet. Maybe she batted her eyelashes and laughed at your dumb jokes—a sign she's faking, by the way, because you're not funny. But who's to say she wasn't planning to stuff you in the trunk of her car and drive you to an underground fight club?"

Parker leaned forward, intrigued. "Ooh, underground fight club. Could be fun, though."

Matty turned his glare on him. "Not helping."

Parker shrugged. "I'm just saying. If she kidnapped you, at least you'd have a cool story."

Matty turned back to me. "You tracked me down, Jace. During my date. And do you know what you did?"

I grabbed the remote, pretending to be super into the game. "Of course, I know what I did. *I* was the one doing it."

"I don't know what he did," Parker offered.

Okay, that was kind of funny. I gave him a high five just because. "I rescued you from a potentially dangerous situation. You're welcome, by the way."

Matty clenched his jaw. "You sat down. At our table."

I nodded. "I did."

"You ordered a drink."

"Thirsty work, tracking people."

"And nachos."

Parker laughed so hard he nearly fell off the couch. "Sorry . . . just making sure I have this straight. You crashed Matty's date and sat down at the table?"

"There was a picture of nachos on the menu. I couldn't resist," I said, completely unapologetic.

Matty groaned, dragging his hands down his face.

I pointed at Matty with my cheese-dusted fingers. "I told her I was his brother so she wouldn't be weirded out."

Matty actually howled in frustration, throwing himself onto the couch beside us like he was being pushed down by the crushing weight of this best friendship. "Before that, she'd asked if we were dating—and then asked if she could watch!"

"What can I say? We're a good-looking pair, Matty. Who wouldn't want to watch us is the actual question. Although, let me be clear, it was offensive that she thought I would ever settle for being a sidepiece."

Parker raised his hand, a smirk on his lips. "I would like the record to reflect that *I* would not want to watch you."

Matty sighed, closing his eyes dramatically like the world was ending. "You're a menace. A psycho menace. And you need to stop tracking me."

I leaned back, popping another cheese puff into my mouth. "No can do, Matty-kins."

Matty groaned again. "Courtney probably thinks I'm freaky now."

Parker snickered. "I mean, that's probably not far off since you're a guy whose male 'companion' showed up at your date and ordered nachos."

Matty sat up suddenly, jabbing a finger at me. "You owe me."

I nodded solemnly. "I'll get you some nachos next time."

He gritted his teeth. "*Not* what I meant."

Parker threw an arm around Matty's shoulders. "Matty, you really should've just texted him back."

"Yeah, look what happened the last time I didn't text *you* back," I told him, a grin spreading on my face because . . . *Darla.*

Matty groaned and sank deeper into the couch. "Point taken."

I offered him the bag of cheese puffs.

He took one.

Victory.

———————

The game was on, Parker was half asleep, and Matty was still sulking about the "Great Nacho Betrayal." All in all, a solid Saturday. If Riley was going to be at the spa with Casey and Nat, this was how I wanted to spend the day.

Parker's phone lit up on the coffee table.

Incoming FaceTime: Walker Davis.

Parker groaned, barely cracking one eye open. "If this is about Cole's *Rolling Stone* article, I swear—"

I snatched up his phone before he could finish. "Ooh, let's see what Big Brother Davis wants."

Matty perked up. "Does this mean I get to watch Parker get bullied in real time?"

"Absolutely." I grinned, answering the call.

Walker's face filled the screen, looking entirely too put together for a Saturday. He was in some swanky hotel room, probably on the road with his NHL team, the Dallas Knights. And sitting next to him, grinning like he was about to cause problems on purpose?

Ari Lancaster.

Star defenseman . . . and possibly my hero and who I wanted to be when I grew up.

Not that I would admit that to him. He'd never let me hear the end of it.

"You *finally* picked up, jackass," Walker said before his eyes focused, his frown deepening. "Oh. Jace?"

I smirked. "'Sup, Walker *Disney* Davis?"

"You don't have to say my full name." Walker sighed.

Matty snorted as Parker grumbled, rubbing his face. "That's not your *actual* name. I hope you know that."

"He wishes it was his full name," I said.

Ari leaned into the screen, pointing. "Thatcher."

I saluted. "*Lancaster.*"

"Question." Ari squinted at me. "Your hair during the last game. Was I imagining that?"

Matty perked up, eyes gleaming. "Oh, I love where this is going."

Parker sat up, suddenly interested. "I love where this is going as well."

I smirked at both of them, because I appreciated their attention. "'As well,'" I mimicked. "So proper, Mr. Big Brain."

Ari snorted, and I preened.

Running a hand through my hair, I rolled my shoulders, completely unbothered. "You jealous of my luscious locks, Lancaster?"

Ari grinned. "Nah, just concerned, buddy. Because last I checked, you're not an Instagram influencer from Miami."

Parker was eyeing me, like he could tell I was getting all giddy inside because Ari Lancaster had called me "buddy."

Walker shook his head and examined me. "Or an eleven-year-old at summer camp."

Matty started dying like Walker had actually said something funny. Which he hadn't.

"Hey, *hey.*" I pointed at the camera. "That was *art*. You think I just woke up with two perfectly symmetrical braids intermixed with the rest of my flowing long locks? That took effort. That took precision."

Ari pressed a hand to his chest. "How long did it take for you to look like a budget boy band member from 2002?"

I shrugged. "Thirty minutes to get the look I was going for. And it was worth every second," I said, raising my eyebrows up and down. "I'll have you know that Riley thought it was *very* sexy."

Walker crossed his arms in front of his chest and shook his head. "I'll bet she did. Although, real commitment is piercing her name into your—"

Suddenly Ari's hand was in front of Walker's mouth, cutting off what he'd been about to say. "Disney, there are children in the room. Let's not give specifics about what true love actually looks like."

Parker's eye roll was outrageously dramatic next to me.

Walker leaned back, shaking his head. "I don't think I could get my hair messed with for thirty minutes. I can barely get through a five-minute haircut without twitching."

Ari snorted. "That's because you have the attention span of a goldfish, Disney."

"Oh, I'm sorry," Walker scoffed. "Did you forget about how you zoned out mid-interview with ESPN the other day?"

Ari blinked. "Blake was giving me the look. You try concentrating in the midst of such perfection. I'm just a man, Disney."

I nodded. Because I understood what he was talking about. The struggle was real trying to concentrate on anything but Riley *Babycakes* Thatcher.

"We should talk about your pregame rituals, too. What is it again? You have to tape your left wrist twice before your right, or you'll suddenly forget how to function like a human?"

Ari rolled his eyes. "That's called *being locked in*, darling Disney. It's science."

Matty, Parker, and I were watching their back-and-forth avidly, like we'd never seen anything more interesting.

"I would just like to state for the record," Ari began, turning his attention back to us. "So there's no confusion. Walker only has big balls because Lincoln's not around. His balls shrivel and get simpish when Golden Boy's in the room."

Walker sighed, and Matty waved a cheese puff at the screen.

"Lincoln Daniels, now *he's* what I call style."

Parker and I glanced over at Matty, suddenly sure there was another *simp* in this conversation . . . and it wasn't Disney.

Ari raised a brow at Matty's comment, but then he nodded. "I can't argue with that," he said solemnly.

I smirked, popping a chip into my mouth. "I bet *Daniels* thought my braids were awesome."

Ari scoffed like I'd personally offended him, and Walker looked behind them . . . hopefully . . . like Lincoln—their star center—was about to walk in the room.

Ari sighed and shook his head. "Don't mind Walker. He just can't wait for the sleepover to start."

"Sleepover?" I asked, intrigued. I loved a good sleepover. Too bad *Matthew* was so against it.

"Logan got a hat trick last night . . . so here we are," Walker muttered, like he wasn't fucking giddy about the prospect of Lincoln sleeping in the same room as him.

Ari side-eyed him. "Don't pretend I didn't see those face masks in your bag, Disney. Plus popcorn. *And* a selection of movies that will emotionally wreck us all because there are dogs involved."

"I also brought *Pretty Woman*," Walker said with a wink.

Ari looked delighted at that revelation. "Ah, yes. A heartwarming tale of an escort, a corporate credit card, and the undeniable power of thigh-high boots." He patted Walker's shoulder. "You brought that because it's my favorite. Finally! The respect I deserve."

Walker nodded . . . unconvincingly, but Ari didn't seem to notice. I had a sneaking suspicion that *Pretty Woman* might have been a Lincoln Daniels favorite as well.

"Anyways . . ." Walker said, suddenly sounding eager to change the subject. "I did have a point in calling."

"Shocking," Parker said, his gaze drifting to the screen where Houston had just scored a touchdown.

Walker gave a cute little growl that kind of sounded like a kitten trying out its meow for the first time. "ANYWAYS . . . Olivia wants to do a Christmas thing this year in between games, and she *specifically* asked if Matty and Jace are bringing girlfriends."

"Yes," I said at the same time that Matty said, "No."

"You could bring Darla," Parker suggested, quickly ducking as Matty tried to pick up a lamp . . . before realizing it was plugged in. He glared at it like it had personally wronged him.

Walker looked confused by Matty's behavior, but that wasn't anything new. Matty confused all of us at one point or another. "Alright, well tell Olivia what you're doing so she can plan. I don't want to be in charge of wrangling you two."

Parker saluted. "Will do, fearless leader."

Ari pointed at me. "And you—whatever this chaotic energy is, keep it up. It's wildly entertaining."

I grinned, feeling a little boisterous now that I knew I was impressing the great Ari Lancaster. "Oh, I plan to."

"And *Disney* . . . have fun at your sleepover," Parker said mockingly, like he didn't think it was the greatest idea ever, and we wouldn't be instituting it at our next away game.

Walker scoffed. "Bye."

And just like that, the call ended.

Matty exhaled, still scowling. "We're not snuggling, Jace Thatcher. So don't get any ideas."

I shook my head at him. "This is why my ranking system exists. So I can judge you when you're a negative Nancy."

Matty groaned and reached for another handful of cheese puffs.

"Love you, too, bud," I said, opening my app to make sure that Riley was still at the spa.

Parker smirked and pulled up the camera footage from Casey's necklace, and I was instantly inspired by him.

I grinned, already scheming on my next gift for Riley. "You know, Parker, sometimes I think you might actually deserve your spot in the rankings."

"The *per se* rankings," Matty added, grumbling, and I hummed in agreement, because sometimes it was best to just go along with him.

CHAPTER 35

JACE

Riley was in full panic mode.

I leaned against the counter in our kitchen, sipping my coffee, watching her tear through her bag like a woman possessed. Her hair was slightly messy from sleep, her face adorably scrunched in frustration as she yanked things out and tossed them onto the table.

"Where the hell is it?" she muttered, rifling through her wallet, her keys clattering onto the floor in the process.

"What's missing, Riley-girl?" I asked, my voice laced with the perfect amount of casual curiosity.

She huffed out a breath, blowing a strand of hair from her face. "My campus ID! I had it yesterday when I swiped in for lunch, and now it's just . . . gone."

I hummed like I was deep in thought. "You sure you didn't leave it in the bathroom? Or maybe the dining hall?"

"No! I already checked the bathroom, and I know I didn't leave it in the dining hall because I remember having it when I got back last night." She turned, eyes narrowing. "Have you seen it?"

I took another sip of coffee, tilting my head as if I were giving the matter serious contemplation. "Can't say that I have."

I absolutely had. It was sitting safely in a hidden box next to a few other things of hers I'd "collected," but she didn't need to know that.

"This is such a pain," she groaned, rubbing her temples. "I need that ID for everything—food, getting into the library, printing stuff. I guess I'll have to go to the campus office and get a new one."

I pushed off the counter, setting my coffee down. "Tell you what, I'll drive you."

She frowned at me. "Why?"

I shrugged. "Because I'm a good boyfriend who enjoys spending time with his girl?"

She narrowed her eyes suspiciously but didn't argue. "Fine. Let me grab my stuff."

I smirked as she turned away. *Too easy.*

Fifteen minutes later, we were at the student ID office. I leaned against the counter while Riley explained her situation to the girl behind the desk, tapping my fingers idly against the surface as I watched.

"Name?" the student worker asked.

"Riley St. James," she said automatically.

The girl typed a few things, then nodded. "Got it. You'll just need to pay the replacement fee, and I'll print it out."

I handed over my card before Riley could protest. She shot me a look, but I just smiled innocently, wrapping an arm around her waist and pulling her into my side. "Boyfriend duties."

She sighed but let me get away with it.

The girl behind the desk hit a few more buttons, then stood and walked over to the machine to print the card. A few seconds later, she returned and handed it to Riley. "Here you go!"

Riley barely looked at it before stuffing it into her pocket. "Thank you so much."

I almost laughed. *Babycakes, you're in for a surprise.*

Later that night, I was lying on the bed, scrolling through my phone, when I heard the sudden rustling of her bag in the other room.

Then silence.

Then, "JACE!"

I bit back my grin, sitting up just as she stormed into our room, her ID held in a death grip between her fingers. "What the hell is this?!"

I blinked innocently. "An ID card?"

She smacked my arm with it. "Why does it say Riley *Thatcher*?!"

I sat up, stretching lazily. "Oh, that's weird. You sure you didn't request a name change?"

She gaped at me, looking personally offended. "You know damn well I didn't."

I finally let the smirk spread across my face. "Huh. Must've been some administrative mix-up."

She wasn't buying it.

Her jaw clenched, and she pointed an accusatory finger at me. "You did this! I don't know how, but you did."

I just shrugged, unconcerned. "Well, technically, I just nudged the system a little."

She let out a strangled sound. "Jace, this is serious! I can't have the wrong name on my official ID! What if I need it for something important? What if I get in trouble?"

I leaned in, lowering my voice, letting the possessiveness drip into my tone. "Relax, babycakes. It's just one less thing I'll have to change once we're married."

Her eyes went huge. "You're insane."

I grinned. "And you're officially one step closer to being Mrs. Thatcher."

She opened her mouth, closed it, then just gawked at me in sheer disbelief as I slid off the bed. Riley was still clutching the ID like it had personally wronged her. Her face was a mix of disbelief, outrage, and something else—something she was trying really hard to fight.

I knew that look. It was the same one she got every time I did something completely unhinged, yet somehow, she still loved me for it.

Her lips parted, probably to tell me just how out of my mind I was, but I didn't give her the chance. Instead, I reached into the nightstand, grabbed the tiny velvet box I'd stashed there weeks ago, and flicked it open with one hand.

Riley froze.

Every ounce of frustration, every lingering hint of her planned verbal assault, vanished in an instant. Her mouth opened, then closed, then opened again like she was trying to form words but had forgotten how.

I smirked. "You good there, Riley-girl?"

She blinked hard. "Jace," she whispered, her voice uneven.

"Yeah, baby?"

Her gaze flicked between my face and the ring—the one I'd picked out for her without hesitation because the second I saw it, I knew. A delicate band, a stunning diamond in the center, and smaller stones woven into the sides like a crown. A queen's ring for my queen.

"Is this . . ." Her voice cracked, and she cleared her throat, trying again. "Are you . . ."

"Oh, this isn't a proposal," I said easily. "It's an *inevitability*."

Her breath hitched.

I stepped closer, my fingers skimming up her arm, feeling the way she trembled slightly under my touch. "You were always going to be mine, Riley. This just makes it official."

She shook her head, but it wasn't in denial. More like she was trying to catch up, trying to grasp the weight of what was happening. "You—you can't just—"

"I can," I interrupted smoothly. "And I did."

Her lips parted like she wanted to argue, but no words came. Just ragged, uneven breaths, the weight of it all pressing down on her. I watched her throat work as she swallowed hard, her fingers twitching at her sides like she was debating whether to hold on or let go.

Like she still thought she had to make a choice.

But, duh, I wasn't letting her choose wrong.

I reached out, tracing my fingertips over her wrist, feeling her pulse thrumming wildly beneath my touch. "You think I don't know what's going on in that head of yours?" My voice was low . . . steady. "You think I don't know that you still wake up sometimes and wonder if this is real? If you really get to have this? If you really get to be loved like this?"

Her lashes fluttered, and I saw the war waging in her, felt it in the way she shook, in the way her breath hitched like I'd pulled something straight out of her chest and held it up to the light.

"I see you, Riley," I murmured, stepping closer, tilting her chin up so she had no choice but to look at me. "I see the girl who fights so hard to believe she deserves happiness. Who spent too long being told she wasn't allowed to want more, to dream of more. Who learned how to survive before she ever learned how to just be." My thumb brushed against her jaw, soft and reverent. "But you don't have to survive me. You just have to love me."

Her eyes burned, wide and glassy, filled with too many emotions to name. She shook her head again, but this time, I saw it for what it was . . . one last desperate grasp at an excuse. At some invisible force trying to pull her back into the doubt she had lived in for too long.

I wasn't letting it win.

"Tell me you don't love me," I whispered. "Tell me you don't want this. That you don't want forever."

A sharp inhale. A tremor in her fingers. But still, no words.

I stepped even closer, my forehead pressing against hers, my voice barely a breath. "Tell me you don't want my last name."

She made a broken sound, something between a gasp and a sob, her hands fisting in my shirt like I was the only thing holding her up. I felt the way her body trembled against mine, the way she was already sinking into me, already surrendering.

I kissed her forehead, then her cheek, then her jaw. "Tell me, Riley."

Silence.

Then, finally—soft, so soft I almost didn't hear it.

"I can't."

I exhaled, my chest easing for the first time since I'd slid that ring into her palm. "That's all I needed to hear, baby." I pulled back just enough to catch her gaze, my lips curving in a slow, knowing smirk. "Now, let's get that ring on."

Her breath hitched, but I didn't miss the way her fingers curled even tighter around the velvet box like it was already hers. Like she knew it was inevitable. Like she had never really stood a chance.

Because she hadn't.

She was already mine.

She always would be.

And now?

Now, the world would know it, too.

She swallowed hard, her eyes never leaving mine. "You're insane," she repeated once more.

I nodded. "And you love me for it."

She exhaled a laugh, choked and breathless.

I reached for her hand, prying the ID from her fingers, flipping it over in my palm. Riley Thatcher. My girl. My future.

Leaning in, my lips brushed against her ear, my voice low and sure. "Welcome to forever, baby."

I pushed a stray piece of hair from her face, watching the way her lips parted, how her eyes were still wide and dazed from everything that had just happened. "Now, how do you feel about getting married in Vatican City?"

She blinked, still gripping the ring box like she wasn't entirely sure this was real. "That's . . . random."

Then, like a light flicking on, amusement sparked in her gaze, her lips twitching as she tilted her head. "Wait a second. Isn't that one of the only places where marriage contracts are binding . . . forever?"

I winked. "You catch on quick, Mrs. Thatcher."

Her breath hitched, and she shook her head, but there was no fight in it, no hesitation—just that quiet, reluctant acceptance she always had when she realized I'd already made up my mind about something.

And I had.

This wasn't just some impulsive, heat-of-the-moment decision. I'd known since the second I met her that Riley St. James was going to be mine. And now, holding her close, watching the way she swallowed hard like she was still trying to process it all, I could feel it—how much she wanted this, too, how much she wanted *me*, even if she wasn't ready to say it out loud.

Yet.

I leaned in, my hands skimming down her back, pressing her flush against me. "Say yes, Riley-girl," I murmured, my lips brushing against hers, coaxing, teasing. "You know you want to."

Her forehead dropped to mine, her breath warm, her body soft and pliant in my arms. "Jace," she whispered, like she was still trying to figure me out, still trying to convince herself this was happening.

I cupped her face, forcing her to look at me, making sure she saw everything I wasn't saying out loud. "I love you, Riley," I said, my voice rough, full of certainty. "It's you. It's always been you."

She sucked in a sharp breath, and I felt it then—the last of her resistance shattering.

I smirked. "Now, are we getting married in Vatican City or what?"

––––––––––

Riley

I stared at him, at the boy who had spent every second since I met him making himself impossible to leave. Jace Thatcher, with his easy smirks and relentless determination, his infuriating confidence and unshakable certainty. The boy who had gotten under my skin so fast, so thoroughly, that I'd never even stood a chance at stopping him.

And now, here he was, standing in front of me, his hands on my waist, his eyes locked onto mine like I was the only thing that had ever made sense to him.

Like he was willing to bet his entire future on me.

A marriage proposal shouldn't have felt inevitable when you were this young. It shouldn't have felt like the next logical step in a series of moments I had already surrendered to. But Jace wasn't normal. He wasn't predictable. And when it came to him, I couldn't resist.

For so long, I had been convinced I wasn't meant for this kind of love. The kind that was all-consuming, the kind that rooted deep and refused to be torn away. I had spent years feeling unworthy, like I was something temporary, like love was something I could borrow but never keep.

I'd grown up being treated like my illness made me less. Like my body's failures meant I wasn't meant for forever, that I was only good enough to be someone's dirty secret.

But Jace never looked at me like I was fragile. He never hesitated. Never treated me like something that wasn't worthy of adoration . . . or showing off.

He fought for me like I was worth everything. And now, he wasn't just fighting.

He was asking me to stay.

It was a stark contrast—Jace, standing in front of me, fierce and unwavering, like I was something to be protected, something to be fought for. And Callum.

Callum, who had only ever fought to keep me small. Hidden. Like a sin he didn't have the spine to confess.

I thought about the reports that had come out after his arrest, the students from Chapel Hill who had stepped forward with their own stories. Girls who had once stood in my shoes, who had believed his lies, who had felt just as powerless in his grasp. He hadn't just done this to me. He had been doing it for years. The weight of that realization made my stomach churn.

I forced myself to meet Jace's gaze, the raw intensity in his brown eyes grounding me. Callum had spent years convincing me that I wasn't enough—that I was weak, that I was lucky he even wanted me. But Jace? He made me feel like I was everything.

My chest ached as I reached up, tracing my fingers along the edge of his jaw, feeling the slight stubble beneath my touch. He didn't move, didn't even breathe, just let me look at him, let me absorb the weight of what he was offering.

Forever.

With him.

The world was so loud—always pulling, always demanding—but in that moment, it was just us. Just Jace, waiting for me to say the words that would make this real.

"Are you sure this isn't the wrong play, Thatcher?" I asked, a smile spreading across my lips.

He huffed. "Do I ever make the wrong play?"

My smile widened, joy bubbling up inside me.

"Yes," I whispered.

His lips twitched. "What was that?"

I swallowed past the lump in my throat and nodded. "Yes."

Jace exhaled sharply, his grip tightening around me. And then he was kissing me, like he was sealing a deal that had already been made long before either of us admitted it.

I let him.

I kissed him back like I had nowhere else to be, like I had finally figured out the truth that had been clawing at my ribs since the moment he walked into my life.

Jace Thatcher wasn't a wrong turn.

He wasn't a mistake.

He wasn't some reckless impulse I would regret.

He was the safest place I had ever known.

And for the first time in my life, I wasn't afraid of staying.

I pulled back, just enough to see the way his brown eyes burned with triumph. "You're feeling pretty smug about this, aren't you?" I murmured.

His lips curled. "Oh, absolutely."

I huffed a laugh, rolling my eyes. "And what if I had said no?"

Jace gave me a look, all dark amusement and pure, unshakable arrogance. "Now *that* would've been the wrong play, babycakes. And with you, I don't do it wrong. I play to win."

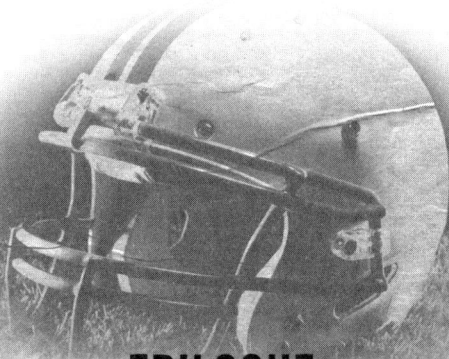

EPILOGUE

RILEY

The first thing I did after Jace left for practice was send an appointment to our shared calendar app on his phone. A notification set to go off the second practice ended.

With this simple message attached:

Track me.

I could already picture the look on his face when he saw it—the smirk, the little huff of amusement. And, of course, he'd listen. Because tracking me had become his favorite pastime.

So, when he finished practice and checked his phone, I knew exactly what he'd done. He'd opened his little app that I'd discovered, zeroed in on my location, and frowned at the little dot blinking at an address he didn't recognize.

> Jace: What are you up to, my lady?

"Riley, we're ready for you," the front desk called. I nodded at the receptionist and stood from my seat, ignoring the rapid-fire texts Jace was sending as I followed him to the back and slid onto the procedure table.

The assistant came in as I was studying the artwork on the walls, and I winced as she swiped antiseptic across my skin. I was nervous, but it was the good kind of nervous. The kind that made my stomach flutter and my heart race, because this? This was permanent. Unlike my parents. Who hadn't even picked up the phone after the news about Callum came out.

But very much like Jace. Because he was forever.

I had finished telling her why I was there, and she had started working, when the door up front suddenly swung open. The wind swept in, along with six feet, four inches of territorial, sweat-drenched football player. He bent over, his breaths coming out in gasps, holding up one finger before he straightened up and looked around for me. Ever the drama queen, as usual.

His eyes lit up when he saw me, and he shook his head in confusion as he stalked over to where I was reclining.

"What are you doing?" Jace's voice was part exasperation, part disbelief when he got to me. His cleats were still on, and his practice bag was slung over his shoulder.

He must have run here.

"Babycakes, you—" He frowned as he glanced around before his gaze finally landed on the stenciled design on my ribs, and his expression did something I wasn't expecting.

It softened.

His name sat just beneath my ribs, exactly where my lungs expanded when I breathed.

Jace inhaled sharply. "Riley."

His voice sounded different—hoarse, almost reverent.

I turned my head, meeting his eyes, feeling the weight of the moment settle over us like gravity itself had thickened. "You did it first," I said softly.

His brows drew together slightly, like he was still struggling to process it.

"The first time I saw my name on you, I thought it was crazy. I thought maybe you were just being your usual reckless, obsessive self." I let out a small, shaky laugh. "But then I realized something. I never once doubted it. I never questioned whether you meant it, whether you'd regret it."

Jace's throat bobbed as he swallowed, his hands flexing at his sides like he wanted to reach for me but didn't want to interrupt.

I inhaled deeply, feeling his name on my ribs, like it was becoming a part of me. "Every time you take a breath, you lift me up. So now, every time I breathe, I'll lift you up, too."

He swallowed hard, his eyes shiny. I tapped my ribs, right over his name. My voice dropped, my words carrying the weight of a truth I'd only just come to understand.

"Let's breathe for each other, Jace Thatcher."

His eyes darkened, and he exhaled like I'd just knocked the wind out of him. His bag hit the floor with a dull *thud* before his fingers brushed the edge of my jaw, tilting my face toward his. "You're really mine, aren't you?" His voice was rough, almost awed.

I smiled, small and certain. "I always will be. Now and forever."

His fingers traced the design, light as a whisper, before he let out a low chuckle, shaking his head. Before he could say anything else, though . . . the artist cleared her throat. "Uh, if you two lovebirds are ready . . ."

I snorted because I'd kind of forgotten she was there.

I lay back, my breath steady, and let the needle carve *Jace* into my skin like he'd already carved himself into my life.

———

Later that night, I found it.

Tucked in the back of the closet, half forgotten but impossible to mistake—a black blindfold. I picked it up, smoothing my fingers over the fabric, and an idea sparked.

Jace had just stepped out of the shower, a towel slung low on his hips, water droplets still clinging to his chest. His hair was damp, messy, the blonde strands curling slightly at the ends from the steam, and his muscles flexed with every lazy step he took toward me.

I needed a second to process the sight.

Because there was something almost unfair about Jace Thatcher when he was fresh out of the shower—like he'd been handcrafted for sin. Every sharp plane of his body, every defined ridge of his abs, was on full display, glistening under the soft light. His tattooed chest was broad, his shoulders unfairly wide, tapering down into a tight, cut waist, the kind of V-line that could make a woman forget all common sense.

I swallowed, my gaze trailing lower, taking in the way the towel barely clung to his hips, hanging loose, taunting. It wouldn't take much—a tug, a well-timed stretch—for it to drop, and that knowledge made my pulse thud a little harder.

And then, my gaze caught on the ink that sat just along his ribs, standing stark against his tan skin. My name.

Riley.

My breath hitched, and I bit my lip, heat creeping up my spine as I imagined tracing my tongue over the letters, tasting the proof of his devotion. My own ribs were feeling tender after their new ink . . . but certainly not enough to stop me from having some . . . fun.

His lips twitched like he could feel my stare, like he knew exactly what was going through my head.

"Enjoying the view, babycakes?"

Cocky bastard. He was eyefucking me just as hard since I was dressed in nothing but a shirt and a pair of underwear.

I huffed, crossing my arms, even though my face felt *way* too warm. "It's not *my* fault you look like this."

His smirk deepened, and he took another step closer, his abs tensing, his towel dangerously loose. "Yeah?" His voice was thick, amused. "Is that why you're undressing me with your eyes?"

Scoffing, my pulse betrayed me with another hard thump. "There's not much left to undress, Thatcher."

His gaze darkened, dropping to my bare legs before snapping back up. "Then why don't you finish the job?"

I sucked in a breath, my knees suddenly *very* weak.

And then—his towel shifted. Not downward. *Upward.*

The thick material lifted, tenting as his body betrayed him, and my cheeks burned, even though I was well acquainted with this monster of a dick at this point.

Jace's smirk turned . . . sinful, and his brown eyes gleamed with satisfaction, enjoying every second of my internal meltdown. "Something on your mind?"

I crossed my arms, shifting my weight, trying very hard to *not* look at the very obvious issue in front of me. "Your towel is . . . um . . ." I gestured vaguely.

He tilted his head, mock confusion clouding his expression. "What about it?"

I glared. "It's moving."

Jace let out a deep, rumbling chuckle, running a slow hand through his damp hair, making the muscles in his arm flex *way* too distractingly. "Huh. Weird. Wonder what could be causing that."

I approached him, the blindfold hidden behind my back, trying to get hold of myself so this game could go how I wanted it to.

"Do you trust me, Jace?" I asked, trying to make my voice at least a little sexy sounding.

He lifted a brow. "Riley-girl, that smile is dangerous."

I grinned wider. "Close your eyes."

Jace's smirk deepened, but he obeyed. "As you wish." I rolled my eyes, because he'd gotten that from watching *The Princess Bride* with me last night.

Stepping closer, I smoothed my fingers over his jaw before slipping the blindfold over his head, tying it snugly. The second the fabric slid into place, his body went rigid.

"They really should have invested in softer material," he muttered under his breath, his jaw tightening like he was suppressing a memory.

Pausing, my hands lingered at the knot. "Jace?"

His smirk returned, a fraction too quick. "Nothing. Just an observation."

I hesitated for a second longer, but his lips curled, like he was daring me to keep questioning him. So I didn't. I had other things I wanted to be doing.

"So, you trust me?" I asked again.

He swallowed hard. "With my life."

"And you can't see anything?" I checked.

He snorted. "Not a thing."

A thrill shot through me.

I stepped closer, my hands skimming over his abs, his breath hitching as I pressed up on my toes, letting my lips brush along his jaw.

"Come to bed, Jace," I murmured, my voice soft, coaxing.

His smirk deepened. "Babycakes, I was just about to say the same thing to you."

I grinned, pushing on his chest so he stepped backward until the backs of his knees hit the mattress. He didn't resist, letting me guide him down, his body sprawled beneath me, all sharp lines and muscle, and deliciousness.

Fuck. He was beautiful.

I climbed over him, straddling his waist, dragging my nails lightly down his chest. "You're awfully compliant," I teased.

He smirked. "This is definitely my idea of a good time, just so you know."

I leaned in, brushing my lips just shy of his. "I'll make a note."

His fingers ghosted up my spine before his hand curled around my waist, pulling me flush against him. My heart pounded, my body humming at the feel of him, the warmth of his skin, the raw intensity in his grip.

Perfect.

I pressed kisses along his jaw as I trailed my fingers up his arm, slow, deliberate, letting my touch lull him deeper into this moment. And then, quick as a flash—

Click.

Jace stilled.

Flexed his wrist. The unmistakable sound of metal rattling filled the room.

"Riley."

I eased back, admiring my handiwork, my heart pounding from the thrill of it. *Gotcha.*

"Yes, dear?"

His jaw clenched. He yanked his arm, his wrist securely fastened by the pink, furry handcuff I'd attached to the bedpost earlier.

"What the hell?" His voice was low, laced with something between exasperation and intrigue.

I clapped a hand over my mouth to stifle my giggle. "I thought it was time for a little payback."

"Riley." His voice dropped into a warning, rough and low. "Take them off."

I pouted, dragging my fingers lightly over his wrist where the pink, furry cuffs were holding him hostage. "Don't like being handcuffed, huh?"

His fingers flexed against the restraints, his muscles pulling tight. "Riley," he said again.

I ignored the tension in his voice, too caught up in the way his body looked stretched beneath me—his arm strained, his bicep flexing, his abs tight and ridged, dipping into that deep V that disappeared under the towel still slung around his waist. My name on his ribs, rising and falling with each deep breath he took.

Mine. All of him was mine.

A thrill shot through me as I traced the ink with my fingertips, watching his stomach clench in response. His body was so responsive to me, and I reveled in it.

"You love being in control," I murmured, dragging my nails up his chest, my touch featherlight.

He swallowed hard, his Adam's apple bobbing as he reached for me with his other hand. "And you *love* pushing your luck, babycakes."

I caught his wrist and pressed it into the mattress as I grinned, leaning in to drop a soft, teasing kiss on the center of his chest. "No touching."

His breath hitched as I dragged my lips lower, kissing over the hard ridges of his abs, my tongue flicking out just enough to taste his skin. He jerked slightly at the sensation, his body completely at my mercy.

His towel twitched.

I bit back a smile as I ran my tongue along his tattoo before moving down to the cut of his hip bone, kissing my way to the edge of the fabric still clinging to him. The strain in his muscles, the way his body coiled beneath me like a loaded spring . . . I loved this.

"I wonder, Riley-girl—" His voice was tight, controlled, but there was desperation beneath it. "If you know exactly what you're doing right now . . ."

I laughed, my insides clenching just thinking about what the danger in his voice would mean for me later on.

I lifted my gaze, and slowly—so agonizingly slow—peeled his towel away.

His cock sprang free, thick and heavy, and a pulse of need shot through me at the sight of him laid out for me like this. "Hmm. No wonder you liked this so much."

Jace's chest rose and fell in deep, controlled breaths as I wrapped my fingers around him, watching the way his jaw clenched at the first firm stroke.

"Fuck," he rasped, his arm tensing against the cuffs.

I dragged my tongue along the underside of his length, slow and deliberate, teasing him as I swirled around the tip, savoring the taste of him.

Jace groaned, his hips instinctively bucking up as his free hand reached out, searching for something to grasp.

I immediately pulled away, so there was no way for him to get to me. "I believe I said no touching, Mr. Thatcher."

His head snapped back against the pillow, his knuckles going white as he yanked at the cuffs again, frustration crackling off him in waves.

I smiled against him, taking him deeper, letting my tongue glide along his length before hollowing my cheeks and sucking him in.

A harsh, ragged curse slipped from his lips. *"Fucking hell—"*

His muscles were tight, his body trembling as he fought not to break. His bicep flexed again, his stomach clenching as I took him deeper, swallowing him down until his thighs shook beneath my hands.

His whole body went rigid, his fingers flexing against the restraint as a growl ripped through him. "I hate this. I hate not fucking *touching* you."

I moaned around him, knowing that sound would drive him insane.

"Riley," he snapped, his voice wrecked. "You better—"

His words cut off into a snarl as I sucked harder, taking him deeper, my hands gripping his thighs, nails lightly scraping along his skin.

"Fuck. *Fuck.*" He yanked his arm again, the bed frame groaning under the force.

My tongue flicked over him once more, slow and teasing, and then . . .

Snap.

The furry cuff ripped free, the bedpost splintering where the wood had given way. The blindfold went flying somewhere off the bed.

And in a blink, his hands were on me.

He flipped us in one smooth, overpowering motion, his body covering mine, pinning me to the mattress before I could react.

I gasped, my heart hammering, but Jace was already on me—his big, warm hands gripping my wrists, shoving them above my head, his weight pressing flush against me, his breath hot against my lips.

He glared down at me, his gaze breathless and burning as he took me in.

I was very smug about the way his chest was heaving, how his brown eyes were dark and filled with something primal . . . something very *fun*. "That was a dirty trick, Riley-girl."

I was breathless, laughing, but entirely at his mercy now. "I don't regret it."

His lips twitched, that signature smirk flickering over his face. "Oh, I know."

His lips slammed against mine—wild, claiming, relentless—stealing my breath the way he always did, the way he always would.

Jace dragged my thighs apart, his body pressing against mine like he couldn't stand even an inch of space between us.

A sharp gasp left me as his fingers curled around the thin lace of my underwear. There was no hesitation, no warning . . . just a low growl and the snarl of fabric as he ripped them clean off my body.

"Jace—"

His mouth crashed back onto mine, swallowing my gasp, his tongue sweeping inside, devouring, as his fingers replaced what he'd just torn away. He slid through my slick heat, teasing, pressing, his touch ruthless, knowing exactly how to pull me apart.

"I don't like not touching you," he growled against my lips, his breath ragged, his control barely there as he pressed his length against me, dragging the tip along my entrance, teasing us both.

I writhed beneath him desperately, my fingers clawing at his back as I tried to pull him closer, deeper.

He slammed into me, hot and hard and so deep I arched, a cry breaking from my lips.

He didn't give me time to adjust, didn't ease into it. He owned me, thrusting deep, filling me completely, stretching me until there was nothing left of me but him.

My nails dug into his shoulders as pleasure crashed through me. "Yeeesss!"

"That's it," he muttered against my throat, his lips dragging down to my collarbone, sucking, biting, marking me. "Take it. Take all of me."

I clenched around him, my body pulling him deeper, harder, and his rhythm turned brutal—relentless—like he had to remind me that I belonged right here, under him, taking every ounce of his obsession.

"You feel so fucking perfect," he rasped, shifting his angle, hitting the spot that made me cry out.

I was unraveling, pleasure coiling deep, burning hotter and hotter, my body tightening, chasing the peak I knew was coming too fast, too hard.

"Baby . . ." My voice broke as the climax ripped through me, pleasure exploding in every nerve, leaving me shattered and shaking beneath him.

"Fuck," he groaned, thrusting once, twice—then burying himself deep, his body locking against mine as he came with a loud, wrecked sound.

We stayed like that, tangled and trembling, his breath warm against my skin, his hands still gripping my thighs like he'd never let go.

His lips brushed against my temple, softer now, his voice hushed, reverent. "I'll get you back for that, babycakes."

I let out a breathless, contented laugh. "I'm looking forward to it."

His fingers traced slow, lazy circles on my spine as he pulled me closer like I was something precious.

I turned my head, my lips brushing over the strong curve of his jaw, my heart full and steady, knowing that this . . . this was where I belonged. *Always*.

SECOND EPILOGUE

JACE

A Week Before the NCAA Football Playoffs

I wiped sweat from my forehead as I jogged back into formation, my cleats digging into the grass. Practice was dragging today. Coach was in one of his I'm-trying-to-kill-you-before-the-playoffs moods, and I was mostly just counting down the seconds until I could get home to Riley.

But at least I had entertainment.

"So, remember Riley's roommate?" I started, shaking out my arms, rolling my shoulders before getting into position for the next drill.

"How could we forget?" drawled Matty, looking a bit growly that I'd even brought her up.

"She texted Riley," I continued, ignoring his rudeness.

"What did Creepy McCreeper say?" Parker asked, sounding intrigued because he'd never actually met Emma. He hadn't seen her staring, and he'd just heard secondhand about her femur fantasies and her love of crazy clowns . . . You really had to meet Emma in person to understand.

I grimaced. "She said her new roommate isn't *nearly* as interesting to watch."

There was a beat of silence. Matty looked *horrified*. Like, full-on, flashbacks to war, thousand-yard stare, kind of horrified.

Which was fair . . . and appropriate considering *he'd* been the one stuck keeping Emma distracted while I snuck into Riley's dorm that night.

He hadn't been the same since.

"She—*she's texting her*?" Matty croaked, like he was moments away from having a full-body shiver.

I grimaced. "Well, not anymore. Riley doesn't even know how she got her phone number. She never gave it to her."

Matty made a strangled noise, looking like he was reliving the moment Emma had told him—dead serious—about her fixation on the taste of human flesh.

"Riley thinks it was Emma's attempt at being sweet . . . like in a definitely-should-have-ended-up-on-a-true-crime-podcast kinda way."

Parker snorted. "Yes, real heartwarming. I bet she's crying herself to sleep at night, clutching the hair she probably cut off Riley's head while she was sleeping . . . like it's an unrequited love story."

That thought wasn't pleasant.

"There's no way she doesn't have a playlist dedicated to Matty—one of those dramatic, longing ones. 'I Will Always Love You,' 'Under My Skin,' maybe 'Every Breath You Take'—really good ones like that," I mused.

Parker barked out a laugh, but Matty threw a water bottle at me.

Minus ten best-friendship points right there. *Per se.*

Coach blew the whistle, cutting off our shit-talking, and we launched into another drill, running routes, cutting past defenders, pushing through the burn in our legs.

I wiped sweat from my neck as we reset for another rep. "Oh, by the way, I recently came into a bunch of money," I announced.

Parker looked confused. "One of your investments?"

"It's strange for me, because I usually just use a paper towel," I finished.

Parker barked out a laugh, but Matty was being suspiciously quiet. Why wasn't he paying attention to me?

I glanced over, frowning when I saw that Matty had frozen on the field.

No sarcastic remarks. No eye roll.

Not even a *Shut the fuck up, Jace-face.* What was going on?

"Hey." I nudged him with my elbow. "Why aren't you appropriately worshiping me right now?"

Matty didn't even *look* at me.

His jaw was tight, his brows drawn, his gaze locked onto something in the distance.

Something out in the parking lot.

I exchanged a glance with Parker, who had also noticed.

"What's up with you?" Parker asked, half laughing, half confused.

Matty's scowl deepened, his voice quieter than usual. "She's not here."

Parker tilted his head. "Who's not here?"

Matty didn't answer right away. Instead, his throat bobbed, his stance stiffening, like something was actually *wrong*.

And then I followed his line of sight.

Right to the spot where that beat-up old car was always parked during every single practice.

Where that girl who was always watching, always waiting—*wasn't*.

The air suddenly felt heavier, like we had all just noticed something at the same time.

Matty clenched his jaw, his voice quiet but full of something I couldn't quite place.

"Why isn't she here?"

"Who?" Parker asked again, looking back and forth between the lot and Matty's face, taking a minute to get it. "Your stalker?" He barked out a laugh. "Isn't that a good thing?"

"Yeah, Matty-boy, maybe she just finally decided to trade up and stalk someone funnier," I inserted helpfully, kind of loving how he seemed to be freaking out right now.

Matty shook his head. "Something's wrong."

I blinked, and then Matty was turning and sprinting off the field.

Like a maniac. Like he'd suddenly picked up a habit of drinking iced milk.

Coach Everett hollered at him, probably done with all the running away his players had been doing lately. The rest of our teammates just watched in confusion.

Parker whistled low under his breath. "Huh. Didn't expect that."

A grin stretched across my face. "Didn't know Matty had it in him. He just gained some bestilicious bro points."

Parker bristled. "For what?"

"For finally doing something cool."

He watched Matty disappear from view and sighed in defeat. "True."

Brooks, one of our running backs snorted nearby. "There is seriously something wrong with you guys."

I couldn't argue with that.

We believed in true love, obviously, and I was proud of that fact. It had gotten me my Riley-girl, after all. And for her, I'd be wrong, insane, and completely fucking psychotic every single day if I needed to be.

Because with her, everything was right.

BONUS SCENE

Want more Jace and Riley? Come hang out in C.R. Jane's Fated Realm for an exclusive BONUS scene! Get it here: https://www.facebook.com/groups/C.R.FatedRealm

JACE THATCHER'S
CHILI RECIPE

SERVINGS: 8

INGREDIENTS

- 2 POUNDS GROUND BEEF
- ½ MEDIUM ONION, CHOPPED
- 2½ CUPS TOMATO SAUCE
- 1 (15oz) CAN LIGHT RED KIDNEY BEANS
- 1 (15oz) CAN DARK RED KIDNEY BEANS
- 1 (8oz) JAR PACE MEDIUM CHUNKY SALSA (MUST BE PACE)
- 1 PACKET ORGANIC CHILI SEASONING MIX (BECAUSE YOUR BODY IS A TEMPLE)
- ½ TEASPOON GROUND BLACK PEPPER
- ½ TEASPOON GARLIC POWDER
- 1 TEASPOON SALT

INSTRUCTIONS

1. PLACE GROUND BEEF AND ONION INTO A LARGE NONSTICK SAUCEPAN OVER MEDIUM HEAT. COOK, STIRRING OCCASIONALLY, UNTIL BEEF IS BROWNED AND CRUMBLY AND ONION IS TRANSLUCENT, ABOUT 10 MINUTES. DRAIN GREASE IF DESIRED.

2. STIR IN TOMATO SAUCE, LIGHT AND DARK KIDNEY BEANS, SALSA, CHILI SEASONING, PEPPER, GARLIC POWDER, AND SALT UNTIL WELL COMBINED. REDUCE THE HEAT TO LOW AND SIMMER FOR AT LEAST 1 HOUR BEFORE SERVING.

3. SERVE WITH SHREDDED CHEESE AND COOKED WHITE RICE AND/OR FRITOS, AND/OR JALAPEÑO CORNBREAD.

ACKNOWLEDGMENTS

Dear Reader,

We've all been in relationships that made us feel like we were too much or not enough. Ones that left scars we couldn't see but carried anyway. Ones that made us question what we deserved, who we were, and whether we'd ever find something better.

This book is for those moments, for the times we've had to untangle love from control, devotion from possession, and desire from destruction. For the times we've had to relearn what it means to be wanted in a way that doesn't break us, but builds us instead.

Riley and Jace's story isn't just about love. It's about finding someone who sees you—the real you—and refuses to look away. It's about knowing, deep in your bones, that you are worth the fight.

This book is dedicated to my husband, who never lets me forget that love should never hurt, that obsession can be soft, and that the best kind of love is the one that never makes you question if you're enough.

XOXOXO,
C.R.

A few thank-yous . . .

To Raven aka My Moon aka Bird aka My Best Friend aka The One Who Always Shows Up Exactly When I Need Her:

Some things in life are just meant to be, and your friendship is one of them. You are a force—steady and unwavering in the way you support and push me. You're the unexpected gift that keeps giving. Brilliant, hilarious, kind . . . and the type of friend people write books about.

Your talent leaves me in awe, your loyalty means the world, and your friendship is one of my favorite things about life. ILY forever.

To my beta readers, Crystal, Blair, and Lisa: Your sharp eyes, honest feedback, and endless enthusiasm have made this book stronger in ways I can't even begin to describe. Thank you for your friendship, every late-night discussion, every reaction message, and every moment you spent in this world with me. I'm beyond lucky to have you on this journey.

To Stephanie, my editor: Your insight, patience, and talent have shaped this story in ways I never could have done alone. Thank you for pushing me to dig deeper, for knowing exactly when to rein me in and when to let me run wild. Your guidance is invaluable, and I'm so grateful to have you in my corner.

To my PAs and BFFs, Caitlin and Sarah: You already know how much I adore you. Always have, always will. There aren't enough words to express my gratitude, but just know—I'd be lost without you.

And to you, the readers who make this dream a reality: I am grateful every moment for you.

ABOUT THE AUTHOR

C.R. Jane is a *USA Today*–bestselling author of romance, fantasy, and whatever else she feels like writing. Her stories are designed to make readers cry, scream, and eventually . . . swoon. Welcome to her world, where heartbreak and happy endings rule.

Podium

DISCOVER MORE

STORIES
UNBOUND

PodiumEntertainment.com